A TALE OF TWO RABBIS

MARVIN J. WOLF

Copyright © 2017 Marvin J. Wolf

All rights reserved.

RAMBAM PRESS, Asheville NC

This is a work of fiction. While certain place names and historical events described herein are true, the story and its characters are entirely a product of the author's imagination. Any resemblance to any person, living or dead, or to actual events, is purely coincidental

ACKNOWLEDGEMENTS

I am indebted to my copy editor, Pat Rolfe for her hard work and many important suggestions. My daughter, Tomi, served as a sounding board for my sometimes far-fetched notions. Most of all, I honor my literary agent, Doug Grad, for his support, his many excellent ideas, and his friendship.

ALSO BY MARVIN J. WOLF

A Scribe Dies In Brooklyn
For Whom The Shofar Blows
Abandoned In Hell
Family Blood
Fallen Angels
Rotten Apples
Buddha's Child
Perfect Crimes
Where White Men Fear To Tread

MARVIN J. WOLF

CHAPTER ONE

The kid under the bridge looked to be about ten, nicely dressed in slacks with a white shirt and tie under a sports jacket. A yarmulke graced the top of an oval head covered with dark curls. His skin was cocoa, with carmine highlights, and his face was so finely featured that at first glance Ben took him for a girl.

A trio of white boys in jeans and running shoes had shoved him against a wall beneath the bridge. The smaller two were almost Ben's height, about five feet, seven inches, a head taller than yarmulke boy. The third kid, old enough to sprout a few sparse hairs on his upper lip, was six feet tall and well over 200 pounds, soft in the middle, and working on a second chin. He was going through yarmulke boy's backpack, dropping books and papers on the ground, tossing an orange to one of his henchman, a bagged sandwich to the other, and then pocketing a cell phone.

Taking this in at a glance from the top of a gentle slope above the bridge, Ben started forward, feeling weak and shaky, but unwilling to be a spectator to what was obviously a robbery or something worse.

It was his first Tuesday afternoon in Pittsburgh Five days earlier, he had kissed Miryam goodbye at Ben Gurion Airport, swapped hugs with her maternal grandparents and a phalanx of cousins, and boarded a plane for Boston. After a night in his Cambridge apartment, Ben had packed his four-year-old Honda Accord and drove straight through to Pittsburgh.

And on the previous morning, Ben had gone to a university clinic to give a bone-marrow sample and the first of what would be a year-long series of weekly injections and blood tests. Afterward, he took a cab back to his rented room in Pittsburgh's Squirrel Hill neighborhood, where he slept all that day and night. At noon Tuesday, weak but hungry, he had made coffee and toasted a bagel. Unable even to consider the five-mile run that for years had launched his daily routine, Ben had settled on a walk, a leisurely exploration of the community where he would live until he learned if the Human Immunodeficiency Virus had been eradicated from his body.

And now this. Three big kids robbing a smaller boy.

Instinctively, he reached up to remove his glasses, fingers fumbling on his face until he remembered that two weeks earlier, in Tel Aviv, he'd had Lasik surgery.

Ben no longer needed glasses.

He lengthened his stride, still walking but now with a purpose, and as he came into earshot, he heard the big kid laughing.

"Hey, you know what *this* is? It's a kigger—a kike *and* a nigger." The big kid laughed at his own joke, and the other two joined in.

Yarmulke boy didn't seem to see the humor.

Ben said, "Hey!"

Four kids turned their heads as Ben approached.

Ben said, "I'd ask what's going on, but I can see that."

The tall kid said, "Nothing on. Just hanging out with my bros."

Ben said, "You've got one minute to pick up all that stuff, take what you've stolen out of your pockets, and put it all back in this young man's backpack. Then you've got one minute to get out of my sight."

One of the smaller kids asked, "Or what?"

The tall kid smiled. "Yeah. Or what?"

Ben said, "Or I kick all your bully boy asses."

Yarmulke boy said, "Go away, Mister. You're making everything worser."

The tall kid said, "Yeah, go away before *we* kick *your* ass."

Ben said, "You've wasted half your minute."

The tall kid advanced on Ben, balling his fists, menace etched into his face. Ben waited, hands loosely at his sides until he was six feet away.

Then he danced forward on his toes, whirling to his left, bending at the waist and bringing his right foot across to land solidly in the kid's midsection.

The kid went down like a sack of onions. Gasping for air, he writhed on the ground.

One of the boys fumbled under his shirt and produced a gun.

Ben snatched it away before the kid could thumb back the safety catch.

Ben said, "Pick up all those things and put them back in the pack." The smaller of the two boys knelt, stuffing papers and books into the bag. Ben turned to the still-writhing juvenile giant and hauled him to his feet, then pulled two cell phones, an iPod and a wad of cash from his pockets.

Ben turned to the boy. "These yours?"

"Not the silver one. The phone, I mean. The black one is mine. And I think the iPod is Joey's."

"Who is Joey?"

"Joey Gordon. He's in my class."

"And the money?"

"No, sir. Not mine."

Ben handed him his things, then turned to the three boys. "You've exceeded my store of goodwill. Get out of my sight—and if I ever hear that you bothered this young man, I'll come after you and make you regret it for the rest of your lives."

He feinted a kick at the tall kid, who turned and ran, the others on his heels.

With a few swift motions, Ben checked to see that the gun was unloaded, removed the magazine, then detached the barrel assembly from the receiver and distributed the pieces among his pockets.

He turned back to yarmulke boy. "You okay?"

"Yeah. Thanks, Mister."

"What's your name?"

"Zach."

"I'll walk you home and make sure you get there in one piece"

"Okay."

Midway up the incline, Ben's adrenaline rush began to wear off. The toll of his exertions had to be paid. He grew lightheaded and nauseous. Spots appeared before his eyes. Each step became an effort. Ben realized that he couldn't go on.

"Have to rest," he gasped.

The boy said, "You don't look so good, Mister. Are you sick?"

"Is there a bench...I...sit...a minute?"

"It's only a little ways more."

 Ben opened his mouth to answer, but no words came out. Breathing became hard. The sky revolved. The world grew dark.

Ben staggered toward the bushes lining the sidewalk.

Zach screamed, "Mister!"

Two Weeks Earlier

Short, but lean and muscular, a man with a reddish crew cut who appeared to be in his late thirties opened the door and flipped a light switch, revealing a narrow bed with an ornate headboard, a highboy chest, a dresser, a table, two chairs. He left and returned moments later carrying a pair of suitcases that he set on the floor next to the bed. A moment later, he was joined by a petite Venus in the full bloom of young adulthood, 102 pounds of sensuality in a slender, bosomy figure topped by long, dark hair, flawless olive skin glowing with health, and the symmetrical face of a cover model.

"So this is where you ravish all your women," Miryam sighed.

Their private joke. Rabbi Moshe Benyamin Maimon—Ben to his friends—giggled.

Miryam stepped into Ben's arms, and they embraced for a long moment.

"Is that a Chippendale chair?" Miryam asked, looking around.

"You have a good eye," he said. "In fact, you have two wonderful eyes."

"And a Seymour table? And—my God, is that a Samuel McIntire highboy?"

"Guilty as charged. How is it that you know about antiques?"

"I took a course in furniture design."

Ben looked confused. "On your way to a graduate degree in early childhood development?"

"Before I transferred to Berkeley," she said. "In Tel Aviv, at the Technion, I was thinking about a career in industrial design or architecture. Then I discovered that I love teaching children."

"Ah."

She turned, searching the room, taking in each piece, eyes narrowing as she calculated. "Ben! If these are real, you have maybe half a million dollars in antique furniture. More, probably. Are they real?"

Ben said. "My insurance company's appraiser thinks so. But I don't think they're worth *that* much—and my grandparents bought each of them for less than a hundred dollars."

"So you inherited all this?"

"My *bubbe*—grandma—came from Vienna in the Thirties. Her brothers started a used furniture shop in Brooklyn; she sometimes worked there. It was mostly junk, but once in a while, they'd buy something worth keeping. These pieces were in my grandparents' guest room, and when my mother and I moved in—I was a baby—it became ours. When I started first grade, Mom used a rollout in the living room.

"A few years after my grandparents died, somebody clued me in that they were valuable. I'd kept them only because I couldn't afford anything newer."

"So that explains your fancy security system."

"That, and I've been solving other people's problems and cleaning up their messes for long enough to make a few enemies..."

"There *is* that. Ben, are we going to get naked tonight?"

"Remember what Bert—Doctor Epstein—told us? That we need to be extremely careful? He wants to see what my virus numbers are. We should wait for my blood work to come back."

"You look pretty healthy to me."

Ben had to smile. "The last six months have been very stressful. There were days when I didn't eat, or I got hardly any sleep, and a few when I got off my drug regimen. The drugs suppress the virus, but can't kill it. HIV is incredibly adaptable. And it's very patient. It's in my marrow—waiting for me to get run down or to screw up my drug regimen. Then it could mutate and start to reproduce. If I can't suppress it again, it's one opportunistic disease after another till something kills me. It's possible that it's already happened. I won't know until my test results are back."

"But what if we used a lot of precautions? A condom *and* spermicide?"

"I suppose we could get *partly* naked. If we're very careful."

"What if Dr. Epstein put me on Truvada? Didn't he say that its FDA approved?"

Ben shook his head. "It has horrible side effects—and the best trial, even when participants used condoms, was only about 75 percent effective in preventing new infections. You have better odds at Russian roulette—and if you lose at that, it's a painless death."

Miryam sighed and moved back into Ben's arms. "Is my hair ever going to grow back?"

"You look gorgeous in that wig."

Miryam ducked her head and pulled off the hairpiece, revealing a head covered with dark fuzz. Dropping the wig on the dresser, she peered at her reflection in its mirror. "I am *sooooo* ugly."

Ben stepped up behind her and circled her waist with his arms. "I've never seen you more beautiful than the day we lost our hair. And you're still awfully cute."

"You walked through fire to save me. How can I ever thank you enough?"

"Live a long and happy life at my side, and we'll call it even."

She turned and looked at Ben. "Let's go look in that box."

"Come on! We just got here."

"I don't want to wonder another minute if you're a *mamzer*."

Ben sighed. Until a few weeks earlier, helping Miryam retrieve an ancient Hebrew codex that had been stolen from her great uncle's home, he never had reason to think that *he* might be a child of incest.

Ben never knew his dad; growing up, he was told that his father was *not* Jewish and that he had died in a mysterious fashion that no one would talk about. Ben was raised in his maternal grandparents' home with his mother, who took her own life when Ben was twelve.

Then, only a few months back, he had stumbled upon his father's tombstone in a Jewish cemetery in California. He learned that his father had been a career swindler with a string of aliases and a long arrest record. Just before leaving California, Ben discovered that he had a half-sister and half-brother. From them, he learned that he was the spitting image of their late father.

Shortly after that, in Brooklyn, Ben renewed acquaintances with an elderly rabbi who had been a close friend of his maternal grandfather, Salomen. To Ben's surprise, Rabbi Zeev at first mistook Ben for Salomen.

But how could he so closely resemble his father, his father's child, and his *mother's* father? The obvious but horrible answer was that his parents were siblings or first cousins, which would make him a *mamzer* and therefore, as many rabbis understood Jewish law, unable to marry a Jewish woman. It might also explain why his mother took her own life. Religious aspects aside, Ben's ancestors, the Jews of northern Europe, were descended from an extremely small population that had intermarried for centuries and were therefore much more likely to carry a gene for a variety of nasty genetic disorders. A child of incest from this group was almost certainly a carrier of at least one deadly gene

Ben's grandparents died within months of each other. Stricken by their loss, he had left everything in their apartment except the steel box where his grandfather kept valuables and family documents. Ben had hired a moving company to ship him the bedroom furniture that he had used as a child and had them get rid of everything else.

For years he had avoided the pain of thinking about his beloved grandparents. Now he was going to see if the papers in the box held clues to the puzzle of his ancestry. He had faced down men with guns or knives, risked his life a dozen times, but the thought of what he might find among his family's documents terrified him.

§

Ben said, "I'm hungry. Can we eat before we tackle the box?"

Miryam smiled. "I'll make something while you get started."

Ben shook his head, no. "There's almost nothing in the house. I've been home only a few days at a time over the last year. There's just a few canned goods and what little is in the freezer. Let's order in, eat, and then look at the box together."

Miryam smiled. "You're stalling. I'll go through your freezer and pantry. If I can't whip something up, I'll go out. There must be a dozen restaurants around here."

Ben sighed. "So that's how it's going to be? You're now my conscience?"

"A manifestation of your highest aspirations. And you're mine. Get the box."

"I'm dreading what I'll find."

"As you once told me, 'Anticipation of pain is usually worse than the pain.'"

Ben smiled. He was cornered and knew it.

While Miryam scouted the kitchen, Ben got a ladder from the service porch, carried it into the bedroom, and then into the closet. He climbed three steps, then turned his upper body and with arms outspread pushed on two sections of ceiling molding simultaneously. A square hole yawned in the wall above the molding.

The box was two feet long, 18 inches deep, a foot high and heavy; he stood it on end and propped it between his head and his right shoulder, steadying it with one hand as he backed down the ladder. He carried the box into the dining area and set it on the table, turning to find Miryam watching.

"You were right. There's nothing much to eat. Where should I go for takeout?"

"How about, The Great Wall of Jerusalem. Around the corner."

"Kosher Chinese?"

"The best in Boston. Hurry up. I'm really hungry."

Miryam stepped close and kissed him on the lips, softly. "I don't care what you find in that box. I just want to be with you."

"That makes me only a little less terrified."

Ben watched Miryam as she put her wig back on, straightened it in a mirror, then took the key card and left.

He opened the box. Inside was a large accordion folder filled with photos, another with papers, and a box of what Ben supposed was his grandmother's jewelry.

He took the document folder out of the box and opened it. Then he rose and went to his home office, returning with a yellow legal pad and three pencils. Then he got a glass of water from the kitchen, drank it, and sat down at the table.

CHAPTER TWO

Ben opened his eyes. A tall, blonde woman in her forties, with blue eyes and a blunt, Slavic face knelt before him. She shined a tiny light in his eyes. "Welcome back. Do you know your name, sir?"

"Ben."

The woman frowned, holding up his wallet and peering at his Massachusetts driver's license. "This says your name is Mark Glass."

"Legal name. Same as ... father. But my fa...um, deserted us. Nobody wanted to say name." Ben took a deep breath. "They called me by my Hebrew name, Moshe Benyamin. Ben."

The woman smiled. "You don't look Jewish."

"Neither did that little yeshiva *bocher,* student, with me."

The woman chuckled. "Point taken."

She held up a card from Ben's wallet. "This says you're a patient in a gene therapy trial at Pittsburgh Medical. And that if you need a doctor, I should call the number on the card."

Ben tried to sit up and found that he was sprawled on the sidewalk. The woman restrained him, a hand firmly against his chest.

"Easy," she said. "Can you tell me what happened? Was it from the fight? Did you get punched?"

Ben said, "No, no. The nurse at the clinic... said that I'd feel weak and nauseous after each treatment. I was to rest. Take it easy for a few days. And that gradually I'd get used... and soon I'd only need to rest a few hours each time. That was yesterday. I'm used to a lot of exercise, so I went for a walk. I, I, guess I tried to push it. Too soon."

"But you weren't hurt in the fight?"

Out of Ben's sight, Zach said, "I told you, Mom. Tommy Rollins never touched him. Mr. Glass put some kind of Kung Fu move on him, and boom! It was over. And then Luther Hoffman pulled a gun, and Mr. Glass like just snatched it away."

"Thank you, Zach."

Ben said, "Please call me Ben. Not Mr. Glass."

"Ben it is. Can you get up?"

Slowly, he hoisted himself to his feet. His head swam, but after several seconds, he began to feel better.

"Thank you for coming to help me."

"Thank *you* for helping Zach. Can you walk a little way? Less than a block?"

"Let's try."

Ben tottered forward, gradually feeling strength returning to his legs. By the time they reached the residential street up the road and turned the corner, he felt nearly normal, although still very tired.

They stopped before a small house painted bright blue. The woman said, "Please come in. I'll check your vitals before I decide whether to call your clinic."

Ben said, "You're a doctor?

"CRNP—a certified registered nurse practitioner. And a neonatal nurse. Abigail Silverblatt."

"Thanks for your help, Nurse Silverblatt."

"Just Abby is fine."

"Wait a minute," Ben said, peering very closely at Abby. "Did you grow up in a three-story house on East 34th Street, off Avenue D in Flatbush? Were the shutters painted royal blue—like this house?"

Abby stared. "How could you possibly know that?"

"Because you have a younger sister, Sara Tamar Silverblatt. Who is now a fellow in pediatric oncology at Duke University's Lenox Baker Children's Hospital."

"Yes! Who are you?"

"Sara was my first girlfriend—in the ninth grade."

"Ohmygod—Bennie!"

Abby burst into tears and hugged Ben tight. After a moment, she released him and then gave him a big kiss on the forehead.

"Let's go inside," she said.

Ben climbed the steps to the porch and followed her into the house. She took Zach into the kitchen, then led Ben to a small office outfitted with medical equipment. He sat in a chair as she rolled a blood pressure meter with an automatic cuff and digital readout over, then took a digital thermometer from a cabinet and slipped on a fresh pair of latex gloves.

Abby asked, "Are you allergic to latex?"

"No."

She fastened the pressure cuff around Ben's upper arm and flipped a switch on the device. Slowly, the cuff inflated, tightening around his arm.

As the cuff filled, she took Ben's pulse. The machine chimed, then slowly deflated, and Abby put the thermometer sensor in Ben's ear and held it until a soft beep sounded. She read the blood pressure readout, detached the cuff and smiled.

"BP is slightly low. Your pulse is terrific. And you're a little warm, 99.4, but there's no reason to call the clinic."

Ben said, "Your son is *Beyta Yisroel*? An Ethiopian Jew?"

Abby smiled. "Yes, his birth mother is from Ethiopia."

"And he's about ten?"

"Almost twelve. Small for his age. He goes to a Jewish day school, not a yeshiva."

"He seems like a fine young man."

"He is. I hate to change the subject, but Zach said that you took a gun from those kids. What did you do with it?"

Ben got to his feet, pulled the clip and both halves of the gun from his pockets and laid them on her desk. "The police should look that over, check the ballistics, and see if it's tied to any shootings."

Abby smiled. "My spouse is a police officer. She'll be home soon. Forgive me for asking, professional curiosity, but what is the gene therapy for? If you don't mind saying."

Ben hesitated. "I consider you a long-lost friend. But do we now have a professional relationship? Healer to patient?"

Abby frowned. "You're talking about patient confidentiality?"

Ben said, "Yes."

"Then, yes, of course. I will keep whatever you tell me in confidence."

"My trial is to find a cure for HIV. The first trial was in Denmark and produced excellent results: Most of the participants show no trace of the virus after one year. But it was a very small study. The second trial was a somewhat larger group, and it's in progress. The interim data looks promising. My virologist thinks the protocol has an excellent chance to genetically modify my T-helper lymphocytes–T-cells. In other words, kill the virus hiding in my marrow. Cure me."

Abby said, "You sound like a scientist."

Ben grinned. "I went to M.I.T., but my B.S. is in electrical engineering. Computers. But many of my close friends and former classmates became doctors."

"You were describing the study. Is there more to it?"

"My cohort is getting somewhat stronger dosages and more frequent injections than earlier groups, and it's double-blind. I won't know if I'm getting a therapeutic series or a placebo until the trial concludes."

Abby asked, "Side effects?"

"It makes me feel tired, nauseous and dizzy. But as I said, that's supposed to pass as my system adjusts."

Abby said, "There are so many, many people in our community that will benefit from this trial, no matter how it turns out. Thank you for stepping forward."

"There's nothing to thank me for. I'm doing this strictly for myself. I hope, after this trial, to be virus-free, which will allow me to marry and have children without worrying about infecting anyone."

Abby's face registered surprise. "Oh. I thought maybe—"

Ben interrupted. "I have great sympathy for every human being afflicted with this virus, but I wasn't infected in the manner that most people are."

Abby asked, "A needle stick? An open wound?"

"In Jerusalem, nine years ago. Almost ten now. A bomb in a café. My wife was killed. Everyone who wasn't dead had multiple cuts, including me. A guy near me was choking on his tongue, so I put my hand down his throat to pull it out, and, of course, he bit me. Not his fault. Then an IDF doctor came. He asked me to stick my fingers into a man's leg wound and showed me how to pinch off his femoral artery until he could deal with the man's other problems. I got a lot of other people's blood on me, and some of it must have been infected."

Abby frowned, her face sympathetic. "It's terrible to lose a wife. Even more terrible at such a young age. Do you have children?"

Ben shook his head. "My wife—Rachel—was in her seventh month. The baby was delivered by caesarean but died the next day."

Abby made a face. "I should never have asked."

"It was a long time ago."

Abby said, "That's why you're still single? The virus?"

Ben said, "I recently got engaged. We hope to marry next year."

"Is your fiancé here in Pittsburgh?"

"In Israel—she's visiting her grandparents. Pretty soon, she'll go down to Argentina to spend some time with her father's side of the family She's coming for Pesach if I'm feeling up to it. Then she's going to Berkeley to take one last class and finish her master's degree."

"I bet you miss her."

"I do. And it's only been a week."

"You must think I'm a Nosy Nellie, but what do you do for a living? When you're not saving little boys from juvenile thugs?"

Ben paused before answering, uncertain of how much he wanted to share.

"Since I became aware of my condition, I've been unable to find full-time employment in the field for which I am trained. I guess you could say that now I do stuff like saving little boys from juvenile thugs."

Abby looked puzzled. "I don't understand."

"I practice *tikkun olam*. I work to heal the world, a little at a time, as and when my help is needed. Usually, the gig is somewhat longer and more interesting than today's little tête-à-tête by the bridge, and there's a fee arrangement."

"I suppose it's really none of my business. But you've piqued my curiosity. You were trained for computer science. Why can't you find work? You're on antiretrovirals, right?"

"After M.I.T., I went to rabbinical school."

"You're a rabbi?"

Ben inclined his head, yes.

"You mean that no *shul* will hire you? Because you're HIV-positive?"

"Every board of directors that I approached decided that their members won't want me around their children. They're afraid that I might infect them."

"That's ridiculous. But you *look* healthy. How would they know your HIV status?"

"Abby, being a pulpit rabbi is not like driving a bus or running a corporate I.T. department. The spiritual leader of a sacred congregation must set a moral example. His behavior, especially in private, must be above reproach. Rabbis are privy to congregants' personal confidences. We must be the one person that everyone knows with absolute certainty they can trust. And to do what is right and proper and morally correct under all circumstances. But rabbis are human. We are fallible. I know wonderful rabbis, beacons of morality and probity. But, sadly, I also know or have met, or read about, rabbis who are thieves, swindlers, adulterers, child molesters, even murderers. One of my rabbinical classmates made a fortune peddling underwater Red Sea real estate. Developing trust between a rabbi and a congregation does not happen easily or all at once but over a long period.

"How could I expect to earn that trust if I began a relationship with my congregation by concealing such an important fact?"

"So you just told them? Is that it?"

"Each time I interviewed for a pulpit. Straight up, including how I was infected. And each time, they apologized for declining to offer me a position."

"That's just wrong. What *exactly* do you do now, Rabbi?"

"I'm sort of a roving troubleshooter for Jewish institutions. Or individuals."

"Sorry. You just told me that, but I didn't get it."

Ben smiled then got to his feet. He was hungry, which he took as a good sign. "Thanks for checking me over, Abby. I feel much better, so I should be going."

"Can't you stay for dinner? My wife will be home soon—I'm sure she'd love to meet you."

"I'd be honored to share your meal. But only if it's kosher."

"We're not a kosher household. But we eat only vegetables, dairy, and fish in this house. No meat or meat products, ever. It's a compromise between my wish to be a vegan and Yolanda's craving for animal protein. We're having fresh salmon tonight—I could use paper plates and plastic tableware if that would make you more comfortable?"

Ben smiled. "Then I accept."

"Wonderful. And I bake my own bread. We even have a bottle of Baron Herzog Zinfandel, if you'd care to try some."

Chapter Three

Abby asked, "Zach, would you lead us in the blessing over wine?"

Gripping a wine glass half full of grape juice, the boy stood up and chanted, "*Barukh atah Adonai Eloheinu Melekh ha'olam, bo're p'ri ha'gafen.*"

"Amen," replied Ben, Abby, and Yolanda.

Yolanda was in her early thirties, tall and shapely, with olive skin, huge brown eyes and dark, silky hair. She had come directly from work and wore a severely tailored business suit that barely left room for a holster and a badge. She had locked both in a safe before sitting down to eat.

Yolanda said, "We've never had a rabbi over for dinner. It feels almost like *Shabbos.*"

Ben said, "It does kind of feel like *Shabbat.*"

Zach asked, "Rabbi, how come you say *Shabbat* and Momma Yolanda says *Shabbos?* Which one is right?"

Ben winked at Yolanda to show that he'd expected the question. "Both are correct. In Modern Hebrew, as it's spoken in Israel and in most American synagogues, we use the Sephardic pronunciation. The most obvious difference is that many words that Ashkenazim would pronounce with the softer 'ess' sound, like Shabbos, Sephardim pronounce with a final 't' sound. 'Shabbat.'

Zach asked, "What's an Ashka Nazim? And a Seffar Dim?"

The adults smiled.

Yolanda said, "The Ashkenazim, as I understand it, are descended from Jews who lived in northern European countries, like Germany and Russia, and the Sephardim came from Spain."

Abby said, "And Portugal."

Ben said, "Almost right. It has more to do with language and customs than where they lived. The way they spoke Hebrew was influenced by the language of their daily lives. For Ashkenazim, that was Yiddish, which is a variant of Old German, but with many Hebrew, Polish and other Slavic words. It's written with the Hebrew alphabet. For the Sephardim, it was *Ladino*, which is based on Old Spanish and written with Roman characters..."

Zach said, "Wait. Why did Jews only *used to* live in Spain? And in Russia and Germany? Don't any Jewish people still live there?"

Ben said, "Another excellent question. Some Jews, a few, now live in Spain, although almost none did until about thirty years ago. A few live in Germany again, and many are in Russia. The better question is, how did they come to live in all these countries in the first place?"

Yolanda said, "I've got this one. The nation of Israel was wiped off the map when the Romans conquered what they called Judea and then destroyed the Temple in Jerusalem. After that, the Jews dispersed and settled in different countries around the world."

Ben asked, "And when was that? When was the Temple destroyed?"

Abby said, "This is wonderful, having our very own rabbi to teach us. The Temple was destroyed in 70 C.E. Now before everything gets cold, can we eat?"

§

After dinner, Abby went with Zach to get him started on his homework. Ben and Yolanda remained at the table, sipping coffee.

Ben said, "Have you always lived in Pittsburgh?"

Yolanda shook her head, no. "I was born in a little town in New Mexico. When I was five, my dad got shot on the job—he was a deputy sheriff—and took disability retirement. He lined up a security gig with Times Square Stores, and we moved to Queens. In New York City."

"I remember those stores. One of the first big discount chains."

"They went bankrupt, and Dad wound up in a civilian position for NYPD: property and evidence clerk."

"When did you decide to convert to Judaism?"

Yolanda stared at Ben. "How do you know that? Because I'm Hispanic?"

Ben shook his head. "If you had grown up Jewish in New York thirty years ago, unless you were Orthodox—and most New York Orthodox are Hassid—you would use the Sephardic dialect."

"And you knew I wasn't Orthodox because…?"

"Because few Orthodox would pursue a career in law enforcement. It would mean working on Shabbat, not always having access to kosher food, and involvement in the kinds of things that most Orthodox try to avoid in their daily life.

"So I'm guessing that you recently decided to convert and that your teacher is an older rabbi, probably raised in the Orthodox tradition but no longer identified with that stream of Judaism. He might be retired or working only part time."

"Wow. You figured that all out from one word?"

"Talmudic logic."

"You should be a detective!"

Ben asked, "What's your family name?"

"Sanchez."

"And your mother's maiden name?"

"Toleadano."

"And what was the name of your original hometown?"

"Bet you never heard of it. Jareles."

"Actually, I *have*. South of Albuquerque on U.S. 85. And now I'm going to go way out on a limb and guess that as a child you never ate pork and that when your mother swept the floor, she swept everything into the center of the room, then threw it outside through a window, never through the door."

Yolanda stared, wide-eyed, at Ben. "Not my *mom*. The sweeping, I mean. But that was what my grandmother did—how she swept up—my father's mother."

Ben smiled. "Now I'll bet that your mother lit candles on Friday nights, but she went into a back room or down in the basement to light them. And that your father had a special set of old knives that were never used, and that he traded shifts or days off so he didn't have to work Saturdays."

Yolanda whispered, "My God, *who* are you?"

"Just a rabbi."

"This is really, really, weird."

"Not at all. Do you know the term 'crypto-Jew'"?

Yolanda shook her head, just as Abby returned to the room.

Yolanda said, "Abby, this is really wild—Rabbi Ben knows more about me than you did when we first met."

Abby pulled out her chair and sat down. "What's going on?"

"Well, he knows about my mom and her candles. And my grandmother's weird way of sweeping the floor. And about my Dad always trading days off at work. And that we didn't allow *carnitas* at our house. And he guessed that I was converting."

Ben asked, "So you haven't completed the process?"

Abby said, "She was supposed to go to the *Beit Din*, and then schedule a trip to the *mikveh*, but Rabbi Geltkern had to leave town. So, when he gets back."

Yolanda said, "He even figured out that Rabbi Geltkern is an older man."

Ben doffed an imaginary hat.

Yolanda smiled. "Rabbi Geltkern is wonderful. Maybe the only rabbi in Pittsburgh that would even consider performing a same-sex marriage ceremony."

Abby asked, "What was that you said about crypto-Jews? A minute ago?"

Ben said, "I asked if she knew what that meant."

Yolanda and Abby exchanged glances. Abby said, "Well, crypto has to mean something like a code, a secret? Secret Jews?"

Ben smiled. "Go to the head of the class, Yolanda. Not everyone named Toleadano is Jewish, but every one that *I've* met, at least a dozen people, were descended from Jews who lived in Spain before and, in some cases, also after 1492. Second, the name Sanchez was very common among 15th Century Spanish Jews. Third, most of Spain's Jews were *not* expelled. Given the choice of losing everything—their homes, their livestock, all their money and even their personal valuables, and then becoming stateless refugees, wandering the world trying to find a country that would accept them—or converting to Christianity, many chose to convert. Even among those who didn't choose Christianity, many of their children were forcibly converted, and many Jewish adults were literally dragged to the baptismal font.

"They were called New Christians. Also converts or converses, and pork-eaters, or *Marranos*. Many went on practicing Judaism in secret. Then came the Inquisition, created to detect heretics, backsliders and, not incidentally, to allow the Church to confiscate their property and split it with the Spanish Crown. It was directed mostly at New Christians and soon became an instrument of terror. Possession of Hebrew books or papers was punishable by death. Thousands of *conversos* were tortured to admit that they still practiced Judaism, forced to implicate friends and even close relatives—and then they were murdered, often burned alive as a public spectacle."

Abby and Yolanda looked horrified.

Yolanda said, "I've heard of the Inquisition, but I never knew—"

Ben said, "It went on for centuries, in a less barbaric form, until the eighteen-fifties. To escape it, many New Christians fled to the New World. So many went to Mexico that Spain barred New Christian emigration, and the Church established the Inquisition in Mexico City. And for decades, it was just as horrific as it was in Spain. Many New Christians moved as far from Mexico City as they could get.

"Today, if you visit graveyards in some New Mexico small towns, and look carefully at old tombstones, you'll find many with a Star of David hidden in the ornamentation around a name or crucifix. You'll find Hebrew words similarly camouflaged on these tombstones.

"And, several years ago, the adult male church members of a parish in your old hometown—Jareles—took DNA tests. Many of them, including a Catholic priest, had markers that proved that they were descended not just from Jews but from the Kohanim, the ancient priestly class established by Aaron and his sons."

Yolanda began to weep. Abby put her arm around her.

Sobbing, Yolanda said, "I always felt like we weren't like other families. Whose mother goes down to the basement to light candles every Friday night? And after my little brother was baptized, when my father thought no one was watching, he wiped the holy water off him! Rabbi Ben, does this mean that I'm actually Jewish?"

Ben said, "Very likely. *Converso* families tended not to intermarry with Old Christian families. Your DNA will tell if you are descended from Jews, but in order to *be* Jewish, you would have to know that you had a Jewish mother. Which would mean identifying several generations of female ancestors as Jewish? It might be done, but it would be expensive and time-consuming. I recommend that you continue on your present path to conversion because DNA analysis and hiring a professional genealogist is expensive and could take years."

Abby said, "Thank you for enlightening us. This means so much to Yolanda."

Yolanda said, "I can't wait to tell Rabbi Geltkern."

Two Weeks Earlier (continued)

Ben heard the door open behind him and felt in his pocket for a handkerchief.

Miryam set a large paper bag on the table.

"Ben! What's wrong?"

Tears rolled down his cheeks. Sobbing, he got to his feet and reached for Miryam. As they held each other, she felt his body shuddering as he wept.

After several minutes, Ben said, "I'm sorry," and went into the bathroom..he returned mopping his eyes and face with a tissue.

Miryam said, "Talk to me. What's going on?"

Ben said, "Everything I thought I knew about my parents and grandparents was a lie. But—I'm *not* a *mamzer*."

He took a deep breath. "I feel better. And hungry. Let's eat."

"But you're okay?"

"Just ... a little shook up."

Ben set out plates and glasses, and Miryam ladled food onto the plates. Ben mumbled a blessing over the food, and they ate in silence for a few minutes, Ben seeming to turn inward, processing his thoughts until he laid his chopsticks down and reached into the box. He took out a hand-tinted photo of a smiling young woman in a jacket, her hair restrained by a snood.

Miryam said, "She's beautiful. Your mother?"

"My *grand*mother."

He turned the photo over and showed her what was written in pencil there:

Chana Teitelbaum, Siget, 1942.

Ben said, "Siget was in the northwestern corner of Rumania."

"But you just said that your grandmother came from Vienna, in 1933?"

"I did. But *bubbe* was not my *mother's* mother. She was my *father's* mother."

"But you told me—"

"Let me start over. What I know, and what I can guess."

Ben reached for his pad. The top page was covered with notes.

"Chana Teitelbaum was born in Rumania in 1925. Starting in 1943, she survived various concentration camps and wound up, very sick and malnourished, in a place called Föhrenwald, in Bavaria, in 1945 or 1946. A camp for displaced Jews."

"And you learned this just now?"

Ben dipped his head. Then he reached for a document at the top of a small pile next to the steel box.

"I had to go online to look up some things. For instance, I'd never heard of Föhrenwald until now.

"After Germany surrendered, Europe was overrun with refugees and displaced persons. More than a million Jews—Germans, French, Estonians, Latvians, Lithuanians, Hungarians, Austrians, Czechs, Rumanians, Poles—Jews from all over Europe. And others—Russian and Polish prisoners of war, slave laborers, Roma—Gypsies—German communists and Jehovah's Witnesses, disabled people, homosexuals—anybody the Nazis tried to exterminate or turned into slave laborers to support their war effort."

Miryam asked, "And Chana was one of those displaced persons?"

"Yes. Most had no documents, nothing to prove their nationality. And their communities were gone, everyone they knew had been murdered, their homes were taken over by others. They had no reason to return to their birthplaces. The Allied armies put them in camps, dealt with their malnutrition, treated their diseases, and tried to find a country that would accept them."

"Why not send them to Israel?"

"Israel did not exist until 1948. When Chana got to Föhrenwald, in the American sector, the British still controlled Palestine. They refused to allow more Jews to settle there. Thousands came anyway, but it was risky and difficult."

"Like that old movie, *Exodus*?"

"That's right. From what I found on the Internet if you were Jewish and you *had* to be in a DP camp, Föhrenwald wasn't the worst place to be. They had a yeshiva, a *mikveh*, or ritual bathhouse, synagogues, schools, a full religious life. And they had the highest birth rate in Europe."

"Chana got married in that camp?"

Ben said, "I found her *ketubah,* marriage contract, written in Hebrew and Yiddish. She married Chaim Sperrah in 1956."

"I don't understand—she stayed in that camp all those years?"

"Until 1960, when she died."

"But why?"

Ben shrugged. "I can't tell. Maybe she had tuberculosis or something, and no country would take her. Or maybe she found a job in the camps, something that she wanted to do. Maybe Chaim Sperrah was an aid worker, not a displaced person. I don't know anything about Chaim except that he was a U.S. citizen born in Hungary. He's listed as my mother's father on her birth certificate."

"What was your mother's name?"

"Tzippe. In Hebrew, Zipporah. She was born in 1960. Her mother, Chana, died of 'complications of childbirth,' whatever that means."

"Chaim brought Tzippe to America?"

"It looks that way. She was naturalized in Brooklyn in 1963. According to her certificate, she had a stepmother, Annalisa Fierro, also a U.S. citizen."

"Fierro doesn't sound very Jewish."

"You never can tell for sure."

Ben consulted his notes again, then ate some rice.

"Let me go on. My mother graduated high school in 1977. The address on her last report card is the apartment that I grew up in. My grandparent's home."

Miryam frowned. "She graduated from high school in 1977, when she was 17?"

"Sixteen years and eight months. I was born less than a year later."

"Was she married?"

"Yes. There's another *ketubah*. And a license issued at Brooklyn's Borough Hall. She married Mark Thompson Glass in June 1977."

Ben reached into an open accordion file and removed a picture of a young man in a graduation cap and gown. The picture had been torn into pieces; then reassembled with clear tape that had yellowed with age. The man wore glasses and looked amazingly like Ben.

"This is my father. The first picture of him that I've ever seen. He was born in August 1952."

Chapter Four

Two Fridays after dinner with Abby and Yolanda, Ben rolled out of bed a little past 6:00 a.m., feeling more energetic and stronger than he had since coming to Pittsburgh. He said the *Modeh Ani*, the morning prayer, aloud, slower and more heartfelt than his usual hurried recitation: "I offer thanks before you, living and eternal King, for You have mercifully restored my soul within me; Your faithfulness is great."

Changing into running shoes and sweats for the cool Pennsylvania autumn, he resolved to run a mile. One mile and he'd turn around and walk home, cooling off as he went. No sense in pushing things again.

He thumbed on his iPhone pedometer, then jogged up Darlington, turned onto Forbes Avenue and dropped into his second gear, a leisurely lope, but as he neared the mile's end at Bob O'Connor Golf Course, where Forbes takes a sharp right turn to the northwest, he felt too good to stop. He lengthened his stride, feeling strong, eager to go on. A*nother mil*e, he told himself. Ninety seconds and a quarter mile later, as Forbes turned again, a dogleg west, he picked up the pace again, reveling in the crisp air and the glorious red and orange foliage.

Behind him, a siren gave a short, intense whoop, and Ben craned his head as an unmarked black Ford Crown Victoria slid past him and stopped on the shoulder. The passenger door flew open and a tall, beefy man in his late forties, with thinning hair, emerged, parting his suit jacket to display a badge.

Ben said, "Good morning, Officer."

The cop said, "Detective. Reason we stopped you, sir, is that you were exceeding the jogging speed limit. You look like you might be from out of town, so I'm officially informing you that the city of Pittsburgh is very strict about this. We don't want any of you running types colliding with cars, or scaring pedestrians, or livestock."

"I see. How fast did you clock me at, Officer?"

The cop glared at Ben. "You trying to get smart? Let's see your jogging license and running shoe registration."

Ben laughed.

The cop roared, and the driver's door opened to reveal Yolanda, giggling as she approached.

"Admit it, Rabbi, we had you going for a minute, right?"

Ben shook his head and gestured toward the far side of the street. "I was just getting warm. That's a golf course over there, and I'm pretty sure I could have hopped the fence and outrun both of you."

The male cop laughed again and stuck out his hand. "Roland Easton," he said, and they shook hands.

Yolanda said, "Detective Easton is my training officer. He's teaching me the basics of field investigation."

Ben smiled. "Roland and Yolanda. Sounds like a dance act."

Both officers cracked up.

Ben said, "Delighted to meet you, Detective. If you're Officer Sanchez's training officer, that makes you her rabbi, right?"

Easton smiled. "Yolanda didn't tell me that you *parlez vous* police."

Ben said, "That's just between us rabbis."

Yolanda said, "Can you come to Shabbat dinnert? Six o'clock?"

"Sure. But I need to get moving again before I cramp up."

Easton said, "We're gonna let you go with a warning, this time. But watch those feet."

Everybody laughed, Ben shook Easton's hand again, and the cops climbed back into their car and drove off.

Ben decided to go just far enough toward downtown Pittsburgh to get warm again, then head back. Half an hour later, covered with sweat but riding a runner's high, he stepped into the shower, wondering if his meeting with Yolanda had been entirely a matter of chance.

§

Yolanda said, "Rabbi Ben, I have a confession to make."

Ben said, "Then you need a priest, not a rabbi."

Around the table, Yolanda, Abby, and Zach giggled.

Yolanda said, "I checked you out on the Internet."

Ben frowned. "The YouTube videos?"

Yolanda said, "Apparently saving Zach wasn't the first time you've kicked some righteous butt."

Ben shook his head. "Everybody carries a cell phone. Everybody's got a video camera. A guy can't even kick a little righteous *tuchas* in private anymore."

Abby asked, "Ben, could you teach Zach to defend himself?"

Yolanda said, "We'll pay you."

Ben paused, thinking. "Until now—thanks to my weekly injections—I wasn't sure if I'll feel well enough to handle the exertion that the martial-arts demand."

Yolanda said, "Of course. It was thoughtless of us to ask—"

Ben interrupted. "Hold on. Actually, you've given me an idea. Assuming that my doctors are correct and that I'll continue to adjust to the side effects, I should be able to manage a few hours a week. And I've been thinking that I should try to find something useful to do while I'm here. I was going to ask somebody at the Jewish Federation about a volunteer gig, maybe a few days a week. Maybe I could start with—how many students in Zach's school?"

Abby thought for a moment. "About 200, grades seven to 12."

"Maybe I could volunteer to teach a self-defense course. Basic stuff. Maybe another teacher could lead a discussion about bullying."

Yolanda said, "That's wonderful. We'll make an appointment to see the director and see how receptive she is to something like that."

Ben said, "Great. Make sure you tell her that I can't handle Mondays or Tuesdays. And that I'll only be here until next September."

Zach said, "Thanks, Rabbi."

Abby said, "Yolanda also discovered that you have an FBI file."

Ben made a face. "That doesn't surprise me."

Yolanda touched his arm. "You're actually kind of a private detective, right?"

"You could say that. But I'm here for medical treatment, not to get involved with another mystery."

Abby said, "But we *have* a mystery, and we need your help."

Two Weeks Earlier (*continued*)

Miryam took a sip of water and thought for a moment. "Wait, my head is swimming, she said. Your father was 25, almost 26, and your mom was 16, almost 17, when they got married?"

"Yes. I was born in November 1977. My mother filed for divorce from my father in December 1977. There's a civil divorce decree from 1977 and a *get*, a Jewish divorce document, issued by a Beit Din, a rabbinical court, in Brooklyn.

"So your father impregnated a 16-year-old girl who was living with his parents, married and then divorced her. Do I have that right?

"Remember the times. I think that when she got pregnant, her father and stepmother kicked her out, and my grandparents took her in. Then it gets weird. After the divorce, before her 18th birthday, Salomen and Hadassah Glass, my paternal grandparents, adopted her."

"What? They adopted their son's wife?"

"His ex-wife."

Miryam said, "That was one screwed-up family."

CHAPTER FIVE

Ben looked at Abby and then at Yolanda, and shook his head. "I've taken a leave of absence from mysteries. I'm just here to get well. And once I am, I intend to seek a pulpit of my own and get married."

Abby said, "We understand. Can you come with us to *shul* tomorrow?"

Yolanda said, "We'd like you to meet Rabbi Geltkern."

Ben smiled. "Is it a long walk?"

Abby laughed. "It's in Berona Township. Too far to walk."

Yolanda said, "We'll pick you up."

Zach said, "You're still sick, right? So it's okay to drive to *shul* when you're sick, right, Rabbi Ben?"

Ben said, "Well, most Conservative rabbis believe that in the world we now live in, many people live too far from their synagogue to walk. Driving is better than not joining your community to celebrate Shabbat. So, if we're going straight out and coming right back afterward, sure, I'll ride with you."

Abby said, "We'll come by about 8:30 tomorrow."

Ben looked out the window of Abby's minivan as it sped along an expressway following the north bank of the Allegheny River. "There must be half a dozen Jewish congregations in Squirrel Hill alone," he said, "Why *schlep* all the way out here?"

Yolanda said, "Because of Rabbi Geltkern. You'll see."

Ben said, "There's an LGBT group, a kind of congregation within a congregation, that meets at Rodef Shalom. Have you ever been there?"

Abby said, "Nice people. But mostly singles. Not many families with kids Zach's age."

Ben asked, "How did you happen to find Rabbi Geltkern?"

Abby smiled. "When we moved here, I took the state licensing exams, but then I had to wait until I was certified before I could start my own practice. While I was waiting, I worked part-time and temporary gigs. One was the Sanok Retirement Home, out in Berona Township."

Ben asked, "Sanok? That was a Jewish town in Poland, right?"

Abby dipped her head. "I think so. As I understand it, about a hundred years ago, before the First World War, several Jewish men from towns around Sanok came to Pittsburgh to work in the steel mills. When they had saved enough money, they sent for their families. At one time, just before World War II, there were about 2,000 people in the Pittsburgh area from that part of Poland. They started a burial society."

In the back seat, sitting next to Yolanda, Zach asked, "Momma Abby, what's a burial society?"

"It's when a bunch of Jewish people put up some money and buy land for a cemetery, and they make sure that, when someone dies, that they get a Jewish funeral and are buried in a Jewish cemetery. Right, Rabbi Ben?"

Ben said. "Exactly. So how did a burial society become a retirement home?"

Abby shook her head. "I'm not sure. The Sanok people, the ones living here, thought that most of their extended families would soon leave

Poland and come here. In fact, in 1938, just before the war, their Rebbe collected money and went back to Poland to bring the rest of the Sanok Jews here, but...."

Ben chewed his lip. "The Holocaust?"

"Yes," Abby said, as she braked, then cautiously steered into the right-hand lane. An off-ramp took them to a high bridge over the river. As they descended to the south bank, Ben saw a golf course, then a subdivision of expensive homes circling a country club. In contrast to much of Pittsburgh, with its weathered buildings and mature trees, the houses looked new. Many had luxury cars in their driveways.

Ben said, "Maybe, after the war, when they saw that they wouldn't need such a big cemetery, they sold some of their land and used the money to build a retirement home. But where does Rabbi Geltkern come in?"

Abby said, "I'm getting to that. The home used to have about 500 people, and they employed a staff doctor. Now it's only about fifty residents. They have a few vocational nurses and an on-call doctor, and they bus residents into Pittsburgh to see their doctors. I was hired to work Fridays, supervise the vocational nurses, make sure patients' charts are kept professionally and residents' prescriptions are current. I also see anybody with an urgent problem and arrange for further treatment if needed.

"They used to have a full-time rabbi. Now, Rabbi Geltkern is there part time. He's on call for emergencies, and he comes Friday afternoons and holds services after dinner."

Ben asked, "And he has his own congregation, as well?"

"It's just a little farther," Abby replied.

They rode on in silence for a long moment. Less than a mile from the river, the new pavement narrowed to older asphalt, replete with potholes. Abruptly, the road veered to the left, and the town of Berona appeared. Above it, a winding lane ascended a gentle, forested slope to a low ridge topped by a long white building with a blue tile roof.

Abby said, "See there, up top? That's the Sanok Home."

Turning off the highway into a street that led past a series of chain-link fences around shuttered manufacturing facilities, Abby found a wide driveway and drove under a rusting arch announcing the Berona Industrial Park, a collection of weathered brick buildings housing machine shops and small factories. Many were shuttered and locked. Near the back of the park, she turned into a crowded parking lot before a two-story building with a hand-painted sign proclaiming the "The Sanoker Shul."

Ben stared. It was an odd name for a 21st-century American synagogue. Was there a connection to the nearby Sanok Home?

TWO WEEKS EARLIER (CONTINUED)

Miryam waited while Ben paused to drink water. "There's one more thing," he said." I believe, it's the key to all this. "My father was the screwed-up one. The Torah tells us, *'If a man has a stubborn and rebellious son who will not listen to his parents, then the parents shall take him to the elders of the city for judgment.'*"

Miryam asked, "So your granddad took your father to a *Beit Din*?"

"My grandfather, Salomen, a revered Talmudist and the chairman of his department at the Jewish Theological Seminary, dragged my father before a *Beit Din*, a rabbinical court, of five rabbis. I can't tell from these papers if my father even bothered to show up for the trial."

"What happened?"

"My father was excommunicated."

"What does that mean?"

"No one in the Jewish community can have anything to do with him. Can't speak to him, help him, support him, have any dealings with him. He's still a member of the tribe, a Jew, but he is forever shunned."

"But what did he do to deserve that?"

"There's a writ from the *Beit Din*. It refers to the *Shulchan Aruch,* the sixteenth-century Code of Jewish Law, and to the Talmudic injunction that one who violates a Torah prohibition is subject to the laws of shunning. I've never seen this kind of document before, not even in rabbinical school. And it doesn't name my father's offense."

"I feel so sorry for your mother."

"Yes. My poor mother. Maybe my father did force himself on her—that could be the Torah prohibition that he ignored."

"And your grandparents, your father's parents, adopted her so that she wouldn't be alone in the world trying to raise his child."

"And then they made up this vague story to tell people about my father getting killed in an overseas plane crash."

"You said he actually died in California?"

"A year or two ago. He had a long, ugly police record. A con man. Sometimes, he called himself a rabbi. He specialized in ripping off synagogues and Jewish institutions."

"Ben, maybe he had already started that life when he met your mother. Maybe that's why he was excommunicated."

Ben considered the idea. "As despicable as it is, I like that a whole lot more than thinking I might be the child of a rape."

Miryam took Ben's hand. "How amazing—your father spent his life hurting Jews, and you spend yours helping Jews."

"I never intended to make a career of this work. I just wanted to be a rabbi, to be the spiritual guide and teacher of a Jewish community. My grandfather, of blessed memory, would say that this is proof of *chesed*, God's loving kindness."

Miryam pushed back her chair and rose to hug Ben.

"Let's see how it goes in Pittsburgh," she whispered. "Maybe you'll get cured. Maybe someday you will have a pulpit of your own, and I will help you by teaching the little ones."

"From your lips to God's ear," Ben said.

Chapter Six

The high-ceilinged interior of The Sanoker Shul was a study in improvisation. Illuminated by long skylights that attested to the building's industrial origin, it was divided into a series of expansive enclosures whose walls ended well below the high roof. The entrance space included rows of wall hooks for coats, a rack that held several tallitot, or prayer shawls, a box of yarmulkes in various styles, and a bookcase with multiple copies of several different volumes.

The sanctuary area was larger, its walls draped with canvases on which Biblical scenes were sketched in a primitive style; to Ben, they had the appearance of a high school theatrical set.

Ben, Abby, Yolanda, and Zach found seats in pews of unfinished pine covered with stuffed red leatherette and arranged in a semicircle around a bimah, an elevated platform built of what appeared to be shipping pallets. At the back of the bimah, Ben saw a gigantic Aron Kodesh or Torah Ark. It seemed very old and was beautifully carved from dark wood. Ben guessed that it had been salvaged from a more traditional sanctuary.

After a few minutes, a dark, kindly-looking, white-haired man in thick glasses mounted the bimah and took his place in front of a lectern. Tapping the microphone with one finger, he waited for the room to quiet.

"I guess we all expected Rabbi Geltkern to return yesterday, but he isn't back yet. I'll update you all by email as soon as I know when he's coming," he said.

"We'll start with the Torah service. Do we have a Torah reader today?"

Ben craned his head, looking around the room, but saw no hands. He got to his feet. "I can read Torah," he said.

Heads swiveled, and the man at the lectern peered at Ben. "You must be new. Would you introduce yourself, please?"

"Moshe Benyamin Maimon," he replied. "I go by Ben."

"Ben, did you take Rabbi Geltkern's Torah reading class?"

Ben shook his head, no. "My first time here. But I can read Torah."

The man at the lectern smiled but shook his head. "I'm sure that you can. But we do things a little differently here, and Rabbi Geltkern wants all new Torah readers to take his class first. See me after services, and I'll sign you up for the class."

Ben said, "Okay, sure," and sat down.

Abby started to get up, but Ben gently took her arm.

Abby whispered, "Why don't you tell them that you're a rabbi?"

"It's okay. I'll tell you later."

The man at the lectern said, "Anybody else who can read Torah?"

A tall, slender, balding young man who had entered a few moments earlier called out, "Hey, Stan, sorry I'm late. I've got the Torah if you need me."

"Wonderful," Stan replied. "Our Torah reader this morning will be Andrew. Let's open our Shabbos prayer books to page one 122.

Ben pulled a book from its shelf on the back of the bench in front of him, noting that it was Mishkan T'Filah, a standard siddur, or prayer book, used by many Reform Judaism congregations. He wondered why Stan — if that was his name — had called it a "Shabbos prayer book." Maybe, thought Ben, he used a layman's term. Two generations after the Holocaust exterminated most of Europe's Jews, Yiddish was spoken mainly by the elderly and the ultra-Orthodox. Combining a Yiddish term with English to describe a Reform prayer book seemed jarring.

I'm making too much of this, he thought. One of the things Ben loved about Judaism was that if someone didn't like a particular rabbi or something about a particular congregation, he or she was free to find another one.

Ben put the issue out of his mind as the service began. In form and structure, the service followed the prayer book and seemed much like those he knew from his visits to Reform temples. As usual in Reform synagogues, prayers were mostly in English, with a few hymns sung in Hebrew—except that the melody used for one was usually associated with Hanukkah, and another was sung to a tune Ben had heard only on Passover. Ben found it strange and jarring, but not a violation of Halakhah, or Jewish law.

In an Orthodox or Conservative synagogue, Ben would have expected seven people to be called to the Torah, one after another, to recite a benediction before and after each Torah passage the reader chanted. Most Reform congregations call only three; Andrew, the Torah reader, chanted passages from a Sefer Torah, the handwritten scroll secured in the Torah Ark, and did a credible job, stumbling over only a few words. To Ben's ears, the young man's trope, the melodic chant that accompanies ritual Torah readings, seemed off, but Ben had heard much worse in Orthodox and Conservative synagogues.

After the Torah reading, it's traditional in most congregations for the rabbi, or some other member, to deliver a drasha, or scholarly lesson, about the Torah. Usually, this is in the form of a lecture, but sometimes it is a discussion led by the rabbi or a lay member. When the Torah service concluded, Stan scanned the room.

"Does anyone have a drasha, a lesson, that they'd care to share?"

The room was silent for a few moments. Then Abby stood up. "We brought a guest this morning. Perhaps Rabbi Ben would like to share some Torah with us?"

With a sigh, Ben climbed to his feet. "I'm a stranger here. Probably you'd feel more comfortable hearing from one of your own."

Stan smiled. "No. Please come up and share some Torah with us."

Several people applauded, and Ben made his way to the bimah. When he reached the lectern, Stan leaned in to whisper to Ben, "Why didn't you say that you were a rabbi?"

Ben said, "I didn't think it would have made any difference. If you have your own rules, I wouldn't think of asking you to make an exception for me."

Stan smiled, and shook Ben's hand, then stood aside to allow Ben to stand before the lectern.

Ben began, "In Haye Sarah, this week's Torah portion, our mother Sarah dies. Our father Abraham goes in search of a place to bury her.

"He goes to the local people, Hittites, and asks to buy a particular field that includes a cave, as a place to bury Sarah. He is introduced to Ephron, a prominent merchant, and they engage in an odd negotiation: Ephron offers to give him the land as a gift, but Abraham insists on paying. Eventually, in an offhand manner, Ephron says, 'You're a prince of God! What are 400 silver shekels between men like us? Just take the land, and bury your wife.'

"Abraham, however, insists on paying the sum that Ephron had so casually named.

"So what's going on here? What was this really all about?"

After a moment, an older woman raised her hand. "Rabbi, what was a shekel worth in those days?"

Ben smiled. "A very good question. A shekel was ten and a half grams of silver. At today's prices, about ten dollars."

A younger man stood up. "Rabbi, if a shekel is ten bucks today, then this guy Ephron asked for $4,000. Wasn't that way too much for that time?"

Ben looked pleased. "This was during the early Hittite empire. Common people relied on barter for most things. They didn't have much cash. Today, silver is an industrial metal. Four hundred silver shekels is about ten pounds of pure silver. From everything that I've read, mining and smelting coinage was a laborious process in that era. A silver coin was far more precious than it is now."

An older man stood up. "You're saying that the price this Ephron guy named was way too much?"

Ben said, "Consider what we know about that part of the world today. Maybe, Ephron expected Abraham to make a counter-offer, to bargain with him."

Another man raised his hand with a comment, and then several more people; the discussion continued for ten minutes, until Ben guided the congregation to the conclusion that perhaps Abraham wasn't merely buying a plot of land, but what it stood for: "God had promised that his descendants would be as numerous as the grains of sand on a beach," Ben summarized. "And God also promised that he would give those descendants the Land of Israel. By buying land, Abraham became the first Jew to own land in Israel. But unless it was acquired by purchase, future generations of Hittites might claim that the land was merely loaned to Abraham and that, after he died, they could take it back. Exchanging silver for land made it a business transaction so that the land would always belong to Abraham and his descendants."

The room was silent for a few moments as the congregation digested his words. As they began to applaud, Ben shook his head and raised his hands for quiet.

"This is a house of study and prayer. What we do here is not a performance, not a show. By worshipping and learning together, we honor the commandment, or mitzvah, to study Torah. The proper way to show appreciation for fulfilling a mitzvah is to say 'yasher koach,' meaning, 'May God give you strength.'

"I thank you for the privilege of helping to complete this mitzvah."

Chapter Seven

After the service, Ben was surrounded by people who seemed genuinely pleased to meet him. They asked where he was from, how long would he be in the area, whether he would be coming back; Ben made small talk, saying only that he was visiting Pittsburgh for several months on personal business.

A light lunch was served in an adjacent room filled with folding tables covered with disposable table cloths. Uncertain that the food was kosher, Ben ate a bagel and nibbled salad, chatting with Yolanda and Abby. Then Stan appeared and beckoned to him. Trailed by Abby, Ben followed him into a large but mostly empty office.

"I'm Stansfield Elk-in-Bushes," he said, "or, as it says on my birth certificate, Stan Bernstein."

Ben shook his head. "You lost me."

Stan smiled, took a seat behind a desk heaped high with unopened mail, and gestured to two folding chairs nearby.

As Ben and Abby sat down, Stan closed his eyes, seemingly lost in thought, then opened them and look directly at Ben. "Back in the '50s, Washington decided to encourage people living on Indian reservations to relocate to cities where there'd be more economic and educational opportunity. The government paid their way, gave them a cash allowance to move, helped get them settled, and provided job training.

"Quite a few Indians took them up on this. One was my mother. She left the Standing Rock Reservation with me—I was a very young fetus—

and my older sister, and we moved to Pittsburgh."

Ben said, "So you're a native American?"

"My mother was an enrolled member of the Standing Rock Sioux Tribe. My biological father—I'm not sure. Anyway, Mom came to Pittsburgh, found a job, met a guy named Jerry Bernstein, and they got married. I was born about two weeks later. So that makes me Jewish by injection. Almost."

Ben smiled. "You're president of the congregation?"

Stan shook his head. "We don't have a president or officers. Not even a board of directors."

Ben looked surprised. "Then who takes care of the business of this place? Pays the rent, does the mailings, maintains the building, collects the dues—all that kind of stuff?

Stan smiled again. "Well, except for the dues—we accept donations, but we don't charge dues—that's mostly me and Rabbi Geltkern.

"I'm semi-retired—got a nice home remodeling business that my sons run—so I have plenty of time to help out here."

Ben said, "I'm really lost. Rabbi Geltkern doesn't get a salary, and he pays the rent, supports this place, all by himself?"

Stan dipped his head up and down. "He must have a source of funding. Whenever I've asked him to get something for the shul—an air conditioner, more tables, a bigger refrigerator—he asks how much it will cost, and when I tell him, he always says, 'Let me see what I can do.' A week, two weeks, and he gets the money."

Abby said, "That's one reason why everybody loves this place. Rabbi Geltkern asks nothing of us except to come worship together."

Ben asked, "So when do I meet this wonder rabbi?"

Stan looked at Abby. Something unsaid passed between them.

Stan said, "We don't know where he is. And that's kind of why Abby and Yolanda asked you to come out today."

Ben said, "Explain that."

"He left me a note a few weeks ago that he had to go out of town for awhile and that he'd check in by phone. A couple of days later, I got a text message on my cell that said he'd be back in time for last week's Shabbat service, but... he never showed. I've been trying to call him, but every time, it goes straight to voice mail. Then Abby and Yolanda told me that they'd met a man who was a kind of private detective. They didn't mention that he was also a rabbi. You are a rabbi, right?"

Ben looked at Abby, shaking his head.

She looked down at the floor.

Ben said, "I told you, I'm here to undergo medical treatment. I'm in no shape to go running around, chasing after missing persons, turning over rocks."

Abby sighed. "I'm sorry. It's just we're really worried about the rabbi, and the police won't look for him until he's been gone a month."

Ben said. "He's a grown man. It's a free country. Unless you have some reason to suspect that he's in trouble, the police can't get involved. Is there something you haven't told me? Something that makes you think he's been abducted or something?"

Stan and Abby shook their heads.

Ben asked, "Have you been to his home? Does he live with someone? Does he have a pet that someone would have to take care of if he left town?"

Stan said, "He lives right here, an apartment on the other end of the building. The entrance is from the outside. Lives alone, no pets that I know of."

Ben asked, "Enemies? Threats? Anything?"

Stan shook his head. "It's just that... I've been doing this, helping him out, since about a month after he got started. I hired the work crews to gut this old building and put up partitions, bring the electric and plumbing up to code, paint it inside and out—and he paid for everything except my time, and I wouldn't let him pay for that."

Against his own inclinations, Ben felt himself being drawn into the story. "How long ago was that? When you started this congregation?"

Stan pursed his lips. "Four years and some. And in all that time, he's never missed one Shabbat, never even took a vacation."

Ben shook his head. "Did it occur to you that maybe he just got tired? That he wanted time away to clear his head, a little personal time? Rabbis are human, you know. We have the same needs and wants and weaknesses that everyone else does.

"Does Rabbi Geltkern drink? Does he have a wife or a girlfriend? Children? What did he do besides hold services here on Shabbat?"

Abby said, "I don't know about the rest of his life, but I got the impression that he was a widower. He never mentioned a family."

Stan said, "Me, too. And I have no idea what he did when I wasn't here. I come out two or three days a week, try to beat the traffic from Pittsburgh both ways, so I'm here maybe four or five hours. I don't see him much during the week—he calls or leaves me notes, or we text. Couple of times a month we'll go out for coffee, here in town. I had him out to the house for dinner with my family a few times."

Ben asked, "How do the bills get paid?"

Stan said, "That's all on him. I'd leave an invoice in my outbox, and he'd take it and write a check or something."

Ben thought for a moment. "Does he counsel people? You mentioned his Torah reading class—when does that happen? What about private lessons?"

Abby said, "It's all in the evening when working people are off. Yolanda took an Introduction to Judaism class in New York, and he was tutoring her, getting her ready for the Beit Din. He came to our house on Tuesday evenings after supper."

Stan said. "He only gives the Torah-reading class a few times a year. I never took it—he says I do plenty as it is, I shouldn't have to worry about that, too. Anyway, it's one evening a week, nine or ten weeks, here, in the sanctuary or in his study."

Ben looked around. "Where is that room—his study?"

"At the back end, next to his apartment."

"Have you looked in there? Maybe he left a note or something?"

Stan said, "I guess I should have tried that first, before asking you.

Ben asked, "Why don't you do that, say, first thing Monday?"

Chapter Eight

On Monday morning, a month after Ben had begun treatment, the protocol called for harvesting a bone marrow sample. Ben was anesthetized and wheeled into an operating room. There, a doctor carefully inserted a long needle into his "iliac crest," a cavity in the rear hip bone that holds a pool of marrow. After a marrow sample was withdrawn, Ben was wheeled to a recovery room.

By noon, he was back in his rented room, dizzy, exhausted and fighting nausea in his queen-size bed. When his iPhone rang, he cursed himself for a fool for forgetting to turn it off, until he recognized the ring tone: *Hatikva*—"the Hope."

Miryam!

Ben asked, "Where are you, my love?"

Miryam said, "On a plane to Buenos Aires. How do you feel, Ben?"

"Rotten. I'll spare you the details. Just generally crappy."

"Want some company?"

"I thought you were on your way to Argentina?"

"Ben Gurion to JFK to Buenos Aires. With a three-day layover in New York. I have to sign some papers at the museum, and then I thought, well, if you haven't found another girlfriend yet, I might pop over and spend a day with you."

"Actually, I have *two* new girlfriends."

"What?"

"Yup."

"Really, Ben?"

"Remember that couple I mentioned? With the *Beyta Yisroel* kid?"

"He was getting robbed, and you chased off the bullies?"

"That's the one. Well, both his parents are women."

"And they're married to each other?"

"Yup."

"You're fooling around with married women now, Casanova Ben?"

"Miryam, I sort of feel like death warmed over, but I should be better tomorrow. When shall I expect you?"

"Late tomorrow afternoon. I've booked three different flights, depending on when I finish at the museum. I'll text the details before I leave New York."

"I'll meet you at the airport."

"Please. If you feel crappy, I can take a cab."

"If I'm dead, I'll have someone haul my corpse to the airport. I don't want to miss even a minute of your visit."

"I love you, Firewalker Ben."

"And I love you, Baldy."

§

When Ronit Khardun, Miryam's second cousin, learned that Miryam intended to meet the board of directors of the Jewish Museum of New

York in the same jeans and sweater she would wear on the flight to New York, Ronit was aghast.

Ronit said, "Do you really think that those museum people are going to give millions of dollars to someone who shows up dressed like a waitress on her day off?"

Miryam said, "All my fall clothes got burned up, and I won't have time to go shopping in New York."

Ronit bundled her petite cousin into a taxi and took her to Tel Aviv's posh Neve Tzedek district. Three days later in New York, again on Ronit's advice, Miryam hired a limousine for the two-mile ride from the Plaza Hotel to the Jewish Museum. Radiantly confident in a bold crimson Dior suit, she alighted at the curb and swept past the secretary sent to greet her. She found the museum director in the lobby, chatting with a small circle of well-dressed men and women, all north of fifty.

After introductions, Miryam was ushered into an elevator and then into the conference room, where she took a seat at a long table. While the others filed in, she skimmed a four-color brochure describing the various forensic examinations performed on ancient documents that she had asked the museum to authenticate.

Miryam asked, "You had a brochure printed?"

Dr. Menachem Rosenzweig, the museum director, smiled. "We did it in-house. It was distributed exclusively to a select group of potential donors, people who are interested in supporting the Museum and its programs."

Miryam said, "I get it. As I said in my email, I'm on my way from Tel Aviv to Buenos Aires. My fiancé, Rabbi Moshe Ben Maimon, is in Pittsburgh, and I intend to spend a day with him before going on to Argentina. So let me save us all some time."

Miryam picked up a brochure.

"This says that the letter from Maimonides to the chief rabbi of Aleppo is authentic; that The Kitab al Khazari, by Yehuda Halevi, an early 12th

Century hand-written book, is authentic; and that my Kurdish Tanakh, the Hebrew Bible, is the genuine article—the ink checks out, you've carbon-dated it to about 1630, you've used molecular spectroscopy and organic analysis to confirm that the sheeps' hides for the parchment were of the Awassi species and that they ate grass that grew in the Mosul area. You even had a panel of *sefer soferim,* scribes with the training and experience to create a Torah scroll, compare the calligraphy with examples of Tanna'it Asenath's writing. And so you are certain that this is the genuine article. Is all that correct?"

"Yes," said Rosenzweig, to smiles and nods around the table.

"Ben and I also did some homework," Miryam said. "In Israel, the Chief Sephardic Rabbi's office denies that a Tanakh, a Torah, could have been written by a woman in Kurdistan 350 years ago. He denies that Asenath Barzani was actually a rabbi and that if she had written a codex, it would not be kosher, and so it could never have been kept in the Great Synagogue of Aleppo.

"So there are no other claims to ownership of the Barzani Tanakh."

Around the table, faces morphed into inquisitive expressions.

"I'm going to keep the Kitab al Khazari and the Maimonides letter, at least for now, although I will lend them to the museum for awhile.

"I called Sotheby's, and they said that they could get me at least $50 million for the Barzani Tanakh. And maybe a lot more."

 Gasps and frowns circled the table.

Miryam said, "I have a plane to catch. And I have no idea what I'd do with that much money, except give it away. So I talked to my Ben, the guy who recovered the Barzani Tanakh, and we decided that you guys can have it. But we want a few things in return.

"First, it needs its own little room in your museum, with my grandparents' names, Naomi and Isaac Benkamal, on that room, along with the fact that they risked their lives to rescue it from an Arab mob in Aleppo, Syria, in 1947 CE.

"Second, I want Rabbi Jason Silber—he's a sopher stam in Queens—to be hired, at the museum's expense, to supervise the restoration of the Barzani Tanach.

"Third, I want the museum to set up a nonprofit foundation in honor of my parents: The Aida and Isaac Benkamal Foundation. I'll be president, and Rabbi Ben will be chairman of the board. The museum can have two seats on that board, and I will name two other people for it. I want you to give us an office in this building and hire and pay a staff for the first two years. Two people should be enough.

"Then I want you to open a Foundation bank account and put $5 million in it. And another million, each year, for the next thirty years."

Rosenzweig's head slowly swiveled left, then right, and Miryam saw each of the people sitting around the table give a tiny nod.

Miryam got to her feet, and everyone else stood up.

Miryam asked, "Do we have a deal?"

Rosenzweig smiled. "We do. You've been very generous. May I ask what the purpose of your foundation will be?"

Miryam said, "We'll give cash grants and assistance in curriculum development to not-for-profit preschools in poor neighborhoods. So they can start or expand free tuition programs, add staff, and include courses in art, music and gentle exercise. We want to make it possible for more low-income mothers to work while their kids get the kind of early education that only well-off kids get now."

Rosenzweig said, "How wonderful!"

More smiles and nods around the room.

Miryam said, "Email me the papers."

Chapter Nine

Ben turned the corner and looked around. The street was somehow both familiar and strangely foreign; he didn't know where he was. He needed to get back to Darlington, a street lined with big trees and old brownstones. If he could find that street, he'd know the house, set back on a little slope. He'd open the side gate and go down the walkway to the stairs that led up to the converted attic he rented.

A glimmer of sun on water caught his eye. The river! He'd follow the river. He started down the block. It seemed to go on forever, much longer than any block he could recall. Ahead skyscrapers peeked through dense fog. The lights of an enormous suspension bridge glowed in the distance behind them. It looked like San Francisco, but he knew that with two rivers joining to make a third, Pittsburgh had many bridges. But where was he? How could he find Darlington Road?

He picked up his pace, aware now that he was being followed. He paused to look for reflections in a shop window, but the street seemed deserted. At the corner, he turned left, toward the river. Again, the buildings seemed hauntingly familiar—but in a different way than they had earlier. Why were the streets empty? Where was everybody? Maybe he could find a cab. Or a bus. He reached into his back pocket for his wallet. He patted himself down. His pockets were empty. And he was hungry. He had to get back to Darlington, to his room.

He should call somebody. He pulled his iPhone from his breast pocket, but the battery was dead. And it was getting dark.

He quickened his pace and was rewarded with another glimpse of light on water. The river must be just ahead. A car went by, then another, and Ben called out, but they didn't stop. The streets filled with people, all rushing toward Ben, passing him, eyes averted as they hurried along. He called to them, but they ignored him.

The street narrowed, and he crossed to the other side, the safer side, stumbling because asphalt had given way to cobblestones. Maybe he was in London? Or Quebec City? He came to the corner. There was the water. Not a river. A lake. Chicago? Maybe Cleveland?

He tried to follow the lake shore, but the streets ran straight while the shoreline curved away. Now he was sure that someone was following him. He could almost feel the footsteps. A scent wafted by on a breeze off the lake. He knew that scent; it was familiar, comforting. But what was it?

He heard footsteps behind him, then a door opening. He turned around. A doorway yawned, and he stepped through it into darkness and the overpowering scent of ... sandalwood. That was it, sandalwood.

Miryam bathed with sandalwood soap. She must be nearby.

Ben opened his eyes to see Miryam bending over him. She smiled.

"You were dreaming."

"How did ... What are you doing here?"

"I came to visit my Ben, the patient rabbi. How are you feeling?"

"You said you were coming tomorrow. I was going to meet you at the airport."

"It *is* tomorrow. It's Tuesday night. Your landlady, Mrs. Meltzer, said you've been here, asleep, since yesterday. How do you feel?"

Ben stretched. His hip was sore, but he felt clear-headed and strong.

"Oh, so much better. Almost as good as new."

"I kind of like the beard. Are you going to let it grow out?"

Ben felt his face. He needed to shave. A bath. Food.

He sat up, put his feet on the floor, and wrapped himself in Miryam's arms.

She whispered, "Ben, I love you, but you need a shower."

"I'm really hungry."

"Mrs. Meltzer made soup. Go take a shower, and I'll warm it up for you."

"I don't have a stove."

"Downstairs. It's fine—just go take a shower."

§

Ben went down the inside staircase and opened the door to the first-floor kitchen to find it filled with women, all talking at once.

"Why didn't you say you were a rabbi?" asked Mrs. Meltzer, a sleek, stylishly sophisticated, widow still a beauty at seventy-something.

Abby said, "We've been calling you since yesterday."

Yolanda said, "Wait till you see what we found in Rabbi Geltkern's study!"

Miryam said, "You clean up so well!"

Ben said, "Where is Zach?"

Abby said, "I dropped him off at the library."

Mrs. Meltzer said, "Sit down, your soup is ready."

Abby said, "I baked some bread."

Ben slid into a chair at the kitchen table, and Mrs. Meltzer set before him a steaming broth thick with noodles, matzo balls and chunks of chicken breast. Abby put a small loaf of bread on a wooden carving board and sliced it in half, then cut a thick slice from one end. She took margarine from a plastic tub and slathered the bread with it. Miryam placed a glass of water near the soup.

Ben said the blessing over bread than attacked the slice, eating with gusto, glancing at the soup.

Mrs. Meltzer said, "Something is wrong with the soup?"

Miryam said, "He doesn't know if it's kosher."

Mrs. Meltzer sighed. "I know you're a rabbi—now I know—and you want to be careful. I make meals for the Jewish Community Center's senior lunches program. Jew or gentile, they get a kosher meal. Rabbi Moller, president of the Pittsburgh *Vaad Hakashrus*, the kosher food supervision authority, kashered this kitchen."

Miryam said, "Eat the soup, Ben."

Ben sighed. "So many mothers, so little time."

He pulled the bowl to him, picked up the spoon and dipped out some broth. He blew on it to cool it. He regarded it carefully, lips pursed.

Ben looked up. Everyone was staring at him. "It's so quiet in here."

Miryam grabbed a spoon and dipped it into his bowl, slurped its contents down and turned her dazzling smile on Mrs. Meltzer. "Wonderful! I'm from a Mizrahi family—we don't do chicken soup this way. Can I get your recipe?"

Ben began to eat.

§

As the bottom of the bowl came into view, Ben put his spoon down.

"It's wonderful," he said, "better than my own *bubbe* used to make.

Mrs. Meltzer glowed with delight. "But why am I the last person on earth to learn that there's a rabbi living under my roof?"

Ben sipped some water. "What would you have done had you known that I was a rabbi?"

"There are so many things in the Torah that I don't understand. And the Halakhah on kashrut, dietary laws, can be confusing. My neighbors are always asking me questions. And my grandson Joshua, he's studying for his bar mitzvah ..."

Ben smiled and held out both hands, palms up. "That's why."

Mrs. Meltzer looked stricken. "You must have so many other things to do."

Miryam said, "Starting with getting well."

Abby said, "And helping us find Rabbi Geltkern."

Yolanda said, "And teaching martial arts at Zach's school."

Abby shook her head. "I spoke with the principal yesterday about that. She doesn't think it's a good idea. We had a little argument, very polite, and she decided that I should join the enrichment committee and see if I can sell my idea to the rest of the committee. So, for the time being, no martial arts classes."

Ben said, "I understand."

Miryam said, "Wait—there's a missing rabbi? And Ben is helping you find him? Ben, we talk by email or Skype almost every day. Why don't I know this?"

Ben sighed. "Because I don't know that he's missing. Because I never agreed to find him. And because investigation isn't my hobby."

Miryam said, "He means that he got six-figures for his last case."

Ben said, *"Seven* figures. *Your* figure was my bonus."

Miryam blushed from head to toe. "We met on his last case."

Yolanda asked, "Six figures? Really? For how long?"

Miryam said. "A couple of months. Which is why he can afford to do some pro bono work once in awhile. If he's feeling well enough to handle it."

Mrs. Meltzer said, "Excuse me for saying so, Rabbi, but at first I thought she was too young for you. But now I see that you and Miryam are a perfect match."

His fate was sealed.

Ben stood up. "Let's go see Rabbi Geltkern's study."

Chapter Ten

It was dark by the time Ben parked his Honda near the only other car in the Sanoker Shul lot, a Toyota SUV. As Yolanda and Miryam got out of the back seat, Ben laid his hand on the Toyota hood. It was cold; the car had been there for some time.

Ben tried the shul door and found it unlocked.

Ben turned back to the women. "Are you coming?"

Yolanda said, "Miryam was just getting to the part where she was trapped in a burning house."

Ben snorted. "Please. She was unconscious when I found her; she doesn't remember anything. If you must know more, catch the YouTube video."

Yolanda giggled. "You're such a romantic!"

Ben asked, "Do you know whose car this is?"

Yolanda said, "It's Stan's, I think."

"Let's do this."

Ben opened the door to a pitch-black interior. He searched with his fingers along the door frame until he found a switch and flipped it.

Nothing happened.

Yolanda said, "The sanctuary light switch is on the far wall." In near darkness, she crept forward, arms extended, until she reached the wall, then found the switch. "This one doesn't work either," she said, her voice barely above a whisper.

Ben said, "Walk back toward the sound of my voice."

When all three were outside, Ben took a flashlight from the Honda's glove box, then removed a penlight, from a side pocket.

He handed the penlight to Yolanda and turned to Miryam. "Get behind the wheel. Lock the doors, and turn on your phone. If anybody shows up, honk the horn and keep honking. If we're not back in five minutes, call 911."

Miryam frowned. "I want to come with you."

"If someone's waiting to ambush us, we need you to call for help."

"But why are you taking Yolanda instead of me?"

Yolanda answered: "Because I'm a police officer."

Ben said, "Are you armed?"

Yolanda bobbed her head. "Always."

"Let's circle the building and look for a circuit breaker box."

They started leftward, playing their lights on the walls. At the end of the structure, they followed the wall around as it turned right. They continued down the wall, almost to the next corner. Ben saw something white, caught in a bush, and turned his flash on it: a sheet of paper.

Yolanda said, "There!" and pointed her beam at a gray metal wall box about five feet off the ground. She cautiously pulled its cover open. Ben probed the interior with his light, found the master switch, pushed it from left to right, then back again.

Light blazed from every window in the building and from a half-open door farther down the wall.

Yolanda said, "That must be Rabbi Geltkern's study."

Ben poked his head inside. "Or his apartment."

It was one large room, the floor covered with cheap gray industrial carpet. There was a couch, an overstuffed chair, an ancient CRT television with a rabbit ears antenna, a battered dinette set of uncertain vintage with a chipped glass top, and three mismatched chairs. In one corner was a small dresser, a nightstand with an old desk lamp, and a twin bed with a box spring. No sheets, pillows, or blankets.

"Jesus Christ!" Yolanda exploded.

Ben offered a wry grin. "Or Moshe *Rabbenu*, Moses our teacher."

Yolanda said, "A hundred bucks in any thrift store. For the whole kit and caboodle, I mean."

Ben pulled out his phone and called Miryam.

"We'll be out in a few minutes," he said when she answered. "Stay in the car."

They pulled out furniture drawers and opened cabinets in the kitchen area, looking for something, anything. There was nothing, not a scrap of paper or a dish or a fork. The refrigerator was unplugged and empty.

Yolanda asked, "What are you thinking?"

Ben shook his head. "A crash pad? Emergency hideout? Or a Potemkin Village that's been cleaned out?"

Yolanda asked, "Potemkin Village?"

"A fake town. Something that looks real from a distance. But in reality, it's a façade. Like a movie set."

"But why?"

"I'm not sure. Maybe Rabbi Geltkern, or whoever lived here, kept enough stuff around that a casual visitor would think he was either poor or very thrifty. And now all that stuff—pots and pans, dishes, blankets, clothing—has been removed. If it was ever here in the first place."

Yolanda said, "I don't understand."

Ben shook his head. "Me neither. Did Rabbi Geltkern just leave? Why? Or was he abducted, and all his belongings went with him?"

"So you do think it's a mystery now?"

"Obviously a mystery. Not so obviously foul play."

"Wait till you see the study."

Ben looked around. In a dimly lit corner of the kitchen was a door.

"Where does that go?"

Yolanda shrugged. "I've never been back here until now. And I've actually never been in the study—just peeked in the door at what Stan wanted me to see."

Ben strode to the corner, opened the door and stepped into Rabbi Geltkern's study. The lights were on, revealing a barren desk and an empty chair.

And absolutely nothing else.

CHAPTER ELEVEN

Yolanda gasped. "There was a computer on that desk, but someone had ripped out the hard drive. There were two cabinets full of file folders. A paper shredder and a great big box full of shredded paper. And a stack of unpaid synagogue invoices on the desk. That's what we found yesterday."

Ben slowly turned his head, peering closely at the room.

Opposite the door to the apartment, he saw another door; Ben tried the knob and found it locked. He examined the lock: a new Schlage. He bent and fished two long, slender pieces of metal from his pants cuff.

Yolanda said, "What are you doing?"

Ben shook his head, concentrating. In seconds, working by feel, he felt the tumblers move. Pocketing his picks, he pulled the door open.

The room was small and dark. Light from the study reflected from a medicine cabinet mirror to reveal the outlines of a bathroom sink. Ben put a hand inside the door, found the switch, and flooded the room with light. To the right of the sink and its small cabinet was a shower stall. Against the far wall was a toilet.

Sitting on the toilet seat lid, slumped against the wall, was Stan.

Ben recoiled, then turned and looked again. Stan had grown a third eye, a hole in his forehead as big as a man's thumb. It was crusted with dried blood. The wall behind the toilet was a rusty-black inkblot of blood and scrambled brain matter. In the middle of the inkblot was a deep gouge where the plaster had been removed.

Chapter Twelve

Ben backed out of the room and turned to Yolanda, his face grim.

"Stan's in there. Dead."

Yolanda paled. "You're sure?"

Ben stepped aside so Yolanda could look. When she turned back to Ben, she was fighting tears.

"He was such a nice old man. Why would anybody kill him?"

Ben shook his head. "You should call the police. I'm going outside to tell Miryam."

He turned to go, then stopped and thought for a moment. He moved to the desk and pulled the center drawer out. It held a small herd of dust bunnies, a rusty thumbtack, four mismatched paper clips and a broken rubber band. Ben took two paper clips and straightened them. He dropped them on the desk.

"What was that for, Rabbi?"

"The cops are going to want to know how I opened the door. You can lie and say that the door was open, or you could say that you were still looking around the apartment when I opened the door."

Yolanda frowned. "And what if I tell the truth?"

"When police find a man carrying lock picks, they assume that he's a burglar. If they assume he's a burglar, they often suspect that he's also a murderer."

"You couldn't possibly have killed Stan. You were twenty miles away in Squirrel Hill until we all came out tonight."

Ben said, "Of course. But I don't want to have to go through the bother of proving that. You last saw Stan alive, when and where?"

"Yesterday, about noon, here."

"So he was shot sometime after about 4:00 yesterday."

"How do you know when he was shot?"

"I don't, exactly, but he's in rigor mortis, which begins three to four hours after death. We found the body, so we automatically became suspects. The police will ask Mrs. Meltzer how she knows that I was in my room from noon yesterday until early this evening, but she can only say that she didn't see me go out or come back. That's not good enough.

"Miryam will say she came from the airport to Mrs. Meltzer's and found me asleep in my room. The police will spend hours or days until they're certain that Miryam wasn't in Pittsburgh until late this afternoon. In the meantime, she'll miss her flight to New York and her connection to Buenos Aires.

"They'll also investigate you, because you're part of my alibi."

"It sounds like a tremendous waste of time."

"It is. And yet they'll be obliged to do it. So let's save them the time. Leave the paper clips on the desk, and if they ask if you opened the door, tell them that you were in the other room when I opened the bathroom door. They'll find the paperclips and draw their own conclusions. Or just say that the door was unlocked."

"What if they ask you to prove you can open that lock with them?"

Ben sighed. He picked up the clips, strode to the door, locked it from the other side, closed it, then slipped first one and then the other clip into the key hole. He turned his mind off, let his fingers find the tumblers. The clock clicked open.

Yolanda gasped. "Forty seconds. How did you learn to do that?"

"It's a long story."

"The Cliff Notes version?"

"A reformed cat burglar, now turned something of a *Tzadik*, a righteous man, gave me a crash course, years ago."

"You're really something! If Miryam wasn't such a sweetheart, and if I wasn't crazy about Abby, I'd jump your bones right here, Rabbi."

Ben shook his head. "Better that you keep such thoughts to yourself. It makes life much easier for everyone."

Yolanda looked stricken. "Oh, God! I'm not thinking very clearly, am I?"

"Pull yourself together, and call the police."

Chapter Thirteen

Ben went back outside the way he had come, pausing in the darkness to throw his picks away, one to the left, the other to the right, then stopped to retrieve the crumpled paper from the bush. He found Miryam waiting outside the car.

Miryam asked, "Where's Yolanda?"

Ben shook his head. "Stan is dead. Shot in the head. She's calling the cops."

"Someone shot him? Why?"

Ben said, "Now that I'm working pro bono to find Rabbi Geltkern, I'll try to find that out, too."

Miryam frowned. "They seem like such nice people. I was only trying to help."

Ben put his arms around her and held her tight. "I know," he whispered. "I'm not angry. I could never be angry with you."

§

Less than five minutes after Yolanda called, a Berona Township patrol car arrived with two patrolmen. Within the next half hour, six more patrol officers, a deputy Allegheny County coroner, both Berona Township's night-shift detectives, and a crime scene investigation team from Troop B of the Pennsylvania State Police were on the scene.

Two officers escorted Miryam, Ben, and Yolanda to the township police station, where they were interviewed separately and asked to volunteer their fingerprints. Then each was asked to empty their pockets and purses so that the officers could see everything they were carrying.

Ben was very thoroughly searched, including his pant cuffs and underwear.

A tired-looking, overweight, nearly bald man with acne scars and wearing a rumpled suit appeared.

"I'm Chief Laurence," he said. "Officer Sanchez, you and Ms. Benkamal are free to go."

Miryam said, "We're not leaving without Rabbi Ben."

Laurence sighed. "This could take a while. Why don't you go into the break room and make yourself comfortable. There's coffee. Soft drinks in the machine."

"Rabbi, come with me, please."

Ben followed Laurence down the hall and into what he knew was an interrogation room.

Laurence pointed at a chair and the two men sat down. He said, "I'm guessing you know why you're here."

Ben said, "The lock to the bathroom."

Laurence said, "There were scratches on the outside face. And the fact that the FBI file on you runs to over 200 pages."

"Have you read that file, Chief?"

"No, sir. And I can't spare anyone to do that just now. We're a small department, and everybody is up at your temple, or whatever it is you people call it."

"Some congregations call their house of worship a temple. Others a synagogue or a Beit Midrash, a house of learning. This one is called a shul, which means 'school' in Yiddish. The terms are pretty much interchangeable. But I'd like to make it clear that it's not my congregation. I'm not a member, not affiliated with it in any way. Until tonight, I'd been there only once before, as a guest of Officer Sanchez."

"And why were you there tonight?"

"As I told your detectives, Officer Sanchez and Mr. Bernstein believe that Rabbi Geltkern, the spiritual leader of her congregation, has disappeared. They asked me to help find him. Yesterday, she and Mr. Bernstein got a locksmith and opened Rabbi Geltkern's study. They wanted me to see what they found, and that's why I was there."

"Do you know who shot Bernstein?"

Ben shook his head. "No idea. I've only met him once, when I visited the shul about a month ago, and he seemed like a smart man, a very nice senior citizen."

"How is it that a rabbi knows how to pick locks?"

"That's in my FBI file. The short answer is, a former burglar who lives down in South Florida taught me. This was long after he'd served many years in prison and became a model citizen."

"Why would you want to know how to pick locks?"

"It's a useful skill."

"For a burglar. Are you a burglar?"

"The FBI file will tell you that I often work with police to help solve crimes."

f"You're a consultant?"

"You could say that. More particularly, I'm sometimes asked by various Jewish institutions, such as a congregation, or a school, to help recover things or to determine what or who caused certain events. Very often I wind up working with the police on these cases. But not always."

"You can open any lock with a couple of paperclips?"

Ben shook his head. "Not at all. But the most common types of door locks are not very secure."

"Ever crack a safe?"

Ben shook his head. "I'm not qualified or equipped for that."

Laurence asked, "Do you use lock picks?"

Ben said, "It's actually quite rare that I need to open a lock for which no one has a key. When the occasion arises, I use whatever I can get my hands on. A jeweler's screwdriver is better than a paperclip."

Laurence reached into a jacket pocket and dropped two paperclips on the table. Both men stood up.

Laurence said. "I'm gonna lock you in this room. If you can pick the door lock, or otherwise get out without breaking a window, I'll let you go home. But we might want to talk to you again."

Ben picked up a paperclip and straightened it against the table, then repeated the process with the other paperclip. "It's unusual to find a really good lock on an interior door."

"Let's see how good it is."

Laurence knocked on the door, which was opened by a patrol officer. He left the room, and the door closed behind him.

Ben looked around the room, then moved to the door and knelt to examine the lock. It was an unusual design, stainless steel instead of brass, and exceptionally well made. He'd never seen another like it.

Chapter Fourteen

Fourteen tries and more than ten minutes later, Ben was still trying to unravel the mystery of unyielding tumblers. And while one part of his mind worked on that, which was about trying to inferentially visualize the device's interior design and then find a way to defeat its intended purpose, another part of his mind was thinking about why he was the subject of this particular trial by ordeal. Ben believed that he could probably jimmy the outside window and pull the sliding half off its tracks, then go out the space that left. That would take a minute, tops.

But that's what a second-story man would do. That's what people who break into houses do. They usually don't have the skill or patience to crack a lock.

Ben took the paperclips out of the lock. By repeatedly bending one in half and straightening it, he broke it in two. Now he had three tools. He shaped the end of each to a slightly different angle. Using three fingers and the thumb of his left hand and two fingers of his right, he forced back the guard tumbler. A tiny, deft move with his right forefinger and the lock clicked. Ben pushed the door open.

Leaning against the corridor wall was Chief Laurence. He held a stopwatch in one hand. "Fourteen minutes, ten seconds," he said. "We respond to silent alarms in this township in under eight minutes."

Ben asked, "Am I free to go?"

The chief offered a half-smile. "Unless you'd care to come to my office for a cup of mint tea and learn why I asked you to pick that lock."

Ten minutes later, after a hurried conference with Miryam and Yolanda, Ben sat across the desk from Laurence sipping tea spiced with cinnamon and honey.

Laurence said, "We're a small town. Most folks call me Jack."

Ben said, "My friends call me Ben."

Laurence nodded. "Now we've got that out of the way, you know anything about the Sanok Home, up there on the ridge?"

"Never been there. I'm told it's a retirement home for people whose ancestors came over from Poland after World War I."

Laurence said, "Assisted living, what they call it now. And we've had six silent alarms from there over the last few months."

"A burglar? What did he take?"

"By the time we responded—about five or six minutes, average—there was nobody around. No jimmied doors or windows, nothing left open. And nothing missing, as far as those folks could tell."

Ben smiled. "So when Yolanda—Officer Sanchez—told you that I opened that bathroom door in half a minute with a couple of paper clips, that got your attention."

"It did get my attention. Especially because you're a rabbi, and those are all your kind of people up there, in the Sanok."

"Are you certain that there's actually an intruder? Some alarm systems can give false alarms."

"We had the same thought. IT guys from Troop B, State Police checked out their system. It works perfectly."

"What sets it off?"

"Any time a first-floor door or window opens and the associated keypad isn't punched with the correct security code within 30 seconds."

"Could it be a someone with a key who forgot the security code?"

Laurence looked hurt. "We may live out in the country, Ben, but we're not bumpkins. We checked that out. Only two staff members on night duty have the keys and know the combination, and they've both been there for years.

"So it's damn odd. And then this fellow Bernstein gets shot, and we were wondering if there was any connection."

Ben shrugged. "It could be, but as I said, I barely knew Bernstein, and I've never been up to the Home."

"But you said you've been looking for that Rabbi, Geltkern, he's disappeared?"

Ben shook his head. "No. I said was that Yolanda and Bernstein asked me to help them—I haven't actually done anything yet. I went to the shul tonight to see what they found in the rabbi's study, but when I got there it had been cleaned out. Except for Mr. Bernstein, of course."

"Tell me, Ben, what are your intentions about this business now?"

"If Yolanda still wants my help, I'll poke around and try to find Rabbi Geltkern. For now, that's it."

"Just so we understand each other, stay clear of my investigation. That's police business."

"Of course."

"We're going to pursue different leads," Laurence said. "One is to learn if there's any connection between that rabbi disappearing and the murder. You have any reason to think that might be the case?"

"Only that nobody's seen Geltkern in several weeks, and the murder took place in his study. At least, it looked to me like it did."

"If you find something related to my murder while you're looking for your rabbi, I'll expect to hear about it sooner rather than later."

CHAPTER FIFTEEN

A little before 2:00 a.m., Ben parked the Honda behind Mrs. Meltzer's house.

Ben said, "Yolanda, do you want to come in?"

"I've got roll call in five hours, Rabbi. I'm going home and crash."

"Call me when you have some time, and we'll talk about Rabbi Geltkern. If I'm going to look for him, I'll need a lot more information than I have."

"I'm really sorry that you had to go through all that at the station."

"Not your fault. The Berona police were just doing their jobs. They don't get many homicides here, so this is a pretty big deal to them."

Miryam said, "It was a pretty big deal to Stan Bernstein, too."

§

Neither Ben nor Miryam wanted to sleep. Instead, they laid on his narrow bed, holding each other, talking, kissing, dozing, until morning light filled the room.

Miryam said, "We should get up. I need to be at the airport by noon."

Ben said, "I need to run. It's been three days."

"Can I come with you?"

"Since when are you a runner?"

"Since high school. And in Israel with my cousin Ronit."

"How far do you go?"

"I'm working my way back to ten kilometers—but recently, only four or five."

"Could you go a little farther?"

"Let's see."

§

An hour later, pleasantly tired and perspiring heavily, Miryam and Ben turned into Darlington Road and slowed to a walk. As they approached the Meltzer house, Yolanda got out of a Ford Crown Victoria parked at the curb.

Ben asked, "Is something wrong?"

Yolanda said, "My captain got a call from Chief Laurence this morning."

"About the murder?"

Yolanda bobbed her head up and down. "Of course."

Miryam asked, "Are you in trouble?"

Yolanda shook her head. "Nothing like that. The Berona force is very small, and for a major case, they get back-up and support from their neighboring townships and from the state police. Chief Laurence thinks that Rabbi Geltkern's disappearance might be tied into Stan's murder, but the Troop B guys say that, since the rabbi's been missing for weeks, his trail is cold, and it's probably a wasted effort. The state investigators want to concentrate on other leads."

Ben said, "I told Laurence that I was going to look for Rabbi Geltkern."

Yolanda said, "Well, he asked my captain if I could help with that end of the investigation. And my captain said that it would have to be on my own time."

"That's good news. Sort of."

"I'm not finished. So then I called Chief Laurence and asked if it was kosher if you help me. And he said the only way that would work out is if the Township hired you as a consultant. That way he could keep control of the case."

Ben said, "But his budget has no money for a consultant."

Yolanda pulled her face into a tight smile. "You're always a step ahead of me."

Miryam said, "That's why he makes the big bucks."

Yolanda shook his head. "I think he meant that, unless you're under contract, you can't have anything more to do with the case. And since there's no money…"

Miryam asked, "What if somebody made a donation to the township police? Enough to cover, say, a month of a high-priced consultant's time?"

Ben said, "Stop. I can't have you giving them money to hire me. That's not right. And I don't need the money."

Miryam smiled and put her arms around Ben. "Let me decide how I want to spend my uncle's stolen fortune."

Chapter Sixteen

Chief Laurence scowled across his desk at Ben. "So let me understand this. This morning a young lady in a thousand-dollar dress goes by City Hall and counts out $9,500 in hundreds and says she wants to donate to the township police budget to hire a consultant.

"And now you're offering to consult on Bernstein for $1 a day?"

Ben said, "Only for a hundred days. After that, it's $0.50 a day."

Laurence asked, "So what do I do with the rest of the money?"

Ben spread his hands, palms up. "Ask City Hall."

Laurence looked thoughtful. "We could use new computers."

Ben said, "If I am to work with you, I have a couple of caveats."

Laurence looked expectant.

"First, I don't work from sundown on Friday to sundown on Saturday. That's our Sabbath."

Laurence asked, "What else?"

"I'm a patient in a medical trial. I go in on Mondays for an injection and a blood workup, and for the next day or so, I'm pretty well useless."

"What are you being treated for?"

Ben shook his head. "I'm not contagious. I'm just saying that I'm not available on the Sabbath or on Mondays or Tuesdays. So I won't be billing you for those days."

Laurence snorted. "What's going on? Why are you so interested in this case?"

Ben said, "You should read my FBI file. And then you should get the one on my father, same legal name, and skim it. If you still have questions, you could contact some of the departments that I've worked with. The names are in the file."

"Your father was also a rabbi investigator?"

Ben shook his head. "He was a roving con man who sometimes posed as a rabbi while he targeted a Jewish institution."

Laurence smiled. "You're trying to live down your old man?"

"In a way. Do you know the Hebrew phrase, '*tikkun olam*'?"

"I'm still trying to learn Spanish so I can deal with our newest residents."

Ben smiled. "Tikkun olam means, 'to heal the world.' Jews believe that God created the world but his work wasn't finished. The task of making the world complete, or perfect, falls to God's last creation. To us. Some people work with the poor. Others heal the sick. Some give money to good causes. My efforts are more to complete God's work than to undo the harm that my father did in his day."

Laurence smiled. "That's an interesting take on things. I'd say that 'healing the world' stuff pretty much covers most police work. I'll have the city attorney draw up a contract. You understand that you're not authorized a weapon?"

Ben smiled. "I never carry a weapon."

"I expect you to work closely with Officer Sanchez but to keep me informed of any developments."

"Of course. When can you read me into the larger case? What the crime scene guys found, the coroner's report, that sort of thing?"

Laurence sighed. "Let's not get ahead of ourselves. Let's get a contract from the city attorney's office and get it signed. Then you'll get whatever you need."

Chapter Seventeen

Ben was on his way out of Berona when Miryam called. He stopped on the shoulder before pulling out his phone. "Let me guess," he said, sans preamble. "My lover is calling because I got her to the airport late and she missed her JFK connection to Buenos Aires?"

Miryam giggled. "Yes, but no. I landed at Terminal Seven about two minutes after my flight was supposed to leave from Terminal Eight, but there's a baggage handler's strike in Argentina, so my plane actually got to New York an hour late. So now I'm all checked in and eating a pretzel because you were too busy this morning to feed me."

Ben giggled. "Poor baby. But that red dress of yours is now famous all over Berona Township. They think it must have cost $1,000."

Miryam gasped. "Almost $4,000! But Ben, the reason I called, aside from to hear the sound of your voice and to enjoy fashion reviews from rural Pennsylvania, was to ask you something about last night."

"You're wondering why all the lights in the building came on when we threw the power switch?"

Miryam gasped. "How do you do that?"

Ben smiled to himself. "The same way you know if a three-year-old needs a nap, a time-out, or a snack."

Miryam sighed. "I do miss all those babies. Go on."

"I also wondered about the lights. Stan got the locksmith to open the study and the apartment in the morning. Then they left.

"Let's work it backward. Iffffffff the master circuit breaker was off, then someone must have set it so. And if the lights came on when power was restored, then someone must have turned them earlier."

Miryam said, "So all that happened the night before."

"Iffffff it happened the night before, then Stan must have come back after dark."

"They're calling my flight now. Can we wrap this up in a few minutes?"

"We can. I think Stan came back after dark, entered through the front door, where we found his car. He turned on lights as he moved through the building to the study. He found it empty, went through the door from the study to the apartment, turned on those lights. At that point, someone outside turned off the power.

"Stan had supervised rehab on that building, so he knew that the shortest route to the circuit box was through the apartment's exterior door. He went outside to check the box, and someone grabbed him, took him back inside, into the study bathroom, and killed him. The killer went back out the way he came in."

Miryam asked, "How do you know that his killer wasn't inside when Stan arrived? Or that he didn't walk in while the lights were on? Why do you think Stan was taken outside and forced inside?

"Because, just before Yolanda and I found Stan's body, I came across a sheet of paper caught in a bush near the power box."

"You never told me that!"

"I never told anyone. It's handwritten in Yiddish, and until I know what it says, this is just between you and me, okay?"

"Wild horses," Miryam said. "I'm now second in line to board. I love you."

"I love you, too. Have a safe flight. Call when you land."

"Bye!"

The connection was broken.

Ben put his phone away and sat thinking for several minutes. Then he checked his rear view mirrors before executing a U-turn across the four-lane highway and heading back into Berona Township.

CHAPTER EIGHTEEN

Ben drove to the Berona Industrial Park and spent ten minutes peering into trash dumpsters behind machine shops and factories. Each was either empty or held only small quantities of refuse—scrap paper, broken plastic, mangled metal, torn wires—or ordinary garbage.

Walking back to his car, he saw a middle-aged man in work clothes locking the door of a machine shop. Ben said, "Excuse me. Do you know when they empty the dumpsters?"

The man turned, glanced at Ben.

"What's it to you?"

Ben stuck out his hand. "I'm a rabbi. Do you know the shul at the back of the property?"

With obvious reluctance, the man shook his hand, seemingly anxious to leave. "Yeah. What about the dumpster?"

"I threw out some trash last Sunday, and now I think something important might have fallen into a wastebasket. I was just wondering if you knew when they pick up trash and where they take it?"

"If you're a rabbi from that temple, or whatever it is, how come you don't know that?"

"Because I'm new. Rabbi Geltkern is on a sabbatical, and I'm just filling in. Are you Jewish?'

The man shook his head. "My wife is. She's been yapping about checking that place out instead of driving into Pittsburgh when she wants to be around Jews. No offense, you understand."

"None taken. What about the trash?"

"Tuesday morning, early. Everything goes to the township recycling center where they sort it: recyclables, garbage, hazardous waste, whatever."

"Thanks," Ben said, and walked back to his car, thinking furiously.

Iffff...when the contents of the study were removed, would the remover carry everything away from the area, or put it into one of the park's many dumpsters?

That would depend on whether it was too much to carry in a car. Or if the remover was in a hurry to leave the area.

And iffff...the remover decided to put it in a dumpster, instead of taking it elsewhere, then he probably knew when it was to be picked up.

So... iffff he used a convenient dumpster, he would know that it would be emptied Tuesday morning.

Which meant...the remover, who might also be the killer, went there on Monday night.

Which meant he didn't expect to see Stan or anyone else.

Which meant the murder wasn't planned. Maybe it was a cover-up for something else.

Ben parked in front of the recycling center. It was dark, but a low rumble issued from the building, and wisps of steam rose from a tall stack at the back.

He got out of his car and followed a Cyclone fence until he could see into an enormous, roofed space where dim lights showed men on forklifts feeding pallets of trash to a furnace.

"Hey!"

Ben turned to find a flashlight shining in his face.

"We're closed," said a male voice. "What are you doing here?"

Ben said, "Do you work for the recycling center?"

The voice said, "What are you doing here?"

Ben said, "I want to know how long trash is here before it's burned?"

The light moved down Ben's body, allowing him to see a tall, well-built man in a security guard uniform. "You're not from Berona," he said. It wasn't a question.

"I'm filling in for Rabbi Geltkern up at the Sanoker Shul, in the Industrial Park. We threw something out last week that we shouldn't have, and I was just wondering if it wasn't too late to find it?"

The guard said, "Wait! I know you! You got up on Shabbos and gave us a *drash* about Abraham buying a burial plot for Sarah."

"Yes."

"Sorry. Didn't recognize you. What are you looking for, and when did you throw it out?"

"A bunch of papers. They were picked up Tuesday morning with the trash."

The tall guard shook his head. "Everything is gone in 24 hours. Clean paper goes to a pulp mill, plastics and metal are compressed into bales, combustibles burned to generate power. Sorry."

Ben said, "Thanks, anyway. You've been a big help."

He turned to go.

"Wait! Is it true about Stan? Did he get shot? Is he dead?"

Ben nodded. "Yes, it's true. I spoke to Chief Laurence about it yesterday."

"It's a damn shame, is what it is. He was a great little guy. Did you know that he was part Indian?"

"Yes, I heard that."

"My name's Mort. Mort Reubens."

"Rabbi Ben is what most people call me. Or just Ben. Either way."

They shook hands, and Ben turned to leave again. "See you on Shabbos," Mort said and stood watching as Ben walked back to his car.

Chapter Nineteen

Slowly driving back through Berona, Ben had another thought: The single sheet of paper he had found near the entrance to Rabbi Geltkern's apartment was written in Yiddish; clearly, it had some connection to Geltkern and the shul. But how did it get there? Someone must have dropped it. Or perhaps a gust of wind had picked it off a stack of other papers that someone was carrying.

Who could have carried it outside the building?

What if, before he was murdered, Stan had removed some of what he found in the rabbi's study? Yolanda had said they found unpaid invoices, filing cabinets full of empty folders, a shredder and a basket full of shredded paper.

Maybe Stan had taken some of that and carried it to his own office. The unpaid invoices, for example, would have to be paid. What if the paper that Ben found had fallen while Stan was carrying it and other papers to his own office?

Ben decided that it was worth a shot. He recalled seeing a craft and hobby store on his earlier drive through town; after driving around for ten minutes, he found it on a street off Berona Road, the main drag. Ben bought a packet of craft needles, a kit of flat blade jeweler's screwdrivers, and a set of metal files.

He found a Dairy Queen in the next block and bought a green salad, a grilled cheese sandwich, onion rings and a diet cola. He drove back to the industrial park, found a dark corner behind a closed factory and ate.

Then he spent an hour working with the file, shaping the screwdrivers and craft needles into lock picks.

Afterward, he climbed into the back seat and slept.

§

His phone's alarm app woke him at 11:00; he left the car, found a place in the shadows to pee, then did five minutes of slow stretches.

There was police crime-scene tape around one end of the Sanoker Shul but none at the front door. A block away, Ben found a lot across from a factory whose brightly-lit windows announced that the night shift was in session. He parked in an area shaded by tall conifers and took a circuitous route to the shul. Approaching from the rear, he slipped around the corner near the front entrance. He waited fifteen minutes until he was satisfied that no one was watching or had seen him approach.

The lock was a Kwikset; it yielded to his picks in thirty seconds.

He checked his watch. He would give himself four minutes.

Inside, he locked the door, threw the previously unused deadbolt, then wrapped his penlight in a handkerchief to dim the beam.

He found his way to Stan's office. The door stood open. Ben held the penlight high above his head and slowly turned, looking for the window. It was covered with a blind; he was fairly sure that this window was at the rear of the building, facing a high cinderblock fence screened by foliage.

Only someone standing directly behind the window could see the light from this office. He thought for a long moment and decided to chance it.

After closing and locking the office door, he flipped the light switch. The office looked much as it had on its previous visit, with an unruly pile of unopened mail covering much of Stan's desk. Looking around, Ben saw four filing cabinets, four waste baskets, three chairs, two desks—

Four waste baskets?

Two were round and battered steel, painted dark green and at least 50 years old. Two were light brown, rectangular, plastic and almost new.

Ben bent to pick up a plastic basket. A sheaf of brittle, yellowing paper, face down, had been shoved into it. Ben gently worked the paper out, revealing a mass of compressed paper strips below it.

Shredded documents.

He looked at the other plastic basket. Also full of shredded paper.

A car door slammed outside.

Ben flew to the light switch, plunged the room into darkness and listened.

Tortured wood screamed from the main entrance.

Ben moved to the window, reached beneath the blinds, unlocked it, raised the bottom half. He grabbed mail from Stan's desk and forced some of it into each waste basket. He dropped one basket to the ground outside, then the other.

A loud snap followed by a crash announced that the front door had been levered open.

Ben went out the window, turned, quietly lowered it, grabbed the two wastebaskets and walked back the way he came, all the while thinking furiously.

If he called the police, he'd have to explain what he was doing in the building and how he gained entry. He'd have to turn over the wastebaskets and their contents.

If he didn't, someone was going to tear the office apart.

Halfway to the end of the building, his reveries were cut short by the sound of the office door being pried open. Holding a wastebasket to his chest with each hand, he ran full-tilt back to his car. After locking the baskets in the trunk, he drove away, slowly, lights out, until he saw traffic signals ahead.

Just as he switched on his lights, a patrol car, lights flashing, turned off Berona Road and sped past him, accelerating.

Ben glanced at his watch: Six minutes and 17 seconds had elapsed since he entered the Sanoker Shul.

Could he have tripped a silent alarm?

Chapter Twenty

Wearily, Ben climbed the stairs to his loft, where he stripped off his clothes, showered, brushed his teeth and flossed, took his cocktail of antiretrovirals, and slipped into bed.

He rolled out of bed at 6:00 and was stretching when his phone rang.

"They got him!" Yolanda said. "He came back to the shul and tripped the alarm. Then he shot it out with them, and they got him."

Ben said, "Slow down. You're talking about the person who killed Stan?"

"Yes, yes! Sorry—I'm just so excited!"

"When did that happen?"

"Last night about midnight. The patrol car came and found the guy in Stan's office. He took a shot at them, and they returned fire."

"Where is the guy now?'

"Uh, the morgue, I guess."

"Are you working today?"

"I work Sundays. This is my day off."

"Let me go run a few miles, clear my head, and we'll have breakfast and talk about this. Ask Abby to join us, if she's free."

"Cool. How 'bout Kazansky's Deli, on Murray?"

"Give me an hour to run and get a shower, and I'll meet you there."

§

Abby and Yolanda were sipping coffee when Ben slipped into their booth.

Yolanda said, "You said an hour?"

Ben said, "Sorry. Miryam called just as I got out of the shower."

Abby said, "She's where now? Israel? Or South America?"

Ben said, "Buenos Aires. She just cleared Customs."

Abby said, "Oy, that's a long flight."

Yolanda said, "She's really crazy about you, Rabbi."

Ben smiled. "I'm just as crazy about her."

Yolanda asked, "Can we order, then talk about last night?"

Ben beckoned to the waitress, who brought Ben coffee, took their food orders and refilled coffee cups. When she was out of earshot, Ben gestured, pointing.

"I was out there last night," he said.

Yolanda asked, "What do you mean?"

"I let myself in, went to Stan's office, and was looking around when I heard somebody breaking down the front door."

Abby asked, "Did you see who it was?"

Ben said, "No. It sounded like he used a crowbar or something to pry the door open. I turned off the light and went out the window. About half a minute later, I heard him start to break down the office door."

Yolanda asked, "And you left without calling the police because you didn't want to have to explain about breaking in?"

Ben nodded. "And because I found something in Stan's office."

Both women stared at Ben. "What?" asked Abby.

Ben said, "Two wastebaskets full of shredded documents, several pages of old papers in Yiddish—and about $3,000 worth of unpaid bills.

"And it's those bills, and the ramifications of them, as well as Stan's murder, that I'd like to talk about first."

"From what I've seen, Stan and Rabbi Geltkern did everything. Between them, they kept the doors open and the shul functioning.

"Now they're gone. If you value your experiences and your attachment to this particular shul enough to save it, then you two must be prepared to become the nucleus of a new management team."

Yolanda said, "I've got a full-time job and a kid to raise with Abby. I can't spend half my time out in Berona Township running a synagogue."

Abby nodded agreement. "And I have a practice that's just getting off the ground."

Ben said, "Find another eight or ten members to form a board of directors and get the members of that board then to recruit about twenty people to serve on committees—or walk away now, find another shul that you like. The choice is yours."

Abby asked, "Where do we get money to run a place like that?"

Ben said, "From its members. Just like every other shul in the world. I want to help. I'm prepared to write a check—enough to cover all the unpaid bills and to pay them again next month. I'm prepared to advise your board. And I'm prepared to lead services for a few months until you hire someone to serve as your spiritual leader."

Abby shook her head, overwhelmed. "How much do rabbis make?"

Ben smiled. "Most brand-new rabbis have just finished four years of college and five more years of rabbinical school. They often have student loans. How much he or she makes is whatever can be negotiated. It could be as much as low six figures for a large congregation or high five figures for a smaller one. Your congregation might have to hire a part-time rabbi, or maybe just a cantor, until you can afford a full-time rabbi. How many families do you have?"

Yolanda said, "I don't know—about eighty or a hundred people come most Saturday mornings. On the High Holidays, it was three times that. People stood in the back."

"Sounds like enough. But this is hard work. You can't do it alone."

Ben reached into his back pocket for a small notebook, then found a ballpoint in his shirt pocket and passed both to Abby. "You'll want to take notes, I think."

He spoke until the food arrived, and for ten minutes afterward, being as specific as he could. Abby filled several pages with notes.

When the waitress had removed the dirty dishes, Ben sat back.

"That's one issue. Next is what happened last night. Did the guy who got shot confess to killing Stan before he died?"

Yolanda sighed. "I don't know."

Ben asked, "Then why do the Berona cops think he was the killer?"

"Because his gun was like the one used to kill Stan. And he had something that belonged to Stan in his pocket—a woman's photograph."

"He was in Stan's office—could the photo have been on the desk?"

Yolanda said, "Of course."

Ben nodded. "Who was this guy? The one they shot?"

"Chief Laurence said he had a record—assault, B and E, that kind of thing."

"Do you recall when we found Stan's body?"

"I'll never forget—I've had nightmares about that."

"Did you see a white gouge in the wall above the toilet tank?"

"Now that you mention it."

"I'm pretty sure that somebody dug a slug out of that hole."

"The slug that killed Stan?"

"The one that passed through his head, yes."

"Why are you asking me this, Ben?"

"Because the Berona police would need that slug to match to this guy's gun. And I think whoever shot him dug that slug out afterward. We can't be sure that the guy who shot it out with them was the guy who killed Stan. But closing the case quickly might seem like a good thing to a small-town police chief."

Yolanda said, "I better go out to Berona and talk to Chief Laurence."

Ben shook his head. "That can wait. Let's spend today trying to find Rabbi Geltkern."

Chapter Twenty-One

Ben asked, "First, do you know Rabbi Geltkern's first name? What kind of car does he drive? Where is he from? If he has a family?

Abby said, "He drove an old Ford wagon. I used to have the same model, a Ford Focus, but mine was a sedan. His is dark red, I think."

Yolanda said, "His first name was Jeremiah. Or maybe Jeremy?"

Abby said, "I think he said he was from Chicago."

Yolanda said, "I'm sure that I heard him say that his last congregation was in New Jersey."

"Jeremiah Geltkern, from Chicago by way of New Jersey?"

Yolanda said, "I think that's right."

Ben said, "I've got a bad feeling about this."

Abby asked, "What do you mean?"

Ben shook his head. "We need to find him in records databases. Is he registered to vote in Pennsylvania? Does he have a driver's license, a car, own a house, have a phone, buy water, electricity or gas from a utility? Does he have a bank account, credit cards, health insurance? Check for things that nearly every adult in the U.S. has."

Yolanda said, "I can do all that from the squad room. We can access public records, and we can ask banks and insurance companies for the rest. They usually cooperate without a subpoena if we're just asking if he's a customer."

Ben said, "Then that's the place to start. And when you do that search, check both for Jeremiah Geltkern and for Jeremy or Jerome, or Gerald Goldkorn. Try different spellings. If he doesn't turn up in-state, you might check Ohio and West Virginia."

Abby asked, "You think he was using an alias?"

Ben said, "Maybe he just 'Yiddishized' his name. Don't forget, I find it professionally useful to go by my Hebrew name. If you searched for me in those databases, you'd need my legal name.

"And one more thing: I need you to find the Sanoker Shul's bank account and its IRS and state records as a not-for-profit house of worship. And see if there's any property, such as the building in Berona, that it owns. Any legal records at all."

Yolanda stood up and opened her purse.

Ben grabbed the check. He said, "I'm buying."

Abby said, "Thank you, Rabbi. We'll get the next one."

Yolanda said, "Thank you. But what are you going to do?"

Ben said, "I'm going to try to find his car. Then I'm going out to see Chief Laurence. I'll call you in a couple of hours."

Abby said, "What about me? I didn't schedule patients today; it's Yolanda's day off. I want to help, too."

Ben said, "Tomorrow, you can introduce me to the people at the Sanok Home. Today, you could start calling everyone you know from your shul and ask them to call all the members that they know and make sure that everyone comes this Shabbat. And let them know that, if they value their connection to the congregation, they'll be asked to do something concrete to help keep it going."

Chapter Twenty-one

Ben walked back to Mrs. Meltzer's home and knocked on her front door. After a moment, it was opened by the lady of the house, who favored Ben with a big smile.

Ben said, "Shalom, Mrs. Meltzer. Do you have a few minutes?"

Mrs. Meltzer said, "Shalom, Rabbi. May I offer you some coffee?"

Ben smiled. "Tea, if you have it?"

"It will just be a minute." She gestured toward the kitchen, and Ben followed her to the table where he'd had soup two days earlier. Half of it was covered with a huge, half-completed jigsaw puzzle.

Ben said, "You do jigsaw puzzles?"

Mrs. Meltzer said, "I love all kinds of puzzles, but jigsaws are my favorite. That was how I met my husband, alev hashalom. He was at the community center, working on a big puzzle, and he came over, introduced himself, and asked for my help. We were married four months later."

"Milk and sugar? In your tea?"

"Please."

The ritual of pouring, sweetening, and stirring took place in silence. When they had each taken a sip, Mrs. Meltzer smiled and gently caressed Ben's cheek. "Oh, if I were only twenty years younger," she said, "and you were single."

"Timing is everything," Ben replied.

"What's on your mind?"

"Do you know a man named Stanley Bernstein?"

"Sure. Bernstein Remodeling. Stan and Eva go to *Poale Zedeck*."

"An Orthodox synagogue?"

"Modern Orthodox. Well, to be fair, it was mostly Eva that went. Stan not so much except for the High Holy Days. Eva died a few years ago, and I don't think I've seen Stan since the funeral. I heard he remarried, a Philadelphia girl."

"I'm sorry to tell you this, but Stan was murdered. Monday night."

Mrs. Meltzer paled. "Oh, my God. How did it happen?"

"We're not sure. It was out in Berona Township—he was shot."

Mrs. Meltzer dabbed at her eyes with a napkin. "He was such a sweet man. How did you happen to know him?"

Ben shook his head. "I met him only once. He was a volunteer at the Sanoker Shul, in Berona."

"The Sanoker Shul? They tore that down thirty years ago, at least."

Ben looked perplexed. "Where was that, exactly?"

"When I was a little girl, right after the war, Berona Township was called Sanoker. It was way out in the country, a little bit of Poland in the middle of nowhere. Maybe 500 families, all Polish Jews. After the war, they renamed it, Berona. Then in the '80s, when the steel mills shut down and we started to clean up this city, some of the smaller factories moved out there. The land was cheap, and there weren't many people to complain about the pollution."

Ben said, "Wait. What about the Polish people in Sanoker?"

"A few years ago, they had an exhibit, with pictures, at the Jewish Community Center. Polish Jews built the town before the war when they thought that all their relatives would be coming. And then..."

Ben said, "The Holocaust."

"Yes. Well, after the war, Pittsburgh people started moving to that area. Not right in Sanoker. Nearer to the river. They built country clubs, golf courses, new tract homes. But I know for sure that they redeveloped downtown Berona and tore down the shul. How could Stan be shot in the Sanoker Shul?"

Ben said, "I guess it was a new congregation, but they took the old name. They met in what used to be an old factory that they fixed up."

"Well, who shot him?"

"The police tried to arrest a man. He pulled a gun. They shot him."

"I know Stan's kids—he had three boys—from when they were little. I went to all their bar mitzvahs. I should call and go see them. And I just made a cheesecake.."

"There's one more thing, Mrs. Meltzer."

"Please, call me Ro."

"Short for Rochelle?"

"When I was a girl, they called me Shelley. But I prefer Ro."

"Then Ro it is. Do you know someone in Pittsburgh who is fluent in Yiddish?"

Chapter Twenty-Two

Doctor George Lewin lived two blocks east, on the other side of Darlington Road and a few doors from the Jewish Community Center. A short man with an enormous head of white hair, he answered the door wearing a suit with a bowtie.

Ben said, "I'm Rabbi—"

"Ro just called. I was expecting somebody older. Come in, Rabbi."

Ben followed Lewin through an expansive house that had been restored to its pre-war splendor, with original wood flooring, wainscoted walls and a huge living room with a fireplace of black basalt. They went through this room and into a smaller one, its walls lined with bookshelves. As they settled into chairs, Ben took a closer look: They all seemed to be Yiddish titles.

Ben asked, "You're a Yiddishist?"

"In my spare time. I'm an internist, although I'm trying to retire."

Ben said, "I'd like to show you some pages I retrieved from an old shul. They're all in Yiddish. Before I ask you to translate them, can you tell me what they are, rather than what they say?"

"Anything for a friend of Ro Meltzer. She was the cutest girl in high school, hands down. And the most popular—homecoming queen, class president, captain of the girls tennis squad and even the girls rifle team. But I was only a sophomore, and she was a senior—I had no chance."

"She's single now."

Lewin sighed. "I'm married. Terribly married. You understand?"

He wasn't sure what "terribly married" meant, but Ben nodded and took out several pages of the yellowing paper he'd retrieved from Stan's office and laid them on the desk. Lewin glanced at the top one, picked it up, glanced at the sheet below it, then the next, rapidly scanning each of the 27 pages in turn.

"Okay. The handwriting is very old-fashioned. Two or three different people wrote these, at different times, and all the writers learned their Yiddish in Europe, probably Poland or Russia. Otherwise, this is simple enough. These are the minutes of some kind of organization: a shul, a burial society, something like that. But they're incomplete, and they're out of sequence. Different dates."

Ben cocked his head, trying to think of a reason why such notes would have been important enough for someone to destroy.

Lewin said, "If you'd care to leave them, I could have a rough translation for you in a week or so."

Ben said, "I'm happy to pay for this. In fact, I insist."

"I don't want your money, Rabbi. If you want to do something for me, find me a doctor in Squirrel Hill who will take some of my younger patients, so I can retire."

Ben thought for a moment. "What about a certified NP?"

Now it was Lewin's turn to think. A long moment passed before he nodded. "Maybe. Maybe. Depends on who. Ninety-five percent of the time, my patients don't actually need an M.D. They need someone to check their vital signs, update their prescriptions, draw blood, interpret lab test results, remind them to lose weight and get more exercise.

The trick would be for this NP to know when it's the other five percent, so they can consult an M.D. or make a timely referral."

"I'll give your card to Abby Silverblatt, or do you know her?"

"She's the gal who started a practice in her house? On Pocusset?"

"That's her"

"Tell her to give me a call."

Chapter Twenty-Three

Ben walked back toward Mrs. Meltzer's, intent on retrieving his car and going to see Chief Laurence. But as he passed the Jewish Community Center, he decided to stop in; perhaps they still had the Sanoker exhibit that Ro Meltzer had described.

The lobby was filled with women of every age and race. A harried receptionist pointed Ben to the director's second-floor office. Next to its door was a desk supporting a stout older woman, who stood as Ben approached.

"And you're here to see the director?" she said. It wasn't a question.

Ben nodded, eyeing the name plate next to an open door. And doing a double-take at the name.

"And whom shall I say is calling without an appointment?"

Ben smiled. "How do you know that I don't have an appointment?"

"And who do you suppose keeps the director's appointments?"

Ben smiled. "Point taken. Tell Rabbi Smolkin that Rabbi Thank You Ma'am has arrived."

"And that would be a nickname? 'Rabbi Thank You Ma'am'?"

"Not the Rabbi part. The rest would indeed be a nickname."

The woman pointed to a row of three chairs. "And have a seat, please."

Ben sat down, watched the woman move at a glacially arthritic pace past him and into the office.

Ten seconds later, a rotund and very short man in his early forties came bounding out. His face lit up when he saw Ben.

"Rambam, Thank You Ma'am!"

Ben jumped to his feet. "Whatchoo Smolkin!"

They laughed, then embraced.

Rabbi Abe Smolkin turned to his aged receptionist. "Mrs. Bender, this is Rabbi Moshe Benyamin Maimon, my Yeshiva classmate."

Mrs. Bender favored Ben with a dim smile. "And a pleasure to meet you, Rabbi."

Smolkin all but dragged Ben into his office and closed the door behind them. "Who are you gunning for?" he whispered.

Ben said, "Excuse me?"

Smolkin said, "Come on. Your reputation precedes you."

Ben shook his head. "I'm afraid you've lost me."

Smolkin's face changed from interest to fear. "I'm clean as a whistle, Ben. You're welcome to dig into any records we have. Look at anything. It's all kosher."

Ben laughed. "I think you've got bad intel on me. I'm nobody's hatchet man. I'm just in town to participate in a medical study at Pittsburgh Medical."

"But it is true that you're some kind of a super-spy detective?"

Ben laughed again. "Not exactly. More of a Jewish paladin. My way of working at *tikkun olam*. My clients are people like you, the leaders of Jewish institutions. They ask for help when they have a problem to solve on the QT. But today, when I decided to come here, I was on my way someplace else. I had no idea I'd find you running the place. Last I heard, you had a second-banana gig in Texas."

"Second banana doesn't begin to describe it. Four thousand families, three rabbis, two cantors, a youth director, a family director. The top banana was in his early fifties and so healthy that he'll probably live forever. The cantor, and the associate cantor, and the family director—they all thought that I worked for them."

Ben frowned. "It doesn't sound like there was much room for advancement. But you said, three rabbis?"

"Number three was a very smart and very pretty woman about our age. But she was number one with the ladies, including the *rebbetzin*, the rabbi's wife. Nobody messed with her. So that left me to handle anything and everything that nobody else wanted to do. Like explaining to Mom and Dad that their precious son can't marry his pregnant *shiksa* in our temple until *after* she converts, and no, a big contribution to the building fund won't change that.

"I had to research Rabbi Englander's sermons and write rough drafts on two different subjects from the same Torah portion every week. I graded papers in the bat/bar mitzvah academy and make sure that no kid's bar mitzvah speech embarrassed anyone. I talked to all the crazy locals who called wanting to know why we don't believe in Jesus. And why we killed their Lord. Or what the passage about Onan in Genesis really means—and when you tell them, they want to argue with you, because their preacher says it means something else."

Ben said, "You looked for another pulpit and wound up here?"

"I went back and finished law school, is what I did. And took the Pennsylvania and New York bar exams. And lined up a job in Pittsburgh.

"And then suddenly this came along. A great job. Great board of directors, a wonderful community. Only about 40 percent of Squirrel Hill is Jewish, but we serve the entire population, from mommy-and-me classes and pre-school to senior exercise. Even a kosher meals-on-wheels program—and a lot more. That's *my* contribution to *tikkun olam*.

"Oh, and I do a little estate work on the side. Wills, powers of attorney, trusts. Once in a while a nice probate job. Keep the bar ticket current—you never know."

"How long have you been here now, Abe?"

"This is my seventh year."

"The reason I stopped by—someone told me that some years ago you had an exhibit on Sanoker, a little Jewish town out in what is now Berona Township."

"I recall reading about it, but it was before my time."

"Do you happen to know where that exhibit is now?"

Abe shook his head. "It's either down in our basement somewhere, or it's in storage. Most likely storage. About five years ago, we cleaned out most of the basement, threw a lot of stuff out, put the rest in storage. Why?"

"It's a little complicated. I've been here in Pittsburgh only a few weeks, but I've made friends. They asked me to do them a favor."

"A rabbi favor or a detective favor?"

"A little of both, I guess. A freebie. I'm trying to find their rabbi, who seems to have disappeared."

"What's his name?"

"Jeremiah Geltkern. Do you know him?"

Abe's face lit up. "I knew it! And he skipped out with, wait, uh—the building fund, right?"

Ben shook his head. "Nothing like that. You know Geltkern?"

Abe's face reassembled into something approaching a snarl. "We've met."

Ben asked, "And what?"

"And I just felt like there was something off about him. Hard to explain. I had to leave the room for a minute—came back to find him looking through my files."

"You're kidding!"

"Said he was trying to save me a few minutes, he knew exactly what he was looking for, didn't think it was a big deal."

"And what was he looking for?"

"I don't know. But it damn sure wasn't what he said it was—a list of the vendors for our Purim fair."

"You think it was something else?"

"Yeah. Which is why I spent about $11,000 of the center's money converting everything more than a year old in this office to digital form."

"Have you ever considered that you made way too much out of that? Maybe he was actually looking for your vendor file?"

Abe shrugged. "There was one more thing about him. I asked if he was Conservative, Reform, Orthodox—whatever. And he got all high and mighty, as if I'd insulted him. Said he'd been ordained by a living saint, that the small differences between the ways different congregations observe the mitzvoth are irrelevant."

"I would agree, up to a point. But—ordained by 'a living saint'?"

"Exactly. If he's taken off, good riddance."

"You don't happen to remember the name of this 'living saint'?"

"No, but I might have written it down in my day planner."

"Abe, how long ago was that?"

Abe wrinkled his brow. "A few years, at least. But I hang on to my old day planners. It's probably in my garage. If it's important, I'll try to find it for you."

Ben thought. "I don't know if it's important or not. But if it's not too much trouble, I'd appreciate it if you could look for that day planner."

"For you, Ben, nothing is too much trouble."

"And what about the Sanoker exhibit?'

"Mrs. Bender will know. But it could get expensive, moving things out of storage."

"I'll pay for it. And I'll make an additional donation to the center."

"You don't have to do that, Ben. But ... the Pittsburgh JCC is always grateful for donations. Now, where are you staying?"

Ben described his arrangement with Mrs. Meltzer, and the friends spent half an hour catching up on the years since they'd last seen each other. At a quarter to one, Mrs. Bender hobbled into the room to remind Abe of his lunch appointment.

Ben said, "One more thing, Abe. What does Geltkern look like?"

Abe scratched his stomach, thinking. "About average height, a little heavy around the middle but not too much. A salt-and-pepper beard, a Semitic nose, big pores, balding, a comb-over, maybe sixty or so. He wore a thrift-store suit, with narrow lapels. And a hideous necktie."

Ben said, "In other words, he looked like half the rabbis we knew at the yeshiva."

Abe said, "Appearances can be deceiving."

Chapter Twenty-four

Halfway to Berona Township, Ben's phone rang. He hung it on the dashboard and put it on speaker before answering.

"Rabbi Ben," said Yolanda.

"How's it going?"

"Well, I have news. And it's not very good, I'm afraid."

"Go ahead."

"Can't find anybody named Jerome or Jeremiah or Gerald or Jerry Geltkern who owns property, registered a car, has a driver's license, votes, has a city utility account, a bank account, a credit card, or an insurance policy in the states of Pennsylvania, Ohio, West Virginia or New York."

Ben asked, "What about Goldkorn?"

"There's a couple of Jerome Goldkorns and one Jeremiah, but according to their Facebook pages, they're college or high school students."

"Anything else?"

"Well, I Googled Jerry Goldkorn and—it's so silly that I hate to mention it."

"The Rabbi of Lud, right?"

"You're still one step ahead of me, Rabbi."

"We'll talk about that next time. Right now, I'm headed out to see Chief Laurence."

"Rabbi, is there anything else I can do?"

"See if you can find his car. Maybe it was abandoned somewhere in Pittsburgh. Or maybe he left at the airport. Then check on the Sanoker Shul financials. Find their bank account, if they have one."

"Okay, yes, I can do that."

"Thanks. I'll see you soon, Yolanda."

Chapter Twenty-Five

Chief Laurence did not seem especially glad to see Ben.

"I called Officer Sanchez and told her that, as far as Berona Township is concerned, the Bernstein murder is closed."

Ben said, "All you've got is a dead guy who was burgling the Sanoker Shul and carrying a gun."

Laurence scowled. "A dead guy with a record of attempted murder, aggravated assault, extortion, and mayhem. A violent ex-felon, carrying a weapon like the one that killed Bernstein."

"Like means consistent with, as in the same general type?"

"Exactly. Forty caliber."

"But you couldn't match the gun to the bullet that killed Bernstein because somebody dug it out of the wall. Am I right?"

"It's not important. He didn't get what he was looking for the first time, so he came back. End of story."

"Who was this guy? The one who tried to shoot it out with your officers?"

Laurence took a file from his desktop. "Julius 'Jake the Heater' Witzelburg, 44, born in Pittsburgh, lived in Youngstown, Ohio. An installer for a heating and air conditioning company reputedly owned by a member of the LaRocca crime family."

Ben shook his head. "Look, I'm not trying to tell you your business. It's just that, like most rabbis, I've learned the value of a certain kind of logic. And this logic poses a question: What would make a guy who worked for a mafia family almost 100 miles away come to your tiny town and break into an obscure synagogue? What was he after? There's never much cash in a synagogue. They had nothing valuable, so far as I know. Why would a hoodlum like that come all the way out to Berona?"

Laurence made a face. "All good questions, Rabbi. But I work for the city manager, and he wants this to go away as quickly as possible."

Ben asked, "What's giving the city manager ants in his pants?"

Laurence chuckled. "That's good! Ants in his pants."

"It's an old Yiddish saying, *shpilkes*."

"I don't know where he gets his ants. I'm not part of the inner circle. Probably has something to do with real estate, judging by the business interests of most of our township council. Maybe somebody wants to buy that industrial park and turn it into big houses for people with too much money. Maybe there's government funding available for something else. All I know is, the Bernstein case is closed."

Ben said, "Then is there any reason that I can't get the mess at the shul cleaned up and have services on Saturday morning?"

"I'm pretty sure you told me last time that you're just a friend of somebody in that temple. Now you're running the show?"

Ben said, "I'm a rabbi. They are Jews. There's no one else available who can pull this together quickly, so I will. But just until they get organized, raise some money and hire a new rabbi."

"That's mighty white of you, Rabbi."

"Any rabbi would do the same. I still want to find Rabbi Geltkern."

"Knock yourself out. You're sure he didn't embezzle their money?"

Ben sighed. "Then it would be a police matter, wouldn't it? The fact is, there is no money. Geltkern never asked his congregation for a dime. Didn't take a salary. Paid for everything himself. And I have to tell you, Jack, that that alone is one of the most curious things I've ever heard."

"Maybe he was filthy rich?"

"Seems unlikely. By the way, there is one thing you might be able to do for me without pissing off your city manager or costing money."

"What's that?"

"Geltkern was seen driving a 2000 or 2001 Ford Focus wagon, dark red. I have a hunch that the car is still in Berona Township. Could you ask your officers to keep an eye out for it? Probably abandoned or left in some parking lot."

"I'll do that much, Rabbi. And I'll have my officers remove the crime scene tape from your building."

§

Three phone calls and an hour later, Ben arrived at the shul to find two men in carpenter's clothing setting a pair of saw horses in front of the main entrance. As he got out of his car, a shop van bearing a locksmith's logo pulled in. Ben spent the next ten minutes walking through the building with the workmen, pointing out the locks, doors and door jambs that needed replacements. He agreed to their estimates, provided that the work was done before 5:00 pm Friday.

While their work proceeded, Ben went into what he still thought of as Stan's office to straighten things up. The window remained as he had left it: closed but unlocked. He locked it. He found bloodstains on the carpet outside the office door, but no bullet holes in walls or furniture, not even in the hallway. Ben found that peculiar. Perhaps police had fired first and killed Witzelburg. Or maybe Witzelburg had fired first, but the cops bullet-proof vests stopped the bullet.

Maybe.

Ben made a mental note to check the police report.

He decided that the rest of the office could wait until the following week, when, he hoped, a committee of members would start taking responsibility for maintaining the building and running the whole enterprise.

He made another mental note to find out who owned the building.

Then he went into the sanctuary, mounted the bimah, or elevated platform, pausing to admire the Old World craftsmanship of the Torah ark. After pulling aside the decorative curtain shielding its ornately carved twin doors, he opened the doors to find three Sefer Torah scrolls. Three Torahs that could be paraded around the sanctuary with solemn joy then unrolled each Shabbat to the proper book, chapter, and verse and read aloud, as the sages of old had established.

He selected the smallest Torah, carefully removed it from the ark, laid it on an angled reading table and started to unwrap it.

"Excuse me, Rabbi."

Ben looked up to find one of the carpenters.

Ben said, "What's up?"

The man held up a bit of plastic, from which dangled a thin wire.

"It was mounted above the door—must have come off with the jamb. If you want it re-installed, you'll need an electrician."

Ben said, "Just leave it," gesturing toward the front of the bimah.

Ben returned to the Torah. He removed the decorative cover, then untied the matching cloth sash holding the twin rollers, each with a portion of the scroll wound around them. He unrolled the scroll a short distance, noting with dismay that many letters were faded or cracked and that the parchment was torn and discolored in several places.

Only a perfect Torah scroll was considered fit for public reading. This one needed extensive repair. If the defects he'd seen on those few pages were typical of the whole scroll, Ben thought they could cost many thousands of dollars to repair. More, perhaps, than the cost of a good second-hand Sefer Torah. He rewound it, tied the two rollers together, put both into the cover and returned it to the ark.

Ben pulled the second scroll out of the ark and examined it as he had the first. It was in worse shape than the first.

He returned the Torah to the ark and pulled the largest Torah out., What his newly repaired eyes showed him was so unbelievable that Ben forced himself to look away, then back to the open scroll.

It was no illusion.

Sewn to each page with broad stitches of black thread was a sheet of ordinary paper with a typewritten transliteration of the Hebrew. That is, English letters arranged into words that when pronounced aloud would render a close approximation of spoken Hebrew.

A Torah for those who could not read Hebrew.

He had never heard of such a thing.

It could only mean that either the man who called himself Rabbi Jeremiah Geltkern was not a rabbi or that he was so lazy and morally bankrupt that he would not take the time and effort to teach even a few members of his congregation how to read from a Torah in Hebrew.

It went a long way toward explaining Stan's refusal to allow Ben to read from the Torah on the previous Shabbat and suggested either that Stan was an innocent who had been taken in by Geltkern's rabbi act. or that Stan had aided and abetted him. Ben thought for a moment and concluded that the events preceding his murder made it far more likely that he was a dupe who'd trusted Geltkern.

But what was his game? Ben wondered. There was no building fund, no bank account to raid. The Sanoker Shul didn't even collect dues from its members. Whatever was going on, Ben realized, had to be much bigger than this small, oddball congregation. He found it hard to imagine what Geltkern was after.

Chapter Twenty-Six

Ben closed the ark, then moved to the front of the bimah and retrieved the bit of plastic left by the workman. He turned it over in his hands, examining it closely. A few millimeters thick and half the size of a business card, its off-white color closely matched the paint above the door. The tiny lens on one side left no doubt in Ben's mind that it was a camera. And the long, thin wire was an antenna.

Ben hunted until he found a tiny switch on one edge. Using a fingernail, he slid it to the "off" position. The person who left this device, he realized, would probably have wiped his fingerprints from the surface. He might not have remembered to do the same inside. He dropped the device into his shirt pocket.

There was one more thing to do. Ben made a quick but thorough inspection of the inside walls near the building's three entrances and found no digital keypad or alarm panel. Then he moved outside, found the phone line coming out of Stan's office and followed it to a junction box. It terminated in a pair of leads connecting to a cable. He followed the cable around the building to where it ran up the wall and then over to a telephone pole.

The only other wires in the terminal box lead to a vacant modular phone receptacle in what had been Rabbi Geltkern's study.

Now he was certain that there was no alarm circuit. Nothing that could be turned on or off by the building's occupants; it was impossible for the police who shot Witzelburg to have responded to a silent alarm. More likely, Ben reasoned, someone monitoring the video feed from the device in his pocket had dispatched the patrol car. Who could have ordered that? Did Chief Laurence send those officers?

§

Rush-hour traffic was mostly headed out of Pittsburgh and toward its eastern exurbs. Ben found the FedEx office in Pittsburgh's Oakland community with time to spare. He wrapped the video device in bubble wrap and overnighted it to friend and M.I.T. classmate Howard Hopper. Then he sent a text message to Howard, a Silicon Valley entrepreneur whose company specialized in developing circuits and software applications for portable devices. Ben asked him to watch for an email that would explain what he had sent and what he needed from Hopper.

Half an hour later, back in his room and fighting hunger pangs, he sent Howard a long email describing where he had found the device and asking him to take it apart, determine its capabilities, and tell him, if possible, who manufactured it and where it was sold.

Hopper didn't respond immediately, but Ben knew that his friend traveled incessantly and might be anywhere in the world. Among Ben's circle of classmates and friends, however, there was no better engineer. And no entrepreneur whom Ben so completely believed in; six years earlier, he had invested what for a self-employed rabbi/detective had been an enormous sum to help Hopper launch his company.

Ben logged off his computer, then called Abby to tell her that, instead of driving out to the Sanok Home, he would meet her there.

Chapter Twenty-Seven

A little before 9:00 the next morning, Ben pulled into the Sanok Home's parking lot. He left his car to admire a magnificent view: the old town and the new suburbs sprawled across the landscape, leading his eye to a shimmering river that curved southwest to a horizon punctuated with the huddled towers of downtown Pittsburgh.

He was still taking in that view when Abby's minivan pulled in.

Together, they entered the long white building with a roof of bright blue tiles. An outer door opened into a long, narrow garden with a walkway to a locked security door; a tall, burly, white-coated attendant in his thirties answered the buzzer promptly and smiled at Abby.

"Good morning, Mrs. Silverblatt."

Abby said, "Good morning, James. This is Rabbi Ben Maimon."

As they shook hands, James said, "Welcome to the Sanok Home, Rabbi. Mrs. Silverblatt told us you were coming, and we've prepared a little show-and-tell for you. That is if you don't mind sitting through a few minutes of multimedia."

Ben smiled. "I guess that won't kill me."

"Would you like a tour first, or go right to the presentation?"

"Maybe the tour would make more sense *after* your presentation?"

James smiled. "I believe it would."

Abby said, "I'll leave you with James, Rabbi. I need to start my rounds."

Ben said, "Thanks, Mrs. Silverblatt."

Abby giggled. "You can still call me Abby."

James led Ben through an expansive open area, a living room in large scale filled with upholstered chairs and low tables, into a corridor leading to an office. James unlocked the door and gestured toward a chair in front of the desk.

Ben sat down and James turned a computer monitor to face him. Over the next ten minutes, he watched a slideshow with photos, music, and narration that told how, starting in 1887, a few dozen young Jewish men from Carpathian Mountain towns around Sanok, Poland, had come to Pittsburgh. Through hard work and thrift, they prospered, sent for their families, and established a rural community much like those they had left in Poland: clusters of small homes, each with a vegetable garden, a chicken coop, and a small pasture for sheep, goats, and perhaps a milk cow.

In that era, rural Pennsylvania attracted few rabbis. The Sanoker Jews made do with an irregular trickle of visiting preachers. They started a burial society, raised money through subscriptions, and bought cheap land on the heights for a cemetery.

The town continued to grow from a steady influx of newly immigrated Polish Jews. In 1910, boasting almost a thousand people, the Sanokers sent a delegation to Poland to invite the younger son of a revered Hassidic rabbi to join them and serve as their spiritual leader. He arrived in 1912, a man of 27 with a wife, three daughters and two sons. Hard luck befell the new rabbi: His wife and children all succumbed to the worldwide influenza epidemic of 1917.

The slide show told how, after the Russian Revolution, Polish Jews were falsely accused of being communists. An anti-Soviet Polish army attacked Jews across Poland, killing at least 30,000. Over the next 20 years, aided by relatives in America, nearly 800 more Polish Jews came to Sanoker, Pennsylvania. But hundreds more, related by blood or marriage, remained in Poland.

During the '20s, the increasingly prosperous Sanoker Jews, through their burial society, bought more land along the ridge, intending to expand the cemetery on the eastern side and use the western slope to build a synagogue, a community center, and communal orchards.

The worldwide economic collapse of the '30s put an end to those plans. But the Sanoker Jews, who owned their homes and raised most of their own food, were better off than most Depression-era Americans. Moreover, before 1914, when the U.S. had temporarily suspended payment in gold for its currency, the Sanokers had converted most of their burial society funds to gold coins; the Depression-era bank failures that ruined millions of American lives had little effect on their community. In 1938, they sent their rabbi to Poland with a fortune in gold coins to bring out the rest of the Sanok Jews and, not incidentally, to find a new wife among the daughters of Poland's Hassidic rabbis.

The Sanoker Rabbi and nearly all Polish Jewry perished in the Holocaust. Among the near-miraculous exceptions, the slide show described were thirty-one who arrived, a few at a time, in late 1938 and early 1939, their passage to America paid for with Sanoker gold.

About 200 Sanoker men served in the U.S. military during World War II. Hundreds more, including many women, left Sanoker to work in Pittsburgh's factories. When the war ended, very few returned to live in Sanoker. In 1950, the burial society decided that many of their members would eventually need someone to care for them in old age. They built a spacious retirement home on top of the ridge and converted their burial fund hoard to an insurance endowment that would support the home until the last of the original Sanokers was gone.

The show ended, and the monitor went dark.

"So you got any questions, Rabbi?" asked James.

Ben said, "Just a few. Who qualified as an 'original' Sanoker?"

James frowned. "I'm not sure, but I think it means anyone living here who was born in Poland, or who paid into the burial society before 1942 when they stopped taking new subscriptions."

Ben nodded. "That makes sense. They probably stopped right after Pearl Harbor. How many of the original Sanokers are still living?"

James shook his head. "I don't think we have any here. The last one was Mrs. Sharpstein, and she died about a month ago. But Mrs. Weinstock, she might know if there are any others."

"Who is Mrs. Weinstock?"

"She's the director. She's on vacation until the first of the month, and then she retires."

Ben nodded to show that he understood. "So you're the new director?"

James shook his head, no. "I'm just one of the daytime attendants. We probably won't get another director. That's the scuttlebutt, anyway."

"You're a Navy veteran?"

James beamed. "Yes, sir. Two tours in Iraq as a corpsman."

Ben said, "Why won't you get a new director?"

James shrugged. "Well, it's pretty much the numbers. We have forty-seven residents now. The youngest is eighty-eight. There's only ten or twelve of them that you could talk to and they'd understand what was going on. One or two die every month. When we get down to thirty-five or 40, the way I understand it, we're going to close."

Ben frowned. "What happens to the remaining patients?"

James shook his head. "They'll be split up. Those who can afford it will go to another private board and care. The state or the county will have to take the rest."

"And Mrs. Weinstock is going to retire just when all this happens?"

James looked thoughtful. "Way I heard, she wanted to retire a few years ago. Before I started. But Rabbi Geltkern, he asked her to stay."

"Do you know where Rabbi Geltkern is now?"

James shook his head. "Maybe Israel? He said he was taking a vacation, would be back to help with the outplacement."

"Do the residents know about this?"

"Well, like I said, there's maybe a dozen, give or take, that understand much of anything about what's going on. But every one of our residents got a written notice explaining what was going to happen."

"When was that, James?"

James squinted, thinking. "About a year ago, I think. And then about two months ago, we sent everyone a second notice."

"There's something I don't understand. The multimedia show—by the way, that was excellent. Did you put that together yourself?"

James shook his head. "No, sir. Rabbi Geltkern and Mrs. Weinstock did that."

Ben said, "Okay. But that show said that the burial society had invested in an endowment policy that was to last until the last original Sanoker resident was alive."

"That's right. And that's just what happened. Last was Mrs. Sharpstein; she passed a few weeks back. But, see, we still have people living here. That's because, a couple of years before Mrs. Sharpstein died, Mrs. Weinstock made arrangements so that there'd be money enough to see us through a while longer and so there'd be enough in an escrow account so that everyone would get what was coming to them when they had to close this place up."

"You're talking about Mrs. Weinstock's retirement?"

"And our severance payments. Everybody who's been here more than four years and stays to the end gets three month's severance and health insurance for a year. I have VA coverage, so that's not a big deal, but for most everyone else, it's mostly about the insurance."

"Do you know where Mrs. Weinstock got the money?"

"Some from Medicare, some from the state, and maybe there was some private funding, but I don't know much about that part."

"James, you've been very helpful. One last question: Who would know about funding, aside from Mrs. Weinstock?"

"We have a bookkeeper, sort of an accountant. She might know."

"You know how to reach her?"

James returned to the desk and lifted the desk pad to reveal several business cards taped to the desk. He pointed to one.

"That's her. Filomina Jenston."

Ben moved the desk, took out his phone, and photographed the card, along with the others around it.

§

Ben said, "Mrs. Silverblatt asked me to fill in for Rabbi Geltkern until he gets back. Will that be a problem for anyone?"

James shook his head. "I'd say that most of the residents, at least the ones who still have most of their marbles, would be happy to have a rabbi around. You're gonna do that thing on Friday night, right?"

Ben nodded. "Shabbat services. Of course. Why don't you give me a quick tour? Maybe I could meet a few of the residents?"

Half an hour later, having walked the length of the building, Ben found Abby in the nursing office, her nose buried in paper.

Ben said, "Got a minute to spare?"

Abby stood up, stretched. "For you, three, if you need them."

Ben smiled. "I know that medical records are confidential. But it would be very useful for me to know the answer to a question regarding all your medical records. May I ask you that question?"

Abby nodded. "Confidentiality is a big issue. But ask the question."

"I would like to know, based on the forty-seven patients still living here, when the first of those patients arrived, and when the last arrived. I do not need to know who those patients are or anything else about them."

Abby sat down, turned to the computer on her desk, brought up a database file, and struck a few keys.

"Of the residents now in this facility, the earliest arrived six years ago and the last about two years ago."

Ben smiled. "That's interesting and useful. Would it also be possible to know if there were other patients who arrived in, say, the last six years, who are no longer here?"

Abby said, "I can probably tell you how many died here, but not how many were transferred to other facilities."

Ben said, "Whatever you can tell me, without breaking any law."

Abby said, "Okay, but that's going to take a little more time than I have right now. Maybe after lunch?"

Ben said, "Fine. And thanks."

Ben's phone vibrated in his pocket, a combination of pulses that meant that he had an email message.

Ben said, "I'm going to go down the hill now. Back after lunch."

Abby shook her head. "Too bad. We're having vegetarian lasagna, and it's the best thing they serve here."

Ben said. "Maybe I'll be back in time to try it."

Chapter Twenty-Eight

Ben got into his car and drove down the winding road into Berona. As the road leveled, he came to a small park and pulled to the curb in the shade of an elm. He took out his iPhone and thumbed through his email. There was a message from Yolanda: Her airport contact had come up empty on Rabbi Geltkern's car.

There was also a message from Miryam, along with a picture of her mounted on a horse and dressed as a gaucho. She looked ridiculous, yet so beautiful that he had to smile.

The next message was the one he had been waiting for: Howard Hopper had put his people on the device Ben had sent them, and they had produced a long report. Ben skimmed the report with interest, especially its conclusions.

He started the engine and headed for the Berona Police Department.

§

Chief Laurence said, "You must have mental telepathy. I was just looking for your phone number."

Ben smiled. "What's up, Jack?"

"We found that car you asked us to look for. The red Ford."

"Where was it?"

"In a ravine on the eastern slope of Mount Sanoker."

"Mount Sanoker?"

"Yeah. Officially it's Kendall Heights, but the locals call it Mount Sanoker. Or Mount Sinai, when they're being sarcastic."

"What can you tell me about that car, Jack?"

Laurence opened the file on the desk before him. "Reported stolen six years ago. Registered to a woman named Marino in Buffalo, New York. The plate is from a junked Pittsburgh car."

"Fingerprints?"

"A bunch, but we're waiting to hear from the state troopers and the FBI. It could take a couple of weeks."

Ben nodded. It wasn't what he'd expected to learn, but it fit the pattern that was emerging about Geltkern.

Laurence said, "And one more bit of news, and it's a pisser."

"What would that be?"

"I told the city manager that you were off the case, wouldn't be working as our consultant, and asked if I could use that money to buy new computers for the department. Ours are over five years old—senior citizens in the computer world.

"Frank Lustig, the city manager, said that I was already over budget and that whatever donation had come in would go toward making up my deficit."

Ben chose his words carefully. "But you don't think that you're over budget?"

"I was projecting a small surplus before the Bernstein murder."

"Come on, you closed that case in a couple of days."

Laurence made a face. "This is a strange place. You ever hear of a guy working as a PD lieutenant and he's moonlighting as a township councilman?"

Ben shook his head. "It doesn't seem unreasonable, this being a small town."

"But did you ever hear of such a thing?"

"No."

Laurence said, "Thirty years on the Greensburg force—that's about fifteen miles south—I retired as deputy chief, then worked private security a couple of years in Pittsburgh. I'm here almost a year when I find out my detective lieutenant is on the council and that, since he got elected, he's been promoted three times:"

Ben said, "And you were thinking that he could have been the chief, but instead they went outside the department and hired you."

Laurence stared at Ben. "Damn, but you are telepathic. That's exactly what I was thinking."

Ben shook his head. "Not telepathy. Logic. If he could have gotten himself promoted to chief but didn't, then he must have had a good reason."

"Overtime," Laurence said. "I don't get any. Everyone else in the department does. And damned if Mr. Councilman Detective Lieutenant Geisel and two of his detectives don't log almost $6,000 in overtime, mileage and per diem working a case that was closed in two days."

Ben said, "Something's not right."

"I'm damn sure of that. Geisel took *both* his homicide dicks, and they all drove to Youngstown, Ohio. Took two cars, so that's twice as much mileage money. And why? To look into why this mafia dude came to our town. Stayed in a nice hotel. Had steak and eggs for breakfast and all like that. Came back and told me that 'Jake the Heater' Witzelburg was mobbed up, that the Youngstown force won't go near the local organized crime establishment and that it was a dead end."

Ben said, "Except that they had a nice weekend and got overtime bonuses."

Laurence sighed. "The township got me cheap. Lustig, I mean. He knew I had a pension from Scottdale, so he offered me $140 a month more than my lieutenant gets—except *he's* eligible for overtime. If I could afford to, I'd quit. But I've got three kids in college, and my daughter's talking about getting married. So...."

Ben nodded sympathetically. "I'm afraid there's more trouble for you, Jack."

"What's that?"

Ben took out his phone and brought up Howard Hopper's email. "The night 'Jake the Heater' got shot. You have a report on that?"

"Don't tell me you want to see it."

"I don't need to see it. But I would like to ask a few questions about it."

"That might be possible, Rabbi. Give me a minute."

Laurence got up from behind his desk, moved to a filing cabinet, extracted a manila folder and brought back to his desk and opened it.

"Go ahead, Ben. Ask away."

"First off, how many shots were fired?"

Laurence peered at the page, turned it over, read the next page.

"Five shots in all. The suspect opened fire with two shots, the two patrolmen each fired one shot, the suspect fired again."

Ben asked, "Did either of the patrolmen get hit? Were they wearing vests?"

Laurence returned to the file. "No hits on the patrolmen. Two shots hit the suspect. Head and chest."

Ben said, "Okay. Next, do you have the coroner's report on Witzelburg?"

Laurence said, "Right here."

Ben said, "How does it describe the gunshot wounds to his body?"

Laurence peered at the page. "Wait a minute. That can't be right."

Ben asked, "What's wrong?"

"Says here, one GSW to the head, stippling and burns observed around the wound, a .38 slug retrieved. And one GSW to the abdomen, 9mm slug retrieved."

Ben asked, "Your patrolmen all carry nine-millimeter automatics?"

"Yeah. Some carry a .38 revolver as a backup, strapped to their ankle."

"Who else carries a .38, Chief?"

Laurence put the file down. "I do. And so does Lieutenant Geisel."

Chapter Twenty-nine

Ben said, "The coroner found stippling and burns. That means the shot was fired from very close range?"

Laurence said, "Exactly what it means. But it doesn't square with the report."

Ben said, "Yesterday, I had some carpenters and a locksmith come to the temple to repair the doors."

Laurence nodded. "You told me you were gonna do that."

Ben said, "I looked around the office very carefully. I found blood stains on the carpet. But no bullet holes in the office, none in the hall outside, none anywhere else in the building. Yet that report says that three shots were fired by Witzelburg and none struck the officers."

"You're sure about those bullet holes?"

"Come up and look for yourself. Chief, how many unfired bullets were in Witzelburg's gun?"

Laurence thumbed through the file. "It doesn't say."

Ben asked, "Does the report say why the patrol car went to the scene in the first place?"

"Responded to a silent alarm."

"Walk me through that. Where does the alarm ring?"

"In a private security office. We've got just two in the township. They either send their own car, or they call us."

"So the security company calls 911, the dispatcher broadcasts, and the nearest car responds. Is that right?"

"We have only two patrol cars out at a time, so we know which one is closest to the alarm."

"Jack, the Sanoker Shul doesn't have an alarm system. I looked all over and couldn't find any mechanism that could have alerted a private security company."

"Then how the hell did the security company know to call 911?"

Ben said, "The men I hired to fix the doors found a small, wireless device that had been attached to the inside lintel over the front door."

"What kind of a wireless device?"

"I sent it to a friend of mine, an electronics expert. I have his report on my phone."

Ben held up the phone. "I'll forward this to you. What it says is that the device was battery-powered, triggered by a built-in motion detector that turned on an infrared-sensing video camera. The video feed from the camera was stored on the device while another component, a cell phone, dialed a number. When that number answered, the device streamed the saved video to the remote phone.

"The device was manufactured in Yonkers, New York, and subsequently modified with a customized software upgrade."

Laurence asked, "Witzelburg tripped a motion sensor and that sent the video?"

'It would seem so."

"And where was the video sent to?"

Ben said, "Phone number is in the report. I'll write it down for you."'

Laurence said, "I sure wish I could see that video."

Ben smiled. "Then let me show it to you."

He got up and moved to Laurence's side, held his phone out in front of the chief. The tiny screen brightened and a figure entered the frame, visible only from above and behind. The image brightened to almost pure white as the figure switched on a flashlight; then it adjusted. Something translucent went over the light, dimming it; the picture adjusted a second time. The light and the indistinct figure holding it moved to the right of the screen and out of view. The screen went dark. After several seconds, the screen came back to life. The scene vibrated, then whipsawed, as though the camera was shaking. The screen went bright and dark and bright as the walls spun. The scene went dark. When an image returned, the camera seemed to be pointing almost at the ceiling. The severely foreshortened figure of a man passed through the frame and disappears. The screen went dark.

Laurence asked, "So there were two perps? One behind the other, a minute or so between them? The first one had a key, the second one broke the door down?"

Ben said, "It looks that way. Keep watching."

After a long pause, the screen brightened. Two foreshortened figures, unmistakably clad in police garb, moved past the camera.

The screen dimmed, but light coming through the broken door showed a ghostly outline of the room. Then, from the right came a bright flash, followed an instant later by another. Several seconds went by, and another foreshortened man moved through the frame and vanished to the right.

The screen dimmed, then another bright flash came from the right.

After a long interval, a figure materialized from the darkness at the right and moved through the frame. A few seconds passed. The room was flooded with bright light. The screen went dark.

Ben said, "That's it."

Laurence said, "I'd like to watch it again, Rabbi."

§

Ben asked, "What do you think we just saw?"

Laurence said, "Looks like there was an intruder, who had a key, who goes into the building, turns on a flashlight and then moves off to the right. A little later, a second intruder breaks down the door and goes off in the same direction. Then two men, probably my officers, come in through the door. There's a bright flash."

Ben asked, "Could that have been a gunshot?"

Laurence nodded. "Probably. Then another man comes in, goes off in the same direction as the others. Another flash. The last to arrive is the first to leave."

Ben said, "I was the first man. I went into the office, intending to retrieve a stack of unpaid bills. While I was there, I heard somebody breaking the door down. I turned off the light, locked the door, went out the window, and ran back to my car. I was almost to Berona Road when the squad car came by, flashing lights, no siren."

Laurence stared at Ben. "You picked the lock?"

Ben said, "I did."

"How long after you cracked the door was it before you saw that squad car?"

"About six minutes."

"So that means there are gaps in this video?"

"It turns on when the motion detector activates it, shuts off after several seconds without movement."

"You never got a look at none of those people?"

Ben shook his head, no.

"You're taking a chance, confessing to breaking into that building."

"A building owned by people who asked me to be their spiritual leader. You can arrest me if you like. But you have bigger fish to fry."

"I'm not so sure I want to troll those waters."

"Did you recognize someone in that video, Jack?"

Laurence shook his head, no. "But I've got two patrolmen who lied on their report. There were three shots, not five. This might still be a righteous shooting. If he pulled a gun. But then it gets all muddied up when that last guy comes and they shoot him again."

Ben said, "Like an execution."

Laurence said, "Maybe, maybe not. Maybe he was shot, but still alive. Maybe he went for his gun again. The question is, Who pulled the trigger on the .38? And who was that last guy, the one who came last and left first?"

Ben said, "It's pretty clear that whoever had the phone that got the video feed was involved in dispatching the patrol car."

Laurence said, "I agree. But that means it's someone in this department."

Ben said, "I think so, too. And I'm betting my life that it wasn't you."

Chapter Thirty

The Sanok Home parking lot seemed to have more cars than Ben recalled from two hours earlier. He rang the buzzer at the front door, and a familiar voice came over the intercom. "We're serving lunch, Rabbi," said James.

In the dining room, Ben saw that perhaps twenty visitors, mostly women or couples in their fifties and sixties, were sprinkled around the tables.

Ben scanned the room until he saw Abby sitting with two women in nurse uniforms. She waved, and he came over.

Abby said, "Sit down, Rabbi."

Ben took a chair next to one of the nurses, a Filipina in her forties.

Abby said, "Rabbi Ben, this is Carmela Bañuelos, and that's Rosa Morales."

Carmela, next to Ben, smiled. "Pleased to meet you, Rabbi," she said. Across the table, Rosa, who might have been Carmela's cousin, smiled.

Ben asked, "Who are all these other people?"

Carmela said, "The ones who have family in the area, mostly in Pittsburgh; their children like to visit."

Rosa said, "Especially now, when we're gonna close soon."

Ben asked, "Do you have a firm date on that?"

Abby said, "Nobody knows yet. I think it will happen when we have so few residents that payments from Medicare and Medical Assistance—what we call Medicaid in Pennsylvania—won't cover overhead. Then we'll notify the county, and they'll make arrangements to take our remaining residents."

A well-dressed woman in her fifties approached their table. She looked at Ben.

"Are you the rabbi?"

Ben said, "I'm a rabbi. But this is my first visit here."

"But you're taking Rabbi Geltkern's place, right?"

Ben shook his head. "Not really. But I thought that the residents might enjoy Friday night Shabbat services..."

"That's well and good, but what are you doing about keeping this place open?"

Ben said, "As I told you, Ma'am, this is my first visit here. I just learned that they'll be closing."

"But you're the rabbi. That's your job! You can't simply abandon these people after taking all their money!"

Ben asked, "Won't you please sit down so we can talk about this?"

The woman glared at Ben. "I'm going to get my husband!" she said and hurried away. Ben and Abby exchanged amused glances until a beefy man about six feet tall stopped at the table and glared at Ben.

"I don't care if you are some kind of rabbi. Anybody who'd talk to my wife like that—I ought to punch you in the nose!" he shouted.

Ben pushed back his chair, rose to his feet, and smiled. "I'm Rabbi Ben. As I told your wife, I don't work here. I'm a first-time visitor. When I asked her to sit down and discuss the problem, she just walked away."

The man looked dubious.

Abby said, "I heard every word of their conversation, Mr. Harrington. Rabbi Ben is my guest here today, and I asked him if he'd lead Friday night services."

Ben said, "But I'd like to know why your wife is so upset. Please, sit down."

Harrington pulled a chair out and sat. "You have to excuse my wife, Rabbi. Heidi's mother is almost ninety, and they've always been close. And now they're gonna close this place. We're just working folks. We don't have money to get her into another place, not one nice as this. And it's not right. She signed over everything—her house and her bank accounts. There's nothing left."

Ben asked, "How long ago was that, Mr. Harrington?"

Harrington frowned, thinking. "I think three, maybe four years ago."

"Do you have some idea what her house was worth back then?"

"I'd say a quarter of a million, give or take. Owned it free and clear, except taxes, of course. And she had twenty grand in savings."

Ben said, "So if she came here, let's say, four years, or 48 months, ago, and her house and savings came to $270,000, that's—"

"—about $5,600 a month," said Harrington. "I just drive a forklift now, but I'm a civil engineer—and I'm still pretty good with numbers."

Abby said, "This is a very nice, very safe, very clean facility. A few years ago, when I went looking for a place for my dad, most of the better ones cost about that much."

Carmela said, "Last assisted living I worked, not so nice like this, was over $6,000 a month."

Harrington said. "But she was supposed to be here the rest of her life. That was the deal."

Abby said, "Everybody who works here is just as sad and angry as you are."

Harrington got to his feet. "Sorry for being a hard-ass, Rabbi."

Ben stood up and they shook hands. "You and your wife are welcome to stay for services," he said.

Harrington shook his head. "That's Heidi's thing. I'm a Methodist. Anyway, I work swing shift. Lucky to have a job. First snow storm, and we'll all get laid off, so I'd best gather my rosebuds while they're blooming."

Ben and Abby exchanged glances, and Ben understood that there might be more to Harrington's complaint than he knew.

Abby said, "I better get back to those charts or I'll never finish today."

The Filipinas also stood. "It was nice meeting you, Rabbi."

"And nice meeting you," said Ben, wondering if there was time enough to find the bookkeeper before Shabbat services.

Chapter Thirty-one

The address on Filomina Jenston's card was a bowling alley, a fact which caused Ben to drive around the block, peering at street signs and address numbers. After two circuits, he pulled into the bowling alley's near-empty lot and went inside.

Except for overhead floods on the far two lanes and a glimmer seeping through the crack of a door at the far end, most of Berona Lanes was dark.

Ben moved toward the light, saw three athletic-looking young men with military buzz cuts drinking beer and bowling on the lighted lanes.

He knocked, then pushed the door open and stood in the doorway.

A pleasant-looking woman about Ben's age looked up from a desk.

"Help you?"

Ben said, "Looking for Filomina Jenston?"

The woman smiled. "Look no further. I be she."

Ben smiled back. "You're a bookkeeper?"

"A CPA, but yes, I also keep books. And yes, this is a bowling alley. Your eyes did not lie, but rent is cheap, and it's quiet during the day. Do you need accounting help?"

"In a way."

"Have a seat," she said, nodding toward a chair. Ben sat down.

Ben asked, "Have you ever heard of the Jewish Federation of Greater Allegheny County? In Pittsburgh?"

Jenston shook her head. "Can't say that I have."

"Are you a Catholic?"

"Is that written on my forehead or something?"

Ben had to laugh. "No, I ask because I wanted to draw some comparisons between a Jewish Federation and a Catholic Archdiocese."

"I bet this has something to do with the Sanok Home."

Ben said, "I'm Rabbi Ben Maimon. Call me Ben, or Rabbi Ben."

Jenston said, "I've kind of been expecting someone like you, Rabbi."

Ben said. "Talk to me."

Jenston stood up, stretched like a cat, stressing a clinging sweater that barely contained her remarkably large breasts.

"I sit all day, Rabbi, so let me take a minute to work the kinks out."

Ben said, "I understand."

After a few minutes of stretching and showing off her lithe body, Jenston reclaimed her chair.

"I guess this is about the mortgage, right?"

Ben looked expectant.

"Or the Sanok Shul thing, whatever that is?"

Ben said, "Start in the beginning, and just lay it all out for me."

"Do you have some kind of ID?"

Ben took out his wallet and handed her his Israeli driver's license.

She looked at it carefully, then passed it back to him.

"You don't look much like a rabbi."

"You mean, no beard, no dark suit, no big black hat."

"And you're much younger than Rabbi Geltkern. A lot cuter, too."

"Thank you. The fact is, I know some rabbis that look like Rabbi Geltkern. My appearance is often helpful for the kind of work that I do."

Jenston smiled. "I get it. Okay, here goes: When I started with the Sanok Home, about fifteen years ago—"

Ben asked, "You've been a CPA since you were twelve?"

Jenston laughed and pushed her hair back from her face. "Thanks. I needed that. And I'm pushing forty."

Ben looked surprised. "I wouldn't have thought so. Anyway, you started about fifteen years ago?"

"They had about 200 residents. Maybe a few more or a couple less, but about that. Rabbi Estrin was the director. Most of their income was from the Sanok Home Trust, and it ran about five to ten percent, annualized, over expenses. At the end of the year, Rabbi Estrin used half the surplus for staff bonuses."

Ben said, "I'll bet he didn't take one himself."

Jenston said, "Did you know Rabbi Estrin?"

"Only by reputation."

"Well, about seven years ago, he retired. By that time, the Home was down to between 90 and a hundred residents. The board of directors voted to make Mrs. Weinstock the new director, and she hired a part-time rabbi."

"Mrs. Weinstock was herself a new hire?"

Jenston shook her head, no. "She was Rabbi Estrin's office manager and had worked for the rabbi before him, I think. She hired Rabbi Geltkern. They were doing okay, financially. Actually, the Trust investments were way up. The last two years of Rabbi Estrin's time, they were able to sock away some rainy-day money.

"Then Estrin retired, Geltkern came aboard, and about four years ago, he started this Sanoker Shul thing. I'm not even sure what it is—Mrs. Weinstock okayed the bills, so I paid them, but she never told me what it was, exactly."

Ben barely suppressed a gasp. Money supporting the shul had come from the Home—funds flowing from the old and sick to the young and healthy. A travesty.

Ben said, "Shul is Yiddish for a school, or a house of study, which is another name, the original name, for a synagogue. Synagogue is actually a Greek word."

"And what's Yiddish, exactly?"

"It was, and still is in a small way, a language spoken by northern European Jews. It's a mixture of Old German, with some Russian, Polish and Hebrew.

"So he started the Sanoker Shul?"

"Yes. And he drew a second salary for that."

Ben said, "They ran through the rainy-day money pretty quick?"

"Sure did. So the board of directors got a line of credit secured by their real estate, and they opened the Home to non-Sanokers."

"What does that mean?"

"Before, only the members and children of original burial society members lived there. After they started the Sanoker Shul, they took in a hundred new residents with no Sanoker connection. That helped their cash flow. For a while."

"For a while?"

"The new residents had to surrender their life savings and their property to the Home. So that was a little over $5 million that came in."

Ben asked, "Is that common in assisted-living facilities?"

Jenston said, "The Sanok is my only board-and-care client. But I think so. And, once those new residents signed their property and their Social Security income over to the home, they were paupers, so they qualified for state Medical Assistance. In addition, they were all on Medicare. So there were two more income streams."

"You spent a lot of time billing the state and Medicare?"

Jenston frowned. "Mrs. Weinstock did all that. I saw the incoming checks, of course, and she sent me the provider bills to pay."

Ben said, "Let me guess: The Medicare and state assistance checks were always more than you paid out to providers."

"Many of the services that she billed to Medicare were performed by staff members. And they hired some new people, at least for awhile, and pretty much everyone got raises."

Ben said, "Let's go back to the $5 million. What happened to that money?"

"Mrs. Weinstock discovered that the Sanok Home had never made provision for employee pensions or severance payments. The board of directors voted to establish a pension and severance fund, and about $3.5 million went into that."

"How many employees qualified for a pension?"

Jenston shook her head. "No idea. They handled all the paperwork. I just cut the check and sent it to K & L Associates, an insurance broker."

Ben said, " Tell me more about that loan."

"A line of credit, secured by a mortgage on the property."

"How much did they borrow?"

"Nothing, until two years ago. The township passed a bed tax."

Ben held up a hand. "You mean a tax on hotel and motel rooms?"

"And on bed-and-breakfast, inns—any establishment that had more than three guest rooms and accepted transient guests."

"Like a board and care? Or an assisted living?"

"Until they changed things up, back when all the residents were part-owners, that couldn't have applied to the Sanok Home. But as soon as they started taking new people, who could stay as long as they wanted to, the city attorney decided that it applied to them, too."

"And this was a tax on the occupied rooms or on all their rooms?"

"Oh, they had to be occupied. And for awhile, there were still a few of the original burial society residents, and their rooms were exempt."

Ben asked, "How much was the tax?"

"When the law was passed, it was fifty cents a night. But then they kept raising it. Now it's $4.00 a night."

"That seems kind of stiff."

The accountant smiled. "Stiff can be very good. I like stiff."

Ben smiled back. "I'm talking about a tax. Four bucks a night?"

"That would be quite a night. I'd like to try that."

Ben laughed.

Jenston said, "You ever spend a night in a Pittsburgh hotel?"

Ben shrugged. "You?"

"When somebody gives me a reason to go to Pittsburgh. The room tax there is seven percent. A nice room is about $200."

"So the Sanok Home was paying, what, $4 times 50 rooms a night?"

"This year, it was around $6,000 a month."

""How much do they owe on that line of credit now?"

"I don't know the current balance, but the line was for $500,000."

Ben stood up. "You've been very helpful. Do you know how to reach Mrs. Weinstock?"

Jenston shrugged. "I'm pretty sure she's with Rabbi Geltkern."

Ben said. "Ah. And do you know where that is?"

Jenston smiled. "You're not married, are you?"

Ben said. "Engaged. But if Mrs. Weinstock is with Rabbi Geltkern, where is Mister Weinstock?"

Jenston came around the desk and stopped very close to Ben. Her perfume was faint but seductive. Her pupils were slightly dilated.

She said, "Her husband died a long time ago."

Ben asked, "Do you happen to have a picture of her? Or of Rabbi Geltkern?"

Jenston said, "I might. Do you want to go to Pittsburgh with me? Tonight? I mean, right now."

Ben took a small step back. "I'm leading services at Sanok Home tonight."

Jenston took Ben's hand and placed it on her left breast. "They're real," she said. "I can wait until you finish up at the Home."

Ben carefully removed his hand. "I'm really sorry, Ms. Jenston, but I'm about to be married to a wonderful woman. I don't think this would work out."

Jenston moved closer to Ben, lightly brushed the front of his trousers with the back of her hand. "I'm not looking for anything past tonight," she said.

For an instant, Ben was consumed by lust. He pictured himself naked with this voluptuous woman, plunging himself deep into her sweet heat. He could almost feel the passion and excitement. Something stirred deep within him, a jolt of almost electrical power that shook him to his core. Miryam need never know.

And with an even bigger jolt, he realized this was what the sages of old had called "the evil inclination."

He recalled his times with Rachel, his beloved, long-dead wife, their bodies entwined, the flesh of two together becoming one, their passion only part of selfless mutual commitment.

Anything less was meaningless.

Not this, then. No. Never. Whether Miryam knew or not, *he* would know.

Ben shook his head. "Sorry. I'm flattered. Women just don't ... with me. But—"

Jenston asked, "You're not really with that Federation thing, are you?"

"I never said that I was."

"Are you actually a rabbi?"

"Yes. And Ms. Jenston, I'm truly grateful for your help. You're a smart, successful and very attractive woman. You don't need to throw yourself at strangers. Please, show some self-respect."

Jenston lowered her face, fighting tears. His passion drained, Ben stepped forward to hold her.

"There aren't any real men in this goddamn town," she sobbed.

"Can that be true?"

"They're all married, and they all fool around."

"Do you go to church?"

Jenston broke free and stepped back, wiping her eyes. "What?"

"If you belong to a church or to a synagogue, you're more likely to meet the kind of man you're looking for."

"I know every Catholic man in Berona. They only go to church when their wives make them. It's not that they're all sinners—I am too—it's their hypocrisy."

"Then get in your car and go to Pittsburgh. Find another church."

"You're a Jew, but you're telling me to go to church? Why not a synagogue?"

"We don't proselytize. Observant or not, it's not easy being a Jew. There's no shortage of people in the world who blame us for their problems and want to see us gone. Or just hate us on general principles. Becoming a Jew, one takes on that burden, among others. We welcome converts, but we don't seek them.

"But, more important, there is only one God. Christians and Jews worship differently but to the same God. You would probably find a synagogue baffling. Much of the service is in Hebrew. But if you want to try it, then do so."

"Mrs. Weinstock swears that Jewish men are the best lovers."

"I've never made love with one, so I really can't say."

Jenston laughed. "You're okay, you know that?"

"If I wasn't engaged to a wonderful woman, and if I thought that you were sincerely interested in Judaism—who knows? I probably would ask you out."

"Did you know that Mrs. Weinstock isn't Jewish?"

Ben shook his head. "I've never met her."

"Everybody thinks she is. Her husband was Jewish, but he died only a year after they married."

"Does she live here in Berona?"

"She has a room at the Home. Weeknights, she usually stays there. But she has her own place, too. Not too far—Pittsburgh, maybe."

"What's her first name?"

"Merry. Short for Meredith."

"I don't suppose you have her address?"

Jenston shook her head. "Never had a reason."

"What did Mrs. Weinstock look like?"

"Not much. Sixty-something, lots of makeup. Big downtown, not much uptown. Wore wigs a lot—her hair is so thin you can see her scalp. But she's smart and focused. She knows what she wants."

"Thank you, Ms. Jenston."

"Come on, you touched my boob. Call me Filomina. Or Mina."

"Thank you, Mina."

"Hey, your turn. Tell me something."

Ben said, "You want to know why I'm poking into the Sanok Home. Why I'm so interested in Weinstock and Geltkern."

"Yeah. What's going on? Who are you, anyway?"

"A rabbi. Some friends of mine belong to the Sanoker Shul. They asked me to help find Rabbi Geltkern. That's it."

"So you're some kind of detective?"

"Sometimes."

"Is this is one of those times?"

Ben smiled. "It is."

"Now that I know a little about you, now that you're not some strange man—are you sure you wouldn't like a night of wild sex in a nice hotel room?"

Chapter Thirty-Two

Ben was almost at the top of the ridge and the Sanok Home when he realized something. He used the parking lot to make a U-turn, then drove back to the bowling alley. Jenston's office door was locked. He tapped on it. Hearing nothing through the door, after a minute he tapped again. Seconds went by, and Mina opened the door to greet him with a dazzling smile. "You changed your mind?"

Ben's face tightened. He shook his head, no. "Mina, I just thought of something. Do you have friends or family out of town? Some place you could stay for awhile?"

Jenston shook her head. "Not really."

"Do you have cash—enough for a room someplace, for a couple of weeks?

"I have a little money saved. What's this about?"

"A man was murdered at the Sanoker Shul last week. Stan Bernstein. He was sort of the caretaker, a volunteer. A month or so after Rabbi Geltkern took off, Stan got a locksmith and opened his study. He found a lot of papers and a shredding operation in progress. When Stan came back the next night, somebody killed him, then took every scrap of paper from that room."

Mina asked, "What does that have to do with me?"

"It appears that maybe Stan carried some of those papers to his own office, at the other end of the building. Two nights later, a thug from Youngstown, a guy with Mafia ties, broke into that office. The police came and shot him dead."

"I still don't understand—"

"You've got records that might show what Geltkern and Weinstock were up to. If someone was willing to kill for his other records, they might decide to go after yours. And if you get in the way, they might put a bullet in you, too."

"What records? The Sanok Home books?"

"All those board minutes. The bills for the Sanoker Shul paid from the Home's account. Millions siphoned from residents, then shuffled off to an insurance broker. There's probably something illegal in all that."

"But I'm just their bookkeeper. I had nothing—"

"The police are not your worry. About Rabbi Geltkern: I'm not sure he's actually a rabbi, and I know for sure his name isn't Jeremiah Geltkern."

"What? Who is he?"

"No idea. But nobody by that name owns a house, a car, or a credit card, has an insurance policy, pays taxes, votes, or can be found in any public record in this state or the ones nearby."

"So I should just leave town?"

"Your records—are they digital or paper?"

"I digitize everything. And it's all backed up, on-site and off-site, too."

"If someone put a gun to your head, would you delete all those files?"

Jenston paled. "Could that really happen?"

Ben nodded.

"What should I do?""

"Change your appearance. Choose a new hair style, a new color."

Jenston thrust her chest out, cradling a breast in each hand. "How do I change these?"

"Buy larger blouses and sweaters. Don't wear a bra. Get a small pillow and a big belt, and strap it around your middle."

She recoiled. "I'll look like I'm fat!"

"Better than looking dead. And the men you attract will be more interested in who you are than your bra size."

Jenston shook her head. "I don't know about this."

Ben reached in his pocket and handed her a roll of bills.

"That's all I've got on me. If I were you, I'd pack a small bag, drive to the Monroeville airport, buy a ticket to Cleveland. Or St. Louis. Anywhere. Use your credit card for that, cash for everything else. Leave your car in long-term parking. Take a bus or a taxi to some small town nearby. Then a bus to Akron or Wheeling, a train someplace else. Don't use credit cards. Stay lost for a few weeks."

"I don't understand—a credit card for this, cash for that. Why?"

"The guy that the police think killed Bernstein was connected to the Mafia. The thing about organized crime is that they're actually organized. They know how to find someone who can, for example, access your credit card purchases."

Jenston shook her head. "How the hell can they do that? There are all sorts of laws against that."

Ben said, "They're criminals. They don't care about laws. They'll find someone they can bribe, or intimidate, or blackmail."

Jenston seemed to collect herself. "So they'll think I bought a ticket to St. Louis, and they'll look for me there?"

"One hopes."

"But wouldn't they also check to see if I was on the passenger manifest?"

"They might. But like all humans, they tend to be lazy. And, thanks to the TSA, since 9/11 it's harder to access airline data than get into a credit card company's computers. Every bank has a way to access those accounts."

"You're some kind of James Bond or Jason Bourne, aren't you?"

"Hardly. I'm only trying to keep you safe."

"Any chance for that wild night in Pittsburgh? When this blows over?"

Ben shook his head. "Not in the cards, really. But please, if I found you, somebody else can, too. I don't have the big picture yet. I don't know what all that business with starting a shul was about. But I do know that Geltkern, or whatever his real name is, is mixed up with dangerous people. Please, save yourself."

Jenston opened her desk drawer, carefully rummaged around, then placed her compact in it. Then she closed it and came around the desk. Sliding her arms under his jacket, she hugged Ben tightly with one arm and lightly stroked his back and buttocks with the other.

"You're very sweet. But you really bring out the slut in me."

Chapter Thirty-three

The Home's parking lot was bathed in late afternoon sun but almost empty when Ben pulled in next to a Toyota pickup with James at the wheel. He waved.

Ben stopped behind his truck and got out.

Ben said, "I'm glad I caught you. Where do I hold the service?"

James said, "They're eating now. When the kitchen staff cleans up afterward, ask them to open the chapel for you. It's off to the side of the dining area."

"Thanks, James. Sorry to sound like a broken record, but one more thing: Does the Home have a board of directors?"

James pointed over Ben's shoulder. "They're all over there, now."

§

Ben watched James drive off, then moved to the edge of the parking lot and peered over a tall hedge at rows of headstones.

The Home's directors, its owner-management team, had all died.

Ben returned to his car, opened the trunk and changed into a long-sleeved blue dress shirt under a navy blazer with silver buttons.

Inside, he found the kitchen and, despite the chef's protest that the brisket prepared and served that evening was kosher, asked for two bagels, some cream cheese and, lacking smoked salmon, black olives. He ate alone in the kitchen.

While two women cleared the dining room, Ben found the sliding doors that ran almost the width of the room and concealed a small but ornate, European-style chapel with, curiously, a new and very inexpensive Torah ark. Ben was struck by the suspicion that Geltkern had taken the ark from this chapel and moved it to the Sanoker Shul, then replaced it with something newer and less expensive.

There were only six rows of pews, about eighty seats; the room's design implied that the dining area, which could seat hundreds with tables removed, would serve as an overflow for days when more people felt the need to worship.

Ben opened the ark and found three Sefer Torahs. A quick but thorough inspection showed that all were in excellent condition.

"So you're the new Sanoker Rebbe?" asked a man's voice.

Ben turned to find an older man with a face like old parchment. Short, slim but erect, he wore an old-fashioned double-breasted suit.

Ben said, "I'm Rabbi Ben Maimon."

"Avi Cohen," said the older man. "You're taking Geltkern's place?"

Ben shook his head. "Just filling in until Rabbi Geltkern returns."

"Which is never," Cohen said. "They'll close this place first."

"You may be right, Mr. Cohen. I'm just here for tonight, or maybe until Rabbi Geltkern can be located."

"He's a fraud, you know."

"We've never met or spoken. What makes you say that?"

"My father, *alev hashalom*, rest in peace, was a rabbi. His father was a rabbi, and his father, and his father—nine generations of rabbis. My older brother, *alev hashalom*, was also a rabbi. His sons were both rabbis. And their sons. I know rabbis."

"But not you?"

"Listen, somebody had to make money, you understand, so that my brothers could study. My mother, *alev hashalom*, died young. Worked herself to death, supporting seven children and a husband who earned almost nothing. So I went to work. I made money. But that doesn't mean I don't know Torah. Or *Halakhah,* Jewish law. Even the Talmud, I learned quite a bit from my father."

Ben asked, "But why do you say that Rabbi Geltkern was a fraud?"

"He doesn't know how to *daven.* To pray. His Hebrew is terrible. He can't read Torah without a cheat sheet. His sermons are so much malarkey. He'll use a Yom Kippur melody for a Shabbos prayer, or a Hanukah tune for Pesach. And he was *shtupping* Mrs. Weinstock, and maybe half the old ladies here, too."

"Those are very serious charges, Mr. Cohen."

"Ask anyone who comes Friday night. Now we don't get even a minion, they're all so fed up with him."

"Mr. Cohen, would you do me a favor?"

"Probably, *boychik.*"

"Two favors, then. One, please don't call me boychik. Eight years ago, I finished first in my class and was ordained a rabbi by the Jewish Theological Society of America. I'm nobody's boy. The second favor is, Would you please tell everyone who might be interested that, if we can muster a minion in the next ten minutes, we'll have time before sunset and the start of Shabbat to daven Mincha, the weekday afternoon service, then Shabbat *Ma'ariv*, the evening service. We'll do Mourner's *Kaddish* twice. A real Friday night Shabbat service."

§

An hour and twenty minutes later, with eleven elderly men and seven women in attendance, Ben completed the service and began his sermon. He spoke for a few minutes about the Jewish responsibility to educate younger generations, to pass on customs, traditions, and learning. Then he paused and looked around the room. And sang, sweetly, the wordless prayer of the soul called a *niggun*.

"Yay dai dai dai, yay dai dai dai, yay dai dai dai dai-d'dai yay yay yay..."

"That's the Bal Shem Tov's niggun. Let's try it together?"

He started again, "Yay dai dai dai, yay dai dai dai, yay dai dai dai dai-d'dai yay yay yay...," and one by one, the others joined. When they had sung together for a few minutes, Ben let his voice trail off into silence. And waited. Finally, he spoke.

"You are among the last of your generation. Together, you hold a vast treasure of Jewish lore, Jewish thought, Jewish learning, study, customs, prayers. I'd bet that among you are fifty *niggunim* that no one else knows, no one else in the world could sing. Knowledge that will die with you—unless you share it. Tomorrow, I will lead services at the Sanoker Shul. I don't know how much you know about the place, but from my one visit, I believe it to be a congregation of earnest young Jews hungry to learn about the faith of their fathers."

Ben looked at Avi Cohen. "I'm also under the impression that they were poorly served by their previous rabbi. I will help them, but I'm in a medical trial at Pittsburgh Medical. On Mondays and Tuesdays, I'm barely able to get out of bed.

"So I invite you all to come to services tomorrow morning. I'll try to arrange transportation. The shul is going to re-organize, starting tomorrow. Have any of you ever served as the president of a congregation?"

Four men and two women raised their hands.

"I hope that some of you will find the time to participate in the life of this congregation, to pass on your special knowledge to future generations, to help and guide the young leaders of this shul so that it will survive and prosper."

A man raised his hand, and Ben nodded to him.

"Rabbi, what kind of congregation is this? Reform, Orthodox, Conservative?"

Ben said, "I would characterize it as sort of Reform. Some of the people who come have only one Jewish parent or only a Jewish grandparent. But they want to learn, and they feel their Jewishness."

A man stood up. "Rabbi, no disrespect, but if someone doesn't have a Jewish mother, they're not Jewish."

Avi Cohen raised his hand. "Hitler didn't ask if your mother was Jewish or not before he murdered you. And he didn't ask any of the Six Million if they were Reform or Orthodox or what. So let's forget about that. We're all Jews, period."

A woman stood up. "Rabbi, I'm Fannie Leftkowitz. We have two minivans here. The attendants have licenses. We can shuttle everyone down for services."

Another woman raised her hand. "Rabbi, you asked if we had time. We have nothing except time. I want to help."

Ben asked, "Who knows how to *lein*, or chant, Torah?"

Four men, including Cohen, raised their hands.

"If you come tomorrow, I'll ask each of you to read. Let's show these young people what a real Torah service looks and sounds and feels like."

It was more than an hour before the members of the Friday Night Minyan would allow Ben to leave. Before driving off, he took a sheet of paper and two Sefer Torahs from the ark and carried them to his car, wrapped in blankets.

Chapter Thirty-Four

Abby and Yolanda arrived at the Sanoker Shul just as Ben was unlocking the newly painted door.

Yolanda said, "We need to talk."

Ben asked, "Can it wait until after Shabbat? This is a day of rest from worldly concerns."

Yolanda said, "I guess it could wait. Sure."

Ben turned to Abby and asked, "Have you ever carried a Torah?"

Abby shook her head. "In my father's shul, women didn't do such things. That's one of the things I love about this place."

Ben said, "In the trunk of my car are two Sefer Torahs that I borrowed from the Sanok Home. Will you each carry one inside?"

Abby said, "Sure, but don't we have a bunch of Torahs already?"

Ben said, "None of them is fit for ritual use. They're in very poor shape and probably too expensive to repair. They'll have to be buried."

Yolanda asked, "That's how you dispose of an old Torah?"

"Anything with the name of God written in it has to be treated with reverence. But that can wait."

He went to his car and handed each woman a Torah, then locked the trunk and led them to the sanctuary, where, one at a time, he stowed the scrolls.

Ben looked at Abby. "Did you talk to any other members?"

Abby nodded. "About twenty. Some are more willing to get involved than others."

Ben smiled. "If you can get half the people in any congregation to do anything beyond giving money, you're a superstar organizer."

He looked at Yolanda. "Because you haven't completed your conversion, you won't be active in the service. As soon as I can clear up all this mystery, I'll be available for tutoring. No charge, of course."

Yolanda smiled. "Thanks, Rabbi Ben. I understand."

Ben turned back to Abby. "Do you know what a *gabbai* does?"

Abby shook her head, no.

"Strictly speaking, the *gabbai* is an all-purpose synagogue helper. Today, we're going to have four *gabbaim*. Some residents from the Home may come this morning, and if they do, I want to pair them up, an old-timer with a younger person. The old-timers will show their partners what to do. One *gabbai* will get the Hebrew name of each person that we call up to the Torah, and the other will announce it. A pair of *gabbaim* will keep track of the Torah reading, prompt the reader if he misses a word or says it wrong. They'll also announce what page we're on in the *Chumash,* the Torah book, or the siddur, the prayer book."

Abby said, "I could do that—announce the names."

Ben said, "I need you for something more important."

He took a sheet of paper from his pocket. "This is a list of the honors—the tasks that are part of the Torah service. I'll find Torah readers, so ignore that. And I'll chant the *haphtarah.* As people arrive, go around the room, talk to them, and try to get two people for each task. Match an older person with a younger person. The older will show the younger what to do."

Abby nodded. "I can do that."

"Good. Here come the first members, so you might as well start."

As Abby hurried away, Ben turned back to Yolanda. "I'd like you to be my personal assistant. Sit on the bimah behind me. If I need you to find someone or something, I'll ask. Otherwise, watch, listen and learn."

§

Fourteen residents of the Sanok Home arrived before Ben started the service. It proceeded much as he had hoped it would: The Torah reading began with a selection from the Five Books of Moses and ended with a haphtarah, a selection from the books of the prophets. Ben led prayers, chanted the first section of the Torah reading, then turned subsequent readings over to the older men who had said they knew how to read. All were enthusiastic readers whose skills varied from excellent to competent. Ben chanted the haphtarah, a demonstration of his rabbinical chops.

When it came time for the drasha or lesson, Ben asked Abby to join him at the lectern.

Ben began, "The Hebrew word for friend is *chaver*. The suffix *im* makes most nouns into plurals. So I begin by saying, chaverim, friends, I bring you news. Some of it is terrible. The other is hopeful. First, as many of you know, Stan Bernstein was murdered last week by an intruder."

A disbelieving murmur swept through the room, and Ben held up his hand for quiet. "Two nights later, police found a prowler in the office, and shot him to death. They believe that he was responsible for Stan's death, and have closed the case.

"A day before he died, Stan, along with Abby Silverblatt, asked me to help find Rabbi Geltkern. I haven't yet succeeded. I have discovered, however, that he was not entirely what he seemed to be, not the person he presented himself as.

"I'm not sure that he was actually a rabbi. For now, let's put that aside. Whatever his motivations, he started this house of prayer, called you together to form a holy congregation. That was a good thing.

"I learned that the funds for this shul are from the Sanoker Home."

A second murmur swept through the room, and again, Ben held up his hands again until the room quieted. "The funds that supported this shul began flowing from the Home at a time when it was running out of money. This was wrong, and I hope that someday they can be repaid, at least in part. In a minute, Abby is going to talk to you about how this congregation needs to proceed if it is to survive as a house of prayer. It requires raising a lot of money, mostly from you. I will do my part. I will donate my services as rabbi for the next nine months, or as long as you want me, and I'll cover the congregation's outstanding bills for the next two months. I will do this because I am sure that the majority of you want to keep this shul going. Beyond raising funds, it will require that each of you pitch in, as much as you can, in whatever ways you can, as a volunteer.

"Abby?"

She spoke in a clear voice for five minutes, outlining what needed to be done, then asked for a show of hands: How many would be willing to come to a meeting here, after Shabbat, to create some temporary committees and begin organizing for the work of creating a congregation?

Nearly every hand was raised.

When she finished speaking, Abby invited questions, and Ben returned to the bimah to help answer them. After everyone had had their say, Ben led a closing hymn. Abby returned to the lectern to make an announcement, and Ben headed for the front door, where he could say goodbye to anyone who cared to on their way out of the sanctuary.

He was shocked to find Mina Jenston, wearing a stylish but modest dress, sitting in a rear row.

She followed him out the door.

Ben said, "You shouldn't be here. It's not safe."

Jenston said, "I came to see if you were really a rabbi."

Ben laughed. "Geltkern fooled these people for years. What makes you think you can tell what a real rabbi looks like?"

Jenston said, "I'll go with my gut. All those people believe in you."

Ben said, "Mina, this is no joke. You need to get lost for a few weeks."

She stepped close to Ben, put her left arm around his waist, caressing his buttock while she shoved her right hand into his front pocket. Ben pulled away.

"Behave yourself."

Jenston said, "The tall blonde—that's your fiancée?"

Ben shook his head. "No. My fiancée is out of the country."

"I'm going to Cincinnati," she whispered. "Call me if you get horny."

A tall man came out of the shul and stuck out his hand. Ben shook it, and then a couple came out and paused to chat. Ten minutes later, when he looked around, Mina was gone.

Chapter Thirty-Five

A little after dark, Ben awoke from his Shabbat nap, his stomach growling. He rolled out of bed and stretched. A tapping noise drew him to his door. "I'm not dressed," he said, through the door.

Mrs. Meltzer said, "I made dinner. Would you care to join us?"

Ben asked, "Do I have time to shower?"

§

Half an hour later, Ben opened the kitchen door to find Mrs. Meltzer ladling soup into bowls, and a stout, motherly-looking woman tossing a salad.

Mrs. Meltzer said, "There you are! Rabbi, this is Bev Lewin. You met her husband, George, the other day."

Ben said, "I did, indeed. I'm pleased to meet you."

Beverly said, "George said that you're some kind of detective?'

Ben smiled. "Some kind, indeed. Right now, I'm the puzzled kind."

Mrs. Meltzer said, "That reminds me, Rabbi. Would you mind moving that puzzle? The one on the table? You can probably find a place for it in the living room."

Ben said, "I'll be very careful."

On close inspection, the puzzle turned out to be a picture of an enormous pile of coins—pennies, nickels, dimes, etc.—a very challenging puzzle, Ben supposed. It gave him an idea, but he decided to discuss it with Mrs. Meltzer privately.

Dinner proved a delight, both tastewise and conversationally. Ben stuffed himself on roasted chicken, sweet potatoes, and salad. Dr. Lewin spoke about some of the Yiddish books in his collection, mentioning authors and subjects that were all fresh and new to Ben.

Lewin said he was still working on translating Ben's pages but promised to finish by Monday evening.

Scrabble followed dinner. By the times the Lewins were yawning, it was past ten. Ben insisted on helping with the dishes; by the time they finished, Mrs. Meltzer was also yawning.

"Something on your mind, Rabbi?" she asked.

Ben said, "I know that you enjoy puzzles. Would you like to try one that's more difficult than any you've ever encountered?"

Mrs. Meltzer smiled. "I've been doing puzzles so long that nothing presents much of a challenge. I do them just to pass the time while I think about my life."

Ben said, "Wait here. I'll be back in a few minutes."

He ran up to his room and returned with a plastic wastebasket, which he handed to Mrs. Meltzer. She carried it into the formal dining room and dumped the contents onto her long, carefully polished table.

Mrs. Meltzer asked, "Is this what I think it is?"

Ben said, "Shredded documents. Are you interested?"

"I can hardly wait to get started."

Chapter Thirty-Six

Ben rose at dawn and ran six miles, feeling good from start to finish. After a leisurely shower, he started thinking about breakfast. His phone rang.

Yolanda asked, "Is this a good time to talk?"

Ben said, "Sure. Are you at work?"

"Roland is in the little boy's room making atonement for last night."

"What was last night?"

"I'm not sure, but it involved a lot of expensive whiskey."

Ben smiled. "Okay, what's on your mind?"

"On Friday, the Youngstown department got a call from somebody cleaning up his yard and smelled something awful next door. The PD broke down the door and found an old woman. They ID'd her as Mrs. Meredith Weinstock. She's been dead for several weeks, at least."

"Cause of death?"

"GSW, they think, but the autopsy isn't until tomorrow. Probably."

"How did you learn about this, Yolanda?"

"Abby told me, months ago, that she thought Weinstock was fooling around with Rabbi Geltkern. She also told me that they both kind of went missing about the same time. So when I went into the system to look for Geltkern's car, credit cards—whatever—I put out a "wanted for questioning" on both names. When the Youngstown cops put Weinstock's name into the computer, my request popped up."

Ben asked, "Do you have an address for the house? Where they found her?"

"I'll text it to you."

Ben said, "Does Abby know about this?"

"I told her yesterday on the drive out to Berona."

Ben said, "By the way, how did it go last night?"

"Great. We had about sixty people show up. Hey, here comes the Duke of Bourbon. Gotta go."

"Bye," Ben said, and hung up.

Half-dressed, he sat on his bed, thinking. Then he fired up his new ThinkPad Helix and Googled a map of western Pennsylvania. Youngstown was about fifty air miles north and west of Pittsburgh. An hour and a half by car, Ben thought.

He went to the closet and got into what he thought of as his rabbi outfit: A dark suit, white shirt, and a new black fedora with a bit more brim than he liked.

A tapping noise issued from the door; Ben opened it to find Mrs. Meltzer in a dressing gown and slippers.

"You're going out now, Rabbi?"

"In a few minutes. Do you happen to know if Kazansky's is open today?"

Mrs. Meltzer smiled. "Come downstairs and have breakfast, and I'll show you the first puzzle I solved."

§

Mrs. Meltzer said, "This one was easy. It's made of parchment, heavier than paper, and a distinctive shade. So I just picked all these strips out and then put them in the right order."

Ben looked at the assembled strips of paper, then took out his iPhone and carefully snapped a picture of a diploma issued in 1972 by the Maharal Rabbinical Academy of Metuchen, New Jersey, and signed by Rabbi Menachem Zelman. It was written in Hebrew and Yiddish, except for the graduate's name: Albert Martin Farkas had been typed in and subsequently covered with a strip of identically hued parchment on which was typed Jeremiah Aharon Geltkern.

Mrs. Meltzer said, "I guess the strip covering the name was glued on, and when the paper was shredded, it came off."

Ben said, "You guess correctly. Now I might have his real name."

"Does this have something to do with that missing rabbi?"

Ben nodded. "It does. I'm still in the middle of things, and it's kind of a long story. Can I tell you what I know the next time we speak?"

"I can see you're in a hurry," said Mrs. Meltzer. "Sit down, and I'll make you some eggs."

Ben said, "You are a wonder. If only I wasn't crazy about Miryam."

"Story of my life," she giggled.

§

With Mrs. Meltzer's help, Ben found a shop in Squirrel Hill that made him a set of business cards in Hebrew and English. While they were being printed, he sent a text message to Yolanda, outlining his plans, then rented a Chevrolet Cruze from a local rental agency. An hour later, as he rolled northwest at 65 mph on the Pennsylvania Turnpike, Miryam called.

"Hola!" she trilled.

"Miryam, my love! Are you wearing your Gaucha outfit?"

"Did I tell you that my cousin Eduardo actually owns a kind of dude ranch? La Estancia de Los Sueños."

"For city folks who want to learn to be a Gaucho?"

"Exactamente! He taught me how to throw a facon—something like a Bowie knife—cut a horse thief's throat with a daga, and throw los boleadoras."

"Boleadoras ?"

"Three balls wrapped in leather on the end of a rawhide sling. They use it instead of a lasso."

"You've come a long way from Brooklyn."

"I miss you, Firewalker Ben."

"And I miss you."

"My hair is growing back," she said. "But one little patch is coming in gray. It's right in front, over my left eye."

"I don't care if your hair is all gray. Or if it comes in green."

"How are you feeling?"

"Great. I ran six miles. Tomorrow—another injection. So we'll see."

"Are you in a car, Ben?"

"I'm driving to Youngstown, Ohio. Since you talked me into accepting the pro-bono, find-Rabbi-Geltkern gig, there've been three murders."

"My God! Have you found him yet?"

"No, but I finally know his real name. At least I think so."

"Stay safe. I'll call you Tuesday when you're feeling better."

"I love you, poquita Marita, mi corazón."

"Benito el lingüisto! I had no idea."

"High school in Brooklyn. You learn a little of everything."

"Bye."

Ben clicked off and brought up his GPS app. The turnoff to Youngstown was less than a mile ahead.

Chapter Thirty-seven

The desk sergeant looked at the card that Ben handed him. "You're Rabbi Mark T. Glass of the Sanoker Home? What's that?"

Ben said, "A board-and-care facility for elderly Jewish people."

"So what can the Youngstown Police Department do for you?"

"A friend, Officer Sanchez, of the Pittsburgh department, told me that Mrs. Weinstock died."

The sergeant looked at Ben again. "What about it?"

"She was the executive director of the Sanok Home."

"You have any idea who'd want to kill her?"

Ben chose his words carefully. "I might. I mean, it's all supposition and inference. But I do have some information that your detectives might find helpful."

The sergeant pointed to a long bench. "Have a seat, Rabbi. I'll let them know."

Fifteen minutes dragged by before Ben was escorted to the Homicide unit, a small room jammed with several desks. A heavy, balding man in his forties pointed to a seat next to his desk.

"I'm Detective Lynch. You have information in the Weinstock case?"

Ben handed him a card and said, "She was executive director of the Sanok Home, in Berona Township. She went on terminal leave several weeks ago."

"Terminal leave? Meaning what?"

"She used up her paid vacation and sick leave, and then she retired."

"What else you got?"

"You should understand that I'm only at the home part time, as a volunteer. I was asked to fill in for their rabbi, who disappeared about the same time Mrs. Weinstock left."

"And you think that the two of them left together?"

"I'm told that there was a romantic relationship between them."

"What's this rabbi's name?"

"He was using the name Jeremiah Geltkern. That's very close to Jerry Goldkorn, the name of a fictional rabbi in a novel published in 1988. But I think his real name is Albert Martin Farkas."

"Why do you think that's his real name?"

Ben took out his iPhone and brought up the picture of the shredded diploma.

"Before he left, Geltkern, or Farkas, shredded a bunch of documents. We were able to reconstruct this."

"I can't read—what is that, Hebrew?"

"Let me zoom in on the name in English."

Ben magnified the name portion.

Lynch looked closely. "The one was pasted on top of the other?"

"I think so. It came off in the shredding."

"Shredding is interesting, Rabbi. Where were you a month ago?"

Ben thought. "I was in Israel."

"Can you prove that?"

Ben nodded. "I expected that someone would ask."

He reached into an inside pocket and came out with his U.S. passport.

Ben said, "You'll find the last two visa entries are my exit through Ben Gurion Airport and my U.S. return at Logan."

"You live in Boston?"

"Cambridge, a suburb."

"And you've been working at the Sanok since when?"

"Just last week: for services and when I'm needed."

"What would be a reason for them to call you?"

"The average age of the residents is about 90. Many are in poor health."

Lynch nodded. "So mostly funerals?"

"Yes. Why did you say you found the shredded document interesting?"

"Because when we searched Mrs. Weinstock's house, most every bit of paper was gone. No phone bills. No utility bills. No pay stubs, bank statements, life insurance, personal letters—nothing. All we found was a few shreds of paper in the bottom of a trash can and a few more under a living room chair."

Ben nodded. "So there's a pattern."

"Could be. What else do you know?"

"I heard that, about a year ago, Farkas, or Geltkern, persuaded Weinstock to take $3.5 million of the Home's reserve fund to start a pension fund. Without that money, the home will probably go bankrupt and close in the next few months."

"Who would draw a pension from that fund?"

"I don't know. But Mrs. Weinstock worked there a long time. What if the pension was a scam? If the only one it covered was Weinstock, and now she's dead, what happens to the money?"

"We'll look into that. Anything more?"

"The chief of police in Berona Township is Jack Laurence. You should call him about the Bernstein murder. And about Julius 'Jake the Heater' Witzelburg, one of your homegrown thugs."

"What about them?"

"Bernstein was an elderly man. He was murdered, shot in the head after he discovered a document shredding operation in Rabbi Geltkern's study. Two days later, Witzelburg, who lived here in Youngstown and was connected to the LaRocca family, returned to the synagogue where Bernstein was shot, broke in and tripped a silent alarm. Two of Laurence's patrolmen responded and shot Witzelburg dead. The Berona police closed the Bernstein case, saying that Witzelburg did it."

"But you don't think so?"

"I think there's more to this than a burglary gone bad."

Lynch favored Ben with a stare. "You're just a rabbi in an old-people's home?"

Ben said, "I never said I was *just* a rabbi. My Hebrew name is Benyamin. I usually go by Rabbi Ben. When you call Chief Laurence, tell him you spoke with me."

"And you have his number, I suppose."

Ben gave Lynch a sheet of paper on which were printed names and numbers.

"What's all this?"

"Some of the police departments that I've worked with during the last few years and individual officers who can vouch for me personally."

Lynch peered at the paper. "New York, Burbank, Los Angeles, Boston, Chicago, Phoenix. You get around."

Chapter Thirty-Seven

Meredith Weinstock had died in a long, narrow, wooden house built in the years before World War I, when Youngstown's steel mills were running full blast. The mills were long gone, and the blue-collar neighborhood north of the business district was dotted with vacant lots overgrown with trees and grass. The streets were potholed; weeds grew in the pavement cracks. Most of the houses on her street were in an advanced state of disrepair. Weinstock's, however, was freshly painted, with a new porch, a new garage, and a new concrete driveway. The low picket fence around the front yard bore fresh white paint, as did the taller fence around the back yard.

Yellow crime-scene tape was affixed to the front of the house.

Hatless and coatless, Ben got out of his rental and headed toward a young white man waxing an eight-year-old Chrysler in the adjacent driveway.

Ben said, "Excuse me, did you know my Aunt Merry?"

The man straightened up and peered at Ben. "You mean old Missus Weinstock?" he asked.

Ben nodded. "Meredith Weinstock. My mom's brother's wife."

The young man said, "Everybody around here knew her. Nice old lady. Now she's dead, and you coming around looking for—what?"

Ben held out his hands. "Never met her. Never knew I had an aunt in Youngstown till my moms told me, three days ago. She's in a nursing home. Asked me to just see was there anything we could do to help."

The young man shook his head. "Cops have the body. You could find out if she needs to be buried proper, or whatever."

"I should have thought of that. Did she have kids? A husband?"

The man shook his head again. "Not that I ever saw. She had a boyfriend, I think. Two or three times, I'd see this guy with a beard over there. But I don't live here; this is my Dad's house. I have my own place now, down in Boardman."

Ben looked at the Chrysler and noted that it had no license plate. "You've got a detailing business?"

The man nodded. "On the side. Half these houses are abandoned. Nobody hassles me for working in the driveway. Weekdays, I'm on the line at Lordstown."

"The GM plant?"

He pointed to Ben's rental. "I probably helped build your Cruze."

Ben said, "Really? That's pretty cool. Say, Aunt Merry's house—looks like she was doing all right."

"Just the last year or so. Came into insurance money, I heard."

"Is your Dad home? Did he know my aunt?"

"Dad's away for a few years. I look after his place. Keep the windows clean, the weeds down. Next spring, I'm gonna paint, inside and out."

"You were the one who called the cops about my aunt?"

"I didn't know she was shot or nothing. I just was mowing the backyard, and there was a window open in her place, around back. First I thought, maybe a skunk, ya' know? Lots of them around here now, along with raccoons and lots of stray cats. Even coyotes, I think. But this was way worse'n a skunk. Terrible. No disrespect."

"No problem. Do you know who I should talk to at the police?"

"An asshole detective named Lynch."

Ben said, "He try to fuck you over or something?"

"Took me in for questioning. Made me miss a whole day's work."

"Just because your dad is ... away?"

"I guess."

Ben shook his head. "Listen, I know what that's like. My old man did a nickel in Mansfield. So back when I was in high school, somebody on the block has a broken window, somebody's pocketbook gets pinched, guess who the cops hassled?"

"Your old man was in Mansfield?"

Ben nodded, yes. "Dumb-shit stuff. Took down a Speedway store in Steubenville for like walking-around money, you know? After he went away, him and my Mom divorced, and we moved to Pittsburgh."

The man looked at Ben again. "What's your name?"

"Mark. Mark Glass."

The man stuck his hand out. "Mo Bartosh."

They shook hands.

Ben said, "Nice meeting you. The cop to see is called Lynch?"

"Yeah. Big old fat fuck detective. Good luck with that."

Ben said, "Thanks."

Chapter Thirty-seven

Ben was eating a grilled cheese sandwich in his car when Abe Smolkin called.

"Hey Ben, it's Abe."

"What's going on, Abe?"

"Hey, I found that day planner. It was from March, four years ago."

"Did you write down the name of Geltkern's 'living saint.'"

"I sure did."

Ben said, "Rabbi Menachem Zelman?"

Abe said, "How did you do that? You knew all along?"

Ben said, "Just found out today. You ever hear of that guy?"

"No. And neither has my father-in-law."

"How is your father-in-law?"

"Mean, nasty and rich as ever."

"What?"

"Kidding. A sweetheart. Has a congregation of 300 families in Elizabeth, New Jersey."

"Do me a favor, Abe. Ask him if he ever heard of the Maharal Rabbinical Academy of Metuchen."

"That's where our missing rabbi was ordained?"

"I think so."

"Never heard of it. What night would you like to come to dinner?"

"How 'bout Wednesday?"

"I'll confirm with Ilene and get back to you."

"Great. One more thing: Did you ever find that Sanoker exhibit?"

"It's in storage. They won't charge much if you go down there and look in the boxes. Fifty an hour to move stuff around."

"Set it up. Wednesday or Thursday would be best."

"I'll take care of it, Ben. Be well."

"Love to Ilene."

"Bye."

Chapter Thirty-Seven

Two hours past dark, Ben drove down Weinstock's street, lights out, at five miles an hour. The road was almost pitch dark; not a single streetlight was lit. No lights were visible in any of the houses on the block. Two blocks west of her house, he turned into a vacant lot and parked, facing outward, under a huge, overgrown sycamore.

Ben waited half an hour, during which not a single car went by. The only living thing he saw was a large white dog that sniffed around the lot for several minutes before depositing a load of stool.

When the dog left, Ben got out of the car, stashed his suit jacket in the trunk, changed into running shoes, and pulled a dark hoodie over his shirt. Keeping to the shadows, he went out the back of the lot and followed an unpaved alley to the rear of the Weinstock house. He stopped behind the house, listening. In the distance, a dog barked. But the neighborhood was so quiet that Ben wondered if anyone still lived in the remaining houses or if they had all been abandoned.

He pulled himself over the fence and dropped inside. Then he found the padlock securing the rear gate and opened it with his homemade picks. He hung the open lock on the hasp and closed the gate. Now he could leave quietly and quickly without presenting a silhouette as he went over the fence.

Just in case.

A new Master padlock secured the garage door; it yielded to his picks in under a minute. Ben raised the door just high enough to slip under it, then lowered it. He pulled out his penlight and looked around.

A new Escalade SUV took up almost half the interior. Its doors were unlocked, and the keys were in the ignition. In the glove compartment, Ben found a registration certificate: Meredith R. Weinstock owned the car. There was no lien holder.

Ben tried the door to the house and found it unlocked. He stepped inside and into a kitchen. Blinds covered the windows, and Ben made sure they were down before taking out his penlight. He pointed it at the floor. In its glow, he saw a large, upgraded kitchen with new, restaurant-quality appliances. A spotless white tile floor, granite counters, and a matching backsplash.

Weinstock had bought a $70,000 car and a kitchen worth at least that. Where did that money come from? he wondered.

The rest of the house was equally impressive, with parquet floors, new furniture in every room, and three full-size baths along with six bedrooms. The house could easily serve as a bed-and-breakfast, although why anyone might want to vacation in this part of Ohio wasn't clear to Ben.

In the first-floor bedroom, he saw a blood-stained bed and blood-spattered walls. The blood had dried dark red, almost black. A large painting in a broken frame stood in a corner. Above the bed, the door of a wall safe yawned open.

Ben found the basement door in a hallway off the kitchen. He went down a flight of stairs, scanning with his penlight. There were no windows, no way for light to escape, so he located the light switch at the top of the stairs and flipped it on, revealing a half-completed rehab project, with big boxes of laminated flooring, bales of drywall, rolls of insulation, cartons of light fixtures. Installed along the wall were a brand-new furnace, a central air-conditioning unit, and a new tankless water heater. Each bore an installer's label: Siragusa Family Plumbing and Heating. That might mean something, Ben decided, and took a picture of a label.

From what had been built so far, Ben decided that this was to be a den or office of some kind, with wood paneling over wallboard and a dropped ceiling with recessed fluorescent lighting.

In the corner opposite the stairs, he found an ancient cast-iron furnace, removed from its former cocoon of asbestos insulation, door welded shut, the entire shell burnished with wire brushes and turned into a curiosity piece, complete with a set of ash shovels, pokers, and brushes. Raised lettering on the furnace door revealed that the design was patented in 1911.

The new wall on the far side of the room ran the width of the house and was framed, but only the upper half had been covered with wallboard. Ben shined his light into the dark beyond the wall and was surprised to see a large, open space.

Then from the direction of the kitchen above came the unmistakable mixture of hum, whine and rumble that only an overhead garage door makes while opening or closing.

Then the low cough of an engine starting.

Ben ran for the stairs.

He raced up to the door.

The basement light went out.

He tried the door, but it was locked.

There was no keyhole on the inside. No way to pick the lock.

He was trapped.

Chapter Thirty-Seven

Turning, Ben tried the light switch. Nothing. He carefully descended the stairs. With the penlight between his teeth, he returned to the furnace and found the smallest poker, about three feet long. One end was flattened and tapered to a dull point for breaking up clinkers—chunks of ash and partly burned coal.

Ben went back up the stairs and jammed the small end of the poker into the narrow crack between door and frame. Setting his feet, he pulled the end of the poker. Nothing happened. He tried again, willing himself to use every last bit of his whole body's strength.

The end of the poker moved a few inches.

A crack appeared between the door and frame.

Flame exploded through the crack. As the door ignited, Ben recoiled. Off-balance, still clutching the poker, he tumbled down the stairs, forcing himself to relax, go limp, let gravity take its course.

He landed in an awkward position on the concrete footing, then rolled away, still clutching the poker. The door was now burning fiercely, sucking the oxygen out of the basement air.

Be calm, Ben thought. Organize your thoughts. Then take action.

His knee ached, but he could still move it. His shoulder throbbed, but he could move it. Ben climbed to his feet, thinking of the space beneath the back of the house. What was that space?

The house was long and narrow. The lot was much wider. Ifffff the house was built after 1911, the date on the furnace, then maybe part of the backyard was a vegetable garden. Ifffff it had a vegetable garden, then during World War II, when essentials were rationed, the occupants of this house probably grew much of their food. Ifffff they depended on this harvest during the winter and spring, then they would have canned vegetables and stored them, along with potatoes, onions, and turnips—anything that could survive the cold of winter in its raw state.

If the dirt-floored space was the former root cellar, then it might have another entrance, an entrance that led up to the garden.

If he could find that entrance, he had a chance to live.

Moving swiftly but deliberately, Ben went through a space in the frame that awaited its drywall cover. The floor was dirt and uneven. The smell of decay permeated even the smoke that was slowly filling the room. In one corner, his light found the skeletal remains of a small animal: a cat, perhaps, or a raccoon.

Ben oriented himself. The yard was to his left, above the wall. The alley was to his front, above and beyond that wall. The entrance, if it existed, had to be near where those two walls met. He moved to the corner, playing his light on the wall.

Pockmarks, chipped brick, and old mortar marked the line alone which a staircase had been attached to the far wall. He pointed his light at the ceiling and saw a square frame of moldering wood.

It was at least eighteen feet above him. He felt the wall with his hands.

No human could climb it without mountaineering equipment.

CHAPTER THIRTY-SEVEN

Ben felt his heart racing in his chest. He took a deep breath, choking a little on the acrid smoke. He struggled to calm himself.

His first semester at M.I.T. had been a challenge. His easiest class, the one whose concepts he grasped almost without effort, was Engineering 101. Engineers build things, he remembered hearing on his first day. He learned how the ancients, with little more than their hands and primitive tools, built the Great Pyramid, the Great Wall, the Hanging Gardens—all the wonders of the ancient world.

He needed a staircase. He would build one.

Ben dashed back to the half-finished wall and ducked through it. He lay supine on the concrete floor and used his legs to batter a wooden crossbar until it broke. He cleared away the remains, leaving a large hole.

Then he began dragging or carrying boxes, bales, bundles and rolls through the hole, the heaviest first, stacking them along the far wall for a foundation. Drywall bundles formed the first two steps. Boxes of flooring formed the next. Stacks of paneling and bales of fiberglass insulation, followed by cartons of lighting fixtures.

His staircase rose six feet. He was out of material.

Think, he told himself.

The smoke was thickening. The half-wall held some of it back, but not for long. He had no more than a few minutes. If the house didn't collapse into the basement first.

Chapter Thirty-Eight

It was the only way, he realized. He would have to build a narrow stairway so steep that he would have to pull himself up each level. It would be shaky and might collapse before it reached the roof. But if he built it against the far wall...

There was no time to pace himself. He ran back to the old furnace and grabbed the smallest ash shovel and the biggest poker. Working like a man possessed, he piled boxes and bales into a steep half-pyramid, each time placing his tools at the top, climbing down for another bale or bundle or box, then hauling it back to the top.

His penlight was dim, its batteries almost exhausted by the time he could reach the ceiling. He stood on tiptoe, feeling the outlines of the trap door. Finally, coughing, almost exhausted, he jammed the poker into the crack between the ceiling as hard as he could and pulled down on the poker.

The wood broke, and a shower of dirt almost knocked him from his perch. But now he could feel the cool night air. He sucked it into his lungs, grateful for the respite. He could also feel the heat, coming through the basement.

He used the poker as a lance, pushing up, making the hole larger, each time being showered with dirt.

A low rumble announced the top floor's collapse into the floor below. Dust filled the basement air. How long before the whole house fell into the basement? Ben dropped the tools, bent his knees, leaped as high as he could—and fell back clutching dirt in both hands, teetering atop the shaky stack.

He couldn't jump high enough. He couldn't climb down and bring up another box. He was two feet from safety. It might as well have been a mile.

Chapter Thirty-nine

"Hey!"

Another shower of dirt fell on Ben. A light struck him in the face.

"Hey," said a man's voice, again.

Ben looked up, squinting into the beam.

"You okay?" said the man.

"For now. Until the house collapses."

"Wait right there!" said the man.

As if he had any place to go.

The light went out of his face. Ben looked up at the hole. He waited, suspended in space and time.

The light came back into his face, and a man's belt—no, two belts, joined—came down the hole.

"Can you climb that?" said the man.

"If you can hold me."

"Go ahead."

Ben seized the belt and began to climb. His shoulder was a burning coal, an agony of agonies, but he had to do this. Hand over agonizing hand, he pulled himself up until strong hands grabbed his shoulders. Slowly, steadily they pulled him into the cool air, dragged him away from the hole.

Finally, panting, he lay on his belly in the garden, near the alley gate.

Two bearded men in dirty rags smiled down at him as the house collapsed into the basement. A fountain of smoke riddled with sparks poured from the hole in the sod that marked the spot where Ben had been moments earlier.

"What were you doing down there?" asked the smaller man.

Ben said, "Trying to get out."

"Looks like you made it," said the taller man.

Ben said, "Where's the fire department?"

The shorter man said, "There's nobody to call it in. Most of these houses are abandoned. They just let 'em burn unless somebody calls."

Ben stood on rubber knees. He ached all over. In the flickering light, he saw that the men who had pulled him to safety were vagrants.

Ben said, "I owe you my life. Can I buy you a meal, give you some money?"

The two men exchanged glances.

"That's not necessary," said the taller man. "You'd have done the same for us."

Ben said, "It would please me to help you. Do you have a place to stay?"

"We have a squat. Next block over. No water, but it's got a good fireplace."

The smaller man said, "Mrs. Weinstock, she lets us get water from her hose. That's why we came. Then this hole opened up, and your arms came flying out…"

The taller man laughed, "He almost shit his pants, brother."

Ben looked around. A few feet away several large plastic jugs lay scattered on the ground. "What are your names? How did you become homeless?"

"I'm Hank," said the smaller man. "I was a custodian. When they closed the school, I tried working as a handyman. Not much call for that around here now."

The taller man said, "I'm Jim. I was an editor at the *Toledo Blade*."

Ben said, "What happened?"

"About nine years ago, I took a buyout. But newspapers are dying. No jobs. I kept refinancing my house until…"

Ben said, "I want to offer you each a job. It comes with a private apartment."

"Doing what?" said Jim.

Chapter Forty

Despite everything that he had been through, it was not yet midnight when Ben rang Mrs. Meltzer's doorbell. After turning on the light, she opened the door and gasped at the sight of the three men on her stoop.

"My God, Rabbi! What happened to you?"

Ben said, "In a minute. This is Jim," he said, pointing, "and that's Hank. They saved my life. I'm giving them my room tonight. May I crash on your couch?"

Mrs. Meltzer shook her head, curls flying. "Come inside this minute," she said, "all of you."

When she had shut the door behind them, she turned to Jim. "There are two guest rooms on the second floor. Each has a bath. Make yourself at home.

"Both of you," she added, looking at Hank.

"Thank you," said both men at the same time.

"Sit down, Rabbi, I'll call Dr. Lewin."

Ben shook his head. "Abby will be here any minute."

Mrs. Meltzer turned back to Hank and Jim. "Please, go upstairs."

Jim said, "He's a *rabbi*?"

Ben said, "That's right."

Mrs. Meltzer took a second look at her visitors. "I'll warm up some chicken soup. And there are fresh bagels. You must be starved," she said.

Ben said, "Even if you're not, it's the best soup you'll ever taste."

Beaming, Mrs. Meltzer turned to Jim. "The room at the top of the stairs—there's a walk-in closet filled with clothes. Shoes, belts, everything. They belonged to my late husband, *alev hashalom*. He was about your size. Take whatever you like."

Hank said, "What's that mean, 'olive ha shall lom'?"

Jim said, "My mother used to say that sometimes."

Mrs. Meltzer said, "It means, 'rest in peace.'"

Ben said, "And Jim, it also means that you're probably Jewish."

Jim shook his head.

Ben said, "Hank, you're about my size. Come with me, I'll get you some clothes."

Chapter Forty

Abby fastened the mask over Ben's face and nose and opened the valve on the oxygen bottle. "You should be in a hospital," she said.

His voice muffled by the mask, Ben said, "In the morning, when I go in for my injection. They'll refer me."

"How important is it that you get your injection tomorrow? Could it wait a day or two?"

Ben shook his head. "I don't think so. And I don't want to leave the study, not after all that I've gone through so far."

Abby said, "Have them use an endoscope to suck the soot out of your lungs."

Ben nodded.

"And get your shoulder x-rayed."

Ben nodded again. "Listen, Abby, there are things I must tell you right away. And Yolanda. Where is she?"

"Home, with Zach."

"Can you call her, put her on speakerphone?"

"You need another half hour on oxygen. Now, rest and be quiet."

Ben lay back on his bed and closed his eyes.

§

Ben opened his eyes. There was something wrong. Everything was white. The walls were close and curved outward. He was in some kind of round space. Maybe a ship? He started to sit up. A man's hand gently but firmly held him down. He needed to get up, he told himself, but his body was so heavy. Maybe if he rested for a few more minutes. He closed his eyes.

§

As Ben's eyes focused, he was surprised to find Abby and Yolanda sitting on either side of his bed. Abby wore pale green scrubs with a stethoscope around her neck. Roland Easton sat next to Yolanda. Standing behind him was a short, balding, dark-skinned man in a white lab coat. Ben realized that he was Dr. Gilbert Rao, the clinician in charge of his study trial. He had never spoken to Ben.

Dr. Rao said, "I didn't realize that I had a celebrity in my study."

Ben said, "Let me guess. Tom Cruise?"

Everyone except Ben laughed.

Ben said, "Who? John Travolta?"

Everyone except Ben laughed again.

Abby said, "He's talking about *you*, Rabbi."

Rao said, "Mrs. Silverblatt recommended that you receive a course of hyperbaric treatments for the soot in your lungs."

Ben said, "What does that do to your study?"

"Not much. The protocol is a series of 48 injections. We space them a week apart to give subjects time to recover between them."

"I understand. When do I get this week's treatment?"

Everyone laughed again.

Abby said, "Your treatment is completed."

Ben said, "What day is this?"

Rao said, "Wednesday."

Ben said, "When do I get my injection? For your study?"

Everyone laughed again.

Rao said, "There was no medical reason not to give you the injection in the hyperbaric chamber. So we got that out of the way."

Ben said. "Thanks."

Rao said, "Next Monday, same time. Skip the fire-walking, okay?"

Ben said, "It's not like I went looking..."

Everyone laughed again.

Rao said, "Our work here is done, Tonto."

Everyone laughed again.

Yolanda said, "How do you feel?"

Ben said, "Like I was run over by a truck. Make that ten trucks. I appreciate everything that you've done for me, Doctor. Can I talk to Abby and Yolanda for a minute before I try to get out of bed?"

Doctor Rao waved goodbye and vanished from Ben's sightline. Abby moved to his bedside, and the bed tilted up into a sitting position.

Ben said, "First, about Jim and Hank. They saved my life."

Abby said, "You promised them jobs. What did you have in mind?"

"The shul will need an administrator. Somebody to keep things organized. Someone with self-starter smarts and computer skills."

Abby said, "I've been talking to Jim about that. Did you know that he was once deputy managing editor of the *Toledo Blade*?"

Ben said, "I knew that he was an editor. Listen, I want to pay his salary for a year. Hank's, too. Whatever the shul leadership can negotiate."

Abby said, "Until we have a membership drive and sign up all that are willing to pay for the privilege of belonging, and then hold an election, we have an ad-hoc executive committee. I have plenty to do, but the others decided I should chair that. So I'll make a deal with him. We can talk about how much it costs you after that."

Ben said. "Hank used to be a handyman. Before that a school custodian. I was thinking we should hire him, too. And I'll pay his—"

Abby said, "Hank and Jim moved into the shul apartment this morning. One of the members is going to take them shopping tomorrow. Hank has a long list of jobs that need doing, starting with their apartment. We'll make a deal with him, too."

Ben said, "You're the best."

Yolanda said, "She raised almost $30,000 from members so far."

Ben said, "You'll need ten times that for the first year. More, if you hope to hire an actual rabbi."

Abby said, "Let me and Mr. Cohen worry about that."

Ben sighed. "Okay. Fine. Now I have to talk about what happened in Youngstown."

Detective Easton said, "Finally."

Chapter Forty

Easton asked, "How did you manage to get yourself locked in the basement of a burning house?"

Yolanda said, "It's his hobby. Did I tell you how he met Miryam, his fiancée?"

Ben said, "Cut it out. Really, those were two very different things."

Easton asked, "How did you get into the house?"

Yolanda said, "His other hobby is picking locks."

Easton said, "But why? It was a crime scene. Youngstown PD was all over it."

Ben said, "I wanted to see what they might have missed."

Easton said, "And?"

Ben said, "A lot. Detective Lynch said there was hardly a scrap of paper in the house. All the records were gone. They found a few scraps of shredded documents, nothing more."

Abby said, "But isn't that exactly what happened at the shul? We opened Rabbi Geltkern's study and found shredded papers, and then later, when we found Stan's body, all the documents were gone."

Ben said, "Exactly what I wanted to tell you. But there's more. There was an Escalade in the garage. Keys were in it. The registration was in the glove compartment. So they missed that. And the car was almost new. Mrs. Weinstock owned it free and clear. A $70,000 car!

"Then there's the rest of the house. This is a ninety-something-year-old house in a neighborhood that looks like a Chernobyl suburb. Vacant lots overgrown with trees. Abandoned homes. No streetlights. Potholes with saplings growing out of them. And she just got a new kitchen, new bathrooms, new flooring, new walls. In the basement, I found a new furnace, a new air conditioning unit and an on-demand water heater. Those three things alone cost $30,000. She put probably another hundred grand in upstairs renovations, plus the kitchen. About $250,000 in upgrades in a house worth, what—$20,000? Less?

"Why would she spend that kind of money on that house? And where did she get it?"

Easton said, "Where do you think?"

Ben said, "Follow the bouncing ball: They could have shot me like they shot Stan Bernstein. Instead, they torch the house. Is there fire insurance? She's dead. Who gets the insurance payout? How much is it worth?"

Easton said, "Wait, the garage was empty, according to Lynch."

Ben said, "It didn't burn?'

"It burned, but it didn't collapse into the basement because under it was a concrete slab."

Ben said, "When I was in the basement, I heard the garage door opening. I ran for the stairs, and I heard the car start, then drive away. Then someone cut the power to the house. I got the door open a crack, and fire just exploded through it."

Yolanda said, "Wait! They cut the power to the house? How do you know they didn't just turn off the basement light?"

"The only switch was inside the door, and the door was closed when the lights went out."

Abby said, "That's what happened at the shul the night Stan was killed."

Ben said, "I was thinking the same thing. Each time, there was shredding, and each time, someone killed the power. Can't be a coincidence."

Easton said, "Lynch says his arson guys found an accelerant: powdered aluminum and ammonium nitrate."

Yolanda said, "What's that do?"

Ben said, "Homemade fire bomb."

Easton said, "Five gets you ten, they sent some cowboy to torch the house, and he couldn't resist taking the car. It's probably been chopped up for parts by now."

Yolanda asked, "But who is 'they'?"

Ben said, "Two more things. Maybe they mean something, maybe not. First, I talked to the guy that got a whiff of Weinstock's decomposing body and called the police. His father owns the house next door. And his father is in prison."

Easton said, "We should see if that guy knew this 'Jake the Heater' that the Berona police took down."

Ben said, "That's a good idea. Here's another one: The cooling and heating equipment in her basement was installed by a company called Siragusa Family Plumbing and Heating. I'm pretty sure that I once read that forty or fifty years ago, the Siragusa family was part of the Cleveland Mafia."

Easton shook his head. "Kind of a stretch. Cleveland is a good ways off, and forty years is a long time. Can't be the only family named Siragusa."

Ben said, "Sure. But what if 'Jake the Heater' worked for Siragusa Plumbing and Heating? Maybe part of the crew that installed that furnace."

Abby said, "You're saying that Mrs. Weinstock sent this Jake the Heater guy to kill Stan Bernstein?"

Ben shook his head.

Easton said, "He's saying that, if this Geltkern guy was involved with Weinstock and if he was hiding out at her place, he might have met Jake the Heater and maybe hired him to clean up a loose end."

Ben said, "Bingo."

Chapter Forty

Ben said, "Pardon me for asking, Detective Easton—"

Easton interrupted. "Call me Roland. Or The Duke of Bourbon."

Yolanda turned bright red.

Ben said, "Okay, Roland. When I went off to sniff around Youngstown, the Berona PD had closed the Bernstein case, and Yolanda was working on her own time, helping me locate Geltkern. Now, suddenly, you're chatting with Youngstown PD about the Weinstock case. Why is Pittsburgh PD interested in two murders, both outside its jurisdiction?"

Easton nodded, a look of approval on his face, "Maybe you really are the Sherlock that Yolanda makes you out. I probably shouldn't say this out loud, but Officer Sanchez has the makings of a top investigator. She's a natural."

Yolanda turned bright red again. Abby beamed.

Easton said, "Now, she's just getting started. Doesn't know enough yet. But my job is to find people like her and turn them into detectives. All while trying to close actual cases, you understand."

Ben said, "Go on."

"So I give her some rope, let her get involved, on her own time, working with you. She keeps me in the loop. How the investigation is proceeding. And the more I hear, the more it sounds familiar, like another case that I worked, or one I knew about or heard of. But I can't place it. Sort of like, when you meet somebody you know but can't think of their name. Or a particular word that's on the tip of your tongue, but it doesn't come. So I went to see my rabbi."

Abby said, "What? You have a rabbi?"

Yolanda said, "It's cop slang, sweetie. He means his mentor. Roland is my mentor, my rabbi. Once upon a time, way back before cell phones, computers, airplanes and TV, he was an innocent rookie who needed training and guidance. Someone to teach him how to drink bourbon. The guy who gave it to him was his training officer, his rabbi."

Easton said, "Careful, Sanchez. Any man considering spending his vacation getting hair plugs is possibly a mite sensitive about his age."

Yolanda said, "Kidding, sahib."

Easton said, "So, anyway, I go see my rabbi. Miles Turlock, like they say, a legend in his own time. I tell him a little about Bernstein, and he scratches his head and wiggles his eyebrows and says, 'All the paper was gone? From a church maybe?'"

Ben said, "Don't tease me."

Easton said, "Late Sixties. Bearded, long-haired kid—maybe eighteen or so– becomes the preacher's right-hand man in some church over in Shadyside. Bennie Abe The Messiah, something like that."

Ben said, "Beni Abraham? B, E, N, I?"

Easton shrugged. "Could be. Jews who followed Jesus, like that."

Abby said, "What we now call 'Messianic Judaism.'"

Ben said, "Which isn't Judaism at all. It's Christianity, with a lot of borrowed—and corrupted—Jewish customs and practices."

Easton said, "You want to hear about his case or argue theology?"

Ben laughed. "Proceed, professor."

Easton said, "Anyway, this kid is a volunteer. Preaches a little, gets involved in the community, works in the office. Babysits for members, runs their errands, brings their meals on wheels—everybody's best friend. For three months.

"One Friday afternoon, he says he's driving to Chicago for the weekend to see his brother. Last they saw of him.

"Comes Monday, preacher tries to get into the office, the locks are changed. They get a locksmith. Every single piece of paper is AWOL. Not a scrap. Paid bills, current bills, accounts, membership rolls, pledges, bank books, ledgers—even, can you believe it, the office phone books. All gone."

Abby said, "And their money was gone, too?"

Easton shook his head. "They made expenses from a weekly collection. Passed the basket on Sundays. And the minister put the arm on the local merchants for donations. Not just money, but food, office supplies—whatever. Whatever cash came in went into a bank account.

"The account was still there. But the bank book—gone. All gone, every piece of paper. And the long-haired kid."

Ben said, "Taking the papers was a smokescreen, designed to sow confusion and keep them tied up trying to keep the place running?"

Yolanda said, "Confusion over what?"

Ben said, "If you don't want your mark to know what you really wanted and why you want it, take everything. Let them figure it out while you run the scam."

Easton said, "Exactly. This wasn't a wealthy church. Not gonna be putting up a cathedral. But the members—they weren't poor. Solid, middle-class citizens, homeowners. Owned neighborhood businesses, worked steady jobs. And, Miles recalls, most were from Jewish families or families that used to be Jewish."

Ben said. "In that way, very similar to the membership of the Sanoker Shul."

Easton said, "I didn't make that connection, but you're right."

Yolanda asked, "So what was the con? What was he after?"

Ben said, "Wait. Was this about identity theft?"

Easton said, "Give that man a cigar! Three, four months after the kid disappears, the sky falls on the church members. Not the church—the members. People lost their homes because someone took a second mortgage on it, pocketed the cash, never made a payment. One day, the sheriff shows up with an order to vacate. Credit cards weren't big back then, but there were a couple—American Express and Diner's Club. And lots of department stores had charge cards. Person or persons unknown use church members' names to apply for hundreds of cards, buy all kinds of pricey goods, never make a payment. The stores came after the people whose names were on the cards."

Ben said, "I didn't realize identity theft was a problem in the '60s."

Easton shook his head. "Not on anybody's radar yet. But it was around. Mostly small time. This was notable. And yes, Sanchez, they had radar in the '60s."

Ben said, "They nail anybody for this?"

"Not really. Months after the kid disappears, some hick-town Ohio PD busts a numbers parlor and finds church records. The numbers operation belongs to a soldier in the Pittsburgh Mafia family. But it takes those hayseed cops almost a year to figure that out, and then where the records came from. Meantime, our long-haired Holy Roller is gone, and a bunch of small-time grifters are using the names, addresses and such to shop till they drop. Miles and his squad made six arrests—shoppers. Locals, no records, average Joes. Five jump bail and disappear."

Ben said, "And the sixth?"

"One between the eyes, one in the heart, small caliber. Put him in a dumpster behind the church, so there'd be no mistake about why he was killed. The son of a respected judge and former state senator, which is why he was paid in lead."

Abby said, "What? What are you saying?"

Yolanda said, "His killers thought this guy would talk. So he was silenced."

Ben said, "What if the long-haired kid didn't sell his paper to a bunch of people? What if he wholesaled everything to one guy."

Easton said, "That's what Miles thinks now. That it was an O.C. move. Some Mafioso puts the kid into the church, pays him a grand or two to grab the paper. The guy goes back where he came from. The Mafioso has phony drivers licenses printed, recruits locals to take out second mortgages, buy cars on credit and go shopping. He has another guy fence the goods. He's got maybe twenty people running around. Any one of them takes $1,000 home for two weeks' shopping, and the boss gets the rest. That's a major score for 1969. And no downside. No way to connect him to the kid or the church. Unless somebody talks."

Ben said, "That's still an open case? The murder?"

Easton nodded. "Statute of limitations ran out on grand theft forty years ago. But not the murder. And the murder vic's family is still prominent in civic affairs."

Ben said, "So the shredding, in our case, is just a way to make paper disappear. Maybe they didn't have cheap shredders in the Sixties."

Yolanda said, "But what's the score with our case? Was Geltkern going to steal identities from the Sanoker Shul?"

Ben said, "I don't think so. Now that I know we're all on the same team, allow me to share still more information that you don't have."

Yolanda said, "You picked somebody else's locks?"

Ben said, "Somebody else's brains. Yolanda, Abby, you recall that the night we found Stan's body, I found a piece of paper in the bushes?"

Abby said, "You told us about that. And that you went back two nights later and found some of the shul's unpaid bills and a wastebasket of shredded papers."

Easton said, "Whoa. I didn't know that."

Ben said, "I told Chief Laurence in Berona about it. I also told him that I found a remote video surveillance device that was stuck inside the shul door."

Easton said, "And I'm just now hearing about this now?"

Ben said, "Laurence wanted to keep that to himself. The video from that device casts doubt on the report that his patrolmen gave when they shot and killed Jake the Heater. There was a third party present. Apparently, Jake never got off a shot. The report said he fired three."

Easton said, "I'd like to see that video."

Ben smiled. "Get me out of here, feed me, and I'll show it to you."

Easton said, "Deal."

Abby said, "I've got patients to see. I'll get your release paperwork started, and Ben, you really need to stay off that knee for a few days.."

CHAPTER FORTY-ONE

Yolanda and Easton watched the video on Ben's phone three times.

Easton said, "Who was the first guy? The one with the light?"

Ben said, "On advice of counsel, I respectfully decline to answer."

Yolanda giggled.

Easton said, "You do B&E as a hobby, or as a sideline?"

Ben said, "If the person on that video was the spiritual leader of the congregation whose building that is, then entering it at any time is no crime."

Easton said, "You got some stones, showing that to me."

Ben said, "Because you haven't paid for lunch yet?"

Easton said, "That, and I swore an oath to uphold the laws of the Commonwealth. What was that first guy doing there?"

Ben said, "He might have been looking to see if the late Stan Bernstein had stashed any of the papers from the rabbi's study before he got murdered."

Easton said, "Who else has seen this video?"

Ben said, "Chief Laurence, and the guy that the remote device sent it to. I gave that phone number to Chief Laurence."

Easton said, "I'm gonna pop over to Berona Township and chat with the chief."

Ben said, "It might be more productive if you ran the phone number first."

Easton said, "Might do that if this guy I know would give it to me."

Yolanda said, "Why are you guys talking like that?"

Easton said, "Testosterone. But Second-Story Rabbi started it."

Ben said, "First Story Rabbi. So now, let me tell you the first story."

Ben then recounted the tale of how the Sanok home came into being from Polish Jews who started a burial society and eventually turned it into a board and care facility."

"Everything went along as planned until about six or seven years ago," Ben added." By that time, only a few of the original Sanok residents were still alive. Their old director, a rabbi, retired, and his assistant, a lonely and horny widow, became the new director. She hired a part-timer who called himself Rabbi Jeremiah Geltkern.

"Geltkern had plans. He got the horny widow to open the Sanok Home to other elderly Jewish people. The newcomers agreed to sign over their life savings and property in exchange for lifetime care. The home took in about $5 million. Had they invested it prudently and managed the Home wisely, it might have been enough to keep them going for quite a while.

"Because, once the newcomers moved in, they were paupers. The Home billed the Commonwealth Medical Assistance for their care, and it received, all told, a significant fraction of its expenses. They also billed Medicare for all sorts of medical procedures, real and imaginary.

"Under Geltkern's influence, the horny widow took $3.5 million cash from the home and started a pension fund. He got her to let him start a synagogue in Berona, for reasons still not clear. The Home paid Geltkern a second salary for this duty, and it paid to maintain the synagogue. These expenses, a new bed tax from Berona Township, and the lump-sum payment to the pension fund were such a drain on the Home's finances that it had to take out a loan.

"Shortly after the last of the original Sanoker Jews died, the widow went on terminal leave prior to retirement. Geltkern also took a vacation at the same time, probably with the widow. Perhaps anticipating a huge pension, she began to renovate her old, almost-worthless home in Youngstown. She might have bought a better home someplace else, but that would have created a paper trail. Then she was murdered. Her papers vanished from the house. Not long after the police found her body, somebody torched her house.

"A curious rabbi, who happened to be visiting that house, barely escaped with his life. By then, the curious rabbi had learned that Geltkern's real name, possibly, was Albert Martin Farkas."

"The end of Part One. Questions?"

Easton said, "The objective of the con was the pension money?"

Ben said, "Could be. Maybe the insurance brokerage that she gave the money to was just a cash laundry and didn't really buy an endowment policy. Three and a half million is a tidy sum, although Geltkern had to work years to get it. But there's something we're missing. I don't think he started the shul just for another thirty grand a year, but I have no idea why he did."

Yolanda asked, "How did you get his real name?"

Ben said, "I gave the bucket of shredded documents from Stan's office to an expert at jigsaw puzzles. She picked out the parchment and re-assembled a diploma."

Ben picked up his phone and showed them the photo.

Yolanda asked, "Mrs. Meltzer did that?"

Ben said, "Took her less than a day."

Easton asked, "Jeremiah Geltkern is really Albert Martin Farkas?"

Ben said, "Maybe. Geltkern might have found it in a trash can. Or bought it in a flea market."

Easton asked, "Why didn't her killer torch the house as well?"

Ben said, "Maybe the shooter wanted time to cover his tracks before the body was discovered."

Easton asked, "Then how did the guy who fired the house know to come there just when the curious second-story rabbi was in it?"

Ben said, "Perhaps when he entered the house, the rabbi was too stupid to look for a motion-sensor-activated cellphone device."

Yolanda asked, "Like the one you found at the shul?"

Ben said, "Probably its twin brother."

Easton said, "So Weinstock's killer could be anywhere. He gets a video over the phone, he calls **YOUNGSTOWN FIRES Я US**."

Ben said, "Which suggests the involvement of a confederate."

Easton said, "You don't suppose that, forty-odd years ago, Farkas was a long-haired kid who had a pivotal role in a mafia scam?"

Ben shrugged. "Or maybe the guy who hired him lived long and bold enough to become the boss of a small-town fiefdom?"

Yolanda asked, "How do you know so much about the pension fund and the new residents and starting the shul?"

Ben said, "Some I got from an attendant at the home, and the rest from Filomina Jenston, the Home's bookkeeper for the last 15 years."

Easton said, "The bookkeeper! Not bad, for a second-story man."

Chapter Forty-two

Awkwardly using crutches to negotiate the stairs to his attic room, Ben felt his phone buzzing against his hip. The ringtone played Hatikva.

He pulled himself up two stairs to the second-floor landing and leaned against the railing before answering.

Miryam said, "You were playing in a burning house without me?"

Ben said, "I should have called earlier. I don't know what Abby told you, but I'm fine."

"Fine, as in hobbling around on crutches with a torn rotator cuff?"

"Partially torn. A very small tear that won't require surgery."

"I don't want to lose you!"

"I'm fine, Baldy. And if you had been along, I wouldn't have needed to be rescued."

"You are either the luckiest man alive, or you have a guardian angel."

Ben smiled. "Molly Malach. She was taking a coffee break Sunday night."

"I'm sorry that I volunteered you for this. I had—have—this image of you as utterly fearless, an invulnerable superhero that no one and nothing can harm. Almost as if you have super powers. I say that out loud, and I realize how foolish I am. Don't be angry with me, Ben."

"Of course not! None of this is your fault. What are you up to today?"

"Don't change the subject. Ben, please, please, please say that you'll be careful."

Ben said, "More now than ever."

So softly that Ben almost didn't hear, Miryam said, "My aunt died."

"Tía Fruma?"

"Yes. My grandmother's sister."

"I'm so sorry to hear that, Marita."

"She had a long life. Mostly, after leaving Syria, a good life. And a good death, with her family all around. It was a wonderful way to leave the world. I'm just sad that I had so little time with her."

"I'll leave tonight and fly down for the funeral."

"No! I want you to get well. Stay, get your health back. Take your injections. Anyway, it's tomorrow morning. You'd never get here in time."

Ben said, "I love you, Calva."

Miryam giggled. "That means 'bald patch.'"

"I try."

Miryam said, "Feel better. I love you always," and hung up.

Before Ben could put his phone away, it rang again.

Abe Smolkin said, "Ben! I've been trying to reach you since Monday. Are you coming to dinner tonight?"

Ben said, "I've been out of touch. Sorry. Text me the address."

Abe said, "And we'll have a big surprise for you."

Ben said, "What it is it?"

Abe said, "If I tell you, it's not a surprise. I promise, a real treat."

§

"Abe promised me a treat," said the tall, athletic and shaggy-bearded Rabbi Arthur Baum of Elizabeth, N.J. "And now, here you are."

Ben said, "He promised me a surprise, as well."

Abe said, "It's two-for-one night. When I told Arthur that you had questions about the Maharal Rabbinical Academy, he decided to come out and meet you."

Rabbi Baum said, "As it happened, I'm speaking at a conference here tomorrow, so I came early to spend time with my grandkids."

Ben said, "Over the years that I've known him, Abe mentions you only with the greatest respect. I'm happy to meet you at last."

Baum said, "Forty years ago, your grandfather, of blessed memory, was my faculty adviser. You look very much like him. But he was a world-class authority on Talmud. I understand that you're some kind of rabbinical James Bond?"

Ben shook his head. "Not at all. I've never killed anyone. No guns, no gadgets, no girls. I'm really more of a trouble-shooter."

"You injured your knee while pursuing this line of work, Rabbi?"

Ben smiled. "It was dark. I tripped and fell down a flight of stairs."

Ilene Baum-Smolkin, tall and slender under a cloud of thick blond curls, appeared in her living room to announce dinner.

Half an hour later, braving a food coma with third helpings of melt-in-your-mouth brisket and mouth-watering zucchini pancakes, Ben and Rabbi Baum watched Abe and Ilene start to clear the dining room table.

Rabbi Baum said, "Come with me, Rabbi," and went out through the kitchen and into the backyard. Ben followed.

Ben said, "Really, sir, anything you want to tell me, you can say in front of Abe and Ilene."

Baum chuckled, then pulled a huge cigar from his jacket pocket. "The Holy Grail," he said, producing another, which he offered to Ben.

"No, thanks. A cigar is your Holy Grail?"

Rabbi Baum said, "Gurkha Holy Grail, a brand name. Eleven-year-old Honduran tobacco. Ten bucks a smoke, if you can find them."

Baum lit up, taking a big puff, holding it in, letting the smoke slowly out through his nose.

"My only vice," he said. "One a day, after dinner."

Ben remained silent, watching night settle on Squirrel Hill, enjoying the feel of the cool night air in his recovering lungs.

Baum said, "The Sixties. Vietnam. The draft. You're too young to remember."

Ben said, "Only what I've read."

Baum said, "It was an immoral war. And bonehead politics. Cemented the military-industrial complex into place for generations to come. As much as I admired Johnson for pushing the Civil Rights Act through, I can't forgive him for that war.

"The thought of going off to die in some rice paddy made young men do all sorts of strange things. Some enlisted and died to protect LBJ's reputation as tough on communism. Or they let themselves get drafted, and plenty of them died for that privilege, too. The smarter ones among us started looking for an out.

"The National Guard was one—if you could get in. The bet was that LBJ wouldn't call up the Guard because it was full of Congressmen's kids, rich men's sons, privileged, well-connected kids pretending to serve their country.

"The Reserves was another out, almost as good, and almost as hard to get into. Parents browbeat or bribed doctors to give their sons a medical reason to flunk the draft physical. The morally upright refused induction and went to prison. The desperate or scared fled to Canada or Sweden. Kids who barely scraped through high school not only enrolled in college but went on to grad school to get a student deferment. If you flunked out, of course, they'd grab you up, shove a rifle in your hands and send you off to fight.

"Finally, the ordinary people of this country figured out what was going on: The sons of the rich and powerful were ducking the draft. There was such anger and outrage that the government ended student deferments. Switched to a lottery. But by then the war was almost over.

"Before that, if you were a Mormon of draft age, you could avoid the draft with missionary work overseas. Not Catholics, not Protestants, certainly not Jews. But Mormons. They made a deal of some kind.

"The other exception was clergy. If you enrolled in a school that ordained priests or ministers, you were safe as long as you were there, and all but safe afterward, because the military rarely drafted clergy."

Ben said, "What about rabbis?"

Baum nodded. "Same deal. Seminary, Bible School, Yeshiva—all treated the same by General Hershey's minions. Divinity students were protected from the draft.

"Naturally, some enrolled with no intention of assuming the pulpit. But if their families could afford tuition, they were safe as long as they stuck it out.

"The draft also created business opportunities. Start a school to train preachers, get yourself accredited by someone—anyone—charge a lot of tuition, ensure that no one flunked out, and you could get rich."

Ben said, "You're talking about diploma mills? Fake schools?"

"Exactly what I'm talking about. And the Maharal Rabbinical Academy, in Metuchen, was one of the most outrageous. A complete fraud. Huge tuition, but they never took class roll. You didn't have to give up your job—and you could 'study' as long as you could pay. When you got to be too old for the draft, or the war ended, whatever—they sold you a diploma."

"Messianic Christianity?"

"More a mishmash of Christian fundamentalism and Gnosticism, with Jewish rituals. It was run by a fake Hassid who knew more Yiddish than Hebrew and not too much of either."

"That would be Rabbi Menachem Zelman?"

"Just one of the names he used. In the '20s and '30s, he passed out handbills on the Lower East Side and in Brooklyn advertising 'World-Famous Rabbi So-and-So' or 'Cantor Such and Such, The Nightingale of Prague' who would lead High Holy Days services, tickets five bucks.

"The famous rabbi or cantor was some beard who couldn't read fifty words in Hebrew. They'd sell 1,000 tickets for a tent or storefront that held 200, except there were only fifty chairs. The 'world-famous rabbi' would begin the service, a couple of 'gabbaim' would work the crowd for those deserving of 'honors' and the suckers would supply all the readers and doers for the service. Half an hour in, the star would 'faint,' the gabbaim would carry him out of the tent, and the service would continue in whatever fashion the worshippers were capable of."

Ben said, "I'm amazed how much you know about an obscure diploma mill."

Baum snorted. "Give me your hand," he said, and when Ben extended his arm, Baum forced his hand down onto his upper thigh.

Baum said, "Squeeze it."

Ben said, "Rabbi—"

Baum forced Ben's hand against his leg until Ben could feel what lay underneath the trousers fabric. It has hard, cold and unyielding.

Ben said, "My God! I never knew."

Baum said, "I wasn't one of the smart ones. I joined the Marines out of high school. I left that leg at Khe Sanh.

"I went to Newark State on the G.I. Bill, and worked summers for the Middlesex County prosecutor's office as an investigator. They had me enroll in the Maharal Rabbinical Academy, and two other diploma mills, to build a criminal case against Zelman."

Ben said, "How did that turn out?"

Baum shrugged. "He was never indicted. I think the fix was in. He paid someone, or maybe several someones."

Ben said, "About the Academy itself, does the name Albert Martin Farkas mean anything to you in that context?"

Baum gave a harsh little laugh. "Al Farkas. Sure. From the Bronx. We were on the high school debating team. And in the chess club. The black sheep of a family of rabbis. Always knew how to make money. Became a bond trader, made an enormous fortune but handed most of it to Bernie Madoff. Almost went to jail half a dozen times for one financial shenanigan or another, but always managed to wriggle out.

"The Maharal Academy was his draft dodge. His family cut him off, and he had to find his own tuition—God knows where. He never pretended to know much about Judaism, went to shul maybe twice a year, but he put his Maharal diploma on his office wall. He just loved it when people called him rabbi."

Ben fought to keep his excitement in check. Could it really be this easy?

Ben said, "Tell me, Rabbi Baum, what does Farkas look like?"

Baum said, "When I knew him, in high school, he was a big, fat, sloppy kid. When he was about 45 and worth $100 million or so—on paper, anyway—his 25-year-old trophy wife, Lois, a blonde shiksa, hired a couple of personal trainers, and they turned Al into a Clark Kent stand-in. Why do you ask?"

Ben said, "When did you last see him, Rabbi?"

Baum took a long pull on his cigar, thinking. "Seven, eight years ago. I didn't actually see him, but he left my congregation half a million dollars, so I went to his funeral."

Ilene appeared in the doorway, silhouetted by the kitchen lights. "Hey, you guys—coffee's ready—Dad, please put that awful thing out before you come inside."

Chapter Forty-three

The next morning, over coffee in his community center office, Abe said, "I knew you and Arthur would hit it off."

Ben said, "He's very interesting. You never told me that he served in Vietnam or that he was a criminal investigator."

Abe said, "Did he tell you that he decided to become a rabbi because of what he learned while investigating those diploma mills?"

Ben shook his head. "We never got that far in our discussion."

Abe said, "In a lot of ways, he's a very private guy. I didn't learn how he lost his leg until a week before our wedding when he tried to talk me into volunteering to serve two years as an Army chaplain."

"That might have been interesting, Abe," Ben said. "Did you even consider it?"

"Ilene said that if I wanted to run around playing soldier, she would move back in with her parents and finish grad school. So that was that."

Ben laughed. "Did you ever meet this guy, Farkas, the one whose name was originally on the diploma?"

Abe scratched his head. "I don't think so. But I met his widow when she came to Arthur's shul for a dedication service—they built a chapel with funds from her husband's bequest. I'll bet Arthur knows how to reach her."

"When does he leave?"

Abe said, "This afternoon, right after his speech. Call him when he gets home."

Ben said, "I will. Shall we go look at the Sanoker exhibit?"

Abe said, "I'll drive."

§

A skinny young man with wild orange hair and tattoos on his arms led Ben and Abe down a wide aisle in an expansive warehouse. Consulting a clipboard, he pointed to a narrow lane between floor-to-ceiling storage bins.

"Both sides, all the way to the top," he said. "I'll call the forklift when you're ready to see the top shelves."

Abe asked, "What do you expect to learn from looking at this stuff?"

Ben said, "I'm trying to find what Geltkern was after. I'm pretty sure he didn't start the Sanoker Shul out of the goodness of his heart. And I'm really glad you came along, Abe. Between these crutches and my shoulder…"

Ben bent to peer at the label on the first box. "Photographs 1894-1919," he read aloud. Abe wrestled the box off the bottom shelf, surprised by its weight. The attendant produced a box cutter, bent over and slit the heavy tape sealing the box.

The first layer was wadded newspapers. Beneath that was a sheet of corrugated cardboard, and beneath that were eleven battered red bricks, individually wrapped in newspapers.

Ben and Abe exchanged glances but said nothing until they had pulled the second box out and opened it. Its contents were nearly identical to the first.

They opened six more boxes and found only wrapped bricks.

Abe turned to the attendant. "Why don't you get your boss," he said. The warehouse manager was named Larry. Burly and bald, his cheerful fifty-something face faded into a portrait of incredulity as he opened box after box.

"This can't happen here," Larry said.

Abe said, "But it did happen."

"But we have layers of security and 24/7 armed guards."

Ben said, "Perhaps you should look into your staff."

Larry said, "Let me go pull the file. It's in the office."

While they walked the length of the building, Ben took out his phone and called Yolanda.

Yolanda said, "I'm working now, Rabbi. Can I call you back?"

Ben said, "Let me talk to the Duke of Bourbon."

§

Larry laid a bulging manila folder on his desk and opened it. "Do you remember when we picked up all this stuff?"

Abe shook his head. "Around five years ago."

Larry turned page after page until he was nearly halfway through the stack.

"Here it is. The Sanoker Jews. You had it delivered to an address in Berona Township."

Abe shook his head. "Not me. I did no such thing."

Larry turned the page. "And then about two weeks later, you had us pick it up and store it again."

Abe's face was grim. "You're mistaken," he said. "I never had anything to do with this except sign the papers to have it stored here."

Larry passed him both sheets of paper. "That's your signature, isn't it?"

Abe peered at first one page, then the other. He shook his head.

"Not even close," he said. He flipped through the stack of papers until he found a storage order that bore his signature and handed it to Larry.

"Tell me that those signatures are the same!"

Larry peered at the license, then the pages. His face paled. "No," he said, his voice barely a whisper. "They're not."

The office door opened, and Easton, trailed by Yolanda, entered, holding their badges aloft.

Easton said, "Somebody call the cops?"

Ben passed him the two pages. "About four years ago, somebody pretending to be Rabbi Smolkin had the whole exhibit moved to Berona, then had it picked up and put back into storage. Between those two events, all the paper turned to brick."

Easton said, "Our friend Geltkern—or is it Farkas?"

Ben said, "Farkas was long dead when this happened. But somehow Geltkern got hold of his diploma."

Abe said, "Somebody nnexttell me what's going on here?"

Ben said, "Remember the time you caught Geltkern going through your files?"

Abe nodded, yes.

"Maybe he wanted to know where this exhibit was stored, which warehouse."

Abe shook his head. "Why would anybody steal this stuff? You can't sell it."

Ben said, "I think he was looking for something, and when he found it, he destroyed everything so that no one else could find it or even know what he found. Then he returned the boxes so that no one would know that the material was gone."

Easton said, "This is one careful, patient dude. Whatever it is that he took, it's gotta be huge to justify all the time and effort he's invested in this score."

Yolanda said, "What could that possibly be?"

Ben shook his head. "No idea. In the meantime, Roland, we have a Berona Township address to check out. And we have some issues to discuss with Chief Laurence. And these boxes and the bricks in them should be processed as evidence."

Chapter Forty-four

Easton drove, and Yolanda gave the front seat to Ben and his crutches.

Easton said, "That phone number you gave me? From the remote video cell phone gizmo?"

Ben asked, "You traced it?"

Easton said, "A prepaid, sold over in Wheeling, no calls out, five calls in, all from the same number, that surveillance device."

Ben asked, "How did the buyer pay?"

Yolanda said, "Cash."

Ben said, "I feel like I'm playing chess, but I can't see the board."

§

Chief Laurence said, "Not that it isn't good to see you, Ben, but trouble seems to follow you."

Ben said, "I guess two killings in a single month is a lot for a small town."

Laurence said, "Three killings, a case of arson, and three disappearances, counting your absent rabbi."

Easton said, "I'm not keeping score. Bernstein was a murder; Witzelburg got shot by your guys. What's happened since then?"

"Since then," Laurence said, "I've watched a video, attempted to question my two patrolmen, and our bowling alley burned down with a woman in it."

Ben's stomach did flip-flops. His throat tasted of bile. "Who was the woman?"

Laurence opened the middle drawer of his desk and took out a half-empty pack of cigarettes and a lighter. "This is a no-smoking building," he announced, before lighting up. "The whole damn civic center is. But somehow they taste better when you're not supposed to have one.

"There's little enough to do in this town, recreationally speaking, and then two nights ago, somebody fires Berona Lanes. Found a woman's body in the rubble. Autopsy to be performed when the coroner's office gets to it."

Ben asked, "Any I.D. on the body? Tall, short, young, old?"

Lawrence took a final drag on his cigarette before grinding it into a jar lid. "No I.D. She was about five feet, three inches tall, and that's all we know right now."

Ben said, "Filomina Jenston had her office in that bowling alley."

Lawrence stared at Ben. "Fire started in her office. How do you know her?"

"She kept the books for the Sanok Home," Ben said. "I mean, keeps them."

Yolanda said, "She came to services Saturday and volunteered to keep the shul's books for free until we can afford to pay her."

Laurence said, "Are we talking about the same woman? She's a Catholic. I've taken Holy Communion with her at All Saints."

Ben said, "I don't think she's looking for God. She just wanted to help."

Laurence asked, "Any idea who'd want her dead?"

Ben said, "The guy who killed Stan Bernstein."

Easton said, "Or the one who killed Mrs. Weinstock and torched her home."

Laurence asked, "Somebody killed Mrs. Weinstock and burned her house?"

Yolanda said, "With Rabbi Ben inside."

Ben said, "Wait—she was murdered weeks ago. Shot. The house burned down Sunday night."

Laurence said, "But you were ... visiting?"

Easton said, "It's his hobby."

Laurence said, "I've seen him in action. Say no more."

Easton said, "Someone knew that he was in that house. When he went downstairs, they locked him in the basement and set off some kind of homemade firebomb: powdered aluminum and ammonium nitrate."

Laurence said, "The state troopers said that the fire in Filomina's office was so hot that it melted the computers and steel cabinets."

Ben said, "Wait. Go back. You said something about trying to interview your patrolmen. And that you've had three disappearances."

Laurence opened the desk drawer, removed the cigarettes, hesitated, then dropped the pack and slammed the drawer shut. "I sent for Petersen and Barger and told them I wanted to talk about their report on the Witzelburg shooting. Informally. Off the record. They said they'd have a lawyer first. That made it formal. I suspended them, with pay, and told them to have their lawyers call to make an appointment.

"I haven't heard from their attorney, and they both skipped town. Neighbors said they loaded their families into cars and drove away."

Easton said, "Do they really think they can hide for the rest of their lives?"

Laurence shook his head. "Maybe they only have to stay lost until I'm gone."

Ben said, "What does that mean?"

"My contract expires at the end of the year. The city manager can renew it, or not. I thought I'd know his intentions by now, but I haven't heard a peep. Asked about it last week, and he said he'd let me know."

Easton said, "Could the missing cops know something you don't?"

Laurence opened the desk drawer again and shook out a cigarette but left it on the desk. "Maybe they do at that. I'll find security work. Somewhere. Corporate honchos love hiring retired police chiefs. But I'd hate to leave with a cloud hanging over my department."

Ben said, "We need to check out an address in your town. Do you have an officer that you'd trust to come with us and keep his mouth shut afterward?"

Laurence said, "Just one."

Chapter Forty-Five

The address on the storage invoice was a woman's hair salon on a street off Berona Road and a few doors down from the shop where Ben had purchased jewelers' screwdrivers and craft needles.

The shop smelled of nail polish and emollients. A plump, pink-skinned woman in a lavender smock and an elaborate coiffure smiled at the three men and one woman who entered.

She said, "Nice to see you, Jack. Are these your new officers?"

Laurence smiled. "Kathy, these folks are up from Pittsburgh, working a theft case, and they have a few questions for you."

Kathy said, "Whatever I can do to help, Jack."

Yolanda said, "I'm Officer Sanchez, this is Detective Easton, and that's Rabbi Ben."

Ben said, "About four years ago, a truckload of boxes stolen from the Jewish Community Center in Pittsburgh was delivered here."

Kathy interrupted. "We were over on Berona Road until last year. Things are a little slow in town, and the rent here is a deal less, so we moved. I'm sorry, but I can't help with your theft case."

Easton asked, "Do you recall who rented this shop then?"

Kathy said, "It had been vacant for quite a while, as I recall. One reason it was lower rent. Talk to Alexis; she manages the property."

Jack said, "Thanks, Kathy."

They left the shop and climbed back into Easton's Crown Victoria.

Ben asked, "Alexis?"

Laurence said, "Alexis Lustig is my boss's wife."

Yolanda said, "She's married to the city manager?"

Laurence said, "And anything I ask her will go right back to him."

Easton said, "What's the problem with that?"

Ben said, "Jack, do you think that Lustig is mixed up with the Witzelburg shooting?"

Laurence said, "Not directly. I think that my Lieutenant Geisel might have been the guy who turned up at your temple that night. Maybe he even shot Witzelburg. And Geisel is Lustig's man on the township council."

Yolanda asked, "He's on the town council, and he's a cop, too?"

Laurence said, "Democracy. A wonderful thing, when it works."

Easton asked, "Chief, do you play poker?"

Laurence said, "Now and again."

Easton asked, "Ever been in a game where you wondered, Which one of these guys is the sucker, the mark?"

Laurence said, "A time or two."

Easton asked, "And?"

Laurence said, "And I was the sucker. I know. This looks like I'm being set up to take the fall. But the fall for what?"

Ben said, "Drop me around the corner from Alexis's office. I'll go in alone."

Chapter Forty-six

Her skirt was too short, her sweater too tight, most of her long blonde hair wasn't really blonde and in fact had once belonged to someone else, and her mask of makeup seemed only to emphasize that her face was familiar with a surgeon's scalpel. Alexis Lustig was a forty-something trying to look like a twenty-something.

A woman fearful of losing her husband, Ben decided. He smiled as he made his way toward her, crutch-clumsy as he could safely manage.

"Morning," he said, letting a tinge of New England color his voice.

"Good morning," she replied, a low rumble. "What can I do you for today?"

Ben said, "If it's not too much trouble, I really need to sit first."

"Of course," she said, leaving a row of filing cabinets to put a chair at her desk.

Ben made a show of transferring from crutches to a chair, apologizing at every opportunity until he sat facing her, his crutches leaning against her desk.

Alexis said, "What happened to you?"

Ben said, "A pothole on the turnpike got together with my rental and a pole."

Alexis frowned. "I'm really sorry to hear that, Mister–did you say your name?"

Ben said, "Mark T. Glass, Textatron Industries. Unfortunately, my iPad, my briefcase, all my tools, including my card case, were in that car. Which is now somewhere between Pittsburgh and Harrisburg, but Avis isn't saying where."

"Gosh, you've had a rough time. What is it that I can do for you, Mr. Glass?"

Ben coughed, wincing. "Sorry. Cracked a rib, I think. Anyway. Textatron. We're the world's fourth-largest operator of call centers."

Alexis frowned again. "Can't say that I've ever heard of your company."

Ben nodded. "I get that a lot. We're a division of TransAsiana. Our call centers are in Singapore, India, Sri Lanka and the Philippines. Or, we *were* a division of TransAsiana. We're right now in the process of a buyout, using an ESOP."

Alexis smiled. "I don't quite understand what I can do for you, Mark. We're a local property management company."

Ben said, "Sure. An ESOP is an Employee Stock Ownership Plan. Textatron's management team—that's me and six other officers—is in the process of buying our company back from TransAsiana and moving operations back to the U.S. Given the poor job market, and state and local tax incentives, our research suggests that we can operate medium-sized call centers in rural Pennsylvania and Ohio for less than in the Philippines or Singapore. So we're looking for suitable space."

Alexis brightened. "What would one of those medium-sized call centers require in the way of square footage?"

Ben nodded. "We calculate that we can find, train and hire about 500 operators within a twenty-mile radius of Berona Township. That's two shifts of roughly 180 operators per shift—we run a seven-day operation, so at any time, two-sevenths of the force is off-duty—times roughly 28 square feet per operator, including the management footprint. That comes to a little over 5,000 square feet, not including our satellite uplink, which is typically roof-sited."

Alexis sat up in her chair. "That's a lot of square feet for a small town to absorb, Mr. Glass."

Ben frowned. "I guess I could try Scottdale or Latrobe."

Alexis shook her head. "What I meant, Mr. Glass, was that it was a lot if it has to be in one contiguous location."

Ben cocked his head as if thinking. "No. I mean, yes, we don't necessarily have to be in one location. In fact, we were thinking maybe two or three locations, to alleviate impacts of employees and parking on parking and local merchant services."

"I could let you look at some comps for our available properties?"

"That would be fine, Ms.— I didn't get your name, either."

"Alexis Lustig."

Ben reached across the desk to shake hands. "Excuse me, you said Lustig?"

"Yes."

"Your father's the city manager?"

Alexis laughed. "My father is Judge Kendall, president judge of the county Court of Common Pleas. My husband is the city manager."

"As I understand, a very capable administrator."

"He is that."

"You must be very proud of him. A man of many parts, is he not?"

"He does have quite a few business interests."

"Exactly. Now, what I'd like to see first are properties along Knox Avenue."

"We manage them all, and none is available."

"I understand. But, if they were suitable, we might approach the present occupants with an offer. In order to do that, I'd need to see the historical data on those properties and on any others along Knox that you might have, including those that are owner-managed."

"I don't see how my business is helped by your company subletting one of my properties."

"I guess I haven't explained myself very well, Mrs. Lustig. Any leasing offer we might tender for any Knox property would include a management fee to your firm. And that is because, if Textatron decides to open a facility in Berona Township, we would be very pleased to do business with the Lustig family."

Alexis stared at Ben for several seconds. Then she burst into laughter. "Boy, you look all big-city business, but you sure know how to talk to us hillbillies."

She got up from her desk and went to the file cabinet, returning with a thick folder. "This is all I have on Knox."

Ben started on the file, scanning each page, in turn, jotting notes on his iPhone. Twenty minutes passed. Yolanda came through the front door. Ben kept his nose buried in the files, not even glancing at her.

Yolanda said, "Excuse me, do you rent apartments here?"

Alexis said, "We're strictly commercial properties. Our residential office is across the street. I'm sure you'll find some lovely apartments."

"Thank you," Yolanda said and left.

§

Half an hour later, Ben struggled to his feet. "Thank you, Mrs. Lustig. We'll be in touch after I've analyzed this data and conferred with my colleagues."

Alexis said, "How many operators did you say this call center would need?"

Ben smiled. "About 500, when we're at full strength."

"Where are all those people going to live?"

Ben shook his head. "Based on the 2010 census, and Pennsylvania Chamber of Commerce data, there are between 15,000 and 18,000 unemployed or under-employed adults within an hour's drive of your township. Some of those people will be our new hires. They'll commute to work."

"What about your management team?"

"That's another story. We'll most likely begin with three to five managers and then, over time, train and promote from the best of our local employees."

"Those three to five managers, where will they live?"

"Mrs. Lustig, are you trying to sell me real estate?"

"How long before your call center would be up and running?"

Ben shrugged. "Nine months to two years, depending on how the ESOP goes and then how quickly we can repurpose existing structures to suit our needs."

"I think your company should plan on buying a few executive residences in our exclusive Kendall Heights development. We're scheduled to break ground late next year. Custom homes from the mid-four-hundreds to a million-two."

"I'll factor that into our proposal."

"It's a good investment. It's also a requirement for doing business in Berona Township."

Ben smiled. "Why, Mrs. Lustig, you look like a hillbilly, but you talk like big-city business."

CHAPTER FORTY-SIX

Ben turned the corner and found Easton's car half a block down the street. He slid into the front seat next to him. As Easton pulled out into traffic, Ben craned his neck to look at the back seat.

Ben said, "Thanks for coming to check on me, Yolanda."

Easton said, "I sent her to make sure you hadn't stepped in a pile of something while I drove the chief back to his office."

"Then, thank you, too."

Yolanda asked, "What did you learn?"

Ben said, "Quite a few things, starting with the fact that the Lustig family seems to be running this town for fun and profit. Mostly profit."

Easton asked, "About the boxes from the community center?"

Ben said, "According to her records, the store was vacant for almost five years before the hair salon rented it."

Yolanda asked, "Geltkern moved in for a couple of weeks, and nobody said boo?"

Ben shook his head. "Try it this way. The vacant property almost certainly had a notice in a window about rental inquiries. The present tenant, a salon, pays $850 a month. Geltkern finds Alexis and says he wants to borrow the place for two weeks, no questions asked, nothing in writing. How much cash will she take?"

Yolanda asked, "A thousand bucks?"

Easton said, "Less, probably. It's tax-free, under the table. Mad money."

Ben said, "So Geltkern has the boxes delivered in the rear, where there's not much chance of anyone getting overly curious. He does what he does, has them come back and pick up all the boxes."

Easton said, "So Alexis doesn't know what he did or who he was."

Ben said, "We need to find the guy who drove that delivery truck."

Easton shook his head. "That's a tough one. It's been five years."

Ben put his head down, thinking.

"You're probably right," he said. "But as long as we're here, can we go up to the Sanok Home for a minute?"

§

Ben said, "Wait here while I talk to one of the attendants—James. I won't be long."

Easton said, "Good. I've been dying for a smoke."

Yolanda said, "I thought you quit."

Easton said, "So did I."

Ben found James in the office, on his hands and knees. "What happened?"

James looked up and grinned. "Mrs. Lasky dropped her coffee, is all. Something I could help you with, Rabbi?"

Ben said, "Do you keep records of the board of directors meetings?"

James frowned. "We had a whole file cabinet full of them."

"Had?"

"Yessir. Then a few weeks ago, I'm dusting in here, and I find that cabinet unlocked. I opened all the drawers, and they were empty. But it doesn't matter."

Ben said, "Someone stole the records, and it doesn't matter?"

"No sir, not really. They haven't held a meeting in all the time that I've been here. That cabinet was just gathering dust, and Mrs. Silverblatt had asked me, just a few weeks before, if we had an extra cabinet for her office. So I gave it to her. Everybody's happy."

Ben frowned. "I was talking to the police. Did you have some false alarms out here over the last couple months?"

James said, "I heard that. But I don't work nights, and from what I know, nothing was missing."

Ben said, "Except maybe those records."

Chapter Forty-Seven

George Lewin was sipping coffee in Mrs. Meltzer's kitchen when Ben returned from Berona, hungry, tired and dispirited.

Mrs. Meltzer said, "Sit down, and have something to eat."

Ben took a chair across from Lewin, and she put a steaming bowl of barley soup before him. Ben took a cautious sip and smiled.

Mrs. Meltzer smiled back.

Lewin said, "Rabbi, I have good news. And I have bad news."

Ben said, "The bad first."

"I'm so far unable to complete your Yiddish translation, although it's well along. The problem is that this is not just Yiddish; it's a local dialect, compounded by the fact that the person who wrote it was a poor speller. I doubt that I'll find anyone who spoke this dialect. There were probably never more than a few thousand people, and most of them died in the Shoah. The passage of time has erased most or all of the rest. It's not impossible, just a challenge, to find Polish words that might have crept into the local dialect. I suspect that some of the Polish was probably a local dialect as well, which makes it even more interesting."

Ben said, "Thanks for all your effort, Doctor. Do you have anything at all that I could look at?"

Lewin shook his head. "Not really. Just a hodgepodge of notes. But let me share the good news, too: I've had conversations with Abby Silverblatt, and I spent the morning observing her interact with several patients. I'm going to offer her most of my practice. Of course, each of my patients is free to choose whomever they like, but I suspect that most will be happy with the hand-off. And that will leave me much more time to pursue your translation."

Ben said, "That's really good news. But, Doctor Lewin, I'm pursuing a killer. Don't be offended. I know you mean well, that you want to help. And the pages I asked you to translate may or may not have anything to do with finding him or with discovering his motives. But they might. So far, at least four people have died because of this man. If it's going to be weeks or months before you have the time available, I'd better try to find someone else. Can you suggest someone?"

Lewin frowned. "Really, I think by the time you found the right person and brought them up to speed, and by the time they realized what was needed, I'd be done. Please, leave the pages. Give me a few more days, a week, perhaps."

Ben said, "Thank you, Doctor. I know you're trying. Is there anything I could do to help you help me?"

Lewin said, "Find me someone who speaks Yiddish with a Malopolska accent, someone from the Subcarpathian Voivodeship."

Ben said, "I have an idea."

Chapter Forty-eight

On Friday morning, Ben rose early, tested his knee, and decided he could do without crutches. By 9:00 he'd showered, put away a bowl of Mrs. Meltzer's oatmeal, and was on the turnpike headed northwest to Berona.

Ben found Avi Cohen in the living-room area near the main entrance, drinking tea and reading a tabloid newspaper.

Cohen said, "Shalom, Rabbi! You're here very early."

Ben said, "I came to speak with you."

"So, speak already. I'm not getting younger."

"Where were you born, Rav Cohen?" he asked, using a term of respect for a learned Jew.

"Tarnow," he replied, "Poland."

Ben knew that nearly all of Tarnow's 23,000 Jews, half the city's population, had been murdered by the Nazis. He raised his eyebrows. "Then you have lived a charmed life, Rav Cohen."

Cohen nodded. "Ha Shem, God, had other plans for me."

Ben said, "Tell me, if you don't mind, how you survived."

Cohen's face changed to an expression of pain. "The Nazis came in September 1939. On the second day, they shot my wife and took me for forced labor. On the way to the forest, the guards shot three men and left them to die. We were given saws and forced to cut trees.

"We stayed in the forest that night and the next. Slept on the ground, without even a blanket. One of my pals, Mayshe Schwartze, a Zionist and a *shtarker,* a big, strong guy, told me that the longer we waited to escape, the harder it would be. So we cut ourselves a little ways into the forest, and when the guard came, Mayshe hit him with a piece of wood, I took his rifle, and we ran. Two or three other fellows took off in a different direction. The guards chased them, I guess, because nobody came after us. We ran and ran. A little later, we heard a lot of shooting, far away. Maybe they shot everybody on the labor gang. I still wonder about that.

"It was a couple of hundred miles to Hungary, but in 1939 they weren't killing Jews there. That came later. We walked, mostly, through Slovakia and into Hungary. Stole food, dug up farmers' potatoes, went hungry most of the time. I had some cousins in Miskolc, and they fed us. Later, we were both drafted into a Hungarian labor battalion. It was bad, but not like what was going on in Poland. They wanted us to work, and if we died, so what. The Germans just wanted us dead.

"So I survived until 1945 when I went to a British DP camp. Then to England, and I came to the States in '47."

Ben asked, "What about your friend, Mayshe?"

Cohen shook his head. "Typhus, in 1942. What's this about? Why are you interested in my ancient history?"

Ben asked, "How far was Sanok from Tarnow?"

"Maybe 200 kilometers, 120 miles."

"Did Sanok and Tarnow speak different Polish dialects?"

Cohen shrugged. "Almost. Probably they had a few local words."

"And Yiddish? The same in both places?"

"Close enough, I suppose. Why do you want to know this?"

"Do you still know Yiddish?"

Cohen raised his newspaper. "Why do you suppose this is called the Yiddish Daily Forward?"

"Would you care to take a ride with me, Rav Cohen?"

"I'm reading my paper."

"Perhaps you could take it with you, sir."

§

Ben said, "Dr. Lewin, this is Mr. Cohen. He was born in the Subcarpathian Voivodeship."

Cohen said, "In Tarnow."

Lewin smiled. "Tarnow? I thought all the Tarnow Jews were murdered?"

Cohen shook his head. "A few hundred, at least, had the good sense or good luck to leave instead of being fed to the furnaces."

Lewin said, "Please sit down, Mr. Cohen. Would you care for tea?"

Ben said, "I'll come back in a couple of hours to take Mr. Cohen home."

Chapter Forty-nine

Saturday morning was wet and windy. Ben parked in front of the Sanoker Shul, and to his surprise found an improvised canopy—a pitched roof of painter's canvases supported by unpainted wooden posts driven into the ground—leading to the entrance. The muddy ground under the canopy was covered with thick rubber mats, making it safer, easier and more comfortable to get from a car into the synagogue. Inside, he found the entrance area bright and welcoming, lit by a dozen low-energy bulbs in a sleek new chandelier.

Jim appeared. "What do you think, Rabbi?"

Ben smiled. "I think that I'm very glad you saved my life, Jim."

Jim said, "Ancient history. What do you think of Hank's new canopy? The chandelier?"

Ben said, "It shows you're both thinking men. These are small but important things, and you provided them. Cheap, functional, and very quick. Just what this place needs until the congregation gets on its feet."

Jim smiled. "I know you think we saved your life, but really, Rabbi, you saved ours. It's been so long since anyone needed us, so long since we could think about anything except getting high or surviving another day. This is paradise, a job, a decent place to live, a steady paycheck. And nice people. We'll never forget what you've done for us."

"That works both ways.."

"Come by tomorrow, and I'll give you a tour. We've really just started, but I think you'll like what you see."

§

An hour later, just as he began the Torah service, Ben looked up from the scroll while Abby, in her role as a gabbai, announced the page and verse so that the congregation could follow the reader. Movement in the back of the room caught Ben's eye, and for a moment he was certain that he was hallucinating. A bearded man stood in the doorway to the sanctuary. He wore an ankle-length *tallit,* or prayer shawl, over a dark suit, and on his head was a *shtreimel*, a circular fur hat, worn by certain Hassidic sects and by eighteenth-century Polish Jews.

Their eyes met.

The man smiled, then turned and vanished through the door.

His mind whirling furiously, Ben looked back at the Torah, focused, and began to chant, forcing himself to stay in the moment, to concentrate on the holy task before him and not the apparition that had appeared and vanished.

After services, Ben joined the worshippers who remained for a light lunch in the adjacent room. Before they started to eat, Ben called for everyone's attention, explained what a *shtreimel* was and what it looked like. Then he asked if anyone had seen a man wearing one in the shul that morning.

A young man raised his hand. "Not in the shul, but out in the parking lot. He was getting into his car."

Ben took the man aside. "What kind of a car was it?"

The man shrugged. "Some kind of big SUV, gray or silver."

Ben said, "Can you describe the man?"

The young man frowned. "He looked a little like Rabbi Geltkern, but I'm kind of new here. I've only seen him once or twice."

Ben thanked the man, then went outside. The rain had slowed to an intermittent drizzle. He circled the building, eyes on the ground, but wind and rain had obliterated any footprints. He turned the corner and knocked on the door to the apartment now occupied by Hank and Jim.

After a moment, the door opened and Hank smiled at Ben. "Rabbi Ben! Jim was just talking about you."

Ben said, "Hank, this may seem like a strange question, but were you here, in your rooms, about an hour ago?"

Hank nodded. "Yeah, when that dude in the funny hat just walked right in."

Ben's heart beat a little faster. "Can you describe him?"

Hank paused, "I'd say about five-feet-ten or eleven, 240 pounds, a beard, that funny fur hat and a big old prayer thingee that some of you guys wear, only really big."

"And he just walked in?"

"The door wasn't locked. He just stepped inside. I was eating cereal and a banana, and I like to choked on it."

Ben asked, "Did he say anything?"

"Yeah, said he was sorry, that he was looking for your office."

"And then what?"

"Well, we're gonna block off that door, maybe next week, and put in a separate entrance for your office, but right now, he'd have had to go all around the building to get in the front door..."

"So you let him in, and he went in there. Were you with him?"

"I sure was. He seemed disappointed that you weren't there, so I pointed him at the hallway that leads to the front door and the sanctuary."

Ben said, "Do you have an opinion about where he might have come from? Any kind of an accent?"

"New York, definitely."

Ben said, "Please listen carefully. This man is very dangerous. I believe that he carries a gun. If you see him again, stay away from him, and call the police."

Hank looked shaken. "Are you being for real?"

Ben nodded. "Absolutely. He may have killed Mrs. Weinstock and sent someone to burn down her house while I was in it."

Hank's eyes were big as saucers.

Ben said, "Hank, this is not a joke. There's one more thing I'd like you to do, and it can't wait. I want you to look in my office, and then near the front door, and in and around Jim's office. There is a good chance that this man may have left something about half the size of a business card. It would probably be on a wall. It's got a tiny video lens in front and the guts of a cell phone inside. There may be a wire attached to it, and it's probably the same color as the wall paint."

"What do I do if I find it?"

"Look for more. Any you find, put them on the desk in my office."

Hank nodded. "Will do, Rabbi Ben. This guy—what did he want? Why did he come today?"

Ben shook his head. "I've got no idea."

Chapter Fifty

Early Sunday morning, Hank called Ben to say that he had searched the building but found nothing suspicious.

After a two-mile run, Ben hit the shower, then called Yolanda.

Ben said, "Is the Duke of Bourbon within shouting range?"

"He's driving."

"Can you put him on speakerphone?"

A moment later, Easton said, "What's going on, Rabbi?"

"I think Geltkern made a mistake. Maybe two. And so did we."

Yolanda said, "What happened?"

Ben said, "Yesterday morning, a man dressed as a Hassid, with a big, round, fur hat called a *shtreimel*, and wearing a prayer shawl, walked into the caretaker's apartment at the shul. A few minutes later, he came into the sanctuary. He stood in the doorway just long enough to catch my eye, then left.

"One of the worshippers saw him getting into a big SUV and driving off. He said that he wasn't sure but the guy looked like Geltkern."

Easton said, "But don't all those ultra-Orthodox guys have beards and kinda all dress the same way?"

Ben said, "They kind of do. But this guy wasn't a Hassid. No Orthodox Jew would violate the Sabbath by so much as carrying car keys, let alone driving a car."

Yolanda said, "Wouldn't Geltkern know that?"

Ben said, "I expect that he would. My point is he was driving an SUV like the one I saw in Weinstock's garage, but a different color.

"We decided that whoever torched the house took the car. But maybe not. Maybe Geltkern sent someone to retrieve it."

Yolanda said, "Why? So he could drive it?"

Easton said, "So he could sanitize it."

Ben said, "That's what I'm thinking. Or maybe he had another use for a $70,000 car: Paint it, put out-of-state plates on it, get a fake registration, and peddle it for a lot more than walking-around money. Can you put out a want on the car without knowing its license plate?"

Yolanda said, "We know the owner and address. I'll get the plate."

Ben said, "It was Ohio, not Pennsylvania."

Easton said, "We're on it. We'll try, but maybe the car has served its purpose. I doubt that we'll find it."

Yolanda asked, "Why would Geltkern go to the shul, make sure you saw him, and then leave? What was that about?"

Ben said, "I don't know. Makes no sense."

Yolanda said, "We'll let you know if we find the car."

Ben said, "Thanks, Roland. And thanks, Yolanda."

Chapter Fifty-one

Monday morning, Ben returned to Pittsburgh Medical, where for the first time, Dr. Rao personally administered the injection. Gripped by dizziness, nausea and muscle cramps, Ben passed two exhausting and unhappy days in his room, relieved only by periodic visits by Mrs. Meltzer with tea and soup. Not until late Wednesday afternoon did he feel well enough to get dressed and go for a walk.

Perhaps guided by his thoughts, after a few minutes he found himself on the sidewalk in front of Dr. Lewin's home. On impulse, he climbed the porch steps to ring the bell. There was no response. After a few minutes, he turned to leave.

Behind him, the door opened a crack. Dr. Lewin said, "Please come back later," and closed the door.

Amused, Ben walked around the block, feeling better by the minute, pleased that his knee seemed back to normal and that his appetite had returned. Instead of climbing the back stairs to his room, he mounted the porch and rang the doorbell, hoping to learn if Mrs. Meltzer had made progress re-assembling shredded pages.

There was no answer. Ben paused on the sidewalk, thinking: Should he walk over to Kazansky's for a very early dinner or a very late lunch? Or return to his room, munch an energy bar or an apple while he tried to make sense of what he knew and what he didn't about the mysterious Rabbi Geltkern?

Then he realized that he had forgotten to call Abe's father-in-law about talking with Albert Farkas's widow. He would go back to his room, he decided, have a snack, and make those calls.

He left the porch, went around to the side entrance and pushed open the gate. He was almost through the opening when movement caught the corner of his eye. Instinctively, he ducked. A baseball bat grazed his shoulders before splintering the gate's wooden top.

As he straightened, Ben glimpsed the bat descending again, and dove forward, the blow glancing off his buttock. He landed on his shoulder and rolled, lashing out with his right leg to strike his assailant's thigh.

The man staggered backward, and Ben jumped to his feet, realizing that he was trapped. There wasn't enough room in the narrow walkway for him to fight or evade the enormous, bearded man before him, a giant well over six feet tall and weighing at least 300 pounds. A man who could choke him unconscious with a bear hug, or snap his neck. A man whom he didn't know but seemed strangely familiar.

Ben said, "Who sent you?"

"How ya like fightin' grownups?" the man growled. "Lil' different' than pickin' on kids—ain't so?"

Ben edged forward, hoping to get close enough to snatch the bat away. The giant raised his weapon.

As Ben leaned forward, his hip grazed the metal of a recycling can. He snatched off its lid, holding it with his right hand.

The bat flew downward.

In an instant, Ben fed the lid to the bat, pivoting on his left foot as the bat flew by harmlessly, then pushing off the wall to pivot on his right foot, seizing the giant's right arm as it descended and pulling him forward until he stumbled, off-balance.

Ben dashed into the backyard, then turned to face the giant, who clutched the bat in one hand as he stalked into the yard, a picture of rage and menace.

The man said, "No damn kung-fu shit ain't gonna save you, asshole."

Ben said, "Why are you here? Who sent you?"

"You hadda go give my nine to the cops? Stupid."

Ben realized that he was facing an older, bigger version of the tall youngster who robbed Zach. Maybe his father or older brother.

Ben said, "What's stupid is giving a kid a gun."

The giant bent to a crouch, holding the bat in one hand as he advanced toward Ben. Ben held his ground in the center of the space, hands at his side, waiting.

Four feet away, the giant raised the bat, then began his swing.

Ben stepped forward, just inside the giant's reach, seized the barrel of the bat with both hands, and whirled to his left.

The giant fell forward, and Ben came away with the bat.

When using a bat as a weapon, those who grow up playing baseball or softball tend to hold it by its lower handle, hands together as they swing, as if trying to hit a ball. Combined with the length of one's arms, this generates tremendous momentum at the bat head, enough kinetic energy to propel a ball hundreds of feet.

Or to crush a skull.

But as Ben's kung fu *xian sheng*, or teacher, had taught, a man with a short stick will land more blows than a man with a long one.

Ben gripped the bat near the middle, big end down, wrapping the fingers of both hands around the barrel, about a foot apart.

He took a step toward the big man, who returned to his crouch. He held a large Buck knife, blade up, in his right hand, a tipoff that he knew knife fighting.

"Rabbi, are you all right?" said a woman's voice from behind Ben.

Ignoring the voice, Ben held the bat with both hands at a 45-degree angle, then advanced on the knife-wielding man.

The giant lunged.

Ben parried with the bat's long handle, blocking the knife thrust. In the blink of an eye, he raised the bat to shoulder level and horizontal, lunging on his right leg and bringing the bat's fat bottom around in a short arc that struck his opponent's right shoulder with a satisfying thud.

The man grunted in pain and took a step back.

Ben swiveled the bat to the vertical and stepped forward as he brought the fat end straight up under the giant's chin.

Blood spurted. Teeth flew. The man toppled backward, dropping the knife.

"Rabbi?"

Ben turned. On the first-floor stair landing stood a woman gripping an old bolt-action rifle. Her hair was down, her makeup a mess and her dress haphazardly buttoned, but it was unmistakably Ro Meltzer.

"I'm fine, Ro. Please call the police."

CHAPTER FIFTY-TWO

"You should have seen him," said Mrs. Meltzer, hovering over Ben as he sat at the kitchen table with Dr. Lewin and Abby. "That ... gorilla ... was three times his size, a real brute, and the rabbi just went right after him, took his bat away, hit him twice, bang-bang, all over."

Lewin said, "He's fortunate to be alive. The big man, I mean."

Ben said, "I'm glad that he'll recover. I'd never forgive myself if I killed someone."

Abby said, "But he would have killed you!"

Ben shook his head. "We don't know that. More to the point, I know that it's wrong to take a life, even if he doesn't."

The back door to Mrs. Meltzer's kitchen opened, and Yolanda entered, followed by Easton.

Easton said, "His name is Colby Howell. The Rollins kid that you ran off when he was robbing Zach—he's the uncle. Works construction once in awhile, but mostly he's muscle for what's left of the local Mob."

Yolanda said, "Howell has a bunch of arrests: assault, robbery, extortion, attempted murder, gambling. But only one conviction: possession of stolen goods."

Lewin asked, "What? He has a great lawyer?"

Easton said, "You don't need much of a lawyer when all your witnesses come down with amnesia."

Ben asked, "Where is Howell now?"

Easton said, "Handcuffed to a bed at Allegheny General. You fractured his lower jaw; he's all wired up, so it'll be a while before we get anything out of him."

Ben asked, "How did he know where I live?"

Yolanda said, "It was on the report I made when I turned in the gun you took from that other boy."

Ben asked, "Would he have access to that?"

Easton said, "His attorney might."

Mrs. Meltzer, hair now perfectly coiffed and makeup immaculate, moved to the stove. "Who wants soup?" she asked.

§

An hour later, after everyone had downed at least one bowl of chicken soup with homemade farfel, and Abby had assured herself that Ben wasn't injured, only Ben, Dr. Lewin and Mrs. Meltzer remained at the table.

Ben looked up from his third bowl to see his landlady and the doctor trading covert, information-laden stares.

Ben asked, "What's going on?"

Lewin said, "What's going on is that my wife has asked for a divorce."

Ben said, "That's terrible."

Lewin shook his head. "The *marriage* was terrible. This has been stewing for years. Finally, she found someone she likes better."

Mrs. Meltzer said, "It's too precious; she left him for another woman, and this woman is half her age."

Ben asked, "And...?"

Mrs. Meltzer blushed. "And I'm glad. It's the best thing that could have happened for all concerned. And I found something that I like more than puzzles."

Lewin said, "And that's why I never finished translating that Yiddish for you."

Ben laughed. "I'm happy for both of you," he said.

Lewin said, "About that translation: I had a very nice chat with Mr. Cohen in Yiddish. He seemed to enjoy it a lot. By the way, he forgot his Yiddish newspaper—he even called me about it—I'll drop it off the next time I'm over."

Ben asked, "Was his Yiddish helpful?"

Lewin shook his head. "I learned a few new words and a new expression or two, Tarnow style. Truthfully, he wasn't much help with the Sanok material, but I found a book in my library, a privately published memoir by one of the Sanok rabbis, that might help. And I may have some other books. I'll work on it over the next few days."

Mrs. Meltzer said, "And I'll get back to work on my puzzles. I've got several pages started and one about half done, but it's very hard—it's Spanish or Italian."

Ben asked, "What? Spanish or Italian?"

"Maybe Rumanian, or Portuguese, what do I know? And the type is tiny, tiny."

Ben said, "That is amazing. Thank you for all your help on this. And, really, over the last few weeks, thank you for your many kindnesses. You've been almost like a mother to me, Mrs. Meltzer."

Mrs. Meltzer said, "Your mother, she's still...?"

Ben shook his head. "Died when I was a boy."

Ben's phone rang, and he glanced at the screen: Yolanda.

Ben clicked on the phone and asked, "What's up?"

Yolanda said, "Howell broke the weld on his bed frame, pulled his handcuffs free, then waited for the cop guarding him to go into the stairwell for a smoke."

Ben asked, "When did this happen?"

Yolanda said, "Less than an hour ago. His jaw is wired shut, and he's in a hospital gown. He won't get far. But keep your eyes peeled."

Ben turned to Mrs. Meltzer. "Howell has escaped. It might be a good idea if you took a little vacation."

Lewin smiled. "what about the Lodge at Glendorn? You'll love it."

Mrs. Meltzer said, "What about you? You can't stay here all alone."

Ben said, "I'll find a hotel out by the airport for a few days."

She frowned. "But how can I take those shredded papers without mixing them up again?"

Ben shook his head. "What you've already done was extremely helpful, but it would take you forever to finish. I'll bet someone, somewhere, has turned a computer loose on this kind of a problem. I'll take it from here. Enjoy yourselves, stay safe. I'll see you in a week."

Lewin asked, "You'll let us know if they catch that thug?"

Ben said, "Of course."

Chapter Fifty-three

Ben was across the river and near the airport when he decided that, until Howell was back in custody, it would be better if no one knew even approximately where he was staying. He got off the Interstate and turned back toward Pittsburgh. An hour later, he was ensconced in a ninth-floor room of the luxurious Pittsburgh Renaissance Hotel, with magnificent views of downtown Pittsburgh and the confluence of the Allegheny and Monongahela rivers joining to become the Ohio.

He ordered room service eggs scrambled with lox and onions, a bagel, and tea. By the time he had showered, the food arrived. He ate slowly, savoring his meal, thinking. Then he plugged in his laptop, logged onto the hotel Wi-Fi, and sent an email to Howard Hopper's personal account, knowing that it would forward to his Smartphone no matter where Howard was.

Less than five minutes later, Ben's cell phone rang: Howard Hopper calling.

Ben said, "Howie, I just sent you an email!"

Hopper said, "Yeah, that's why I called. You'll understand why I didn't email back when I tell you that I'm considering buying, or at least investing in, a startup that has a set of proprietary algorithms and a very cool scanner that together, supposedly, will do exactly what you need."

Ben said, "They can reassemble shredded documents?

"So they say. And in any language. I'd like to know if their software is for real, and your little project opens the door to a good test of their capabilities."

"Shall I send my shredded paper to them or to you?"

"To me. I'll bring it to them and see what they do with it."

"What do they charge?"

Hopper said, "They don't have a business model, let alone a fee schedule. Not yet. If I buy in, we'll work with them on that. So let's call this a courtesy job for a potential investor; after all, you still own a nice piece of my shop."

Ben said, "Thanks, Howie." He looked at his watch. "If I can get to the FedEx office at the Pittsburgh airport in the next hour, you'll have them tomorrow."

Hopper asked, "Do you have an idea what's on these shredded documents?"

Ben said, "Not a clue. This is a real puzzler."

"What kind of a case are you working?"

Ben said, "Missing person and possible embezzlement. Sorry to be abrupt, but if I hope to make the last FedEx shipment from the airport, I've gotta jet right now."

"Go, and we'll catch up soon."

Chapter Fifty-four

Ben called the concierge and asked for two large FedEx boxes. He found, however, that he could stuff all the shreds into just one. After addressing an air bill to Hopper's company, he took both boxes, retrieved his car from the hotel garage, and headed for the airport.

Getting on I-279, Ben glanced at his mirror, noticing the taxi behind him—and behind it, the shuddering single headlamp of a motorcycle. It was a bit over sixteen miles to the airport; by the time he took the exit for Airport Boulevard, Ben was sure that the motorcycle was following him. If so, he reasoned, it might be in company with a taxi that passed him, changed lanes, slowed to allow Ben to pass him, and remained a quarter of a mile behind him.

Ben parked in a structure across from the Landside Terminal and glanced at his watch. If he was being set up for a snatch-and-grab, he might have enough time to work around it. If it was anything else, he'd worry about FedEx another time.

He got out and went around to the trunk, found the unused box, which he had intended to return. He stuffed wads of paper towels inside, making a slight bulge in the center. Then he sealed it. He took the lug wrench from its place beneath the trunk carpet, then concealed it up the right sleeve of his jacket.

Leaving the real shipment in his car, he trotted toward the terminal, gripping the box by a corner with his left hand, arms at his sides. He paused at a walkway across the four-lane road. The light turned green, and he stepped into the street glancing both ways but without moving his head.

At the far curb, perhaps fifty yards to his right, a taxi pulled out, burning rubber, heading straight for him. Ben stopped just shy of the median stripe and let the tire wrench slide into his right hand as the speeding taxi flashed by him.

The sound of its approach covered by the taxi's roar, the motorcycle rolled toward Ben from the other direction.

As Ben brought the wrench up and pivoted to his right, the motorcycle passenger snatched the FedEx box from Ben's left hand.

The wrench hit the rider full in the face, and he fell off the bike.

As the motorcycle sped away, Ben retrieved the box and hurried into the parking structure. He stopped just long enough to pull out his phone and remove the battery, then returned to his car, turned his reversible jacket inside out, put on a Red Sox cap from the trunk, put the other box under his arm and hurried to the walkway. A small crowd watched as paramedics loaded a man on a stretcher.

Ben crossed the street, found the FedEx office and sent the package.

Instead of returning to Pittsburgh, he got back on the Interstate and headed north, away from Pittsburgh. After a few miles, he left the Interstate and drove secondary roads until he was sure that no one was following. All the while his mind was churning, wondering, worrying:

Whoever they were, they'd known where to find him.

The snatch-and-grab was a professional job, involving at least three people. But not *that* professional: There was no backup plan. So they were probably thugs, thieves, not government operatives.

But who the hell were they? Howell's gangster pals? Why would they want a box of shredded documents? Would they risk jail to avenge a man who lost a fight?

And then he realized that maybe, Howell didn't attack because of what Ben did to his nephew. But whoever had sent Howell wanted Ben to think that he did.

So this could only be about Geltkern and the murders.

He had stepped into something a lot bigger than a missing rabbi. Was it bigger than a scam to siphon $3.5 million from the Sanok Home?

It must be, he reasoned: Otherwise, Geltkern wouldn't be hanging around.

Ben had told no one that he was at the Renaissance Hotel. Or that he was going from there to the airport to send a package to California via FedEx.

Yet someone knew.

He might have been tracked to the hotel by hacking his phone GPS. Or someone in law enforcement could have been bribed or coerced to track his credit card purchases. Or both.

But who? Why? What was going on?

§

About 4:00 the next morning, Ben parked in the hotel's secure parking area and slipped into his room. As he packed his suitcase, he noticed the tray and the dirty dishes from his evening meal on the floor next to the door.

He stopped packing and picked up each dish, turning it over.

He found the device, about the size of a dime, glued to the concave bottom of the teapot.

Now he saw how his pursuers knew that he was headed for the airport.

Ben used a butter knife to pry it loose, then examined it closely to locate the faint outline of its battery compartment. He removed the battery with a pair of tweezers from his toilet kit, dropped the bug and its battery in a hotel envelope, and tucked them into his pocket.

He checked out of the Renaissance, then crawled into the backseat of his car and took a nap. He arose at 9:00; in the next hour, he found a Radio Shack, where he bought three cheap prepaid cell phones for cash.

He parked in the Squirrel Hill Jewish Community Center lot and walked to Mrs. Meltzer's. After a quick shower and a bagel, he went to the smaller of her second-floor guest rooms, where he turned on his iPhone, plugged it into its charger, and set up call-forwarding to relay incoming calls to one of his new prepaid phones. Now he had a stationary repeater. Anyone trying to find him by using his iPhone's GPS would assume that Ben was in his room.

An hour later, he was at the Sanok Home. With Avi Cohen's help, he concealed one of the prepaid phones, connected to its charger, in an unused room. As he had with the iPhone, he used call forwarding to route incoming calls to his other prepaid phone. Now, all incoming calls to his iPhone would be bounced to the Sanok Home before being bounced again to his second prepaid. It was crude, and it wouldn't deter a sophisticated hacker, but it would buy him some time if anyone tried to track him with his own phone.

The third prepaid was a backup, in case the one he used was compromised.

With the help of James, he used the Home's phone to call Abe's father-in-law, Arthur Baum, in Elizabeth, New Jersey. A polite woman in the congregation's office took the call and said that Rabbi Baum was out. She would ask him to call Rabbi Ben back as soon as possible.

As he walked toward his car in the Home's parking lot, his phone rang: Miryam, calling from Buenos Aires.

"Hello, my love," Ben said. "I'm in the middle of something and can't talk."

Miryam said, "Mrs. Meltzer said you were attacked by a brute. Are you okay?"

Ben laughed. "I'm fine. He never laid a finger on me. It's wonderful to hear your voice, but I really have to call you back. I love you, Marita."

"Promise me that you'll be careful, Ben."

"I promise."

"I love you. Bye."

"I'll talk to you soon."

Chapter Fifty-Five

Ben found Chief Laurence in his office, staring into the dregs of his coffee cup. He barely glanced up when Ben tapped on the frame of his open door. After a long moment, he sighed, then gestured for Ben to come in and sit down.

Laurence said, "I've sort of been expecting you."

Ben frowned. "Why is that?"

"Petty criminal name of Colby Howell. There was an all-points on him for escaping from the jail ward at Allegheny General."

Ben said, "I'd heard that he escaped."

Laurence said, "He was arrested for trying to brain you with a baseball bat and then stab you with a Buck knife."

Ben asked, "Did you find him?"

Laurence nodded. "I'm just a small-town cop, Rabbi. How is it that he was trying to brain you with a ball bat and stab you with a knife? Was it both at the same time or one after the other?"

Ben nodded. "I had to take the bat away from him before he hurt someone. Then he pulled a knife, and I used the bat to protect myself."

"Protect yourself as in fracturing his mandible and knocking out four teeth?"

Ben said, "Yes."

Laurence shook his head. "Never understood how it's always the little, wiry ones that the big bullies like to pick on. Did you really have to break his jaw?"

Ben said, "I feel bad about that. But please understand, when a big guy with a knife comes after me, my goal is to stay alive. The sooner I end the fight, the better it is, usually for both of us."

Laurence sighed. "Well, it doesn't much matter now. Patrol found his body early this morning."

Ben said, "He's dead?"

"One to the chest, two to the head. No casings, no bullets."

Ben shook his head. "I'm sorry to hear that, Jack."

"Where were you about 11:00 last night, Rabbi?"

"At the Pittsburgh Airport. I dropped off a FedEx package."

"Can you prove that? I mean, if you had to?"

Ben took out his wallet and found his copy of the air bill, which he passed to the chief. The chief looked it over and handed it back.

"Sorry, Rabbi, but I had to ask. You understand."

"I do. No offense taken."

Laurence scratched his head. "Seems like I saw something on the wire. An incident at the airport last night about 11:00. Guy on a motorcycle—the passenger, not the driver—tried to snatch something from a pedestrian and fell backward off the bike and broke his nose."

Ben said, "I saw the ambulance when I came out of the parking structure. The paramedics were putting someone in their ambulance."

"You don't know how he fell off backward and broke his nose?"

Ben shook his head. "Does sound a little strange. But maybe he turned to try to break his fall."

Laurence frowned. "Just a coincidence that you showed up then?"

"They close at 11:00. I had to get my package to the counter before then."

"You must admit, Rabbi, that lately, almost every time somebody gets killed or hurt, you're not far away."

Ben shrugged. "I came by just now to find out if there'd been an ID on the woman who died in the bowling alley fire."

Laurence pulled a face. "Not yet. State troopers send part of her remains off to the FBI to try to pull some DNA. But Filomina Jenston is missing. Nobody's seen her since the day before the fire. Found her car over at the Monroeville airport."

Ben shrugged. "Maybe she's just out of town for a few days."

Laurence frowned again. "Hope to God you're right."

Ben said, "No other women missing?"

"Not from Berona. I talked to Matt Ender, the fellow who manages the bowling alley, and he said he'd hired a cleaning crew, off the books, and there might have been a woman with them."

"Off the books, as in no green cards?"

"I didn't ask, and he didn't tell."

"Ender owns the bowling alley?"

Laurence shook his head. "Manages it for the Kendalls. Judge Kendall's clan."

"Clayton Kendall?"

"That's him. You've met his daughter, Alexis."

"The commercial real estate lady. Your boss's wife."

Laurence nodded.

Ben asked, "Speaking of your boss, any word on your contract?"

"Just hung up the phone when you barged in. Mr. Lustig thinks a younger man would do a better job, what with all the killings lately. Between now and the end of the year, I'm to use up my vacation and sick days. First of the year, I'm out."

Ben shook his head. "I'm very sorry to hear that, Chief."

"I'll be okay. They weren't paying me that much, and next summer I start on Social Security."

Ben stood up and put out his hand. "It's been a pleasure knowing you, Jack."

They shook hands, and Ben turned to go. Then he stopped and turned back.

"If you don't mind telling me, Jack, how was Howell dressed?"

"Jeans, work shirt, Steelers cap."

"And where was the body found?"

"Same place we found that car you asked about—the ravine below Kendall Heights."

Ben frowned. "That's public land?"

"The ravine is. Everything above it, both sides of the ridge, belongs to your people. The Sanok Home has owned that land for more than fifty years."

Chapter Fifty-five

Ben parked at the Jewish Community Center and, after speaking with Abe, left his car in an underground parking area reserved for management. Then he borrowed Abe's personal cell phone to call Miryam and ask her to call Abe's office. They spoke for ten minutes; Ben left nothing out as he described what had transpired since their last extended conversation.

Miryam said, "I feel like I'm letting you down. I should come and help you."

Ben said, "Absolutely not. It's not safe. Let's stick with the plan: You work on your thesis and get to know your family, I'll lose my virus, and in my spare time, I'll find Geltkern."

"I worry about you, Ben."

"Picture that resolute, resourceful man that braved a school of fearsome nuns and an overgrown puppy dog to leap into your backyard. The guy who could handle anything except a 99-pound beauty queen."

"A hundred and two, dearest. Did you know that you had me at, 'Put some clothes on'?"

"I must be slipping. Usually, my women faint when they see me dressed as a priest."

"I thought about fainting, but I was worried that I'd crush the tomato plants."

"Darling Marita, please don't even think of coming now. I'm close, I'm sure of it. If I wasn't, Geltkern wouldn't try so hard to stop me."

"Bloodhound Ben!"

As Ben hung up the phone, Abe pushed the office door open and peeked in. "All done?" he asked.

"Thanks for the use of your office, Abe."

"Guess who just called on my cell."

"The rabbi formerly known as Jeremiah Geltkern?"

Abe giggled. "I wish. The rabbi presently known as Arthur Baum. He gave me a number: the former Lois Farkas, now Lois Seligman."

Ben said, "She landed a banker?"

"Different branch of the family. Her husband is ten years her junior and makes enormous avant-garde sculptures out of industrial junk."

Ben shook his head. "It must be nice."

"Actually, he's been quite successful. He gets a million or three apiece, sometimes more, but you need a city lot just to exhibit one. Most of his clients are Fortune 500 outfits or municipalities."

"Give me her number, Abe."

Chapter Fifty-Five

Lois Seligman had a personal secretary, and the secretary had an assistant who screened calls. All that aside, Ben's use, twice, of the magical title "rabbi" and the fact that caller ID showed that he was calling from the Jewish Community Center, short-circuited the screening process. After less than five minutes, a pleasantly modulated voice with a fake mid-Atlantic accent came on the line.

"This is Mrs. Seligman," she said. "This is about Rabbi Farkas?"

Ben said, "This is Rabbi Ben Maimon, a colleague of Rabbi Arthur Baum."

Lois said, "You're calling about my late husband?"

Ben said, "In a way."

Lois said, "You do understand that he wasn't actually a rabbi. I mean, he had a piece of paper from some New Jersey diploma mill, but Al Farkas barely made it to shul on Yom Kippur unless I promised him a pastrami sandwich."

Ben laughed. "Actually, it's that piece of paper that I was calling about. The diploma from the Maharal Rabbinical Academy of Metuchen, New Jersey."

Lois snorted. "I gave it away, years ago."

Ben said, "It turned up again. The reason for my call is that I'd like to know who you gave it to."

Lois snorted again. "Oh, shit. Excuse my language, Rabbi. I gave it to one of Al's relatives, a man named ... wait, I'll think of it ... Yes, his name was Bernard Buchler. B-U-C-H-L-E-R. What has he done?"

Ben said, "I'm not sure that he's done anything. Why do you ask?"

Lois snorted again. "He said he was Al's cousin, and he wanted something to remember him by. Turns out he was actually some kind of a landsman, grew up in the same street in the South Bronx with Al. He was the ex-husband of a cousin by marriage, some kind of shirttail relative. But he was very smooth and convincing. A very slick ganef."

Ben said, "A thief? What did he steal?"

"My husband Al, *alev hashalom*, was a very funny guy. Not ha-ha funny but odd-funny. Secretive. He made a lot of money by kind of operating on the fringes, in the gray areas. And he was sure that one day he'd get caught out, that he'd lose everything. You understand?"

"Go on."

"So, Al stashed money all over the place. He had mailboxes in five different storefronts around the city, that I know of, and he kept bundles of cash in them."

Ben said, "He hid money behind his diploma, is that it?"

Another feminine snort rang in Ben's ear. "A Rembrandt. A little sketch of a fisherman, in brown ink, worth about half a million."

"How did this man, Buchler, know about that?"

"Beats me," Lois sighed. Her mid-Atlantic accent had given way to the comparatively nasal tones of Queens, New York. "But he *did* know. He went to London and tried to sell it, but it was a goddamn Rembrandt, you see, and Al had bought it from a dealer, and there was a record of the transaction, so they stalled him and called the art police, or whatever they are in England."

Ben asked, "Did you recover the sketch?"

"That bastard Buchler—he took off. They didn't know his name—the gallery, I mean—so he got away. Couple weeks later, he's back in the States, he calls, says he went to put the diploma in a nicer frame, and found a Rembrandt behind it, and would I like to have it back?"

Ben asked, "How much?"

"He asked for $20,000, but he took $5,000."

Ben said, "You've been very helpful, Mrs. Seligman. I just have a few more questions."

Lois said, "I'm not even sure that his name was really Buchler. Police said that he used a different name in London, Gold Coin, Korngold, something like that."

"What did he look like?"

"Oh, about average height, give or take, a spare tire and love handles. Bad skin. Balding on top. A ten-year-old suit. Big Jewish nose."

"How old was he?"

"Younger than Al. He'd be about sixty now, I think. Maybe a little more."

Ben said, "Is there anything else you recall about him?"

"He said that he was Al's classmate at that same rabbinical school, the diploma mill, but dropped out before he graduated. That was another reason he said that he wanted the diploma."

Ben said, "Did he say why he dropped out?"

Again the snort. "He didn't have to. He dropped out as soon as they stopped sending people to Vietnam. Al said that when they switched to a draft lottery, most of his classmates quit."

Ben said, "You've been extremely helpful, Mrs. Seligman. I very much appreciate both your time and your candor."

Lois said, "You're at Beth Israel, with Rabbi Baum?"

Ben said, "Not now. I went to the Jewish Theological Seminary with Rabbi Baum's son-in-law, Abe Smolkin."

"Which shul are you with now, Rabbi?"

Ben said, "Actually, I'm doing consulting for a Jewish Community Center."

Lois said, "I don't know what that schmuck Buchler did, but I hope you nail him. Let me know. I'd be happy to make a donation to your community center."

Ben said, "That's not necessary, Mrs. Seligman, but thank you."

"But you'll still let me know if you catch him?"

Ben said, "I just thought of something. Do you still have the Rembrandt?"

"On my bedroom wall."

"Did you have it appraised? I mean after Buchler returned it?"

Lois gave a little gasp. "Rabbi, do you think he gave me a copy?"

Ben said, "Ten years ago, you could get a high-quality Giclée copy for $100. Maybe a little more, if you had to match the paper. He could have found a private collector to buy the original for half its value."

"That sonofabitch!"

Ben said, "Please don't jump to conclusions. Have it appraised."

Lois said, "I will. And thank you, Rabbi."

§

Abe said, "Will you please tell me what's going on? I mean, I know some things. I know that Geltkern, whatever his name is, stole our Sanoker exhibit. I know that someone attacked you and that you think someone's using your phone's GPS function to track you. But what's the rest of it? What the hell is all this about, Ben?"

Ben said, "I'll give you a full briefing. But first, would you get your father-in-law back on the phone? I've got a question for him."

Abe pulled out his phone and speed-dialed. When Rabbi Baum answered, Abe handed Ben the phone.

Ben said, "Rabbi Baum, this is Ben. Thanks for connecting me with Lois Seligman."

Baum said, "What did she tell you?"

Ben said, "She recalls a guy named Bernard Buchler, who matches my missing rabbi's description. She said that he was a kind of distant relation to Farkas and that he asked for Al's Maharal Academy diploma as a keepsake. Turned out, though, that her husband had hidden a Rembrandt sketch beneath the diploma, and Buchler knew it. She said that he was Al's classmate in Metuchen but didn't graduate."

Baum remained silent so long that Ben feared the connection had been broken. "Rabbi Baum?" he asked.

"I'm thinking," Baum said. "Just wait a minute, will you?"

Ben heard him put the phone down.

He waited.

After several minutes, Baum came back on the line. "Sorry about that. I had to go find the file."

Ben asked, "What file is that, Rabbi?"

"I kept a copy of my investigation. I always thought that one day I might go back and try to see what I missed."

Ben asked, "Is there anything about Buchler?"

Baum said. "Bernie Buchler was Menachem Zelman's son-in-law. He enrolled to avoid the draft but spent most of his time hanging out on college campuses to recruit new students for Zelman."

Ben asked, "So he was part of the conspiracy?"

Baum said, "You should have been a lawyer! If the Middlesex County prosecutor had brought conspiracy charges instead of trying to build a case for fraud, he'd have gotten an indictment and put those ganefs on trial."

"Did you ever meet Buchler?"

"A few times. Why do you ask?"

"Do you remember what he looked like?"

"Like half the kids on campus. Long hair, a beard, thrift-store clothes."

Ben said, "Thanks for your help, Rabbi. Just one thing more: Do you suppose that Bernard Buchler was not his real name?"

Baum said, "I had no reason to suspect that he used an alias. He was still a kid, not much more than nineteen or twenty."

"Thanks again, Rabbi."

"Not at all. If you're ever over this way, stop in."

"I will do that."

Ben gave the phone to Abe. "Can I get something to eat first?"

Abe said, "For me, Kazansky's will deliver any sandwich."

Ben smiled. "Get me a corned beef on rye, with extra coleslaw, and let me ask Abby Silverblatt to come over so I don't have to go through all this again for her."

§

Ben swallowed the last bite of his sandwich, took a long pull on his Dr. Brown's ginger ale, and sat back in his chair in front of Abe's desk.

Next to him, sipping coffee from a paper cup, sat Abby.

Speaking slowly and carefully, thinking as he went, Ben described how the diploma was from a fake yeshiva and how it came to be in the possession of "Rabbi" Geltkern, whose real name might be Bernie Buchler, and what he knew and didn't know about "Geltkern's" involvement with the Sanok Home and the Sanoker Shul—the deaths of its board of directors, opening the home to new residents, the loan, the pension fund, and the murder of Merry Weinstock. He also recounted the similarities between what Geltkern seems to be up to and the activities of a young man who insinuated himself into a Pittsburgh church so many years earlier,

Ben paused and looked at Abby. "And then, today, the chief got fired," he said.

Abby said, "Yolanda says that he's a very nice man."

Ben said, "And an honest cop. There's something strange going on in Berona Township, and I think that it's somehow mixed up with whatever Bernie Buchler was up to.

"Chief Laurence suggested that the city manager, Lustig, controls the township council, instead of the other way around. His point man on the council is Lieutenant Geisel, head of the PD detective squad.

"Lustig's wife, Alexis, is a real estate mogul. She managed the vacant storefront where Buchler had the stolen Sanoker exhibit delivered. Her father is an important local judge. I approached Alexis in the guise of a businessman interested in renting a lot of space in downtown Berona for a call center, and she said that the price of doing that kind of business was to buy four expensive houses in a tract that isn't built on land that she doesn't own."

Abe asked, "A shakedown?"

Ben nodded. "Very likely."

Abby asked, "Why do you think the township is involved with Buchler?"

Ben paused to think. "First, there's this bed tax thing. Who ever heard of a bed tax on a board and care? Usually, that's only for hotels and motels, but the town council suddenly decides that the Home has to pay, and Weinstock goes along. So maybe that's a payoff of some kind, disguised as a tax payment."

Abby asked, "A payoff for what?"

Ben shook his head. "Police protection of the scam? For services yet to be rendered? I've got no idea at this point.

"When I got back to Berona Township yesterday, I learned that Filomina Jenston's office, which was in a bowling alley, had been torched. The police found a woman's body in the ruins. But they still haven't identified her body. It might be someone else.

"A few days later, at Mrs. Metzger's, Howell jumped me. He said it was revenge for kicking his young nephew's butt. But it turns out that he has ties to the local mafia. He escapes from the hospital, but then someone kills him and dumps his body in Berona Township. So maybe he didn't really come after me to avenge his family honor. Maybe someone sent him to kill me. Maybe that was Buchler.

Abby said, "I should never have asked you to get involved."

Ben said, "Water under the bridge, Abby. You couldn't have known what would happen. To finish, last night, before I learned about Howell, I checked into a downtown hotel. Around 10:30, I drove to the airport to send the shredded paper I recovered from the shul to a firm that reconstructs documents. I was followed to the airport. Three men tried to snatch the FedEx box. When I went back to the hotel, I found a listening device in my room.

"My conclusion is that Buchler is not working alone and that he has enough manpower and money to mount a sophisticated approach to whatever he's up to.

"I've also concluded that he wasn't out to kill me."

Abby asked, "How do you know that?"

"The guy he sent, Howell, had a record, but not as a killer. He's a strong-arm guy. Assuming that he ties back to Buchler, we know that Buchler had no trouble killing Stan or Mrs. Weinstock. Possibly, he ordered Witzelburg killed. If he wanted me dead, he'd have sent someone with a gun. Instead, I got one with a baseball bat.

"Then there's the incident at the airport. They didn't try to kill me, though they might have run me down. They didn't try to abduct me. They tried to snatch the FedEx package.

"They knew what was in it—the shredded documents I took from the shul—because they planted a bug in my room at the Renaissance, and they knew I was going to the airport to send them to somebody who could reconstruct the documents. So it was more important to get those documents than to kill me.

"Now that the documents have been sent, Buchler might change his objective and come after me."

Abe asked, "So now what?"

Ben said, "I've got a couple of theories. I'm going to test one, but I need more information. Abby, do you know how the shul gets its mail?"

Abby shook her head. "That's something I meant to tell you. Hank has been getting calls from creditors asking for payment, but we haven't had mail in weeks. I've got another member, a volunteer, trying to find out if we have a post office box."

Ben asked, "And what about bank accounts?"

Abby shook her head. "None in any of Berona Township's banks."

Abe said, "Why would they even need a bank account if the Home was paying all their bills?"

Ben nodded. "Good point. Abby, can you check with James, at the Home, and see if they get mail for the shul? That might be the answer."

"What if they do?"

"Get it to Jim, and have him go through it. Also, I'm going to write a check for the shul. Get someone to open a shul bank account. That will require some kind of paperwork, and you should put Jim on that as a priority. The first thing he should do is to find out if the secretary of state, or the Department of Corporations, whatever it's called in Pennsylvania, has issued the Sanoker Shul a business license as a nonprofit. Nonprofit status comes from an IRS filing. If there's nothing on file, hire a lawyer, or find one to volunteer. Otherwise, the shul won't be able to start a bank account. And it could be taxed on its income."

Ben dug out his checkbook, wrote two checks, and handed them to Abby. "If the shul can't open an account within the next week or so, cash the check made out to you, and tear up the one made out to Sanoker Shul. Open a checking account, and use that to pay salaries and bills. I'll cover any tax liability you incur."

Abby blinked away tears. "With all that's going on, you're still concerned about the future of this shul! I find that amazing."

Ben said, "This has *always* been about the shul. Find our rabbi, you said. And then Bernstein, who held the whole thing together, is murdered. Everything I've done since then has been about saving the shul. But don't dwell on it. It's *tikkun olam*, and I can afford the money."

Abby said, "Wow. Is there anything else?"

"Yes. Please bring Yolanda and Roland up to speed on what I've told you. And when you get home, would you make me four peanut butter and jelly sandwiches and half a dozen hard-boiled eggs? And throw in some apples and bananas, if you have any."

"Sure, but why?"

"I'm going to be a ghost for a few days, and I'll need some vittles that won't require going to a store or a restaurant."

"How can we reach you?"

"Unless it's a four-alarm emergency, don't. If it is, I'll give you a number to call when I come by for the food."

Abby got up to leave, and Ben followed her to the office door.

"One more thing," he said. "Have Roland call me here, as soon as he can."

"Not Yolanda, but her partner?"

"In this case, yes."

Chapter Fifty-six

Abe got up to stretch.

Ben said, "I need another favor. The center closes at 9:00. Is there a place in the building that I could sleep tonight? It needn't be fancy."

Abe gestured toward his couch. "Sleep here. Use my phone and computer. There's a shower in my bathroom. Towels are in the bathroom supply cabinet."

"Thanks, Abe."

"Why do you need to stay here tonight?"

"My room at Mrs. Meltzer's isn't safe. Apparently, Buchler has friends who can track my phone and my credit card purchases. That means hotels are not safe. Here you have landlines, a switchboard, and hard-wired Internet service. I can work here, try to get some information, go out fresh in the morning, maybe sleep in my car for a night or two. Maybe, by the weekend, I can wrap this up."

"You really think so?"

"No. But if I'm off by myself for awhile, I may be able to think this through in a way that helps me connect the dots."

"Ben, there's an awful lot of dots."

"More than I can keep track of, actually. The presentation I just gave you and Abby was as much for my own edification as for yours."

"Maybe you could explain something to me."

"If I can, sure."

"If Buchler didn't try to have you killed when you had the shredded documents, why would he want to kill you now?"

"Because his first priority was to get the documents back. Now he knows, I think, that I sent the papers to someone who could reconstruct them. If they are successful, and the pages provide some indication of what he has done or is doing, it probably won't be apparent to anyone except me. Or so he might think. As of now, I have to suppose that I'm at the top of his hit list."

"But now Abby and I know pretty much what you know."

"Exactly. So if anything happens to me, go to the police. Take Abby with you."

Abe glanced at his watch, then opened his desk and handed Ben a pair of keys. "This will get you in and out of the building and my office. I'm going to leave a little early today, do some shopping. And I'm going to send Mrs. Bender home, too. On my way out, I'll tell security that you'll be in the building tonight and that you may want to leave and come back."

"Thanks for everything, Abe."

Chapter Fifty-seven

A little after 6:00, Ben tapped on Abby's kitchen door. A moment later, it opened a crack and Zach said, "Rabbi Ben is here!"

He held the door wide, and Ben slipped past him into the warm, cheery kitchen. Yolanda looked up from the sink and smiled.

"We have your food. Abby's taking a bath. Can you stay for dinner? I made ceviche with fresh white fish, and Abby made a salmon loaf."

Ben said, "I haven't had salmon loaf since I was in short pants. My grandmother used to make it at least once a week."

"So you'll stay?"

"Honored, delighted, and very hungry."

"Roland is coming, too."

"The Duke of Bourbon!"

"Don't call him that anymore. He just joined a 12-step program."

Ben said. "That will be good for him. And I'll watch my tongue."

A living room window shattered, and something buzzed past Ben's ear to bury itself in the wall above the refrigerator.

As Ben pushed Zach and Yolanda to the floor, a second shot thudded into the wooden façade of the front porch. Then a third shot, much closer, and a fourth.

Ben got to his feet and ran to the door.

Easton crouched on the porch and fired a shot at a car burning rubber as it sped into the night.

Yolanda flew out of the kitchen, clutching her automatic. "You hit, Easton?"

Easton staggered to his feet. "Not this time."

Ben said, "Did you see who did the shooting?"

Easton shook his head. "I was climbing the stairs, my back to the street, when they fired. By the time I got behind a pillar and returned fire, they were driving off."

Ben said, "Any ID on the car?"

"An SUV, dark color, red, white and blue plate."

Yolanda said, "An Ohio plate?"

Easton said. "Probably. First three letters were OAQ. Or maybe DAO."

Yolanda said, "I'll call it in."

§

"Take us through it from the top," said Captain Ross, a balding man in a good suit with a lapel pin representing the Navy Cross.

Easton said, "I got a message from Miles Turlock that he wanted to see me."

Captain Ross said, "Tell me who that is."

"My T.O. Retired from homicide in the early '90s."

"So you went to see him. Where?"

"Shadyside. A little brick house off the corner of Howe and Walnut. When I got there, I saw smoke coming from the second floor and called 911. Then I ran inside.

"Miles was in the hallway next to his room. I carried him outside and called for an ambulance."

Ross asked, "Was Turlock conscious this whole time?"

Easton shook his head. "Not at first. I gave him CPR, and he came to about when the ambulance arrived. He kept trying to say something."

Ross asked, "What was that?"

Easton frowned. "Couldn't quite make it out. He said it three or four times, and finally I recorded with my phone. Sounded like 'Naaheddicharl.'"

Ben said, "Not Heddy, Charl?"

Ross frowned. "Rabbi, we agreed that you could listen but not speak. One more outburst, and you will leave, understood?"

Ben nodded his head, yes.

Ross asked, "Then what happened?"

"The ambulance took him away. When I got to the hospital, a doctor had pronounced him dead. There was nothing to do but get drunk, so I went to a meeting, and then I headed over here."

Ross asked, "What kind of meeting?"

Easton said, "I'm a friend of Bill's, sir."

Ross said, "Go on."

"On the way to Officer Sanchez's house, I became aware that I was being followed by a man on a motorcycle."

Ben opened his mouth to speak but thought better of it.

Ross asked, "Can you identify the motorcyclist?"

"Leather jacket, helmet with dark goggles. It was dark; I didn't really get a good look at his face. I parked down the block from Officer Sanchez's house and started walking. The motorcycle buzzed by, and a few seconds later a big SUV stopped in front of her house. I went up the stairs, and someone started shooting.

"I took cover behind a pillar and returned fire. Don't think I hit anyone."

Ross scowled. "You said you got a message. What kind of a message? Email?"

Easton frowned. "Miles was old-school, sir. Computers, even just email, baffled him. He called the squad, left word with my boss."

Ross said, "Do you know why Turlock wanted to see you?"

"I called him back. He said it wasn't right for the phone. See, he had cancer. Small-cell lung cancer. End-stage. Docs gave him months, maybe weeks. I kind of got the feeling that he wanted to say goodbye."

Ross said, "We'll stop here. Rabbi, I have some matters to discuss with Detective Easton that don't concern you or Officer Sanchez."

§

Ben and Yolanda waited in the parking lot for Easton to finish. He appeared exhausted as he climbed into Yolanda's car.

Easton said, "If I'm alone tonight, I'm probably gonna drink. Do you have a couch where I could crash?'

Yolanda nodded. "Stay in our guest room."

As she steered out of the lot, Ben said, "What did Ross ask you?"

"Just some bullshit about Miles."

Yolanda said, "What?"

"If I knew that Miles had been forced to retire. If I knew that he took Mob money to look the other way on certain cases."

Ben said, "Is that true?"

Easton shook his head. "All bullshit. I never heard anything like that. But that's Internal Affairs. They start an investigation, even if there's nothing to investigate. The file never goes away."

"What did Miles do after he retired?"

"He'd saved a little money. Bought a newsstand. Downtown, the hotel district."

Yolanda said, "How could he save money on a detective's salary?"

Easton said, "He never married. Lived with his mother until she died. His mom wasn't rich, but she had some kind of income—an inheritance, something like that. Miles didn't drink, or at least not much. Not that I ever saw him buy a round. He smoked, but believe it or not, he rolled his own because it was cheaper. We'd stop for lunch, and he'd pull out a sandwich that his mother packed him. Got his suits at thrift stores. Bought an old Chevy pickup for $600 and drove it almost twenty years. Never had a girlfriend for very long, mostly because he was such a cheapskate. Hell, yes, he could have saved the money."

Yolanda asked, "Was he gay?"

Easton sighed. "That was another thing Ross asked. Hell, I don't know if he was gay. But not that I ever saw."

Ben said, "Could his newsstand have been a front for a book?"

Easton bit his lip. "Possibly. Miles always denied it, but ... he seemed to know a lot of street guys. Once in awhile, he'd tell me something. It always checked out."

Ben said, "Like what?"

"Like who took down a certain score. One time, just before Christmas, a furrier got robbed and lost forty mink coats. Miles gave me the fence, and with a little boost from me, nothing physical, the guy gave up the robbers. Another time, a judge got hit. Miles knew who pulled the trigger, not that that it ever did me any good."

Yolanda asked, "He was your CI?"

"Nothing formal. Never gave him a dime. You run a downtown newsstand that's open late, you keep your eyes open and your mouth shut, you hear things. He was a good friend, is all."

Ben said, "Let me change the subject. Do you recall the name of the murder victim in that old identity-theft case?"

Easton said, "He mentioned it. Right now I can't think of it. Why?"

Ben said, "A thought occurred to me. Something I want to check."

Yolanda asked, "Wouldn't all the names be in the original file?"

Easton shook his head. "Ross has the files from every case Miles ever worked. He'd never let me look at them."

Yolanda turned the corner and stopped in front of the Jewish Community Center. "Your hotel for the night?"

Ben got out of the car and stepped to Easton's window. "I'm sorry for your loss, Roland. It's always painful losing a friend."

Chapter Fifty-Eight

Although it was nearly midnight by the time Ben returned to Abe's office, he turned on his desktop computer. First, he emailed Miryam to tell her that he would be moving around and keeping a low profile so he'd be unreachable by phone for a few days. He Googled Allegheny County government until he found a public database of property records. Then he opened a second window and used Google Maps to find the Sanok Home address.

Listed as a not-for-profit under the "church" category, the Home paid township assessments but no property tax.

But the documents Ben wanted, records of ownership changes, were not available: Everything before 1986 was on paper. These were public records, but they were stored in a county assessor's office.

§

At 8:00 the next morning, Friday, Ben left his car in secure parking under the JCC and boarded a bus for downtown Pittsburgh. His first stop was a private bank which concealed its presence behind an inconspicuous office façade in an innocuous five-story building next to a Catholic school. Ben's principal banking connection was a private bank in California which maintained reciprocal relationships with select private banks around the world. He was almost out of cash; he might have used an ordinary ATM, but that would limit the amount he could withdraw in any 24-hour period, and it would leave a record in a national banking network. The Bank of B. Cohen, in Burbank, California, and its partner banks, maintained separate and highly secure private networks. With an ID and two passwords, there was no limit to the cash that Ben could withdraw from his funds. And almost no one would know about it.

Ten minutes later, with $5,000 distributed between his pockets and a backpack, he left the building and walked three blocks to the Carnegie Public Library.

There he found a reference librarian and asked for microfilm from the *Pittsburgh Post-Gazette* for 1968 and 1969.

The librarian explained that she was permitted to give him only one box of film at a time. Each box held approximately four months of every page in the so-called home edition of the newspaper.

He loaded the first roll of microfilm into its viewer, an antiquated arrangement of spindles, rollers, light and viewing screen, then scrolled through the pages, stopping at each front page and at subsequent local news pages. He wanted an account of the church robbery and subsequent identity thefts of its members, followed by the related murder, because such accounts usually include names.

Maybe, just maybe, Ben reasoned, he might find the name of the young man who stole the documents.

It was tedious work that made Ben grateful for the eye surgery he'd had several weeks earlier.

By noon, he had scanned two boxes of microfilm. Hungry, he left the library and strolled a few blocks to Mellon Square, where he bought a cup of bad coffee from a cart, then sat down and ate two of Abby's hard-boiled eggs, one of her peanut butter and jelly sandwiches, and a banana. He might have gone to any of downtown Pittsburgh's fine restaurants, but he knew people were looking for him. Ben wanted to be out in the open, where he could see anyone approaching him.

When he finished eating, he returned to the library.

By 3:00, he was almost through 1969 without finding mention of a church robbery. He'd have to leave soon, take a bus back to change clothes, rent a car and drive out to the Sanok Home. For a moment, he considered not going. He pictured the disappointment of the small flock of learned and observant elders whom he had called on to help him turn the Sanoker Shul into a real congregation.

No way he would abandon them.

The reference librarian appeared. "We close at 3:30, sir. I'll need all your materials back by twenty after."

"Of course," Ben said. He had two rolls of 1969 film yet to inspect. Carefully threading the next-to-last into the machine, he began to scan.

Near the end of the roll, he found it, published on the Tuesday following Thanksgiving 1969: a church burglarized over the four-day Thanksgiving weekend. Congregation B'nai Abe Messiah, a Shadyside congregation of Messianic Christians. A teenage volunteer was sought for questioning. His name was Buddy Butcher.

Buddy Butcher. Bernard Buchler. Not a great alias, but then he was just a kid.

Now, Ben thought, if I can only find the name of the man who was murdered.

"I'm sorry, sir, but I have to ask you to stop now," said the librarian.

Ben turned to look at the woman. "Are you open Sunday?"

"Not since the latest budget cuts. And just so you know, we used to be open until nine on Fridays."

Chapter Fifty-nine

Ben got off a city bus about a mile west of Squirrel Hill, walked to a local car rental agency, and rented a two-year-old Toyota, leaving $2,000 in cash as a deposit instead of a credit card transaction. Then he headed for Berona Township.

At the Sanok Home, he learned that Avi Cohen wasn't feeling well and that James had taken him to a doctor in Pittsburgh that morning.

After the Shabbat service, he shared pound cake and tea with the worshippers, then found Carmela Bañuelos, the night nurse, and asked about Cohen.

"He was admitted to Pittsburgh Medical this afternoon," she said. "He's in the ICU. More than that I can't tell you."

§

When he left the Home, Ben drove his rented car over back roads on a roundabout return to Pittsburgh. He parked on a street two blocks from the Community Center, slipped into the building by the back door and told the heavy-set, middle-aged guard that he was back.

Then he went up to Abe's office, where he dined on boiled eggs and stale peanut butter sandwiches. After eating, he stripped off his clothes and headed for the shower. Afterward, drying off, he glanced out the window of the second-floor office and realized that he had made a terrible mistake.

It was almost midnight on a Friday evening. On Shabbat. Every office in this building should be dark. Buchler might not be a rabbi, but he would surely know that much. Ben switched off the light, dressed, stuffed his belongings into his backpack and cautiously opened the office door, listening.

It was utterly quiet.

Ben paused, thinking. He had three times passed the guard's desk after hours. Each time, the guard was watching a portable television set.

Maybe the guard had turned off his TV while making his rounds.

Ben slipped on the backpack, quietly locked the door behind him, and headed for the rear stairs, intending to go out the back door. But as he neared the elevators, he heard the unmistakable hum of an ascending car.

But the elevators were locked down when the building closed.

Ben turned and dashed back into the darkened front stairwell. He heard the elevator bell chime as the car arrived.

The stairwell lights came on, and he heard the sound of footfalls from below. Two men, from the sound, were slowly climbing toward him.

He had only a few seconds to make a move.

Pressing his ear to the door, he listened as someone wearing squeaky shoes approached from the direction of the elevator.

When the squeaks were almost at the door, Ben flung it open, then leaped out.

For a fleeting instant, he thought he'd attacked the guard.

But the man who fell backward, his nose spouting blood, the man wearing the guard's jacket and cap, was younger and thinner and, until an instant earlier had been carrying a pump shotgun.

Ben scooped it up and sprinted for the rear stairs.

§

Reaching the stairs, Ben heard shouts. As the door closed behind him, a bullet shattered the fireproof window.

He leaped down to the first landing, took the second flight three steps at a time to the ground floor and was out the door and on the street before the second shot ricocheted down the stairwell.

He looked around, then shoved the barrel of the shotgun into the inch-wide space between the brick wall and the heavy-gauge steel rain downspout. He tugged on the stock until he felt something snap.

He dropped the gun and ran.

He was almost a block away when he heard a motorcycle engine winding up behind him. Instinctively, he ducked into an alley, taking cover from street lights in the deep shadow of a garage, meanwhile silently cursing himself for a fool for tossing the gun.

The motorcycle blew by, affording Ben a glimpse of a driver and a passenger gripping another shotgun.

Ben waited until the motorcycle's engine faded into the city's background noise, then cautiously moved back to the street and peered around the corner.

"Gotcha!" yelled the man who Ben had knocked flat. Ten feet away, the thug leveled the broken shotgun at Ben. In the yellow, other-worldly light of sodium-vapor street lamps, the blood on his face was black.

"Finish him, and let's get the hell out of here," said a man behind the gunman, out of Ben's sight. The nearer man raised the shotgun to eye level, pointed it at Ben.

Ben said, "I don't think that's a good idea—"

The gun exploded. Ben felt the heat of buckshot speeding past his cheek.

The gunman's face was a mass of blackened flesh. Gripping the ruined shotgun, he screamed as he stumbled in a slow, tight, circle before collapsing to the pavement.

A siren sounded in the distance. Then another, and another.

Ben turned and dashed back into the alley. He was halfway down the block, running flat out when he realized that he was behind Ro Meltzer's house.

The wooden picket fence was six feet high. The gate, he knew, was padlocked on the inside, so Ben grabbed the top of the fence, pulled himself up, swung his legs over and dropped into the yard. The house was silent and dark.

He climbed the exterior staircase, checked the door to his room. The tiny scrap of paper he'd jammed between frame and door was right where he left it.

He used his key and entered, moving carefully, lights off.

He locked the door, stripped off his clothes and sat on his bed.

Then he found his Radio Shack phone and dialed Abe's home.

Abe answered on the first ring. "Ben?"

Ben said, "Yes. Listen, there's been a break-in—"

"The police just called, a minute ago. Are you okay?"

"I'm fine. Your office is locked, there's nothing of mine in it. But the cops will find some blood on the second floor, near the front stairwell. It's not mine. They might also find a body around the corner from your place. His blood will match."

Abe said, "You killed someone, Ben?"

Ben said, "I was trying to escape. He aimed his shotgun at me. I tried to warn him that the gun was broken, but he pulled the trigger, and it blew up in his face. He might still be alive, but there was another gunman, so I didn't stick around."

"But you're okay?"

"All good. I'm worried about your guard, though."

"Cops have him. The robbers got the drop on him, put him out with an injection of something. But he's gonna be okay."

Ben said, "Thank God for that. I'll call you after Shabbat."

Abe said, "Where are you now?"

Ben said, "Better that you don't know."

Chapter Sixty

Yolanda waved as Ben got out of his rental car in the Sanoker Shul parking lot. She left her own car and came over to say, "I wasn't sure you'd be here."

Ben smiled, "And why is that, Officer Sanchez?"

Yolanda smiled back. She wore the blue uniform of a Pittsburgh police officer. "I have to go to a funeral this afternoon."

Ben asked, "Miles Turlock?"

She nodded. "What can you tell me about what happened last night at the JCC?"

"I was using the director's office and foolishly turned on the lights."

Yolanda said, "And that shouldn't happen in a Jewish building on Shabbat. Do you think Geltkern—I mean, Buchler—was watching?"

"It's a block from Mrs. Meltzer's. If he had someone in the neighborhood and they knew what to watch for…"

"We have the break-in on video. They rang the bell, and when the guard went to the door, they put a shotgun in his face and threatened to kill him if he didn't open up. Then they took his hat and jacket and injected him with heroin."

Ben said, "They didn't see the video camera and get the tape?"

"According to Rabbi Smolkin, when the JCC upgraded its video about three years ago, they moved the recording device to a remote location, camouflaged the camera, and left the old equipment, which used VHS tapes, in place as a decoy."

Ben said, "I've got maybe five minutes before I have to prepare for the service. Can we talk afterward?'

Yolanda shook her head. "My funeral is at one o'clock. St. Mary's in Bloomfield. Tell me what you can now, and we'll talk again tomorrow."

Ben shrugged, then described his encounter in the JCC building and afterward. "

Yolanda said, "Did you know the gun would explode?"

Ben shook his head. "I didn't want to carry a gun because police might take me for one of the robbers. But I couldn't just leave a loaded shotgun where anyone could find it. So I tried to disable it. I didn't intend for anyone to try to use it, and I'm sorry that it killed the gunman."

Yolanda smiled. "You're really something! Guy tries to murder you, and you feel sorry for him."

Ben said, "Hillel teaches us that to save one life is to save the entire world."

"Then I've got good news. The guy's name is Pete Casalnuovo, from Youngstown, and he needs a new face—but he's alive and talking."

Ben said, "Youngstown again! He's in the Mob?"

Yolanda said, "His uncle is a capo. Killing you was to be Pete's initiation. He was gonna make his bones, and you were to provide them."

Ben frowned. "Then I will have an even better reason to say *Birkhat Ha Gomeyl*, the prayer for surviving great danger. And I better get started because I also need to think up something to use as a sermon."

CHAPTER SIXTY-ONE

Ben said, "Shabbat Shalom!"

The congregation responded, "Shabbat Shalom."

Ben said, "Today, I want to do some things a little differently. Instead of delivering a lesson after the Torah reading, I'll take a few minutes now and update you on what I have learned about Rabbi Geltkern."

In a few sentences, Ben described how he had unmasked Geltkern as a fraud, traced his activities back to the New Jersey diploma mill in the '60s, and shared his opinion that Geltkern was behind the repeated attempts on his life.

"I tell you this now because, if I am a target, then being here puts each of you at risk. So I'm going to leave the room for a few minutes, and your elected representatives can ask you if you want me to continue as your volunteer rabbi. I should also suggest that, if a majority wants me to stay on for a while, each of you is still free to decide for yourselves whether you want to share this space with me or whether you and your families would feel safer by leaving."

Ben pulled off his tallit, or prayer shawl, and left the room as a stunned Abby hurried to the bimah.

Ben stationed himself in a corner of the foyer. After a few minutes, a man and a woman, each carrying a toddler, hurried through the space, looking neither left nor right. A moment later, a second family, with one child, followed them out.

Ten minutes later, a tall, robust young man that Ben recognized as Mort Reubens, the security guard from the township recycling center, found Ben waiting near the front door.

Reubens said, "Rabbi, a few people left, but for the rest of us, it was unanimous. We want you to stay."

Chapter Sixty-Two

Ben spent that night in a bed-and-breakfast in Scottdale, a tiny town southeast of Pittsburgh whose only claim to fame was the birthplace of one of the founding fathers of network television. Early Sunday morning, he drove his rental over back roads toward McKeesport, a Pittsburgh exurb. The town straddled the Monongahela River; as he neared the waterway, a low ridge came into view. It had been cleared, and a network of streets was laid out between home sites in various stages of completion. A roadside billboard declared that Riverview Heights would offer ninety luxury homes priced from upward of half a million dollars.

At that moment, things clicked into place. Ben knew what Buchler's con was and who was probably in it with him.

§

Ten minutes later, after crossing the bridge, he entered a warm, cheery café, where he found Yolanda and Roland drinking coffee.

Easton said, "Good timing, Rabbi. We just got here."

As Ben joined their table, a waitress appeared. When they had ordered, Ben looked at Easton. "Your text said good news?"

Easton said, "Casalnuovo, your now faceless friend, identified four guys with him at the Jewish Community Center, including the two waiting outside for you. Youngstown PD grabbed all four yesterday."

Ben asked, "But who sent them? Is he in custody?"

Yolanda shook her head. "Casalnuovo says his uncle, Nick Siragusa, ordered the hit. The PD brought the capo in, and an hour later, he posted a million-buck bail."

Ben said, "I'd like to know why the mob wants me dead."

Easton frowned. "Probably because they're in for a piece of whatever it is that Buchler's after."

Yolanda said, "They may try again, Rabbi. You still need to be careful."

Ben said, "If Casalnuovo is talking, maybe he knows who killed Mrs. Weinstock. Or who torched her house."

Easton produced his notebook. "I'll add that to the list. He's scheduled for surgery today. It may be awhile before they let me talk to him again."

The waitress appeared with plates of food. The next several minutes passed in near-silence as three hungry people ate.

§

The plate empty, Ben pushed it away. "I think I know what Buchler's con is about—at least part of it—and why he's still hanging around."

The two officers leaned forward.

"There are a couple of things I'll need to check before I can be sure, but part of it is a real-estate swindle."

Easton said, "How do you figure?"

Ben sat back in his chair, choosing his words carefully. "The Sanok Home is a nonprofit managed by a board of directors chosen by its residents. But over the last four years, one by one, the only residents who could serve as directors all passed away.

"My guess is that Buchler and Weinstock were waiting for that. When the last one died, they took control, probably by creating a phony board comprising living residents who knew nothing about it. Or about much of anything else. Residents, maybe, who couldn't tell you what year it was.

Then they forged board minutes to give them legal cover to make changes. For example, the board supposedly authorized the establishment of the Sanoker Shul, along with Buchler's second salary and expenditures for the Shul.

Easton asked, "Where does the real estate come in?"

"I have to make sure of this, but I think the Home owns that ridge, both sides. On the eastern half, below the cemetery, is a wooded area. The western side gets beautiful sunsets and views of downtown Pittsburgh, the river, and the countryside. The township has struggled for years, but I met someone in Berona—Alexis Lustig, the township manager's wife—who described a development of luxury homes on land that now belongs to the Sanok Home. There's even a brochure! She's counting on selling homes to hundreds of families and sparking a business boom and pump lots of tax money into township coffers.

"On my way here this morning, I passed a hill about half a mile from the river. It's maybe half as high and half as long as the Sanok property. They're building ninety luxury homes on the slope facing the river. I think you could put 300 large homes on the western slope of the Sanok property. That pencils out at upward of $150 million, minus construction, land acquisition, and development. If they steal the land, they could clear at least $75 million. Or they could just flip the property to another developer for a quick $50 or $60 million. And those numbers are very conservative."

Yolanda said, "Buchler plans to steal the property and develop it?"

Ben said, "Sort of. He's a con artist, a thief. Buchler, if that's really his name, is tied up with Alexis Lustig's husband, the township manager, and maybe Alexis's father, a judge. They're going to steal the Sanok property, though I don't know how yet."

"This morning, on the drive up, I remembered that Chief Laurence told me that the Sanok property is officially called Kendall Heights."

Yolanda half-raised her hand. "So the township manager and his wife already have plans for that property? How can that be?"

"Buchler will deliver it to them, for a price."

Easton smiled. "That explains the mob's interest. Either they're in for a piece of Buchler's take, or partnered with Lustig to develop it. Or both."

Ben said, "Of course! Roland—you're a genius! Why didn't I see that? They can wash dirty money through Lustig's company, skim the developer's proceeds, and make another big profit on the back end."

Yolanda said, "I don't understand how Buchler gets the property."

Ben said, "I think it could be why he looted the Home's cash. He wants to force it into bankruptcy so their principal creditor takes it over. Mina Jenston, the Home's bookkeeper, told me that they were so broke that Weinstock took out a line of credit."

Easton said, "If we knew who issued that loan—"

"I'd be very surprised if it wasn't someone named Lustig or Kendall. But Jenston's office and records went up in smoke when someone torched her building. She said that everything was backed up, off-site, but not where."

Easton asked, "Where's Jenston now?"

Ben frowned. "I don't know. A woman's body matching her general description was found in the office. As of the last time I spoke with Chief Laurence, no positive ID. By the way, he's out of a job. Lustig put him on leave until his contract runs out."

Easton said, "Another good reason to suspect that Lustig is involved in all this."

Yolanda said, "Explain this: Buchler needed Weinstock to do all this stuff. First, why would she do it? Second, this sounds like a long, complicated scheme. Who walks in the door with all this under his hat?"

Ben nodded. "Fair questions. Second question first: I have a former classmate, David Siegel, Rabbi David Siegel, who's doing hard time in Illinois for selling Red Sea condos to investors. Condos that could never be built except underwater.

"I stay in touch with him. I send him kosher food, and I drop in to see him once in awhile. He claims to have repented and intends to dedicate the rest of his life to making amends to those he swindled. The Red Sea caper was hardly his first or even his last. So maybe David has reformed. Maybe."

"Anyway, David once told me that most guys go into their first long con with a plan, and stick to it, come what may. These guys are called 'inmates.' In prison, they meet their betters and learn to improvise, to react to sudden opportunities."

Easton said, "You think Buchler had something else in mind when he got himself hired at the Home?"

Ben nodded, yes. "I'm not sure what, maybe a Medicare scam or something else. Maybe he wasn't sure, either. Maybe Weinstock just seemed like a pigeon that he could fleece or use. Or maybe he had a scheme in mind but later changed his objective. Or maybe it was more than one. To start, he got himself two part-time salaries that were more than enough to live on while he considered his next moves."

Easton asked, "If he was the same guy that ripped off all those church members in the '60s, was he maybe looking to do something like that with the synagogue's members?"

Ben said, "I hadn't thought of that. But not much of a payoff for a four-year con."

Yolanda asked, "What about Weinstock? How did she figure in this mess?"

Ben sighed. "She was a widow whose husband died very young. She was not an attractive woman, and she was lonely. Owned a crappy house in a dying neighborhood with a two-hour commute. She had nothing but her job, and when that ended, she'd be out without a dime for her years of service. Then along comes a silver-tongued rabbi who lavishes attention on her and promises her not just love but a secure retirement, a chance, finally, to have the good things in life."

"That had to be hard to resist. So she went along. She facilitated."

Yolanda said, "That's why Buchler kept the place open?"

Ben said, "I think so. It was also a way to get cash. They required new patients to sign over their estates in exchange for lifetime care in a first-class establishment. And that came to about $5 million. For a long con, that's a nice payoff. He got Weinstock to invest most of that in a so-called pension fund."

Easton said, "Who else at the Home qualified for a pension?"

Ben said, "That was the beauty of the scheme. Only Weinstock. But to keep the other employees happy, Weinstock promised them severance payments and medical insurance for a year after it closed."

Easton said, "If there's anything left in the fund, that is."

Yolanda said, "I'm really starting to hate this guy."

Easton asked, "The bookkeeper told you all this?"

Ben said, "She did. I haven't seen the documents, but she said the money went to something called K & L Associates, supposedly an insurance broker. We need to find them, see what they know."

Easton asked, "Could the 'L' be Lustig?"

Ben said, "If it is, then the 'K' is probably Kendall—Alexis Kendall Lustig or her father, the judge."

Yolanda asked, "But if Weinstock collects her pension, how does Buchler get his hands on it?"

Ben frowned. "I've been thinking about that for weeks. And I just realized that I've been inspecting the trees and ignoring the forest."

Easton said. "Lay it on us, Rabbi, so we can all feel stupid together."

Ben said, "She was a frumpy widow. Buchler made her feel beautiful and desirable, and he was sleeping with her. She was about to come into a pension worth millions. So he married her."

Chapter Sixty-three

Yolanda said, "If they got married, there has to be a record of that somewhere—if not in Pennsylvania, then surely a nearby state."

Easton said, "We'll have to search the marriage records in every county."

Ben said, "Before you do, ask yourself this: You're a sixty-something widow. You've been alone for forty-odd years. Now this wonderful, charismatic man puts millions in your purse and asks you to marry him. And to keep that quiet for awhile. Are you going to have a civil ceremony in some nearby cow county?"

Easton asked, "If Lustig and his wife are in this, why doesn't she have her father, the judge, perform the ceremony?"

Ben cocked his head. "Maybe. But does Buchler really want his pigeons to know about each other?"

Easton frowned. "He was hustling the Lustigs, too?"

Ben spread his hands wide. "We have to assume that there's always something in a con that whoever's running it wants to keep quiet. I can't believe that he would let Weinstock know that he was buddies with the Lustigs. Or that he'd tell Lustig that he was marrying Weinstock after she collected a $3.5 million pension."

Yolanda said, "Las Vegas. Or maybe Reno."

Ben said, "Bingo."

Yolanda said, "I'll make some calls as soon as we get back to Pittsburgh."

Easton said, "I've got this. My ex-wife's cousin is a Clark County deputy."

Ben said, "See if they left a permanent address on the marriage license application. A place to mail the certificate."

Yolanda asked, "You think he was that dumb?"

Ben shook his head. "You never know. Or maybe Weinstock filled it out."

Easton swallowed the dregs of his coffee and got to his feet. "We should be getting back," he said.

Ben stood up. " We need to make a stop on the way."

Yolanda asked, "How long is this going to take?"

Ben said, "First, I need to look up an address. After that, four minutes, tops."

Chapter Sixty-Four

The parking lot of the big church on the corner overflowed with cars; by noon, a few drivers began edging out of the lot through an alley behind the church lot that led to a cross street.

At 12:09, the church doors opened, and people spilled down the stairs and headed for their cars. At the wheel of Ben's rental, Yolanda turned into the alley a block south of the church and drove north, toward the church.

She stopped halfway up the block.

At 12:10, Easton backed into the other end of the same alley, blocking its entrance. He turned off the engine, got out and raised the Crown Victoria's hood.

At 12:11, wearing a dark blue blazer over blue slacks, Ben got out of the rental and tried the gate on the sixth house south of the church. It was unlatched, and he entered the yard, leaving the gate open.

In the yard, he pulled a ski mask over his head.

He ran to the kitchen entrance and opened the screen door. To his surprise, the door behind it was ajar. Cautiously, with a gloved hand, he pushed it open to find himself in a tiny space, six feet square, empty except for two bundles of newspapers and a pair of women's galoshes. The kitchen door beyond it was open.

"Mina?" he called. There was no response.

He stepped into the kitchen. Directly ahead of him, fastened to the refrigerator door and half-hidden amid a clutter of notes and cartoons, was a tiny cellphone and camera device like the one he'd first found at the shul. He ignored it.

The kitchen was a wreck. Pots, pans, broken dishes, glasses and tableware were scattered across the floor and counters. Every cabinet drawer was open.

He picked his way through the mess as fast as he could, counting silently each second as it passed. The dining room was a fair imitation of the kitchen. The living room and a tiny office were likewise trashed, drawers pulled out and contents dumped on the floor. He ran up the stairs to the second floor and found similar chaos and vandalism in the two small bedrooms and a bathroom.

There was no sign of Mina.

The clock in his head was at four minutes, 12 seconds when Ben heard the first siren.

He hurried back downstairs, pulled off the ski mask as he stepped into the yard, then ran through the open gate down the alley. He got in beside Yolanda, and she edged forward to join the traffic jam leaving the church. At the other end of the alley, Easton dropped the hood, climbed into his car and drove away.

Siren howling, a Berona Township patrol car braked at the corner, threaded its way through the jam of homebound churchgoers and stopped at the sixth house.

Ben said, "Four minutes and forty-some seconds."

Yolanda said, "You didn't mention the half an hour in traffic."

Ben said. "The house was trashed. Went through every room."

Yolanda said, "Mina wasn't there?"

Ben shook his head. "If she's not dead, she's hiding."

Chapter Sixty-Five

Ben got out of the Crown Victoria, said goodbye to Yolanda and Easton, and entered the hospital, where a security guard checked his ID, then directed him to Doctor Rao's office on the seventh floor.

When the elevator door opened, he found Rao waiting.

Ben said, "Thank you for meeting me on a Sunday, Doctor."

Rao smiled. "Not at all. I usually come in Sunday afternoon to review data."

Ben said, "Why are you out here, instead of in your office?"

Rao sighed. "I went to the restroom and locked myself out. I left my phone inside, as well. I couldn't go downstairs to find the guard because I was expecting you. So I decided to wait until you arrived, and we could go downstairs together."

Ben laughed. "Give me half a minute."

He fished in his jacket pocket for the modified jeweler's screwdrivers, worked the lock on the office door for a few seconds, then held the door open.

Rao was dumbstruck.

"I've seen that in the movies, but...."

"It's a matter of a little knowledge and a lot of practice."

Inside, Ben waited for Rao to seat himself behind the desk.

"I need to ask a favor, Doctor."

"Actually, you might not need to. I went over your data this morning, and I want to make some adjustments in your treatment schedule."

Ben cocked an eyebrow.

Dr. Rao said, "Oh, it's good news. Recall that we took some marrow from your iliac crest a few weeks back?"

Ben nodded. "Not as painful as I'd feared. What did you find?"

Rao smiled. "It's what we didn't find. No virus."

Ben's eyes widened. "I'm cured? Just like that?"

Rao shook his head. "It's not that simple. But a very positive step nonetheless. If this were not a controlled trial, I would say you were in remission, schedule follow-ups at six-month intervals, and, barring complications, pronounce you cured after five virus-free years. Then I'd write a paper and collect my Nobel Prize.

"But that is not our situation. This is the same phenomenon that we observed in an earlier trial. We, therefore, anticipated that, at this stage of the treatment cycle, a small fraction of the larger group—in this case, eighteen individuals—would appear to be virus-free."

Ben opened his mouth to speak, but Rao held up a hand.

"Keep in mind that the virus is extremely small and that while our instruments are far more sensitive than those available even five years ago, we cannot be sure that we have eliminated every last virus. Specifically, in a previous trial, some of those who initially tested zero virus later showed a significant level of the virus. Others remained at or near zero. Also, keep in mind that we sampled marrow from only one part of your body. What were you going to say?'

Ben smiled. "It was not important."

Rao smiled back. "Tell me anyway, please. I've heard that you are a keen observer with a very logical mind."

Ben shook his head. "It's nothing like that. Do you know of the Jewish fascination with *gematria*?"

Rao shook his head, no

"It's numerology. The Hebrew alphabet uses letters for numbers: Aleph is one, beit is two, gimel is three, and so forth. By adding the values of its letters, every Hebrew word has a numerical value. The letters of the word hai, life, total eighteen. You said you found eighteen patients with no virus. That was my first thought: Life means no virus.

"As I said, not important."

Rao smiled. "But interesting, nevertheless. In any event, had you not contacted me today, I would have spoken with you tomorrow. We want to create a group within the cohort—the eighteen virus-free patients—and alter your protocol somewhat."

Ben said, "What did you have in mind?"

"We'd like to take marrow samples from several parts of your body on the same day. We'll also sample your T-cells to see how gene-therapy has changed them. If we find no measurable virus and your T-cells are in order, we'll suspend further gene therapy and follow you with periodic marrow samples for the rest of your treatment year."

"That would mean that I should also stop antiretrovirals?"

"Yes. Because that would involve some risk, we would want to do an iliac crest marrow draw monthly to assure ourselves that the virus hasn't returned."

Ben thought for a moment. "All this sounds very promising. But if you're going to take all that marrow from different sites in the same day—"

"—We'll want to keep you here for a day or two afterward while you recover."

Ben said, "I'm pleased to participate."

Rao smiled. "Now, what was it that you wanted to ask me?"

Ben said, "In the past few weeks I've been attacked three times by what the police say are organized-crime figures. I've been hiding out, moving around from place to place. It would be a big help if I could stay here tonight, before beginning my treatment tomorrow."

Rao looked shocked. "Three attempts on your life?"

Ben nodded. "I was locked in a burning house, assaulted in the backyard of the home where I rent a room, and then attacked in the Squirrel Hill Jewish Community Center by five gunmen."

Rao slowly shook his head. "I'm sorry, Rabbi, but you can't stay here tonight."

Ben said, "Can you say why?"

Doctor Rao said, "I understand your desire to hide, but I don't have a bed available. I'd have to refer you to another department, and frankly, there's no medical reason for them to admit you. And it would be much more expensive than a hotel room."

Ben smiled. "Most hotels insist that you register and give them a credit card. The people looking for me found me that way once. They can find me again."

Dr. Rao looked thoughtful for a moment. "Why don't you make yourself comfortable here in my office while I go down to the lab. Use the computer, whatever you like. I'll be back in a little while, and you'll come home with me. We have a very nice guest room, and my wife is Jewish. I'm sure we will find much to talk about.

"Tomorrow, after your marrow draw, I can give you a bed here for up to three days while you recover."

§

After Rao left, Ben switched on the computer, logged on to one of his traveling email accounts and sent Miryam a brief message: He had some exciting news to share about his virus and would try to call her later in the day.

To his surprise, Miryam answered within seconds:

Abby told me all about your adventures at the JCC. Call me on Skype!

Ben replied that he was on a borrowed computer with neither a camera nor a microphone. He sent the hospital phone number and Rao's extension.

Half a minute later, the phone rang.

"Fugitive Ben!" Miryam said. "I'll never forgive myself if anything happens to you."

Ben said, "Stop that. None of this is your fault. And I'm fine. I just needed to hear your voice. Now, tell me what you've been up to."

Miryam sighed. Ben thought he could hear her weeping. He remained silent until she found her voice again. "In spite of all the time that I spent worrying about you, I'm almost finished with my thesis."

"That's wonderful news!"

"I just need to edit my citations and then proofread everything. It wasn't as hard as I thought it would be."

"Does that mean you might come back before Pesach?"

"I could come today if you want me."

"Let me nab this guy first. There's apparently still a contract out on me."

"What does that mean, 'a contract'?"

"It means somebody wants me dead, and they're willing to pay for it. What about your online class? Did you finish that, too?"

"They let you take the lessons at your own pace, so I did one a day until I finished. And I think you just changed the subject."

"I want to talk about my virus."

"Tell me."

"Don't get too excited, because it's going to be months before we know for sure, but Doctor Rao says he found *no* virus in my marrow. We're doing a follow-up tomorrow, and they'll take biopsies from different parts of my body."

Miryam gasped. "Is this for real? Are you maybe cured?"

Ben said, "The operative word is 'maybe.'"

"When will you know for sure?"

"Rao won't say that his instruments are sensitive enough to detect every last living virus, so he's playing down the possibility that I'm out of the woods. It might be another year before he's ready to say it on the record. But he's optimistic."

"I should come to Pittsburgh."

"Stay in Buenos Aires until I clean up this mess. It won't be much longer."

Miryam said, "Make it soon Ben."

"I love you, Marita."

"I love you, Ben."

Ben replaced the phone in its cradle and wiped his eyes. When he looked up, he saw Dr. Rao standing in front of the desk.

Chapter Sixty-Six

Ben was about to climb into Dr. Rao's Ford Escape when a horn honked behind him. He turned to see James at the wheel of a minivan.

James said, "We've been looking for you, Rabbi."

Ben said, "What's up?"

James said, "We left a whole bunch of phone messages on your voice mail. Then Mrs. Silverblatt said to try you here, but I didn't know what extension to call."

Ben said, "What happened?"

James blinked away a tear. "Mr. Cohen passed this morning."

Ben said, "Where is he now?"

James said, "We have a mortuary at the Home, and we called a mortician."

Ben said, "What about his family?"

James shook his head. "Didn't have nobody left. You know he was a hundred and two?"

Ben shook his head. "I didn't think—no. The late eighties, I figured."

"He wanted to be buried at the Home, near Mr. Schy or Mrs. Gohlke."

Ben said, "Wait a minute, while I tell Dr. Rao that I'm going with you."

§

Ben took the fresh clothes and laptop he'd grabbed from his room and left the Accord in a far corner of the Home lot. Inside, James led him to an unused room, where he changed into jeans, a sweatshirt, and running shoes. Then he made his way to a small outbuilding beside the cemetery on the eastern slope, where white-haired Rilee Given, a mortician, waited with the late Avi Cohen.

For the next two hours, Ben worked with Given to prepare Cohen for burial in accordance with Jewish law. In so doing, Ben became part of one of Judaism's most ancient traditions, meanwhile fulfilling a mitzvah, a commandment, that was utterly without reward except for the performance of the act itself.

When they had finished, Ben asked Given to stay until Ben could cleanse himself and eat something. No Jewish corpse should be alone until it is buried, and Ben intended to return for an overnight vigil.

But when he opened the door, he found three elderly residents seated on folding chairs.

Chaim Grinspan said, "Rabbi, help us settle this. I deserve the honor of taking the first shift with Avi because I've known him the longest."

Leo Wise shook his bald head. "I was once his business partner. No, it was twice. Anyway, he wouldn't have come here if I hadn't persuaded him to join me."

His deeply lined face stern and his upper lip trembling, Dan Brin held up both palms. "We're family. My nephew's son married his niece's step-daughter. I should take the first shift."

Ben said, "Each of you, take a coin and hold it in your closed hand."

The three men rose, fumbled in their pockets until each clasped a coin.

Ben turned to Grinspan. "Open your hand."

The hand opened to reveal a nickel, Jefferson's face up.

Ben turned to the next man, Wise. "Open your hand."

Wise's palm held a Lincoln penny, face down.

He looked at Brin, who opened his fist to show a Kennedy half-dollar, face up.

Ben turned to Wise. "You take the first shift."

He looked at Grinspan. "Jefferson came before Kennedy. You get your choice of the remaining shifts."

Wise sighed. "We could have done this ourselves."

Ben shook his head. "But instead you decided to quarrel over who goes first. That's not the way to serve God and honor Avi's memory."

§

Including nearly half the adult members of the Sanoker Shul, more than a hundred people joined the Home's residents and staff in the Monday morning fog and mist to say goodbye to Avi Cohen. Aided by recollections from Wise, Brin, and Grinspan, Ben delivered a brief eulogy, describing Avi's life from his early years in Tarnow, his escape from the Nazis, his ordeal in a Hungarian labor battalion, his rescue and redemption, years of prosperity in New York and Pittsburgh and, most of all, Cohen's dedication to an observant life and community service.

Only Ben knew that it was the first time that he had led a funeral service.

Avi Cohen was buried two spaces from Bernie Schy and six from Goldie Gohlke, both natives of Tarnow.

After the coffin was lowered into the earth, after each mourner had taken a turn shoveling a little soil onto it, after everyone else had retreated to the dry warmth of the Home's dining room for tea and cake, Ben walked the rows of tombstones, pausing here and there to read one, musing over the tiny ripples in the stream of life that sent one man to a death camp and another to freedom, the accidents and coincuences and innocuous choices that meant one Jew would die young and full of vigor and another would live past the century mark.

Did it even matter? he mused. Six million went to the furnaces. doctors and bricklayers, accountants and housewives, dairymen and dentists, husbands and wives and childen and grandparents—six million men, women, and children dead before their times, and without even a stone to mark their passage to the next world. Six million without a grave where their family might come to remember them. Because most of their families went to the same furnaces.

But some had survived. Some had fled Europe in time. A very few had survived the camps. Yet all these years later, even those who escaped the Nazi death machine had joined their kin in death. They were buried here or in cemeteries around the world. All dead.

It did matter, Ben decided. It mattered greatly. These people had lived and loved and hated and striven and were defeated and had striven again and succeeded. They had worked, each in their own greater or lesser way, to help heal the world. If they had children and grandchildren and great-grandchildren who might know nothing about them, still they all mattered.

Life mattered.

The cemetery descended a gentle slope; Avi Cohen slept about two-thirds of the way down from the top row. Below him were the newer graves, and as Ben walked the bottom row, he saw stones inscribed with the now-familiar place name, Sanok, followed by what he guessed was a nearby village or community within Sanok's civil jurisdiction.

There lay Moisheh Averbakh of Sanok-Pisarowce. Here was Malka Carlebach of Sanok-Czertez. Next to her Abe Frankel of Sanok-Lizna.

Ben had a sudden thought. He straightened up, counting the graves in each row. Eighteen. No less, no more. Eighteen for hai. Even in death, eighteen for life.

Cold and wet, he'd never felt more alive. He returned to the last two rows, reading the names aloud: Jacob Auer of Sanok-Miedzybrodzie, Ursula Stern of Sanok-Tyrawa, Dov Günzburg of Sanok-Nowosielce, Selma Katznelson of Sanok-Dolny, Yaakov Hildesheimer of Sanok-Dudynce, Eda Sinzheimer of Sanok-Wislok, Zelda Sapir of Sanok-Kostarowce, Nachum Rozenkwit of Sanok-Zablotce, and Schlomo Seigafuse, Esther Eibeschütz, David Anscher and Saul Gurevich, all of Sanok. Just Sanok.

He walked back the way he came, looking at gravestone dates. There were three empty spaces in the first row; the other fifteen held the remains of those who died in the previous four years. Each was from in or around Sanok. Here lay the Sanok Home's last board of directors, its movers and shakers. He recalled the multimedia show. These fifteen were probably among those rescued just before the war by the Sanok Rabbi, ransomed or bribed to freedom with burial society gold.

Ben traversed the ground a third time, noting this time that, except for Avi Cohen, who did not yet have a stone, the four newest graves were not adjacent to each other, that each tombstone said only Sanok and not a village. And that the people under those stones had died within a seven-month span, the first less than a year previous to Avi Cohen, the last only about four months ago.

That was strange. By ancient custom, the year following a death was a time of mourning. Normally, usually, and almost always, no gravestone was emplaced before the end of that year.

Yet, there they were: four graves with stones. Four graves less than a year old.

Was it because Weinstock knew that these four had no families to mourn them and to erect a stone? Or was there another reason?

He looked again, this time memorizing the dates. They had died one or two months apart, all on one of the first five days of a month. After their Social Security checks were deposited to the Home's account.

It was too much to be a coincidence.

Could all four have been murdered?

And if so, why?

Chapter Sixty-six

By the time Ben went back inside the building, nearly all the mourners had left. He found his borrowed room, changed his wet clothes. And as he looked around the room to see if he had left anything behind, he glanced out the window.

As if by magic, a man's head appeared behind Ben's car. The man walked away, not hurrying, went out the parking lot gate, crossed the road, and stopped.

A moment later, a beat-up pickup stopped for a few seconds, then drove away. The man was gone.

Ben's blood ran cold.

He went to the front desk and asked James to call the police.

"What do I tell them, Rabbi?"

"Tell them that you think someone put a bomb in my car."

§

The bomb squad was from the Pennsylvania State Police and had had to come forty miles from their barracks. By the time they arrived, James had moved all the Home's residents to the east side of the building, where they would be safe from flying glass and debris, while Ben and the Home's other employees emptied the parking lot of cars, driving each in turn out of the lot and down the road.

A burly man in black body armor found Ben waiting under an umbrella.

"I'm Lieutenant Rooney. What makes you think there's a bomb in your car?"

Ben frowned. "Over the last few weeks, there have been three attempts on my life. Detective Roland Easton of the Pittsburgh PD can confirm that for you.

"I held a funeral service this morning, and by the time I was finished, my clothes were wet. I went inside to change and happened to look out the window. I saw a man's head sort of materialize on the far side of my car."

Rooney said, "*Sort of materialize*? What does that mean?"

"One second he wasn't there, and the next second, he was. I think he was under the car or kneeling beside it and then stood up."

"Can you describe this man?"

Ben closed his eyes, picturing the scene. "He was about five-ten or five-eleven, thin, wearing a dark blue coat, a blue or black watch cap. Long, thin nose, very pale complexion. He walked away down the hill, and then an old Ford F-150, dark blue or black, stopped and he got in. They drove away."

Rooney scowled. He had been enjoying a rare quiet day, catching up on the endless paperwork his job demanded, and now this. "We'll get the mirrors out while we wait for the dog," he said.

Two officers in body armor took long poles with mirrors on one end and carefully placed them under various parts of the car. They saw nothing unusual.

Meanwhile, the morning mist worked its way into a driving deluge.

Finally, a squad car turned into the lot and stopped in the opposite corner from Ben's car. A cop got out, opened the back door and a large, gray, mixed-breed dog bounded out and followed the cop to Ben's car.

"Seek!" called the K-9 officer, and the dog approached the car, head down circling, sniffing the tires, the doors the hood, the trunk.

The dog handler turned to face Rooney and shook his head.

Ben said, "Would the rain be a factor in how well the dog functions?"

Rooney considered the question for a long moment. "Possibly," he said. "Give me the key; we'll look inside."

Ben handed him his keys.

Before Ben could stop him, Rooney pushed the button of the remote entry device on the key ring, which generated a radio signal that unlocked the car doors.

Ben said, "If a bomb was wired to a lock, you may have armed it."

Rooney bristled. "You're a bomb expert?"

"I took a class from the Israeli Defense Forces in anti-bomb measures. I also have a degree in electrical engineering from M.I.T. You should wait a few minutes before approaching the car."

Rooney set his jaw. "I've never seen a bomb armed by a remote entry switch."

Ben asked, "How many car bombs have you worked on?"

Clearly irritated, Rooney scowled at Ben. "Enough. And I see after-action reports describing every bomb found in this country."

Ben said, "I know you don't want my help, and I assume that you're proficient at your work, but what would it hurt to have the dog sniff again?"

"Why?"

"Because if there is a bomb and if it is now armed. The arming device may be a simple time-delay fuse that is now burning. We have a minute or two."

"If there is a bomb. And if it has a time-delay fuse."

"It's the easiest kind of bomb to install."

Rooney glared at Ben, thinking.

Ben said, "Is it really that much trouble to have the dog out again?"

Rooney was now furious. "Go inside and stay there!"

Ben turned to go, and as he did, he saw Rooney gesture to the dog handler. From the shelter of the doorway, Ben watched the dog circle the car.

The dog sat down.

The handler hollered something and ran, the dog on his heels.

Rooney went prone on the wet pavement.

A modest explosion blew out the Honda's windows and sent its doors flying. The car began to burn.

Two cops with big fire extinguishers ran up and put out the fire in less than a minute.

Back on his feet, Rooney eyed Ben suspiciously. "You know way too much about bombs. Who was that Pittsburgh detective again?"

Chapter Sixty-Seven

It was a bomb, Ben realized. A bomb in the café. That's why he was in a pile of rubble. Why he was covered with blood. It was the reason for the screams and moans that filled his ears. And the sirens. And the screaming. Now someone was pawing him, shaking him.

Ben opened his eyes.

Dr. Rao said, "How are you feeling, Rabbi?"

What was going on? Ben thought. One minute he was in a Jerusalem café, and now there was this dark-skinned man in a white coat standing over him.

Dr. Rao said, "You're in Pittsburgh. You're fine. Everything is fine."

Ben tried to sit up, but waves of agony drove him back.

Dr. Rao said, "Are you still in pain?"

Ben said, "Ache all over—my arms, my legs, my back."

Dr. Rao said, "We took marrow from both your thighs, your iliac crest, and your forearms."

The world turned, and Ben grabbed it. He was safe in Pittsburgh. Rachel was long dead. Miryam was in Argentina. He was safe.

Ben said, "I remember going into surgery. What day is it?"

Rao smiled. "Wednesday. You've been sedated since Monday."

Ben pushed through the pain to work himself into a sitting position.

Dr. Rao said, "You should get up and walk around."

Ben swung his feet over the side of the bed, gathered himself, and stood. He took a wobbly step, then another. "I'm hungry," he announced, "starving."

Dr. Rao said, "Your friend, the police detective, is here."

"Easton?"

Dr. Rao nodded. "Before you go, I need to speak with you."

Ben sat down on the bed.

Dr. Rao said, "You were moaning and cursing. Thrashing around in your sleep. Classic nightmare symptoms."

Ben sighed. "I have PTSD. Ten years ago, I was in a Jerusalem café that was bombed. I lost my wife. There were cuts all over my face and chest, mostly superficial. There was blood everywhere. That's how I was infected with HIV."

Dr. Rao said, "Ah. I wasn't sure that you were aware of your condition. I could prescribe something for anxiety if that would help."

Ben shook his head. "Tranquilizers don't help. My best drug is exercise; between weekly injections and the rest of my life, I haven't had enough lately."

Dr. Rao said, "It will get easier now. I want you back next week to go over the results of your marrow biopsy, and if they are as I expect, you won't require further gene therapy injections for at least a month. Or perhaps never."

Easton poked his head into the room and smiled at Ben. "Get dressed. Sanchez is meeting us at Kazansky's."

Chapter Sixty-Eight

A squad car was parked in front of Kazansky's Deli. Easton passed it, went to the corner and turned right, then right again into the alley, and parked in the employee lot behind the restaurant. A second squad car pulled in next to Easton's Crown Victoria.

Easton said, "This way," and led Ben through the kitchen to the dining area. The place was packed, except for a vacant booth next to the kitchen. Ben sat down, noting the booth's unobstructed view of the front door and the street beyond.

He sat across from Easton and shot him an inquiring glance.

Easton said, "So this cowboy, Rooney, the bomb squad L.T., thinks you planted a bomb in your own car."

Ben snorted. "Come on!"

"I set him straight. I think. But now the ATF wants to talk to you."

Ben shrugged. "If it helps, sure, I'll talk to them."

"Few things first. Rooney's commanding officer at Troop B put out a press release: unidentified man critically injured by a bomb in his car, yadda, yadda, yadda, on life support at Allegheny General's burn unit."

Ben said, "If Miryam sees that, she'll be on the next plane."

Easton shook his head. "Not much chance of that. Didn't identify the Sanok Home, just a board-and-care near Monroeville. No age, no description of the car."

"But you think the bomber will see it?"

Easton nodded. "Yeah, they usually watch for stuff like that. Take clippings and all. By the way, we found that black pickup—the Ford—on the shoulder in front by those abandoned factories off Berona Road."

"And you've got eyes at Allegheny General?"

Easton smiled. "Two uniforms in front of a room with a CPR dummy fitted out with all kinds of tubes and monitors. And two men in scrubs roaming the hallway."

"I bet that they won't send anyone. Safer to just let me die."

"We'll see."

Easton looked up from their booth at Kazansky's and waved. "Here comes Sanchez with your lunch date."

Yolanda slid into the booth next to Ben. Behind her stood a man in his early fifties, no more than five feet tall, and weighing perhaps 120 pounds. His short hair was dark and limp. He wore an Armani suit.

The man said. "McKey Kerton, ATF."

"I'm Rabbi Ben."

Easton scooted over to make room. "Sit down, Agent Kerton."

Ben said, "I haven't eaten in three days. Let's order."

§

Sated, Ben pushed his plate away. "Sorry to keep you waiting, Agent Kerton. How can I help you?"

Kerton produced an envelope from a pocket and laid it on the table. "Please describe the man you saw near your car."

Ben said, "An inch or two under six feet, pale, slender, with an aquiline nose."

Easton said, "Aquiline? Really? Because you're talking to a Fed?"

Ben shrugged.

Kerton said. "What age, approximately?"

Ben shrugged. "He was wearing a watch cap that covered his hair, and I was too far to notice much about his skin except that it was light."

"Anything else you noticed?"

"I'm not certain, but he seemed to favor his left leg, just a little. But maybe the pavement was uneven going down to the road."

Kerton opened the envelope and took out four small photos, all taken at a distance with telephoto lenses. "Do you recognize any of these men?"

Ben looked closely at each in turn, then shook his head.

Kerton collected the pictures, returned them to the envelope, and took out the second envelope. He showed Ben three more pictures. "Any of these familiar?"

Ben pointed to the second picture. "I think I've seen this man, but he wasn't the one by my car last Monday."

Kerton collected the images and put both envelopes away. "Is there anything else you can tell me about what happened?"

Ben said, "I've been thinking about this. Maybe I'm splitting hairs, but I don't think that I'd describe the device in my car as a car bomb."

Easton said, "If the agent isn't confused, I am."

Kerton smiled. "The rabbi is on to something. Go on, please."

Ben paused, choosing his words carefully. "I think of a car bomb as a massive device, hundreds of pounds of explosives. A terror weapon, designed to inflict great damage, to kill many people, and take down structures. But the bomb in my car was very small: a quarter pound of TNT or a few ounces of Semtex. Deadly at close range—meant to kill the driver—but it didn't even break a window at the Home."

Kerton smiled again. "Correct. This is perhaps why Lt.Rooney didn't recognize the device signature—he had big car bombs in mind.

"Actually, we—the ATF—have seen bombs similar to this one. In New York, New Jersey, and in the Philadelphia area. But none in a car. And we think that we know *what* the bomb's maker is but not *who*."

Ben said, "One of those pictures you showed me—the one I thought I'd seen?"

Kerton asked, "What about it?"

"That was the dog handler I saw Monday at the Home, wasn't it?"

Kerton smiled again but didn't reply.

Easton asked, "So this bomb maker is some kind of cop?"

Kerton continued to smile but remained silent.

Ben asked, "Does ATF assume that the person who makes these bombs also installs them?

Kerton pursed his lips. "That's not always the case, but we have reason to suspect that this bomber usually installs his own devices."

Ben said, "Because installing them means concealing them, and setting the trigger can be dangerous."

Kerton smiled yet again. "Very possibly."

Yolanda asked, "Were his previous bombs associated with organized crime?'

Kerton said, "Possibly, in New York."

Ben asked, "Maybe in Manhattan? On the West Side?"

Kerton got to his feet and extended a tiny hand to Ben. "A pleasure, Rabbi."

Easton stood up and shook hands with the agent. "I'll walk you out to your car," he said.

Yolanda said, "Glad to meet you, Agent Kerton."

Easton was back in seconds, shaking his head as he sat down.

"Wouldn't tell me a thing."

Ben said, "I think he told us a lot. The man who built that bomb is probably associated with law enforcement, has built and placed similar bombs previously, all along the Eastern Seaboard, and is probably Irish or Irish-American."

Yolanda asked, "Why Irish?"

"Because the dominant gang on Manhattan's West Side, the Westies, is an Irish-American outfit. They've had strong ties to Ireland, and especially Northern Ireland, for more than a hundred years."

Easton said, "And those Irish, the Northerners, have a lot of experience with bombs."

Ben said, "Exactly. And, the fact that this guy is associated with East Coast organized crime suggests that the local mob is desperate to kill me but either lacks resources, so that they had to go outside their organization, or that they went outside their organization to avoid involving their own higher-ups."

Easton said, "There're three more things to share, Rabbi. First, Cousin Mike, a.k.a. Deputy Michael Paladino of the Clark County Sheriff's Office, was using some vacation days to paint his house. He called me back late yesterday and is now looking for a marriage license with Buchler and Weinstock's names on it. If he finds one, he'll fax a copy to my office.

"Second, Officer Sanchez took it upon herself to check every data backup service she could find within twenty miles of Berona Township."

Yolanda said, "Turns out there's only four. Mina Jenston used a service in Monroeville. The day after her office burned down, a woman called, claiming that she was Mina. She said her company was in bankruptcy; they were to cancel her contract and delete all her data. The person who took the call reminded her that she owed the full contract balance. The caller said to get in line with the other creditors."

Ben said, "So they deleted all her data?"

Yolanda said, "That they did."

Ben said, "Well, that sucks. What's the other thing?'

Easton said, "You're leaving town before someone kills you. Your friendly Pittsburgh PD, with Troop B of the Pennsylvania State Police, and the ATF, will take it from here. I booked you a seat to Los Angeles; your flight leaves at 9:17 tonight. Officer Sanchez will see you off."

Ben said, "That's nonsense. You can't order me to leave town."

Easton sighed. "I was ordered to put you in protective custody. Bars on the doors and windows. I stuck my neck out and told my captain that I'd talk to you about taking a vacation for a few weeks. By the way, you don't have to go to L.A. You could go to Seattle. Or Boise. Anyplace where it will be hard to find you for a while."

Yolanda asked, "How 'bout Argentina?"

Ben smiled. "Bingo! But it will take about a week to get a visa."

Easton said, "First, I'll see if I can sell that to my captain. If he bites, I'll ask the Feds to expedite a visa for you. Until then, you have Officer Sanchez as a bodyguard, along with a plainclothes detail, 24/7."

Chapter Sixty-eight

Abe Smolkin came bounding out of his office even before Mrs. Bender could shuffle to its doorway.

"Ben!" he cried and threw his arms around him in a bear hug. "I read that your car was bombed and that you were in intensive care?"

Ben pointed his chin at the door to Abe's office. Trailed by Yolanda, they went inside and closed the door, where Ben explained the situation in a few terse sentences.

Abe asked, "So this is goodbye?'

Ben said, "Just for awhile. I'll be back after the police nab the elusive Mr. Buchler."

Abe said, "I almost forgot. I have a message from you from Lois Seligman—remember, the former Mrs. Al Farkas?"

Ben said, "What did she say?"

Abe dug around on his desk until he found a Post-It. "She said, 'My Rembrandt is worth a hundred dollars, including the frame.'"

Ben sighed. "Another Buchler mark. He stole her Rembrandt sketch, sold it back to her but replaced it with a copy."

Yolanda said, "I hate to be a cold shower, but Rabbi Ben has several stops to make before we get to the airport."

Ben said, "Unless her training officer can persuade his captain to give me a few more days here, I'm leaving tonight."

Abe threw his arms around Ben again. "Stay in touch," he said.

Ben said, "Abe, I do need one last favor."

"Anything."

"This is Yolanda Sanchez. Her family lived in New Mexico for many generations. I'm pretty sure that her ancestors were conversos. She was enrolled in a conversion program taught by Rabbi Geltkern, aka Bernard Buchler. You know what that was worth. Yolanda lives in the neighborhood. Can you find her a tutor or get her into a class?"

Abe smiled. "I teach Introduction to Judaism here at the center. Come see me, anytime, Officer Sanchez."

§

The tiny hair that Ben had left across the door frame at ankle height was exactly as he'd left it, but Yolanda nevertheless insisted on inspecting his room before she allowed him inside.

He laid his suitcases on the bed and began filling them from dresser drawers.

Someone tapped on the door. Yolanda drew her weapon.

"Who is it?" she said.

Mrs. Meltzer pushed the door open and poked her head inside, recoiling at the sight of Yolanda in a shooting stance.

Ben said, "It's okay, Ro. Come on in."

"Rabbi, I read in the paper that someone put a bomb in your car and that you were horribly burned," she said.

Ben sighed. "I wasn't in the car. The police put that story out so that whoever planted the bomb would think they succeeded. They never mentioned my name."

Mrs. Meltzer paled. "George and I put two and two together. Excuse me, I have to call Miryam. She must be worried to death."

Mrs. Meltzer ran down the stairs, and, after a quick look outside, Yolanda shut the door.

Ben moved to the closet and resumed packing. He took his second-best suit out, held it up, thinking about wearing it for the trip, then changed his mind. He removed the hanger, spread the suit on the bed and began to fold it when he felt something in the left front trouser pocket. He reached in and came out with a tiny plastic rectangle with a Wal-Mart logo. On inspection, one end concealed a USB receptacle. It must be a flash drive, he realized, one that he'd never seen before.

Someone knocked on the door, and Ben slipped the plastic in his pocket.

In a hoarse whisper, Ben said, "That's probably Dr. Lewin."

Yolanda took out her gun again and pointed it at the door.

Ben said, "Come in!"

The door opened and in came Lewin, carrying a manila folder.

Ben asked, "Dr. Lewin, have you met Officer Sanchez?"

Lewin peered closely at Yolanda, then smiled. "Of course! You're Abby Silverblatt's partner."

Yolanda said, "Abby's wife."

Lewin smiled. "How wonderful."

Ben asked, "What did you bring me, Doctor?"

"Your documents, my translations, and Avi Cohen's Yiddish newspaper."

Ben shook his head. "Avi died last week. His funeral was Monday."

Lewin's voice failed him for a moment. When he recovered his composure, he said, "We were away. I didn't know."

Ben took the papers and lay them on his bed. "More than a hundred people came to his funeral," he said. "I didn't know this until he died, but Avi was 102 years old. He had an interesting and useful life."

Lewin said, "May he rest in peace."

Ben said, "Thanks for the translations. Find anything interesting?"

The doctor shook his head. "As I first supposed, these were random pages from 1938 and 1939—the minutes of some organization. They had one thing in common: Each page noted the arrival of someone from somewhere in Poland."

Ben said, "I'll look at them at the airport. Or maybe on the plane."

Lewin said, "Ro said you were leaving. Is it for good?"

"Just until the police find the guy who put a bomb in my car."

"Rabbi, we wanted you to be the first to hear this: Ro and I are getting married, just as soon as my divorce is final."

Ben and Yolanda beamed. "That's wonderful news," she said.

Lewin said, "We were hoping, Rabbi, that you would perform the ceremony."

Ben said, "I'm honored. So you had a nice time up at the Lodge?"

"We hiked, rode horses, ate some wonderful meals, and she even taught me to shoot a rifle."

Yolanda asked, "She taught you to shoot?"

Lewin laughed. "Ro was co-captain of her high school rifle team. They have a range at the lodge, and she gave me a couple of lessons."

Ben said, "She's a remarkable woman. I'm so glad you found each other."

Yolanda said, "I hate to break up the reunion, but the Rabbi has a few stops to make before we get to the airport."

Ben said, "The first one is right downstairs. I want to get my iPhone out of her guest room."

Chapter Sixty-eight

Trailed by two plainclothes officers in a Ford SUV and preceded by Yolanda in an unmarked Chevy Cruze used for undercover work, Ben returned his rental car, then slid in beside Yolanda.

Yolanda said, "Abby is expecting us for an early dinner. What else must you do before we leave for the airport?"

Ben asked, "Heard anything from Roland?"

"Not yet. Where are we going?"

Ben said, "Downtown: the Office of Property Assessments."

§

Yolanda said, "Let me handle this. A badge can clear away a lot of red tape."

Ben stepped aside and followed Yolanda into the office. They found a dozen people at a counter served by one clerk. Yolanda went to the end of the counter, held up her badge and parted her jacket just enough to show the holster on her belt. A middle-aged woman, clearly a supervisor, rose from her desk and hurried over.

"Something wrong, officer?" she asked.

Yolanda said, "I'm not sure. We need to see a property record."

"Do you have a parcel number?"

Yolanda said. "Show me a map of Berona Township, and I'll find the parcel."

Ben sat down next to Yolanda at a table in the records area. Two minutes later, the supervisor laid a file folder in front of them.

Yolanda said, "Okay, that's my end. What are we looking for?"

Ben said, "I'd like to know when the Sanok people acquired that property, who they bought it from, and who has a lien against it."

The documents in the file were in chronological order. The earliest was a Homestead Act deed dated August 14, 1881, that gave the title to 160 acres, a square mile, that included all of present-day Berona Township, including the ridge, to one G. Parker Kendall. Ben wrote the name and date down.

The next record showed that, in 1887, G. Parker Kendall began selling off half-acre parcels on the flat land below the ridge.

In 1922, title to the remaining land was transferred to Randall Kendall.

In 1928, he divided the ridge into three parcels and sold the smallest, seven acres along the crest, to the Sanok Burial Society.

In 1944, the remaining land passed to Parker G. Kendall. In 1952, he sold the remainder of the western slope to the burial society.

Finally, in March 1970, Parker Kendall sold the remainder of the original parcel, the ridge's eastern slope, to the Sanok Home.

The final item in the file was a first trust deed. The Sanok Retirement Home had taken out a mortgage with K & L Associates, a limited liability company. The whole property, 113 acres, was pledged as surety for the loan.

Ben wrote all the dates and land transfers on a pad, then turned to Yolanda. "Would you ask that supervisor if you could use a computer for a few minutes?"

"What do I want to find?"

"See if you can access the Pennsylvania Department of Corporations. They should have a database that lists corporate officers. We need to identify the officers or owners of K & L Associates."

While Yolanda spoke with the supervisor, Ben broke out his iPhone to access an online perpetual calendar. He looked up the dates of the various land transfers.

When Yolanda returned, she handed Ben a page torn from a steno pad with a list of names and titles.

"K & L Associates is a holding company for a general insurance agency, a property management company, and a land development corporation," she explained. "The president of all K & L and of all three subsidiaries is C. Clayton Kendall, the secretary is Alexis Kendall Lustig, and the treasurer is Frank A. Lustig."

Ben pursed his lips. "So when the Home defaults on their loan—and they will—Kendall, his daughter, and her husband, the township manager, get back all the land that Kendall's family sold to the Home."

Yolanda looked angry. "That's what Buchler was after?"

Ben said, "I think so. And one thing more. Take a look at this."

He handed her his iPhone, still showing the perpetual calendar.

"What am I looking at?"

"August 14, 1881. Note the day of the week."

"Sunday."

"This was the date of the filing of the original Homestead Act deed issued to G. Parker Kendall. Six years later, he sold off lots to the original Sanok families."

Yolanda looked at the iPhone again. "I don't understand."

"Under the Homestead Act—one of Abraham Lincoln's lesser-known accomplishments—anyone could get free title to a section of unoccupied Federal land—160 acres, or one square mile—by living on or farming it for five years. When you took up occupancy, you made an initial claim. Five years later, you signed an affidavit that you had been there the requisite period. The government then issued a deed."

Yolanda shook her curls. "I still don't understand."

"August 14, 1881, was a Sunday. Have you ever heard of a government office being open on a Sunday?"

Yolanda looked at the calendar, then at Ben. "So this deed is...?"

"A forgery. G. Parker Kendall latched on to a bunch of Polish greenhorns and sold them land he didn't own. Then he forged a deed to show that he did own it."

Yolanda paled. "How could he get away with that?"

Ben turned the stack of papers over and inspected the Homestead Act deed. In the corner, he found a handwritten notation and a seal. The date was April 2, 1888. "He didn't record the fake deed until after he'd started selling off lots."

Yolanda asked, "So the Sanok Home doesn't actually own that land?"

Ben shook his head. "Most likely, the state or federal government owned the land. Many people were homesteading then. A small bribe to the right person would have been enough to avoid suspicion. Most courts now hold that, if no one contests land ownership over a ten-year period, the land goes to whoever has claimed ownership. I doubt that any judge would try to undo a nineteenth-century land transaction. But I find it interesting that the original sale was fraudulent."

Yolanda said, How can we help the Home keep its land?"

Ben said. "The Home needs a lot of money and a good lawyer."

Chapter Sixty-Nine

Yolanda held up her badge. The reference librarian hurried over.

"How can I help you?" she asked, her eyes darting back and forth between Ben and Yolanda.

"We'd like to see all the *Post-Gazette* microfilm for November 1969 through December 1970."

The librarian looked at Ben again and pursed her lips. "Normally, we allow each viewer only one box at a time," she said. "We do have our rules."

Yolanda smiled. "We also have rules. We charge people with obstruction of justice when they fail to cooperate with an investigation."

Trembling, the librarian pointed at a row of microfilm readers. "The last machine is the newest and best. I'll bring the film as soon as I can."

Ten minutes later, Ben threaded the roll that held the newspaper account of Congregation B'nai Abe Messiah's burglary. There was only one more day of the Post-Gazette on the roll, and it held no mention of the robbery.

Ben loaded the last roll from 1969 into the machine and wound it forward, looking for the December 1, 1969, edition.

The film on the roll was blank.

He took the first roll from the next box and without loading it, pulled out several feet of film, then held a section up to the light.

It was perfectly opaque.

Ben shook his head. "This is how Buchler operates. We've seen it over and over from him. I should have expected something like this."

Yolanda said, "There's a branch library in Squirrel Hill."

Ben said, "If he went to the effort of removing the film from this library, why wouldn't he do the same at all the branch libraries?"

Yolanda chewed her lip. "What do we do?"

"We go to the *Post-Gazette*, and you wave your badge again."

§

Yolanda said, "I think this is what we're looking for."

Ben got up from his microfilm viewer in the Post-Gazette library and peered over her shoulder at the screen.

March 4, 1970

SON OF BERONA TOWNSHIP JUDGE MURDERED

Special to the Gazette

The body of Edward Clayton Kendall, 25, son of Judge Parker Kendall and Mrs. Vivian Kendall of Berona Township, was discovered by sanitation workers behind a Shadyside church that was robbed last Thanksgiving.

Late last year, burglars entered Congregation B'nai Abe Messiah and stole files with personal information about individual members. The information was later used to obtain department store charge cards, to take out bank loans and buy new cars. Police estimate that the value of merchandise and loans will exceed $200,000.

Kendall had been arrested in connection with the thefts and was free on bail.

The cause of death has not been disclosed. An autopsy is pending. Arthur Mills, one of the sanitation workers, made the grisly discovery while emptying a dumpster. Mills told a reporter that he observed what looked like several gunshot wounds on the corpse.

Edward Kendall is survived by his parents, and a twin brother, Charles.

Funeral services are pending.

Ben said, "There it is: the missing link."

Yolanda turned away from the screen to look at Ben.

"I don't see it."

Ben said, "Print it out while I tell you what I think this means."

While Yolanda fumbled with the unfamiliar controls of the antiquated machine, Ben pulled out his iPhone and thumbed through several menus.

Yolanda said, "I'm waiting."

Ben held the phone up and touched the screen.

A voice said "Naaheddicharl."

Yolanda asked, "What's that?"

"That was me, repeating what Roland said were Miles Turlock's last words."

"Play it again, Rabbi."

Ben touched the phone screen, and the voice repeated, "Naaheddicharl."

Yolanda asked, "Not Heddy, Sharl?"

Ben said. "Could be. But what if it was, 'Not Eddie, Charles'?"

"Eddie as in Edward?"

Ben said, "As in *Edward* Clayton Kendall. The twin of Charles Clayton Kendall. Now Judge C. Clayton Kendall. And the 'K' in K & L Associates."

Yolanda said, "This is confusing."

Ben said, "I've been driving myself crazy trying to find why a judge would get involved with a swindler like Buchler. Now I think I know.

"Back in 1969, a kid named Buddy Butcher, whom I strongly suspect was really Bernard Buchler—"

Yolanda said, "Not much of an alias."

Ben smiled. "Also my first thought. Anyway, Buchler steals the church records and hands them over to a gangster. The gangster hires a bunch of people, including one of the Kendall twins, to get charge cards, loans, and so forth. Big score. Then Miles Turlock busts six of those people. Five jump bail and disappear. The sixth is found dead behind the church. The cops identify the body as Edward.

"Roland said he thought that this guy was killed because the mob thought a judge's son would probably finger the guy who hired him. The mob suspected that he'd take a deal—probation, maybe, or pleading to a misdemeanor instead of a felony—in exchange for his testimony."

Yolanda said, "Okay, so far so good."

Ben asked, "What if the mob killed the wrong twin?"

"Deliberately?"

"Probably not. But if it was the wrong one, and Miles knew it?"

Yolanda frowned. "And never told anyone?"

"Charles was on bail. If Eddie gets shot, who'd identify the body as Charles?"

Yolanda said, "The cop who made the original arrest."

Ben said, "Exactly. So what if Turlock went to their father, to Judge Parker Kendall? He's just lost one son, and the other has a felony hanging over him. What if Miles told Judge Kendall that nobody has to know that the dead son is Eddie?"

Yolanda said, "That would leave Charles in the clear. No prison, no mob."

Ben said, "It might also explain the income that Turlock's mother had: It was a payoff to her son. And it could explain why, a few weeks after Eddie died, Judge Kendall sold the rest of Kendall Heights to the Sanok Home: to fund that payoff."

Yolanda asked, "Why wouldn't Miles want all the cash at once?"

Ben said, "Turlock was smart. He didn't want to have to explain how a junior detective winds up with a pile of money. And Kendall, a judge, a man of the world, would need assurances that Miles wouldn't keep coming back for more. So he put the money into an escrow account that made regular payments to Turlock's mother. As long as Miles kept the secret, money would come every month, Miles would never have to explain it, and Judge Kendall's last son would be safe."

Yolanda said, "So then, forty-odd years later, Buchler turns up, calling himself Rabbi Jeremiah Geltkern. He finds Charles, now known as Edward, and makes him an offer he can't refuse: a way to recover the property that his father and grandfather sold to bribe Turlock, land that's now worth a fortune."

Ben said, "If Kendall doesn't bite, Buchler threatens to expose him. Eddie jumped bail in 1969. He's still a fugitive. If that ever came out, he'll lose his judgeship, and no one will want to do business with his company. He'll be ruined."

Yolanda sighed. We have no proof. This is all guessework."

Ben smiled. "It's Talmudic logic. We can get proof in an hour."

Yolanda asked, "How?"

"Identical twins have different fingerprints. Judge Charles Kendall's prints are in the system. So are the fugitive Eddie Kendall's prints. If they match, confront him. Maybe you can get him to give up Buchler. Maybe Buchler will give up the Youngstown mob guys."

Yolanda's face lit up, then fell. "We can nail Judge Kendall as a fugitive. But unless he implicates Buchler, we have no proof of a conspiracy. Weinstock is dead. Without the Home's financial records, we have no proof that Buchler, Weinstock, and Kendall conspired to send the Home into bankruptcy. It's all circumstantial."

Ben said, "Arresting Kendall might panic Buchler. It's not much of a stretch to see Kendall giving us Buchler for blackmail and extortion."

Yolanda thought for a long moment. "Worth a shot," she said.

Ben said, "But first, and this is important, we have to get Roland into the loop. He won't like hearing about Turlock's dirty hands, but he should probably go to Captain Ross before he tries to arrest anybody."

Chapter Seventy

Yolanda said, "I ran the prints through the FBI's fingerprint system, IAFIS. An eighteen-point match: Judge Charles Clayton Kendall is actually the fugitive Eddie Clayton Kendall."

From behind the wheel of his Crown Victoria, Easton shook his head. "That doesn't prove Miles Turlock knew it."

Ben asked, "Who would have identified the body?"

Easton sighed. "It was found behind the church, and Miles was working the church case, so yeah, the responding officers would have called it in, and Homicide would have sent Miles to the scene. But that wouldn't have been enough for the coroner. He'd have asked next-of-kin to make positive ID"

Ben said, "And there you have it."

Yolanda said, "Judge Parker Kendall would know which son was dead because the other one was still alive."

Easton's face turned beet red. "It doesn't prove that Miles knew! He could have mistaken one twin for the other."

Ben asked, "Would the father make the same mistake?"

Easton exploded. "He'd lie to save his other son!"

Ben said, "You're forgetting one thing: In 1969, there was no FBI supercomputer to match prints in twenty minutes. But one twin was alive, and the other was dead. If anyone in Homicide, and I mean Miles Turlock, was worthy of standing behind a gold shield, he'd have taken the dead man's fingerprints and had the crime lab match them to his booking prints. And that would have exposed the switch. If that didn't happen, it was because Turlock made it so."

Easton took a deep breath, let it out. "Okay. Yes. I see that. But what if Turlock didn't get around to that until after the father had ID'd Eddie as Charles?"

Ben said. "I'll give you that. It could have happened that way as easily as the other. But it's a distinction without a difference."

Easton asked, "Huh?"

Ben asked, "Have you read Don Quixote?"

"I'm only a homicide dick. You'd need a federal agent for that."

"What does it matter 'if the pitcher hits the stone, or the stone hits the pitcher? Either way, it's bad for the pitcher.'"

Easton's response was a blank stare.

Yolanda said, "Roland, say Kendall lied about which son was dead, and Turlock found out. Did he report it? Does it matter if Turlock went to Clayton Kendall and shook him down, or if Kendall offered a bribe and Turlock took it?"

Easton's chin sunk toward his chest. "I just really hate the idea that Turlock was dirty. I knew him all those years, and never once…."

Ben said. "I understand. He was your teacher, your friend, your partner, maybe even a kind of second father. You have this … image of him as above reproach. You try to emulate him in your own professional life. And now this. It's hard, but you have to accept it."

Easton sighed again. "I guess. But hold on. Maybe Turlock knew, but how does Buchler know that Eddie is actually Charles?"

Yolanda asked, "Did they know each other from 1969?"

Ben said, "Possibly. Let's think this through. Would Judge Parker Kendall tell his son, Eddie, that he bribed a cop to save his skin?"

Yolanda said, "He must have. But maybe he didn't say which cop."

Easton grunted agreement.

Ben said, "But if Miles sold his silence in 1969, was that the end of it? What if, decades later, after his mother died and the Kendall money stopped after Parker Kendall dies, and Miles is old and sick and needs money, did he sell Kendall's secret to someone else? Did he go to Eddie and demand another payoff?"

Easton cracked the sedan's door, got out, stretched, began to pace in the street. After a minute or two, he climbed back into the car, cleared his throat. "Miles was pretty broke, there at the end. The newsstand business went to hell when the Internet came along. He sold out about eight years ago and got almost nothing."

Yolanda asked, "Did he go to Eddie and demand money?"

Easton said, "Risky. A retired cop trying to blackmail a sitting judge? The judge could turn it around: 'Take me down, and you also lose your pension. You lose your medical coverage, your reputation.'"

Ben asked, "Who else would pay for this secret?"

Easton turned to look at Yolanda in the backseat. "What do you think, Officer Sanchez?"

Yolanda said, "Someone with business before the judge's court."

Ben said, "Or somebody with reason to buy a secret and sit on it until he needed it. Or until he could set up a big score that required Eddie's assistance."

Easton said, "Bingo. We've been thinking, all along, that Buchler went to the mob and cut them in. Maybe it was the other way: They brought Buchler in."

Yolanda said, "They brought him to Pittsburgh to run the scam?"

Ben said. "Hold on. Six years ago, the bottom was falling out of real estate values. Not the right time to pull off that kind of a scam. So the mob and Buchler wait. Meanwhile, Buchler gets Weinstock to run the Home into debt while he keeps the doors open until property markets recover. Along the way, he skims off some gravy: the $3.5 million that Weinstock stole for a 'retirement' fund."

Yolanda asked, "That's just gravy?"

Easton said, The land's worth $75 million or more to a developer."

Ben said, "So at some point, Buchler approached Kendall with not only a way to get this valuable property for next to nothing but with development financing."

Easton said, "And Kendall didn't need to know it's dirty money."

Yolanda said, "If Kendall turns him down, Buchler calls him Eddie."

Ben said, "I think it had to go down pretty much like that. I just wish the Home's financial records hadn't gone up in smoke.

"And one more thing: We've been talking about the mob like it was some giant, faceless institution. But if I understand correctly, there were never more than a handful of hardcore wise guys here in Pittsburgh. How hard can it be to figure out which ones were around in 1969 and are still around today?"

Easton said, "Here's the thing. In the '90s, pretty much the whole Pittsburgh wise-guy establishment went to prison or left town. The two or three made guys who didn't go down with the bosses took up residence in Youngstown."

Yolanda said, "Siragusa or one of his underlings."

Easton shook his head. "I've been to see our Organized Crime squad. They said that Siragusa used to be part of the Cleveland mob. Went down on a murder rap and got out eight years ago. He wasn't here in 1969."

Ben said, "What if one of the Pittsburgh guys who went to prison is out now. Somebody that Turlock knew back in the day, someone who didn't have the juice to pull off a complicated scam but could get to Siragusa?"

Yolanda said, "Roland, that's why you should go see Captain Ross. The guy we're looking for might be in an old Internal Affairs file."

Easton said, "Before I go to that prick, I'm gonna talk to *my* captain. Maybe we don't involve Internal Affairs at all. That's above my pay grade.

"In the meantime, Rabbi: You're on a plane tonight."

Ben shrugged. "A man's gotta do what a man's gotta do."

"Now I have to say thank you. I'm amazed at the way you put all this together."

Ben said, "We put this together. All three of us. But, if this all goes sideways and somebody has to be the sacrificial goat, sign me up.

"By the way, have you heard anything from Las Vegas?'

Easton scowled. "Weinstock and 'Geltkern' got a marriage license all right. He gave a Pittsburgh address. I looked it up: Allegheny County Mental Health. Ha ha."

Roland shook his head. "This is gonna be an unholy mess. Guess what happens when you expose a judge as a fugitive and take him off the bench?"

Ben said, "Everyone who ever came before him and didn't like the result will demand a new trial. But, since he became a judge after he became a fugitive, I don't think too many appeals will get traction."

Roland shrugged. "We'll see. But I don't much care."

All three people climbed out of the Crown Victoria. Easton looked up the street to where the SUV with the security detail was double-parked. "Go home and eat dinner with your family, Sanchez, then take our rabbi to the airport. Stay with him until his plane takes off."

Yolanda sighed. "And after that?"

"We're gonna need a warrant for Judge Kendall, and it best is signed by someone a lot higher up the food chain than he is. We might have to call Harrisburg. I'd say mid-morning tomorrow, earliest. So take the rest of the day off."

Chapter Seventy-one

Halfway up the two-lane approach ramp to the I-376 bridge across the Monongahela River, the shortest and most direct route to the Pittsburgh airport, Yolanda abruptly braked the Cruze and stopped in the right lane behind the security detail's SUV. A procession of cars and trucks swerved around her, horns honking.

"I don't dare open this door, Rabbi," she said. "Can you see if they need help?"

Ben pushed his door partly open, slipped sideways into the narrow space along the guard rail, then edged down to the SUV. The passenger window rolled down, and a plainclothes officer looked out. "All the engine lights came on at once," he said. "Looks like it overheated and seized up."

Ben asked, "What do you want Officer Sanchez to do?"

"We called for a tow truck and a replacement vehicle. Go on ahead, and we'll catch up with you at the airport."

Ben slid back into the Cruze next to Yolanda and repeated what the cop said.

"I don't like this," she said.

"You could ask Roland to light a fire under the tow truck."

"Too soon. Let's get you out to the airport first," she said.

Yolanda backed up a few feet, then waited for a break in traffic before revving the engine and pulling out. A delivery van braked sharply, stopping just short of slamming into the compact; The Cruze burned rubber as it sped away.

Twenty minutes later, Yolanda nosed into a space on the half-empty roof of an airport parking structure. As Ben pulled suitcases from the trunk, Yolanda peered at his ticket in the strange, green-tinted orange of the sodium vapor lighting.

"You're on American to Chicago, then you change for L.A."

"When we get settled inside, I'll fire up my computer and make a hotel reservation."

"I thought you had family in L.A."

"My sister and brother are in Israel this year."

"You don't have anybody in L.A. that you could stay with?"

"It's kind of short notice. But I've got a lot of friends in Chicago. What if we change the ticket?"

"No problem."

Instead of checking his bags with a skycap, Ben carried them into the terminal and joined a long line at the American Airlines counter. Yolanda pulled out her phone and speed-dialed the security detail. After a few terse sentences, she broke the connection and looked at Ben.

"I really, really, don't like this."

"What?"

"Couple minutes after we left, a big rig jackknifed trying to make the turn onto the ramp. It's gonna be at least an hour before they can clear it away and get that replacement vehicle to the security team. The only other way to the airport is to take Liberty Bridge and the tunnel and go around the jam. This time of day, that adds an hour to the trip."

Ben said, "You think a jackknifed truck might not be an accident?"

Yolanda shrugged. "I'm just saying. I don't like it."

"Call Roland, and let him know."

Yolanda speed dialed again, then spoke urgently into the phone.

"Call went straight to voicemail."

"He's probably on the other line, talking to Harrisburg."

"I feel like a sitting duck. Wait here. I'm gonna move this along."

Ben watched Yolanda walk to the end of the counter and hold up her badge. An airline employee approached her, listened for a few seconds, then picked up a telephone and punched in numbers.

A minute ticked by until a bulky, dark-skinned woman in a Transportation Security Agency uniform appeared. She spoke with Yolanda, who then turned toward Ben and beckoned him over.

Yolanda said, "This is Agent Chysum. She knows that you're a witness in an organized crime investigation. She'll see you to a secure waiting area while I deal with your ticket."

Ben said, "Thank you, Detective."

Yolanda shot Ben a secret wink, then headed for the counter.

Chysum escorted Ben around the security screening lines and into the American Airlines terminal waiting area, where she used her walkie-talkie to summon a male agent to unlock an almost-invisible door in a wall panel. It opened to reveal a small, well-lit space with a low coffee table, comfortable chairs, and a view of the runways.

Chysum said, "I'll bring that detective when she finishes your ticketing."

"Thanks, I appreciate your help."

Both agents left, and the door clicked shut behind them.

Ben took his ThinkPad Helix from its case and booted it up, then opened his browser and made a reservation at Chicago's Ramada Plaza. Even though he was certain of a warm welcome, he wasn't about to inconvenience a friend without notice of his arrival.

After logging off the Web, he got to his feet and searched in his pocket for the tiny plastic rectangle he'd found in his suit trousers. He plugged one end into his computer's USB port.

A window with a series of numbers, a file name, popped up. Ben clicked on it.

Instantly, his screen filled with an unfamiliar logo. After a moment, a menu appeared. Peering at it closely, Ben felt his heart beating faster. Excitement growing by the second, he realized that he was looking at the master income and expense ledger for the Sanok Retirement Home. Scrolling through menus, he saw pages for month-by-month accounts of almost 15 years of the Home's finances, including a raft of documents with labels indicating that they were the minutes of the Home's board of directors. Another menu brought up a trove of Home payroll documents.

This must have come from Mina, he realized. How did it get into his trousers?

He thought back to the last time he saw her, in the doorway of the Sanoker Shul on a Shabbat morning.

She had flung an arm around him and shoved her other hand deep into his pants pocket. He remembered pushing her away.

That had to be it. Dead or alive, Mina had given him everything needed to pursue a fraud prosecution against Buchler and Kendall. But first, he had to find Buchler.

Chapter Seventy-Two

The door opened, and Yolanda stepped inside.

"How are you doing, Rabbi?"

"Fine," he replied. "Come see what I found."

Yolanda sat next to Ben, and he turned the screen toward her.

"What is all this?"

"The financial records of the Sanok Home, going back more than 14 years."

"What? How did you—?"

Ben laughed. "Mina! The last time I saw her, she shoved this tiny flash drive into my pocket. I didn't know it was there until I packed my clothes today."

"I wish I could tell Roland!"

Ben looked up, instantly alert. "Why can't you tell Roland?"

Yolanda shook her curls. "He doesn't answer his cell phone. I called the squad, and they said he left two hours ago."

"Maybe he's eating or taking a shower."

"Or getting drunk?"

Ben shook his head. "Maybe he's at a meeting. What about the security team?"

"Still stuck on the ramp."

"Nothing to be done but keep our heads down until it's time to board. Let me copy this data onto my computer, email it to you, and then I'll give you the flash drive for safe keeping and evidence."

"While you do that, I'm going to check on your flight. The plane was delayed leaving Atlanta."

"Get me some coffee?"

"Sure."

Yolanda left, and Ben began copying the data to his hard drive. It was several gigabytes; while the copy was in progress, he opened Avi Cohen's Yiddish newspaper and thumbed through it.

Ben understood a little Yiddish; it was written in Hebrew letters and without vowels, so he could pronounce words, many of them similar to German, a language that he'd studied as an undergraduate. Ben's eyes slid down the page, past a photo of a long-dead Hassidic rabbi, then leaped back to focus on a familiar word in the accompanying headline: Sanoker. Ben studied the text, puzzling out the meaning. As near as he could tell, the small story in this months-old paper was about a huge insurance payout from a pre-war policy written by an Italian company. The beneficiary was the Sanoker Rebbe, pictured in 1937.

How could that be? Ben wondered. The Sanoker Rebbe died in the Holocaust.

Ben looked at the paper again. Someone—Dr. Lewin? Avi Cohen?—had turned the corner of the page down. He read the story aloud, searching for familiar words, but could glean little aside from the amount: almost $1 million.

The door opened, and Yolanda appeared, carrying two coffees in tall paper cups. "I spoke to Roland," she smiled. "He was over in

Organized Crime, looking for local wise guys from 1969 that might still be alive, and his phone battery died."

"Anything new?"

"The bridge is still a mess. They're sending another team; they'll take the Liberty Bridge route. They should be here in about an hour."

Ben's computer chirped: The upload was complete.

He dropped the file into his Hightail app and sent it to Yolanda's office email, then dismounted the flash drive and handed it to Yolanda. "Evidence," he said.

Yolanda said, "You still have over an hour to kill."

Ben said, "I'm going to try to Skype Miryam."

He brought up the program, which activated either the tiny camera in the computer lid or the bigger one facing away from the machine, then clicked an icon representing Miryam's account. A message appeared: Temporarily Out Of Service."

Yolanda asked, "What does that mean?"

Ben said, "Her computer is turned off."

"You have an iPhone. Why don't you call her and use Facetime?"

Ben smiled. "Won't work in Argentina. Many countries don't have the broadband infrastructure to handle that much video data."

Ben took out his phone and auto-dialed. Waiting for the call to go through, he smiled at Yolanda. "So I'll just call her in the usual way."

A tone sounded in his ear, and a pleasant female voice said, "All circuits are busy. Please try again later."

Ben sighed and clicked off. "The circuits to Argentina are busy."

The door slid open, and Agent Chysum appeared. "Detective, there's a call for you in the TSA office—that's in Concourse C."

Yolanda jumped to her feet. "Why would anyone call me there?"

Chysum said, "It sounded like a child—said his name was Zick, something like that?"

"Zach?"

"That's it."

Yolanda said, "Wait outside. I need to speak to my witness."

When the door closed, Yolanda leaned close to Ben. "This is all wrong. Zach would know to call my cell. He does it all the time."

Ben said, "What if someone grabbed him? If they took his phone?"

Yolanda dropped to one knee and pulled up her pant leg, revealing an ankle holster. "Do you know how to use a gun?"

Ben said, "I don't like guns."

"But do you know how to use one if you had to?"

"I was once a pretty good shot, but it's been a few years."

Still on one knee, Yolanda carefully extracted a .22 caliber Smith & Wesson revolver from an ankle holster and handed it to Ben.

"Six shots. Double-action. Half-cock is safety."

Ben said, "Better give me the rig, too."

Yolanda pulled off the Velcro strap, then strapped it to Ben's right ankle before climbing to her feet.

"That door is locked from the outside and can only be opened by security personnel. Don't leave until I come back."

Chapter Seventy-Three

The door clicked shut behind Yolanda, and Ben turned back to his computer. A blinking light caught his eye: A Skype paging notice.

Miryam!

The smiling face of Howard Hopper appeared on Ben's computer screen.

Hopper said, "You were expecting someone better-looking?"

Ben smiled in spite of his disappointment.

"I was expecting someone younger, better-looking, female, and anxious to jump my bones," he said. "But it's good to see you, anyway."

Hopper said, "They re-assembled your shredded documents. I just sent you a link to the unscrambled pages. You can view them and download what you want."

Ben said, "That was pretty quick."

"Yeah, the hardware still has a few wrinkles to iron out, but their software rocks. I'll talk to my board about buying a piece of that company. After you've looked at your pages, tell me what you think."

"You emailed my Yahoo account?"

"I sent a link to Hightail. You can download from there."

"I'll look them over and get back to you with my take. And thanks for this. I can't tell yet if it'll be important to my investigation, but I suspect that it might be."

"Good hunting," Hopper said, and the screen went blank.

Before logging into his mail account, Ben tried Miryam on Skype again. When she didn't answer, he set his computer to auto-dial her every fifteen minutes, then opened Hopper's message.

Ben found a link that took him to where the re-assembled pages were stored as Adobe PDF files. He downloaded and opened the first file to find an old-fashioned-looking document written in Italian, topped with the words Assicurazione Equità in half-inch faded red type. Google's translation feature turned that into "Equitable Assurance," which Ben took to be the name of an insurance company. Continuing down the page, he found the company's address in Trieste, a strategically placed Adriatic seaport in Italy's northeastern coastal fringe. A tiny bell went off in Ben's mind, and he scanned the document, noting that each paragraph in Italian was repeated below with a paragraph each in German, a Slavic language that he supposed was Polish, and then another that might have been Hungarian.

Ben found a name, Schlomo Seigafuse, and confirmed his suspicion that this was indeed an insurance policy. A handwritten date indicated that it had been issued in November 1938.

There was something familiar about that name, Schlomo Seigafuse. Ben put that thought aside and concentrated on recalling what he knew about Trieste and insurance. Annoyed with himself, he Googled the two words and was rewarded with a Wikipedia article that said that, until after the First World War, Trieste had been part of Austria-Hungary, and that several large insurance companies had set up shop there. Many of these were owned by Jews; they hired agents in the Jewish regions of Middle and Eastern Europe and sold all sorts of insurance policies to their co-religionists.

That was enough to focus the recollections that Ben had been dimly aware of: Starting in the last decades of the 19th century and continuing right up to the Holocaust, millions of Jews had purchased a variety of insurance policies. For example, dowry policies, purchased at birth and payable after 20 years, provided funds for a daughter's wedding or a son's education. More affluent Jews found that purchasing certain types of front-loaded policies, such as an endowment, was almost the only way they could send a substantial sum abroad in anticipation of leaving Poland, Hungary, Czechoslovakia or Germany.

Ben returned to the open file and searched for some indication of what type of policy this was. It appeared to be an endowment. He found a number, 28, followed by a string of zeros. More Googling produced the value of a 1938 Polish zloty. Making a rough calculation, this particular policy cost, in 1938, about 22,000 U.S. dollars.

Which could be worth as much as twenty times that much today. Plus compound interest for almost 80 years.

Ben recalled the Yiddish article that he'd puzzled over earlier, which mentioned an insurance payout to the Sanoker Rebbe of almost a million dollars.

He scanned the document before him, looking for a beneficiary, and recognized it in the German text: The Rabbi of the Sanoker Congregation in Sanoker, Pennsylvania, United States of America.

What was now Berona Township, Ben recalled, was then known as Sanoker.

He closed the file and pulled up the next. It was similar to the first, though written by a different company, Generali. He wrote the name of the insured, checked to see the beneficiary: The Sanoker Rebbe. He went on to the next document file.

By the time he had written six more names, he knew what was on the shredded documents that he had taken that night in Berona Township. And he realized where he had seen the names: Abe Frankel, Jacob Auer, Ursula Stern Schlomo Seigafuse, Dov Günzburg, Selma Katznelson and Zach Hildesheimer. They were chiseled into gravestones in the cemetery next to the Sanok Home. The names of people who had died there in the last four years.

The names of people whose families had sent some of their wealth out of Poland by purchasing endowment policies for their sons and daughters as each escaped Europe on the eve of the Holocaust.

And all were payable to the Sanoker Rebbe.

That was Bernie Buchler's big payday. It was why he had started a synagogue, and carefully named it the Sanoker Shul: By dint of forged minutes from the Sanok Home, he, Buchler, became the Sanoker Rebbe. A scheme requiring great patience to wait for each of the elderly people who had escaped the Holocaust as children to die of old age.

There were fifteen graves, Ben recalled. Fifteen insurance payouts of large sums that had grown enormously, thanks to inflation and compounding interest on the original investment. Millions of dollars paid to the Sanoker Rebbe. But not the brave, God-fearing Rebbe who bought freedom for a handful of Jewish children. The money went to his successor, the poseur and confidence man, Bernard Buchler.

Ben heard the door open behind him, then close.

Ben said, "Yolanda, you're not going to believe what I just found."

A man's voice said, "Officer Sanchez has been detained."

Ben looked over his shoulder as Chief Jack Lawrence stepped into the room.

Chapter Seventy-three

Ben said, "Jack! What are you doing here?"

Jack closed the door behind him.

"Against my better judgment, I'm trying to save your life. Again."

Still holding the computer, Ben jumped to his feet.

Jack moved past him to stop in front of the low table.

Keeping that table between them, Ben realized, was to prevent him from kicking the antiquated but deadly .38 caliber revolver out of Jack's hand. Jack might be older, but he was shrewd and dangerous.

The computer in his lap, Ben touched a key as he sat down, then set the Helix on the table between them. "What are you talking about?"

"First time I laid eyes on you, I almost wet my pants. You not only look like your old man, you sound like him. The way you parse your sentences. Your tendency to lecture—vintage Mark Glass. Mark Glass, Senior, that is."

Ben's head swam. "You knew my father? How can that be?"

"We worked together, off and on, for thirty years. And the only reason you're not dead now is because he stuck his neck out for me, and I mean more than once. He also broke out his wallet. Last time I saw him, he put up a hundred large for my bail, knowing that I was headed for

Mexico the minute I took off the jumpsuit and that he'd never see dime one of the bond."

Ben's head swam, and he struggled to speak.

"First time we met was in New Rochelle. That was 1973, and he was calling himself Marty Thompson. He cut me into the score and had me join St. Michael's."

"What was the game?"

Jack smiled and sat down across the table. "Your dad taught me the virtues of the long con. That a clever grifter could do much better with one good con, even if it took a year to set up, than with a dozen quick scores. And if you set it up right, got to know the people, made them like you, a church or synagogue would let you rip them off and maybe never go to the cops. Or at least not until it was much too late.

"So I joined St. Michael's and volunteered for this and that, and over about six months' time, I worked my way onto the lay advisory board. I told the chairman that I knew a man, a retired doctor, who'd put up as much as $100,000 to build a new rectory. And this was 1973 when a good doctor earned that much for a year's work."

Ben smiled. "But the catch…?"

Jack smiled back. "My donor would match anything the church raised, up to the hundred K, but they had only six months to do it because he needed the tax deduction for that year."

Ben said, "In cash, of course."

"Of course. We raised a little over seventy-eight grand. The day came when we were supposed to show this to our anonymous donor. We hired a real New York actor for this—tall, gray hair, wearing a great suit—he was terrific. Comes into Father Lopez's private office, big smile, praising God. He meets the members of the fund-raising committee and shakes hands with each one. Then we count the money that we've raised, and he takes out a checkbook and very slowly writes out a check for the same amount, puts it on the stack of money, shakes hands all around a second time, and leaves.

"Two minutes later, Father Burke from the New York Diocese, Cardinal Cooke's personal assistant, turns up, furious over our unauthorized expenditure of funds, livid that the young priest, Father Lopez, had never bothered to ask the diocese for permission to build."

"Burke was my father?"

"He had an extraordinary gift for accents. So there he was, all red hair and righteous anger, spouting Church doctrine, lecturing Father Lopez on canon law, going on and on about how the Diocese, under Cardinal Cooke's guidance, decides what to build or tear down and when and how to do so."

Ben was genuinely shocked. "He made off with the money?"

"Had a real Brinks truck waiting outside with a couple of real guards. Far as I know, the priest never went to the cops.

"A couple of days after I met you, when I got into your FBI file, I read about your caper in Brooklyn. Dressed as a priest, proper Belfast accent and all, you conned a bunch of nuns into letting you make a security inspection—right there I decided that you were a chip off the old block. Then all that business picking locks—if only your father had been able to walk through doors, we'd have made a killing every week!"

Ben shook his head. "I'm not running a con."

Jack smiled. "Look at it my way. On various occasions, your father called himself Rabbi Mark, Rabbi Glass, Rabbi Marcus, and Rabbi Tomashevsky. And those are just the rabbis I remember. So when you turn up near the end of a long game with a big payday in sight, what was I supposed to think?"

Ben shrugged. "How did you get to be Berona's chief of police?"

Jack laughed. "Laurence had retired from the Greensburg force and was working corporate security and hating it. So we fixed it that he won a free trip to Belgrade, where his wife's family came from about a hundred years back. Had someone meet him at the airport there, some local muscle with a car, and that was that. We had someone else send postcards to his kids for a year afterward.

"The day he and his wife left Greensburg, we went into his house, found the documents that we needed, and made Frank Lustig an offer that he couldn't refuse."

Ben said, "A minute ago, you said 'save my life again'. What did that mean?"

Jack snorted. "The night you broke into the temple. The shul."

Ben sat forward. "You shot Jake the Heater?"

"He had orders to kill you. My guys nicked him when he was about to go out the window; I came as soon as I could. I couldn't arrest him—he had ties to Siragusa, he could implicate me in the land game. I had to shoot him and lay it on trigger-happy patrolmen."

Ben said, "And when I showed you that video, told you that the police report was wrong, you told those cops to get lost for awhile?"

"A couple of all-expense vacations with pay. Chicken feed."

"Why would Jake want to kill me?"

"He thought you were Geltkern. And Siragusa thought Geltkern had double-crossed him. Which he had, by the way. So he had a guy stake out the shul, and when you went in through the front door... "

Ben said, "Geltkern can't be his real name."

Jack smiled again. "Raphael Rabinowicz."

Ben digested this for a long moment. "Then you must be Bernie Buchler."

It was Jack's turn to be surprised. For an instant, his face froze in a snarl. Then he laughed. "Your dad would be so proud of you."

"In 1969, you called yourself Buddy Butcher for a few months?"

Again Jack's eye's narrowed. And again he chuckled. "Wow. You're good. I'm starting to think I missed something. That you are actually running a con."

Ben shook his head. "It's exactly as I told you the first time we met: Mrs. Silverblatt asked me to find a missing rabbi. So far, I've failed. But I kept finding things that made me think that Geltkern—Rabinowicz—was running a scam."

Jack nodded. "I've known him at least twenty years, and he was very convincing at whatever grift he was working. Came from a religious family and knew enough of the mumbo-jumbo to pull off the rabbi, so we brought him in for the role. Best of all, he'd never been arrested. He was to keep the Home going until the real-estate market recovered. And get a line of credit with Kendall's bank, secured by their land, and borrow thirty or forty thousand on it. And to disappear the original charter paperwork, all the records, so that when the Home became insolvent, Lustig could take it over, with Kendall making sure there were no grounds for a legal challenge. Then we develop the land for residential use, sell the homes, and retire, rich and legit. Like your father did."

"How did he do that, exactly?"

Jack asked, "You really never knew him?"

Ben shook his head. "My parents divorced when I was born. Never met him."

"Well, he was what I'd call a strategic thinker. For twenty-some years, every time he made a good score, he found someone—a woman, usually—in a different part of the country or in Canada and bought something: a piece of real estate, a fast-food franchise, a service station, a car dealership, a refrigerated warehouse, a trucking company, even a diamond-cutting operation in Manhattan. Highly diversified. Kept everything in his partners' names, gave them most of the operating profit to manage things. When he retired, he sold his half of each asset to the partner, or else they liquidated it. Wound up in California with a bundle. A big bundle. Got married again. Five years later, wham. Major heart attack, all done."

Ben said, "Maybe you could tell me something about my father that I've always wondered about: How does the son of a Talmudic scholar from Poland wind up with a name like Mark Thomson Glass?"

Jack laughed. "I asked him that myself. Not that I know it's true, but here's what he told me. His father—your grandfather, came from a tiny shtetl in Poland."

Ben nodded. "Go on."

"It was a very poor town. In the 1890s, when there was more anti-Semitism than usual, they took up a collection and raised enough to send one young man to America. He was supposed to come here, find a job, save his money, and send for the next young man, who would do the same. They sent the smartest kid in town. Years went by, things got worse and worse, and they never heard from this guy. So they took up another collection and send a second boy, and then a third. They never heard from any of them.

"Then, just before the start of World War I, the first guy returns. He's rich, and he pays to have every young man who wants to leave come to America."

Ben said, "And one of those was my grandfather?"

"Correct."

"What does that have to do with naming his son Mark Thompson?"

"Everything. This guy, the one who came back rich, had found a job working for an Irishman in New York who owned a printing company that made calendars. The Polish kid convinced him to make Jewish calendars, sold advertising on them, and distributed them free through synagogues. The Irishman made a fortune, and by 1912, when he died, the Polish Jew was his partner. He sold the company, and went back to Poland to help the people who had sent him to America."

Ben said, "And the name of the Irishman was Mark Thompson?"

"That's what your father told me."

"Except that my grandfather was born in Warsaw in 1913, and came to America with his mother and older brother in 1928. I have his immigration papers."

"That was your old man—a great story for every occasion."

"Are you really here to save me?"

Jack looked grim. "Against my better judgment. I owed your Dad, big time. By the way, he was always lucky. Just like you: the fire, the bomb, the hit squad at the JCC. By all rights, I shouldn't have to do this, because you should be dead."

Ben said, "Geltkern—Rabinowicz—he's dead now, isn't he?"

Jack said, "He was supposed to keep the doors open and wait. We promised him ten percent of the big score—at least five million, and probably more, every dime legal and clean as a whistle, and a capital gain to boot. Time goes on, the market is still in the toilet, and he starts a Medicare scam at the Home. Same with the state assistance money. And we let him do it. Let him keep it all and said nothing. He promotes himself a second salary with that shul of his, and we let that go, too—it's chump change, and it helps set up the bankruptcy.

"But then he takes out three and half million for Weinstock's pension. And, he stole my Rembrandt."

"Wait. You had a Rembrandt?"

"A sketch. He swapped a high-quality scan for the original. It was months before I noticed. He denied it, of course, but nobody else even knew that I had it."

"The same Rembrandt that you stole from Al Farkas' widow?"

Jack's face grew dark. He clenched his teeth and his mouth curled into an angry sneer. Then he shook his head and laughed.

"You're unbelievable! How could you possibly know that?"

"You have the police and FBI reports. I have a network of old rabbis. But please continue. Was that why you killed Rabinowicz?"

"That wasn't me. Swiping my Rembrandt was disrespectful, but it was strictly between the two of us. I asked him nicely to return it, and he said that he never had it, but that if he had actually taken it, it would have burned in Weinstock's house. So that was that.

"What got him whacked was her pension—$3.5 million. That was over the line, and Siragusa wouldn't stand for it. He's old-school. Took the fall on a murder rap for Jack Licavoli, the Cleveland don. Did twenty-two years, straight up, in Marion. Maximum security. Could have turned state's evidence, gone into Witness Protection, had some kind of a life in Oshkosh or Boise. Someplace. Not Siragusa. He got out ten years ago. Licavoli's dead. Siragusa's pretty young wife is fat and middle-aged, and his kids don't know him. But now it's his time. He takes over the Pittsburgh action—girls, drugs, gambling, numbers—but stays in Youngstown, where he's got some cops and a judge in his pocket.

"But now he's six years into this Berona thing, he's spent a ton of money, and if anyone is gonna take a few million out, Siragusa wants his share. The lion's share.

"If Rabinowicz had come to him, Siragusa would have let him keep a million. But he thought that nobody knew about that money. Weinstock put it all into a Metropolitan Life annuity, names some of her cousins as heirs. Rabinowicz even marries Weinstock, but she won't cash out. Won't put the money into something liquid that he could steal.

"A couple of Siragusa's guys talk to her for an hour or so, and she decides to move the whole thing to K & L Insurance. Then the Don has her whacked. We split up the take, with a taste for Kendall and Lustig.

"That scares Rabinowicz. He tries to make a deal. Siragusa is a hard case, but he's not heartless. He gives Rabinowicz a shot: Take you out of the picture, and he's free. He gets nothing, but he's out, and he's alive. So he sets up a hit but he does it on the cheap—sends a moron with a baseball bat to break your bones. You kicked his ass.

"Then he sends a crew to the Jewish Center, but that blows up in his face, or rather in the nephew's face. And finally, the car bomb and even that fails. Rabinowicz has nothing more to trade—or so we thought. So then he's gone."

The loudspeaker in the ceiling crackled to life, announcing that Ben's flight for Chicago was now boarding.

Jack got to his feet. "That's our cue. Siragusa's guys are in TSA uniforms. They'll pull you out of line, take you somewhere on the airport and finish you."

Ben asked, "How did they get uniforms? How can they bring weapons through security without credentials?"

Jack sighed. "Do you know how much a baggage handler makes? Or a TSA screener? For a few thousand, you can find someone that will bring anything you want through security."

"So now what?"

"Siragusa knows you figured out the land deal. He wants you gone before that blows up or Judge Kendall decides to walk away rather than worry about spending the rest of his life in a cell."

"How did Siragusa know that Charles Kendall is really Eddie Kendall?"

Again Jack looked shocked. "Where did you get that?"

Ben shrugged. "Talmudic logic. There had to be a reason for a respected judge to crawl into bed with a notorious Mafioso. I read the old papers. How did Siragusa know?"

Jack sat back down. "He had a bookie here, a retired cop. The bookie was sick and broke. The only thing he had to sell was a secret, that Judge Kendall was a fugitive."

Ben said, "What's your end in this?"

"I hatched the scheme and kept an eye on things. Siragusa fronted the money; he takes half. Twenty percent to Kendall and Lustig. The rest is mine."

"And you'd give that up?"

"Won't have to. But there's no reason you have to die for these people. Disappear for a while. South America, Israel. Wherever. Next year, the land will be ours. In two years, we'll be selling luxury houses. In three, we'll be rich and respectable."

"So—what, you'll escort me out of here while Siragusa's goons stand around in the boarding area?"

"If we go now, you're long gone before they figure out you've ditched them. I've got a car for you. Drive to Akron or Cincinnati, wherever. Get on a plane, and go see your girlfriend in Buenos Aires."

"And that's it?"

"No, damn it, that's not it. Rabinowicz had one more score. He figured to rake in at least eight million."

"Why do you think that?"

"Because we had a bug in Weinstock's bedroom when he told her. He never said what or how. It's all in those shredded documents you took. Give me that score, and as a way to repay a favor to your late father, I'll give you your life."

Chapter Seventy-four

Ben asked, "What about Yolanda?"

"She's in the trunk of her car. We put a tracking beacon in it this morning, and fortunately, she parked on the roof, where it was easy to find."

"Why wouldn't you kill her?"

"She can't prove anything, and Siragusa doesn't kill cops. Brings too much heat."

"When do we leave this room?"

"As soon as you tell me what the scam was."

"Pre-war life insurance policies. In 1938, the Sanok people sent their rabbi to Poland to bring back as many of their relatives as he could. He died in the Holocaust, but not before he got some people out. Mostly kids, from wealthy families. Back then, the only way a Jew could move money out of Poland was to buy an endowment policy with an international insurance company, and pay the full premium up front."

Jack said, "I thought the statute of limitations ran out on Holocaust insurance claims. Wasn't there a class-action settlement a few years ago?"

Ben said, "That was for Holocaust *victims*. For those who died in the Holocaust. All these people were here and survived the Holocaust.

Their policies paid on their death or when they were cashed in by the insured. I'm pretty sure none of these individuals even know about the policies; they were kids, and the arrangements were handled by the rabbi and their families. Fifteen of them died over the last four years. All buried at the Sanok Home."

Jack asked, "How could Rabinowicz know about this, and how could he get his hands on the payout?"

"He stole a museum exhibit that included the Sanok Burial Society's documents and records. That's probably where he found the policies. I think that's why he started the shul: All the policies paid benefits to 'The Sanoker Rebbe.' As the rabbi of the Sanoker Shul, Rabinowicz made himself the Sanoker Rabbi. By not charging dues or collecting money from the members, they had no way to fire him."

"So he waited for those people to die, then claimed the insurance proceeds?"

Ben nodded. "That's it."

"Where's the money?"

Ben shrugged. "No idea. Did you search his home?"

"He kept a crib in Monroeville, a doublewide, but we went over it with a fine-tooth comb. No money. And nothing at that so-called shul."

"What about Weinstock's house?"

"There was a safe over the bed, but there was only about twenty Gs in it."

"She'd just finished a whole-house makeover. Maybe there was another safe, under the floorboards, or in a wall?"

"We went over the whole house with a portable ultrasound. No safe, no hidden room, no voids in the walls. Nothing buried in the basement. Nothing in the yard."

"Maybe he didn't claim it yet. Or maybe it's in a safe deposit box somewhere."

Jack set his jaw. His eyes narrowed to slits. "Not in any bank in Ohio, Pennsylvania, New York or West Virginia. At least not in any of his known aliases. He used five Social Security numbers, and the Youngstown cops didn't turn up a thing."

Ben shrugged. "Then I wouldn't even know where to look. Unless it was in one of the vacant lots around Weinstock's house. Some of them are overgrown."

"We looked there, too."

Ben shrugged again. "Then I'm out of ideas."

"You're lying. You know more than you're saying."

Ben shrugged. "I never found Geltkern—Rabinowicz. I never spoke to him, never communicated with him. I don't know where he lived, aside from with Weinstock. Your people carted every piece of paper out of the shul and burned down the house."

"Not every piece of paper. You took some of it."

"It was the insurance policies, all shredded. Either he didn't need them anymore because he'd filed the claims and been paid, or they were worthless."

Jack stood up and pointed the .38 at Ben. "Time to go.

Chapter Seventy-Five

Walking through the half-empty terminal with his hands cuffed behind him, Ben's mind raced furiously. By the time the parking structure elevator rose to roof level, he had worked it out: Even if Yolanda was still alive, Jack would never risk letting her go. And he certainly wouldn't take a chance on anyone else who knew the whole scheme, chapter and verse. No, he would certainly kill them both.

Prodded by Jack's gun barrel, Ben stepped out of the elevator. The near part of the parking area was dark and the lot was empty except for seven cars, among them Yolanda's Cruze. The far end of the space was bright under the harsh, other-worldly glare of sodium vapor lamps. Glass crunched underfoot as Jack urged Ben forward.

In the far corner, half a football field away, a big man slid out of a light-colored Escalade. Another, almost as big, climbed out of the back passenger door and yanked Yolanda out to stand in front of him.

Ben flexed his knees, preparing his move.

A whirring, whistling sound, like a cyclone in a small space, came from the darkness to his left. As he turned his head, something came whirling from the shadows.

Something that glanced off his left leg.

Something serpentine that seized Jack's legs and wrapped itself around them.

Ben whirled, breaking Jack's grip as the older man's feet were yanked sharply to the left and he toppled backward.

Ben landed on Jack's solar plexus with both knees, then bounded back to his feet, kicked the .38 into the darkness, and turned back toward the Escalade.

The bigger man fired and something whizzed by Ben's ear to ricochet off the concrete and shatter a windshield. An instant later, a soft pop sounded from behind a nearby car, and the big man dropped his automatic and reeled, clutching his shoulder. A second soft pop and the other man screamed in pain and went down. Yolanda scooped up his fallen gun and sprinted toward Ben.

Easton came bounding out of the stairwell, followed by four uniformed cops with military rifles and wearing S.W.A.T. vests. They swarmed the two gunmen while Easton handcuffed Buchler.

Yolanda threw her arms around Ben. "Are you all right? I was so worried!"

"Good shooting, Ro," said Miryam, stepping from the shadows, still gripping the rawhide strap of los boleadoras, the Gaucho's lasso.

Mrs. Meltzer appeared from behind a car, clutching her target rifle.

Miryam said, "Are you okay, Yolanda?"

"I'm fine," she said.

"Then unhand that redhead—he's mine."

Yolanda said, "Let me get my cuffs off him, and he's all yours."

Chapter Seventy-Six

After the S.W.A.T. police took Buchler and his two wounded gunmen away, everyone left on the roof tried to talk at once:

Yolanda said, "I was so stupid. I should have called Abby before I left Ben alone."

Miryam said, "Mrs. Meltzer called and said that your car was bombed and that you were in intensive care, so I got on the first plane."

Easton said, "When you called me, Mrs. Meltzer, you said that you were on the way to the airport to pick up Miryam and to meet you on the parking garage roof to help the rabbi. You never said anything about a gun!"

Mrs. Meltzer said, "I'd forgotten that I'd left it in the trunk. But I had only five bullets, and I had to use two on the lights."

Ben said, "Jack Laurence is really Bernard Buchler."

Miryam said, "We know. Everyone saw the live video of him that you streamed through Skype."

Yolanda said, "Not everyone. Chief Lawrence is Bernie Buchler?"

Easton said, "You could have waited two more minutes, Rabbi, and we would have handled this."

Ben shook his head. "In two more minutes, Yolanda and I would have been dead, or in a car leaving the airport, and if you caught up to that car it would have meant a gun battle."

Miryam said, "And, I wouldn't have been able to show Ben what a good gaucha I am. And if you had come two minutes later, I would have already stuck my daga in Buchler's corazón negro."

Easton said, "I carry a 9mm. How do I explain the .22 slugs in those mutts?"

Ben knelt and released Yolanda's ankle holster and its .22 revolver. "Ro, what did you do with your brass?"

Mrs. Meltzer reached into her parka pocket and came out with four tiny expended cartridges. Ben unfolded a handkerchief, and she dropped them in it.

Ben said, "Get me the other round, the one in the rifle."

While she went to her car, Ben unloaded the revolver, handed four bullets to Miryam, wiped down the expended cartridges and carefully loaded them into the revolver. Miryam gave the four bullets to Meltzer while Ben wiped down the pistol, put it in the holster, and gave both to Easton.

Ben said, "Yolanda, you saw Laurence take me to the parking lot in handcuffs, and followed us through the terminal. When we got on the elevator, you took the stairs, and that's where you met Roland.

"Roland, your 9mm jammed when you loaded it, so you borrowed Yolanda's backup gun."

Easton nodded, thinking.

Ben said, "Ro, you and Miryam got to the roof after all the shooting. You didn't see anything.. Don't leave any prints, and dispose of those bullets someplace far from your house. Then go home, clean your rifle and lock it up. Wash the clothes you're wearing, including the parka, and take a shower. A long shower. Wash your hair, too."

Mrs. Meltzer smiled. "It's just like 'Murder, She Wrote!'"

Ben said, "Roland, talk to the uniforms, and then write it up the way it should read. We'll all support you."

Chapter Seventy-Seven

Miryam said, "After all the money you've spent on this, you really want to spend more on a crazy hunch?"

Ben laughed and pulled Miryam to him, feeling the warmth of her body through layers of wool and nylon. "Not a hunch," he said. "A reasoned conclusion reached through the application of *pilpul*. If I'm right, it's a way to keep the Home and the shul going for a long time."

Miryam kissed Ben, hugged him tightly. "Talmudic reasoning is never wrong?" she said.

Ben said, "Of course not. A faulty premise can be taken to its logical conclusion as well as a factual premise. And this wouldn't be the first time I got the facts wrong."

"But this time, you're certain of your premise?"

"Not a hundred percent. But pretty sure."

The roar of a diesel engine interrupted their conversation. An eighteen-wheel flatbed tractor-trailer rig negotiated the corner and stopped in front of the pile of blackened rubble that had once been the Weinstock home. On the truck was a skip loader.

Two men got out of the cab and began removing chains from the skip loader's wheels. A minute later, an enormous dump truck came around the corner, stopped halfway down the block, then backed slowly toward Ben and Miryam.

The men from the flatbed laid a pair of long steel plates, each three feet wide, to form a gentle ramp from the truck bed to the street. One man backed the loader down the ramp, turned it around, and drove to the edge of the rubble.

Ben approached him. "Start in the right front corner, go down until you hit unbroken concrete, then straight ahead for about twenty feet. Stop if you hit metal."

"What are you looking for, boss?"

"A furnace. Cast iron, about six feet high and five feet square. It might be laying on its side."

"If it's down there, I'll find it."

"One more thing: When you get down to the concrete, I'd like to look at what comes out of the hole at that level."

"You got it, boss."

An hour later, the first dump truck left with its load. As a second truck took its place, the loader driver dragged a load of rubble out of the hole, then backed several feet into the street before lowering the bucket to the street. He cut the engine as Ben and Miryam came over to look.

Ben said, "What do you see, Senorita La Gaucha?"

Miryam snorted. "Broken furniture. A desk, I think. And a chair."

Ben said, "Broken, but not burned."

Miryam flashed her thousand-watt smile. "Now I understand."

Ben signaled to the driver, and the excavation resumed.

The second truck left and was replaced by a third.

After almost four hours of careful digging, a pit eight feet wide, more than a dozen feet deep and twenty feet long had been carved out of the rubble. The loader operator shut down his engine, climbed down from the seat and lit a cigarette.

Miryam said, "How do you feel about this now, Digger Ben?"

Ben said, "Nothing's changed. We just keep digging till we find it."

A black Crown Victoria with Pennsylvania government plates stopped behind the eighteen-wheeler. Easton and Yolanda got out, and she went around to the trunk, returning with a carry-out tray with four cups of steaming coffee.

"Yours is in the trunk, with the doughnuts," Yolanda said to Ben, then went into the street to hand cups to the equipment operators and dump truck drivers.

Miryam said, "I'll get your coffee," and headed for the Crown Victoria.

Ben turned to Easton. "How did it go?"

Easton grinned. "Aside from the fact that I'm now known as 'Dead-eye Dick' in the squad room, everything went well.

"The judge was waiting for us with his attorney. We executed a search warrant and booked him into the downtown jail. He made bail, and his lawyers are trying to work out a deal on the fugitive charge. The real-estate scam will be harder to prove, but I'll bet that one of these mugs will want to save his butt and talk. And I bet I know which one.

"Frank Lustig put a half-million in a satchel and took off. They found his car in Harrisburg, and the state police took him off a commuter train in Allentown wearing a wig and a fake soup-strainer."

"And Siragusa?"

"Old-school hoodlum. Put on his best suit, had himself driven to Cleveland, had a nice lunch with his younger mistress, and turned himself in. Bail hearing tomorrow."

Ben asked, "Why Cleveland?"

"Like I said, old-school. If he surrenders in Youngstown, he knows they'll transfer him to Cleveland anyway, so he might as well go in style as ride the prison bus. Cleveland has way more judges, so it'll be easier to find one who might be encouraged to give him bail. There's a waterfront, so if he decides to skip, he can get on a boat. Also, Cleveland has the most comfortable jail cells, the best Italian restaurants, and his lawyers have their offices downtown."

Ben smiled. "All good."

Miryam returned, handed each man a coffee and offered the doughnut bag. Ben shook his head, but Easton chose one with chocolate frosting. He took a big bite, chewed and swallowed, washed it down with coffee.

Easton asked, "Exactly what are we doing here? You never said."

Ben said, "I asked you to come because I want police protection while I move a few million dollars to the Sanok Home's bank."

"Suddenly, you have a few million dollars, Rabbi?"

"I think I know where Rabinowicz—'Rabbi Geltkern'—stashed the cash from the insurance payouts."

"Here? Yolanda told me how the insurance scam worked, and I've watched the Skype recording of Buchler's confession, but Buchler said that Siragusa's men couldn't find any of Rabinowicz's money except what was in the wall safe."

Ben shook his head. "Siragusa didn't know about the insurance. When he went looking for Rabinowicz's money, he was thinking small, maybe a million or so. It never entered anyone's mind that it could be five or ten times that. Buchler suspected that Rabinowicz was into something else, but he had no idea that it was insurance."

Easton said, "If he hid cash in Weinstock's house, what makes you think it didn't burn up in the fire?"

Ben smiled. "Showing is always better than telling."

Easton said, "Let's say you find it. Who owns that money?"

Ben said, "The Sanoker Rabbi was the employee of the Sanoker Burial Society, the Home's predecessor corporation. Because the insured were all children, the beneficiary of each policy was the person in that position, rather than any specific individual. Therefore, the Home owns the proceeds. If not, then it's my money."

Miryam asked, "How could it be your money?"

"Because right now, I'm the rabbi of the Sanoker Shul, the Sanoker Rebbe."

"Hey!"

Everyone turned to face the skip loader.

The driver said, "I think I hit metal."

Ben said, "I brought two shovels."

Easton said, "Now we get to the real reason you asked me to come."

Ben and Easton climbed into the loader's steel bucket and were lowered into the hole. They shoveled debris away from an ancient cast-iron furnace until it stood free on the concrete floor.

"Let's take a little break," Easton gasped. "While you tell me why this cash didn't burn when the house went up," he whispered.

"It was in the basement. The fire started on the first floor, burned upward to the second. The second collapsed into the first, and then the whole thing fell into the basement."

Easton shook his head in wonderment. "And that filled the basement, drove out the air, and left everything under it unburned? How did you know, Rabbi?"

Ben smiled. "I was here, remember? I watched it happen."

"Let's finish this," said Easton and both men slipped behind the furnace, seized a ridge that ran around its top, then rocked it back and forth until the bottom was high enough off the concrete to slip the bucket's steel lip under it. Then they slowly tipped the furnace into the bucket.

The bucket was raised above street level; the loader backed up and deposited the furnace gently on its side on the lawn.

Ben and Easton rode the bucket back up and climbed out.

Ben took an envelope from his pocket and handed it to the loader. "Thank you, we're done here."

The loader operator said, "You're just going to leave that?"

"It's more than a hundred years old and after I hose it down, pretty much perfect. Two years ago, one like it, but smaller, sold to a New York collector for $32,500. After a little cleaning, let's just say I'll have no trouble finding a buyer. I'll get a panel truck to haul it off."

Ben watched the crew put the loader back on its trailer, secure it, and drive off. When the street was clear, Ben went to his car and returned with a small sledgehammer.

Three blows broke the furnace door hinges. A fourth shattered the door weld. Ben pulled the door off, borrowed Easton's flashlight, and put his head and shoulders inside.

After several seconds, he backed out carrying a fiberglass bundle.

Yolanda asked, "That's it? A roll of insulation?"

Ben said, "Miryam, your daga?"

She stepped forward and pulled out an ornate dagger.

Ben said, "Go ahead."

Miryam pushed the blade a few inches into the bundle, then pulled it sideways to make a foot-long incision.

She parted the two halves, glanced inside and smiled.

Ben crawled back into the furnace and handed out eight more fiberglass bundles. Miryam put the first into Ben's new Chevy Volt, and the men loaded the rest into the Crown Victoria's capacious trunk.

Then Ben and Easton rolled the furnace back into the excavation and shoveled debris on it.

When they had finished, Easton and Ben stood together behind the big car.

Easton said, "You're really gonna give all this to the Home?"

Ben said, "We're going right to their bank in Monroeville."

"They'll have to report it. You'll be up to your ass in revenuers."

Ben smiled. "That's why I'm glad I was able to get the policies reconstructed. The IRS will no doubt send a flying squad. The Home's new attorney—my friend, Rabbi Smolkin—will show them police reports, policies, reconstructed board-of-director minutes from the '30s, death certificates, all that jazz, and it will sort itself out."

"What's next for you, Rabbi?"

"Tomorrow, I have a doctor's appointment, and after that, God willing, I'm going down to Buenos Aires to meet Miryam's family."

"So this is goodbye?"

"Not exactly. I'll see you at the Farmers and Merchants Bank of Monroeville in about two hours."

"Sorry, I almost forgot."

"With all eight bundles."

"Eight?

§

Once they had cleared Youngstown and found the turnpike for Pittsburgh, Ben pulled onto the shoulder. Miryam enlarged the hole in the bundle and pulled an unlocked Zero Halliburton aluminum case from its fiberglass cocoon.

Miryam raised the lid, revealing an oversized padded envelope, a Costa Rican passport and bundles of hundred dollar bills.

Miryam held up the passport. "Enrique Acosta, he called himself."

She grabbed the envelope and Ben raised his hand. "Be very careful when you open that."

"You know what's inside, Swami Ben?"

Ben held out his hand and she handed him the envelope, which he placed against his forehead and closed his eyes.

"A sketch of a fisherman, brown ink on vellum."

Miryam burst into laughter. "A new act! I haven't seen this before!"

Still holding the envelope against his forehead, Ben intoned, "By Rembrandt Harmenszoon van Rijn."

He handed the envelope to Miryam, who carefully opened it. "Omigod!" she squealed. "It *is* a Rembrandt!"

Ben nodded. "The property of Mrs. Lois Seligman, of New York."

Miryam shook her head again. "Another of your conquests?"

"We've yet to meet, though I'm told she's quite the dish. Why don't you count the cash?"

"Each bundle is ten grand. This has to be at least a million."

Ben said, "I looked it up. You need a space about eight by six by thirteen inches to hold a million in hundred-dollar bills. This case is much bigger."

Miryam said, "Speaking of money, Yolanda ran into another of your girlfriends. She gave her a check for you. Eight hundred dollars. It's in my purse."

Ben said, "One of my girlfriends?"

Miryam smiled. "Mina something. She's taking an Introduction to Judaism class at the JCC with Yolanda."

Ben smiled.

Miryam said, "Mina said to tell you that 'Wheeling, West Virginia, is lovely in autumn, but she still dreams of that wild night in Pittsburgh with you.'"

Ben laughed.

Miryam said, "Is there anything you'd like to tell me, Casanova Ben?"

Ben smiled. "I met her in a bowling alley, and she confessed her sins. She was the bookkeeper for the Home. I told her that she needed to make herself scarce, that the bad guys might want to kill her. She thanked me and offered her body. A very nice body, I should say. I told her that I was more than flattered, but my heart belongs to a certain Jewish Gaucha who is handy with los boleadoras and with a daga, and who also possesses a body to die for."

Miryam smiled. "Why did she owe you $800, Banker Ben?"

"I gave her all my cash so she could leave town for a few weeks."

"And you did all that in character, with your Belfast brogue?"

"In my fake Yiddish. Now shush, woman, and count the loot."

Miryam giggled, then started to tally the bundles, counting down to the bottom of a stack, then ticking off the rows. And stopped.

"Treasure Hunter Ben!"

"What?"

"There's almost two million in this! If all the others are the same, that comes to about seventeen or eighteen million. That's too much!"

Ben said, "What are you thinking?"

"Geltkern—I mean Rabinowicz—couldn't have taken in that much from the insurance alone. Where did the rest come from?"

"Figure it out. Use pilpul."

"How do I start?"

"Begin with what you know: The money was hidden in a house where a big-time swindler lived. A man in his late sixties, a career con artist, never arrested."

Miryam placed her right hand over her eyes. "Ifffff this was his life savings, all the money he stole over decades.... He planned to wait for spring, buy a yacht in Cleveland, sail it through the Great Lakes and out the St. Lawrence Seaway into the Atlantic, then south to the Caribbean, the Cayman Islands, where there are banks that don't ask questions."

Ben laughed. "Not bad! It's possible, at least. Did you really use Talmudic logic to come up with that?"

"No, Scholar Ben. I used my feminine intuition."

"That's not logic."

"It usually works for me. And if we're going to be together for the next hundred years or so, you should get used to it."

"Now that is logical."

-the end-

ALSO BY MARVIN J. WOLF

For Whom The Shofar Blows

A Scribe Dies In Brooklyn

Abandoned In Hell: The Fight For Vietnam's

Firebase Kate

Where White Men Fear To Tread

Rotten Apples

Family Blood

Fallen Angels

Perfect Crimes

Buddha's Child

About The Author

Marvin J. Wolf, a Vietnam combat veteran and a *Los Angeles Times* best-selling author, is a three-time American Society of Journalists and Authors book award winner. He was also honored with the US Marine Corps Combat Correspondents' prestigious Dennig Award and by the Greater Los Angeles Press Club, among many other writing awards. The author of many nonfiction books, including best-sellers *Where White Men Fear To Tread* and *Fallen Angels, Chronicles of Los Angeles Crime and Mystery*, Wolf had a brief career as a screenwriter before segueing into fiction with his Rabbi Ben Mystery series, and the Chelmin and Spaulding Army CID Mystery series.

Wolf's Website at www.marvinjwolf.com offers personal history, photos, reviews from his many books, and a way to communicate directly with him. See https://www.facebook.com/Koshercrimefighter/

and w@RabbiBenMystery (Twitter).

MARVIN J. WOLF

Printed in Great Britain
by Amazon